BLACK CITY DEMON

ALSO BY RICHARD A. KNAAK

Black City Saint

BLACK CITY DEMON

RICHARD A. KNAAK

an imprint of **Prometheus Books**
Amherst, NY

Cover design and illustration by Jacqueline Nasso Cooke
Cover design © Prometheus Books

Inquiries should be addressed to
Pyr
59 John Glenn Drive
Amherst, New York 14228
VOICE: 716-691-0133
FAX: 716-691-0137
WWW.PYRSF.COM

21 20 19 18 17   5 4 3 2 1

Library of Congress Cataloging-in-Publication Data

Names: Knaak, Richard A., author.
Title: Black City demon / Richard A. Knaak.
Description: Amherst, NY : Pyr, an imprint of Prometheus Books, 2017.
Identifiers: LCCN 2016047703 (print) | LCCN 2016058639 (ebook) |
    ISBN 9781633882751 (softcover) | ISBN 9781633882768 (ebook)
Subjects: | BISAC: FICTION / Fantasy / Urban Life. | FICTION / Fantasy / Historical. |
    GSAFD: Fantasy fiction.
Classification: LCC PS3561.N25 B57 2017 (print) | LCC PS3561.N25 (ebook) |
    DDC 813/.54—dc23
LC record available at https://lccn.loc.gov/2016047703

Printed in the United States of America

For my father

CHAPTER 1

I'd failed her. I'd promised to keep her safe, and I'd failed her. Now, I could do nothing but stare down at her grave again and murmur a prayer in which I only half-believed.

As I did that, I sensed Fetch pacing back and forth just beyond the wall lining the Lawrence Street edge of Saint Boniface cemetery. Being of Feirie, he couldn't enter, but he kept as close as possible. I knew he stayed nearby out of concern for me, not that I'd ever encouraged him. There was nothing he could've changed, not even when she'd died. Her death had been my responsibility, as if I'd been the one whose hand had done the deed.

The mid-November moon was still full, but I didn't need its light to see what I wanted. I'd demanded *his* eyes tonight, and he'd given them to me without argument. That was another reason Fetch was anxious. I generally only trusted in the dragon's power when absolutely necessary, and even then I thought about it twice. But here I was, burning eyes fixated on the symbol of my impotence, the nighttime world a bright, sharp emerald shade. I didn't question his quick acquiescence; he knew that I blamed him as much as I did myself for what had happened to her.

"I'm sorry," I muttered as I knelt down beside the stone. "I'm sorry."

I'd repeated those same two words more often than I could count, but still I felt not even the slightest easing of my conscience. In frustration, I reached forward to shove aside some loose foliage that had obscured part of the headstone.

Her name glared back, accusing me. I swallowed, but didn't look away.

Clarissa O'Halloran.

Another swipe cleared the date of my failure. October of 1871. The Night the Dragon Breathed. The night the city of Chicago burned.

That more than fifty years had passed since then hadn't made the guilt lessen any. Up until last month, I'd not missed coming out here on a regular basis since I'd seen to her burial all those years ago.

"But she's alive and well again, Master Nicholas!" Fetch had reminded me all the way here. *"She's alive and Oberon's a cinder! It's all ducky now!"*

I knew that he had a point, that *Claryce* was a living, breathing woman, which obviously meant that Clarissa's spirit should have moved on. Still, my guilt wouldn't die easily, if it would ever die at all. In fact, coming here only verified that I'd done the right thing when I'd chosen to do my best to avoid Claryce entirely after the incident with Oberon. I was certain that if only I kept her at a distance, kept her away from my dangerous life, she would escape the fate of not only Clarissa, but each and every previous reincarnation.

"You dwell too much in death, Georgius. Life offers you another chance, and you run from it."

Immediately, my eyes reverted to normal. I gritted my teeth as I rose. He'd never materialized here before, but I should've known the cemetery would be open to him. It was as hallowed ground as any church.

I turned to face Diocles. He was always the same. Gray-haired. Rough-hewn features with an eastern European cast akin to my own. Regal robes worthy of a Roman emperor, which made sense given that was what he'd been. If not for the fact that I could see through him, he would have looked in the prime of health.

Of course, that was the thing with ghosts. Sometimes they looked a lot better than the living.

Sometimes.

I'd only met a handful of ghosts in my existence, with only Diocles a reoccurring frustration. I'd avoided Saint Michael's in part because I hadn't wanted to confront him. Too often of late, Diocles had tried to be my conscience where Claryce was concerned, an ironic choice considering his lack of conscience when he'd ordered me executed some sixteen hundred years ago.

"Go back to the church," I ordered him. "You were smart enough not to ever follow me here before. You should've kept being smart."

He frowned. Long ago, when he'd been emperor of the Roman Empire and I a lowly soldier, we'd managed a cordial friendship based on respect and trust. But then, that had been before I'd become a legend by slaying a mythic beast and before I'd become a symbol of the young religion Diocles had chosen—under another's persistent suggestion—to persecute.

"I made no such choice, Georgius," he responded, insisting on using my old name despite constant corrections on my part. Of course, *Nick Medea*, as I was known now, had been chosen by me to forever remind both of us just where I'd lost my head.

"What's that supposed to mean?"

"I do not know this place. I could not even sense it until a short time ago. One moment, I was drifting through Saint Michael's . . . the next I found myself drawn here."

He had no reason to lie, but I also had no reason to listen. Out of sheer obstinacy, I walked right through him. As I did, I heard the expected snickering in my head.

Enjoyed that, did you? I silently asked.

No less than you, my ever-present companion, the dragon, smoothly replied, sibilance stretching the second word a bit. *Eye have no animosity toward this one.*

You have animosity toward everything, I countered. He could not argue with that. He hated all things, me most of all.

The voice quieted. I wish I could've said the same for Diocles.

"I have never been able to follow you to such places before," the ghost persisted. "Always in a house of worship. You know that, Georgius. Always a house of worship. Nowhere else."

"'Nick,'" I angrily reminded him. "Always 'Nick Medea' now. Especially to *you*."

I didn't have to look at him to know he suddenly wore a darker expression. Although Fetch and others called me "Nicholas," it was only by "Nick" that I actually went by. For Diocles, it was always meant as a reminder of that fatal moment between us. Fatal for me, actually, as Nicomedia had been the Roman realm where my ghostly friend had so kindly had me beheaded for refusing to give up my faith.

Diocles started to mouth his usual apology, but then caught sight of the headstone. While he did not have the dragon's eyes to help him see, apparently as a ghost the gloom of night didn't hinder his view in the least. "So, this is where you laid her to rest."

"Go back to Saint Michael's, Diocles," I growled.

The robed phantasm cocked his head as he looked at me again. "Why come here for penance when she is with you once more? Why dwell with the dead—which you do enough, Georgius—when life is still yours . . . and hers? This grave is an empty thing—"

Without thinking, I slashed at him with one hand. I don't know who was more surprised—Diocles for my sudden anger, or me when I realized that long claws now graced my fingers, fingers which had themselves become twisted and scaled.

Take it back! I quickly ordered. *I haven't asked for this!*

But you did . . . just not with words. . . .

To my relief, my hand quickly reverted to normal. I felt his presence sink deep back into my mind.

That still left Diocles, who never seemed to get the hint about leaving. His gaze had drifted back to the grave, which only served to stir my anger anew.

"'Empty thing,'" I muttered. "You still retain your fine respect for the graves of your lessers, Emperor. . . ."

He rippled, a sign of distress on his part that I found at that moment quite satisfying. Diocles knew exactly what I meant. "I ordered that your burial be respected. You deserved that much—"

I'd deserved better than being beheaded in the first place, but that was another argument. "Your orders didn't mean too much, did they?

Especially to Galerius. His men ransacked the tomb the moment they had the chance, and even took my armor and weapons."

That event had had more repercussions than either of us could have imagined. The very spear I'd used to slay the dragon had eventually ended up—just recently, in fact—in the hands of Oberon, the exiled king of Feirie. He'd made a good try of impaling us with it.

"I can only try to apologize over and over, Georgius. I am beyond being able to rectify my sins . . . or those of Galerius, may his bones never rest."

Diocles's sins went far beyond just my execution. He had let himself be influenced by the same Galerius into beginning a bloody persecution of the entire young Christian faith . . . of which I had become, without meaning to, one of its standard-bearers. Galerius might've been the proverbial devil whispering in the emperor's ear, but Diocles had been the one to willingly give the decree. For that alone, he should have been cursed to forever walk as a ghost, but for reasons I could not entirely accept, it appeared that *my* beheading meant more where his fate was concerned. No matter where I'd followed the Gate, Diocles had always been waiting for me in the nearest church.

A chill wind rose up. I tightened the collar of my overcoat and looked around. Diocles's presence had left me with no more desire to be here. Besides, I had an appointment farther on the North Side—a young couple called the Nilssons who continually heard footsteps on the upper floor of the old house they rented. They thought it was the ghost of the first owner, who'd hung herself after her husband perished in the Great Fire.

I knew better. It wasn't a ghost. If they'd seen my ad, seen the offerings of Nick Medea, investigator and debunker of the supernatural, then they had a far worse problem than ghosts. They had one of the *Wyld* lurking around their home.

There was plenty of time to reach my clients, since the appointment was set—for more than theatrical reasons—at midnight. It wasn't hard to convince anyone who needed my services that I needed to come at the witching hour. They'd be desperate for any help at this point, no doubt having exhausted the usual charlatans.

"There was a visitor to Saint Michael's this evening," Diocles muttered.

I looked back at him. Diocles seemed to think it his duty to keep me informed on all newcomers to the church. "Who?"

"A surly Celt. He had the look of—what does that mongrel of yours call them?—a 'hood.'"

"Celt" was the term Diocles used for an Irishman. Around Chicago, it wasn't surprising to have someone of Irish blood popping up, but not on a night when Father Jonathan, Saint Michael's current priest, didn't have a sermon. Diocles's description sounded like it might be one of the North Side gang. Several of them were pretty religious despite their bootlegging ways, but this didn't sound like someone in need of a blessing. I'd just recently had some run-ins with both Moran's and Capone's boys—the latter the North Side's main rivals—but had thought that both gangs had better things to do than track down a "ghost hunter."

Maybe I'd been wrong. "Did he talk to the Father?"

"Nay. He stepped inside, looked around, then left. Perhaps a minute, no more."

It could've been nothing. It could've just been coincidence.

I no longer believed in coincidence. "If you ever see him again—" Diocles vanished.

I swore an oath that would have made Fetch proud. Diocles and I already had a tenuous relationship built only on the fact that we were bound to one another by our sins. For him to vanish without warning like that did nothing to help.

A slight rustling from deeper in the cemetery caught my attention . . . and made my skin instinctively crawl. My left hand went into my overcoat even as I summoned forth the dragon's eyes again. What I suspected shouldn't have been possible in so hallowed a place . . . but then again, in Chicago these days, it was hard to keep any place hallowed. The gangs had done a good job of tainting everything with their bloody battles for territory, which might have opened the way now for something *worse*.

I risked a low, brief whistle. A moment later, a short bark arose from beyond the fence. Fetch understood.

A part of me wondered whether I was just being paranoid, but after Oberon's return, I trusted nothing. The cemetery should've been safe . . . but then, if someone had somehow destroyed the sanctity of this location, *anything* could be lurking around.

Despite all that, I was loath to draw Her Lady's gift in the cemetery unless I had absolute reason to.

That drew a rebuking laugh from inside my head. *Too little too late, Eye say . . . if one of them is already here. . . .*

The dragon had no name, but because of my constant use of his vision, he had come to refer to himself by the odd title. I never argued his choice. To be truthful, I didn't care, so long as he behaved. It was hard enough hunting the Wyld without concerning myself over his plotting. He chafed to be free, no matter what the cost to me or anyone else.

Still, he had a point. I slowly pulled my hand from my overcoat, at the same time drawing forth Her Lady's gift. Its drawing was accompanied by a brief crimson flash. The Feirie-forged sword had a long, jagged edge that had made quick work of some of the worst of the Wyld, but much of the weapon's true power came from within the golden hilt. There, a pattern of moon-colored stones circulated the ancient magic with which the queen of Feirie herself had imbued it.

"Georgius?"

I glared at Diocles, who abruptly stood in front of me. "Either stay or go, but get out of the way. . . ."

Again, I heard faint rustling. This time, I was certain I sensed at least a touch of Feirie nearby. I moved cautiously toward the direction. In the distance, I noted the slight patter of paws, an indication that, while he could not yet find a place where he could enter, Fetch at least tried to keep pace. With the cemetery possibly compromised, he now had an opportunity to enter.

Then I saw her.

She stood near the edge of one of the other headstones, her attention on the moon. Her face was obscured by shoulder-length hair and a small cap out of style for several years. In fact, as I studied her more, I noticed that her entire outfit was out of date by some twenty years or more.

She shimmered . . . exactly the way Diocles sometimes did.

Most of what people thought were ghosts were actually the most primal of the Wyld, creatures of the Feirie realm's most raw energies. However, what I saw in front of me was one of those rare few true spirits like Diocles.

At that moment, my own personal ghost whispered, "What is it? What do you see?"

I frowned. "Can't you see her?"

"I see nothing."

I didn't bother with him after that. Whatever the new ghost's reason for being where she was, there still remained the question of that trace of Wyld I sensed. I crossed another grave, careful to avoid actually stepping on the departed . . . and then she turned to face me.

I stepped back in shock.

To my left, something moved.

"Georgius!"

Diocles's warning came far too late. A force shoved me forward. I tried to keep my balance. Despite my best efforts, my foot came down on the next grave.

The ground gave way.

Holding onto Her Lady's gift with all my might, I fell *into* the grave. There hadn't been an open one near me. Instead, something had emptied out this one, then covered it over with what seemed the original sod so that no one would suspect it was hollow. I couldn't imagine it'd been done for my sake, but that hardly mattered as I landed hard at the bottom. The force of the collision made me tumble over onto my back.

If I'd had my own eyes, I'd have not seen anything ready to drop down on me. With the dragon's, I made out the impossibly thin stick figure falling into the grave. Even the head was nothing more than a stick. I'd found my Wyld, lucky me.

Before I could raise Her Lady's gift, a pile of dirt blinded me. The Wyld had evidently noticed I could see in the dark, so it'd done the logical thing and removed *all* my view. I was reduced to swinging the sword back and forth, hoping for even a graze. It wouldn't take much more than that for Her Lady's gift to do its work.

There was no squeal, which meant that I'd missed. More dirt spilled over my face, into my mouth, almost choking me in the process.

A savage growl filled my ears. It was followed by a hideous hiss that had to come from the Wyld. Another growl came in response. The sounds of a violent struggle ensued.

Wiping away the dirt, I beheld the stick figure struggling with a massive beast, something like a cross between a sleek greyhound and a savage wolf. Fetch was far, far more than either, though, a once powerful servant of Feirie now reduced to skulking around the streets of Chicago when he wasn't assisting me.

The stick figure's left arm abruptly sharpened to a point. The creatures of Feirie were often very fluid of form, especially those spawned nearest the realm's primal forces. The Wyld thrust its limb at Fetch with a lunge worthy of Douglas Fairbanks's Zorro. Fetch managed to dodge the strike, then moved in again.

I jumped up. In my head, the dragon all but roared, *Unleash me! Unleash me! Eye will burn it away!*

I was sorely tempted, but I fought down the suggestion even as I closed on the Wyld. Unleashing the dragon might cause far more calamity than one denizen of Feirie.

The stick figure turned as I reached it. Instead of attacking, though, it *leapt* straight up, then landed on the outer edge of the grave. I jabbed as it moved, but missed.

Fetch did his best to climb out after the thing. Unfortunately, by the time we both made it up, there was no sign of our quarry. I surveyed the area, but couldn't even sense a trace.

"Fetch?"

He sniffed the air. "Not a whiff, Master Nicholas! Looks like it's taken it on the lam!"

I let Fetch's penchant for human slang pass as I extended Her Lady's gift as far as I could reach. Nothing.

"Shall I give chase?"

"Where?" I turned the sword around and returned it to my overcoat. It went back into that dark space Her Lady had also provided for it, enabling me to move unencumbered.

And then, I saw her again.

I didn't know if she'd vanished and returned or just stood there all through our brief struggle with the Wyld. I vaguely wondered if there was some link between her and what had happened, but then she looked my way again and all I could do was stare at her face.

Her face.

"Master Nicholas? Be ye all right? Does something ail ye?"

Instead of answering, I dared tear my gaze from her long enough to look over my shoulder. Of Diocles, there was no sign. I didn't know if that meant anything, but once more, it paled in importance to *her*.

Thankfully, she still stood there, staring in my direction. I belatedly noticed the sadness in her eyes.

"Master Nicholas . . . this isn't copacetic! What ails ye?"

"You don't see her, either." I waved off the reply Fetch started. With the utmost caution, I took a step toward her.

Naturally, she disappeared.

Swearing in more than one of the fourteen languages I remained fluent in, I rushed toward the spot.

There were no footprints, of course, not that I'd even really been looking for them. With her gone, there was only one thing I wanted to see.

And there, on the stone, was just that. A name. Below it, a date that began only a year after the Great Fire and ended barely twenty years after that, right during the Columbian Exposition. Just long enough to verify my fears. Just long enough for the damned cycle to begin anew yet again a few years after that.

Her first name had been *Claudette*. Her last name really didn't matter. It could've been anything. The first name was enough, a variation on a damning theme.

Cleolinda. Clarissa. Claryce. All names for the same old soul, the woman who I'd rescued from a dragon and who then had rescued my heart. There'd been others with such names, spread far apart through the centuries. I'd known each and every one of them. *Lost* each and every one of them save for Claryce . . . so far. They'd all had different backgrounds, different lives, but always the same face.

A face identical to that of the ghost.

Claudette had been another incarnation, one right *before* Claryce.

An incarnation, despite our supposedly intertwined fates, I'd *never* met.

CHAPTER 2

I waited near the headstone the rest of the night, hoping for her return. Fetch sat patiently next to me the entire time, no small feat for him, especially once a rabbit passed nearby. Fetch squirmed for a moment then, but that was all.

If I'd been a better person, I'd have let him give chase, but all I could think about was another chance to try to speak to her . . . to Claudette.

Diocles hung around for a while, too, not that I'd encouraged him. After being as silent as the dead for an entire fifteen minutes, he'd begun voicing his opinion on not just my choice here, but other related matters.

"It will probably not materialize again, Georgius. Manifestation is a matter of strong will at the best of times." When I said nothing, he'd switched to the topic I'd been trying to avoid thinking about. "And again, what does it matter? Even if some vestige of this poor woman does remain, if she is the princess reborn, then her true soul, her true essence, now resides in Claryce Simone . . . with whom you have decided you will not have anything to do."

Fetch could neither see nor hear Diocles, but he could certainly see my reaction. Ears flattened, he'd had the sense to scramble away as I'd spun on the emperor. "Leave. Leave now."

Diocles had done just that. We'd both known that there was nothing I could do to him, but he'd likely seen that it was better for both of us if he let me be. I'd glared at the empty space where he'd stood, then silently went back to my vigil.

Of course, he'd been right. She'd never reappeared. I'd finally left the cemetery just as the first hints of light had begun showing up on the horizon. With Fetch eagerly sitting in the seat next to me, I'd driven the Packard roadster I'd inherited from my battle with the former king of Feirie back to the gray Queen Anne house that I used for home and base in this particular century. The neighborhood was a quiet one not far from the heart of the Cabbage Patch, once the center of German immigration in Chicago and a place that had managed to at least in part survive the Great Fire intact.

Fetch rode along merrily enough in the car, but the moment we reached the house, his ears flattened again.

"You coming in?" I asked him as we pulled up. We'd had a short but rough period after Oberon . . . the enticements of Feirie very strong for an exile like Fetch . . . but he'd come through in the end, and that'd made it easier to forgive his lapse.

"I thank ye, Master Nicholas, but I'll not be stepping in there for a time. *Her* taint's still on this place. Gives me the heebie-jeebies, it does. . . ."

I couldn't blame him. The house had been brought to the ground by Oberon's human goons, then reconstructed in its entirety by his former love, the queen of Feirie, without my neighbors even realizing it. In the process, she'd given herself a portal of sorts into our world. However, after I'd destroyed Oberon, I'd made certain to have her remove all aspects of her power. The house was the house, but even I didn't trust that there might not be some lingering traces of Her Lady's magic.

Still, I suspected that Fetch had another reason, one that we'd silently agreed not to speak about during the drive back. "How is she, Fetch?"

"I've done just as ye asked, haven't buzzed her once since you said to leave her be."

"'Buzzed'?" Before he could translate his latest verbal acquisition, I pressed on. "You've seen her. Just admit it."

"But, Master Nicholas, what good would that be? I cannot speak with her unless you're near, ye know that! Only ye and Kravayik can jaw with me!"

Kravayik was an exile like Fetch—an exile from Her Lady's Court, in fact—who'd gone through an even greater change since crossing to this side of the Gate. Kravayik, once a senior enforcer of the Court, had found *God*. He had converted to Christianity and even now served in Holy Name Cathedral as an unofficial caretaker.

Fetch, too, had acted as an enforcer of sorts for Feirie. In fact, his last mission for Her Lady had been my intended assassination. Fate had changed courses for both of us, and Fetch had ended up being left for dead himself by the Court. I'd managed to keep him alive, and he'd been grateful ever since . . . or at least as grateful as any of the Feirie folk could be.

"But you *did* see her, didn't you? Even after I warned you to steer clear? Admit it."

He let out a short whine. With the power of Feirie behind him, he'd been a powerful shapeshifter, a thing lupine in nature but also almost manlike. Without it, he couldn't even change from the hound he appeared as now. That didn't seem to bother him too much, though. What did, evidently, was possibly angering me by disobeying my orders where Claryce was concerned.

"You saw her." I no longer questioned him. I knew. The thought suddenly got my blood stirring.

My anger must've shown more than I thought. Back arched, fur stiff, he responded, "She didn't see me! I swear!"

He was a terrible liar. Still, I fought down my fury. "How—how long has this been going on?"

"Only a week. . . ." Fetch straightened. "She misses ye something fierce, but she's a tough egg, Master Nicholas! She's pushing on even after Oberon."

I couldn't deny that I was glad to hear she was okay, but I still felt betrayed. Naturally, that brought a snicker from my unseen companion, who had remained oddly silent since the cemetery. I didn't like how no one seemed to be listening to my demands anymore, but I let that pass as my curiosity got the better of me. "She's okay, then."

"Other than not seeing ye, she is."

"Is she still at Oberon's?" In the guise of businessman William Delke, Oberon'd lured Claryce to him by offering her a position in his company. Having had encounters with me over the previous centuries, he'd recognized her as the reincarnation of Cleolinda and used her for bait. Of course, much to his ultimate misfortune, Claryce'd proven to be pretty independent bait.

"Nay. She lives over a bookstore."

I'd expected her situation to change, but not quite so quickly. "She's no longer with Delke Industries, then."

"For a bit, still, but she said—"

He tried to cut himself off, but he'd already said one word too much. Anger rushed through me, stronger than ever. "So you *did* meet with her? You were supposed to stay away from her! I ordered you to!"

Fetch leapt out of the roadster and didn't stop until he was across the street. I gripped the wheel with one hand as I fought with the notion of throttling him.

I heard a wrenching sound from near the wheel. Glancing there, I saw that I'd just crushed the top of the wheel. Worse, my hand had grown longer . . . and scaled to boot.

I'd let a part of the dragon out without even noticing.

"Take it back," I growled. "Take the power back. . . ."

The dragon said nothing, but my hand reverted to normal in an instant. I shuddered. Once again, I'd lost control. This time badly. For a brief moment, I'd actually wanted to kill Fetch.

I looked back to Fetch, who stood with his tail between his legs watching me warily. I started to beckon him back, but the moment I raised my other hand toward him, he turned and raced off.

Inside my head, the dragon snickered.

"Damn you," I whispered, not quite certain if I meant the dragon or myself. I finally jumped out of the Packard and headed inside the nondescript house.

The furnishings inside could be called eclectic at best, some of them simply timeworn, others obviously antiques of tremendous value. I hadn't tried to collect things over the sixteen hundred years of my service to the Gate, but it'd happened anyway. Each piece, even the most innocuous one, had some bit of personal history. It might've seemed mad to anyone else that over the centuries I'd gone through the trouble of sending carts and boats across Asia Minor, Europe, and then the Atlantic just to keep these, but somewhere along the way I'd decided I was owed that much.

The dragon never mocked this eccentricity on my part. I'd wondered if it had anything to do with the stories of his kind hoarding gold and other things they found valuable, but had never bothered to ask. He wouldn't have given me a straight answer, anyway. I only knew that on occasion I sensed he took some little comfort in these bits of our history, too.

I should've gotten some sleep, but the incident in the cemetery still lingered with me. I glanced at the pile of newspapers atop an oak table that'd been an antique back when the States had still been colonies and finally grabbed one. Pulling up a chair, I started scouring the headlines.

There was no one factor that made me decide which articles to cut out. I went by feeling. The story of a theft at a bookshop was my first choice. After checking the back of the page to make sure there wasn't a story of more interest, I removed the news item from the paper and placed it on the side. Over the next half hour, I added three more, one concerning local politics and the other pair about minor incidents overseas. There was a good chance I might never look at them again . . . but then again, I might.

In another room, there stood file cabinet after file cabinet of organized clippings. Some of them were well over a century old. Unlike my furnishings, they were a necessary part of my endless task. Through the articles I stored in them, I tried to glean any threats somehow related to the Gate. Wyld might lurk for generations before they dared mischief. The theft from the bookshop—and I did wonder if it was the same one Claryce now lived over—could concern a book containing ancient words of power. The money stolen might've been merely a cover. I couldn't take a chance.

I pulled over yesterday's *Daily News* and started anew. On the lower part of the front page, I noted a story about a body found in the Chicago River. Male, but so long in the water not much else could be said about it. The police believed it part of the bootlegger wars, which meant that they wouldn't follow through with an investigation unless someone came along with different information. I suspected the same as the police, but cut it out, regardless. Oberon had had ties with Bugs Moran's North Side mob; other Wyld might try to do the same with either Moran or his rival, Capone.

Thinking of Moran, I pulled the latest issue of the *Herald Examiner* next. It was an open secret that the mobs also ran the newspaper distribution for several of the papers, including the *Herald Examiner*. Running that distribution meant pressuring stands and stores to carry one paper over another.

But exhaustion overtook me at some point, and only when the candlestick telephone in the front hall rang did I realize I'd never gotten past the second page. I dropped the paper and jumped to my feet. Only then did I remember my appointment. I glanced at my wristwatch, a recent addition, to find I'd just slept long enough to miss my preliminary appointment with my latest "clients."

Quickly putting the receiver to my ear, I picked up the phone and answered. "Hello?"

"Master Nicholas. . . ." came a rough voice. I'd never asked anyone to call me by such a title, but there were three who insisted. Two, including

Fetch, did so because they'd been spawned serving the Court of Feirie, where, even with its dark excesses, it always insisted on formality.

The third, though, was a man . . . more or less. "Barnaby."

Barnaby had long ago delved into what some might've called the magical arts. He'd done it with the best of intentions, seeking to help his family and friends. Barnaby hadn't managed to achieve much with it and had eventually satisfied himself with collecting bits and pieces that intrigued him as he built up a profitable auto repair shop. In the end, it'd turned out that tinkering with cars had proven a more satisfying outlet for Barnaby than tinkering with the supernatural.

A shame the same couldn't have been said for Joseph.

"Forgive me for calling. I wouldn't have . . . but with my Emma gone, there's no one else who'd understand."

I frowned. Barnaby only mentioned his Emma—dead twenty years—in regard to one subject. "You've seen Joseph?"

A sigh preceded his answer. "I know, you did warn me that it wouldn't do much good, but it was Emma's birthday, so I couldn't help trying to talk with him about her. I thought that maybe his mother's birthday of all days might stir him up."

"And did it?"

"No. He just kept staring at my shadow on the wall. Just like always. Just like since the Wingfoot crash six years ago."

The pain I heard in his voice kept me from further reprimanding him for wasting his time on Joseph. I'd managed to save Barnaby's son from his own ambition, but at a tremendous cost. Yes, Joseph had survived the dirigible's crash into the Illinois Trust and Savings Building, but in the collision he'd suffered a terrible head injury. Barnaby had no choice but to consign his only child to Dunning.

Officially, it wasn't called Dunning anymore. In the hopes of whitewashing its past, the county had renamed it the *Chicago State Hospital* and put out a bunch of pretty announcements about its services.

But most people still called it Dunning.

It wasn't a pleasant place, but it was the only choice for those like Joseph. Joseph had been there for more than five years now with little change. Yet, Barnaby continued to hope.

I'd lived too long to believe in such hope.

While I could sympathize with Barnaby, there wasn't much I could do for his situation, which made me wonder why he'd called. "Did something else happen at Dunning?"

His pause lasted long enough to put me on edge.

"Joseph's had a visitor."

I gripped the receiver tighter. No one knew Joseph had been committed to Dunning except for Barnaby and me. No one knew Joseph even lived. "Who?"

"I don't know. I can't decipher the signature. I tried asking the staff on duty, but no one seems to remember anything except that someone asked for Joseph." He paused, then added, "I never thought to forbid anyone from seeing him. I never thought anyone but me ever would visit him, Master Nicholas."

He had a point there. I'd never considered warning him to do any such thing either. Those involved with Joseph had died before and during the Wingfoot disaster. There should've been no one else interested in Barnaby's son. "How long ago did it happen?"

When he told me, I shuddered. The same night as the Frost Moon and Oberon's plan to make Feirie and the mortal world into one big mess. It didn't surprise me that Oberon might've been involved with Joseph somehow. Oberon's plots had gone all the way back to the day after I thought he'd burned to death during the Great Fire . . . or as those of Feirie often called it, the Night the Dragon Breathed.

The night I'd decided it was better to fully release the dragon and let a city go up in flames in order to save it and everything else.

I mentioned Oberon to Barnaby. Oddly, he sounded relieved at the suggestion. "Then, it's nothing to worry ourselves about. That's all over with His Lord gone. Thank God for that."

"Just the same, I'd like to see the signature when I get the chance. Do you feel like going out to see Joseph soon again?"

"Always. He's still a part of my Emma. He's still my son."

I had no reply for that. I'd not met Emma. I'd met Joseph when he'd been of his own mind. I couldn't imagine him being any part of a woman Barnaby'd described as so loving, so caring.

"I'll call you when I know what's best for me. It should be nothing, but I'd just like to verify."

"Thank you."

"The Packard runs great," I added for lack of anything better to say.

"Glad to hear, Master Nicholas. It's the least I can do."

I hung up. If the unexpected nap hadn't been enough to get me going again, the call had. I couldn't be bothered with the clippings. I needed to get out.

I needed, despite everything I'd told myself over and over, to see Claryce.

The dragon snickered.

CHAPTER 3

I made one quick call before leaving, an apologetic one to the young Mrs. Nilsson about my missed appointment. I understood enough concerning their situation to know that they were still safe from the Wyld likely lurking in the recesses of their house. Unless extremely powerful—like a member of Her Lady's Court—it took time for them to rebuild their power once they crossed into the mortal world. This one clearly hadn't been here long enough. Still, I promised I'd take care of the situation tonight, and I would.

There was no sign of Fetch outside. He'd probably kept running until he was near the State Street restaurants. The Loop was one of his favorite haunts, with the restaurants supplying the bulk of his meals. The cooks didn't actually come out and feed him; Fetch lived for the most part on the robust population of vermin thriving on the trash in the back. He'd also fed regularly on the cats that'd come hunting the rats until I'd put a stop to that.

When she'd only known him as her boss, William Delke, Claryce had accepted his offer to use one of his homes in the city after her own place had suffered a fire. We'd both come to realize that the fire had been set by Oberon's human hoods, but that still had meant that she'd had to stay at the house for a time after I'd settled with the former king of Feirie. Naturally, I'd checked out the place one more time to make certain Oberon'd left nothing behind, then turned my back on Claryce for what I thought was the last time.

I should've known better.

I pulled up near Fetch's favorite haunts, found a spot, and decided which alley to try. After parking the Packard, I left the bright streets of Chicago for the eternal darkness of the alley. Fetch always chose the latter, the better not only to be left undisturbed as he ate, but also so that no one might actually see that he *wasn't* some mere stray dog.

The moment I entered the alley, I could sense the presence of Feirie. It was a gift, so to speak, of my merging with the dragon. The guardian of the Gate had to be able to sense intrusions. If I'd been on the Feirie side, I would've been able to do the same with a human intruder there. That happened less than the former, but it did happen.

As a precaution, I summoned the dragon's vision. The emerald world it revealed made me certain that Fetch would find quite a bounty here. Several meals scurried from view as I stepped deeper into the alley.

Then, something that *wasn't* a rat or even Fetch briefly separated itself from one pile of trash. It was as tall as my waist, but twice as wide as my arm. It moved on all fours, and the three amber orbs it turned in my direction revealed that it knew very well it'd made a mistake by moving.

I had Her Lady's gift out in one sweep. The Wyld hissed, then backed a step away. It did not want this fight. It was clearly new to this world, probably having slipped in during one of Oberon's plots. For now, rats and trash were sufficient food for it, but I couldn't wait for it to grow strong enough to hunt human prey.

Unlike the stickman at Saint Boniface, this Wyld seemed to have no appendage that could act as a weapon. Instead, it kept hissing and tried to stand as straight as it could.

A bug to step on, the dragon commented disdainfully.

I had to admit that it wasn't much of a menace, but it was still a Wyld. I raised Her Lady's gift and approached.

"Nay, Master Nicholas! Leave him be! He's jake! I swear!"

Fetch came barreling down from the opposite direction. As he neared the Wyld, it suddenly dove into hiding behind the trash cans. Fetch ignored it, his attention entirely on me.

"What's going on here?" I demanded, sword still ready. "What's that one doing with you, Fetch?"

"He's on the lam from the Court! Her Lady's purging all who had any sort of loyalty to Oberon from Feirie!"

His revelation didn't exactly shock me. Her Lady had moved cautiously when she'd not been certain of Oberon's death after the Great Fire. Now, though, with absolute proof that her former mate was only a scorched memory, she'd evidently begun making Feirie over entirely in her own image.

I'd expected more activity among the Wyld with Oberon gone and Her Lady fully in charge, but I'd thought it would take longer to begin. We'd barely gotten past Oberon and the Frost Moon. Her Lady'd clearly been looking forward to this day for a long time.

That still didn't explain everything I'd just seen. "You're shielding a Wyld, Fetch."

His ears flattened, but he held his ground. "Not all are Wyld, Master Nicholas. Some of us . . . we just want to live."

This is not allowed. . . . It must be slain. This is our purpose . . . you know that . . . Eye know that. . . .

"Quiet," I muttered.

"I swear this one's no danger!" the shapeshifter insisted, clearly aware to just who I'd been speaking. "He's harmless! Just a Palooka!"

I lowered the sword, but kept it pointed toward the trash. "Call him out, Fetch."

He hesitated, then let out a single bark. When nothing happened, Fetch barked once more.

The creature slowly shifted into the open. The three orbs looked from Fetch to me.

I took its measure. I hadn't always adhered to the demands of the Gate over the centuries. Fetch and Kravayik were two examples of the exceptions I'd made. Of course, in some ways, I could identify with them. They'd been soldiers in service to the Court.

With Her Lady's gift, I cut a swath in the air before the creature. In its wake, an astounding transformation took place. The four-legged thing became a short, thin, almost human figure with two wide silver eyes, silver hair pressed against the skull, and an extremely narrow face. At first glance someone seeing him would've maybe mistaken him for a nude child crouched on hands and knees. Maybe.

The image faded, replaced by the original creature. The sword had given me a glimpse as to the thing's ultimate nature. While not a high-ranking servitor of the Court, this was still a being through whom flowed the blood of some randy member of the high caste. The ruling class of Feirie had a habit of doing what they willed with the rest of the realm's denizens, and in a magical place like Feirie, that often created half-breeds like this.

By human standards, he was probably hundreds of years old, but by Feirie's probably still pretty young and not so adept with his powers. He couldn't have survived so intact in Feirie without the favor of whoever his high-caste parent had been, favor which didn't necessarily equate to love. *Fondness* maybe, like a favored pet, not an offspring.

I still should've dealt with him. That was part of my duty. Certainly, Her Lady wanted him dead. Still, I didn't serve the queen of Feirie, despite what she thought.

The dragon didn't hide his disgust with my hesitation. I didn't care. Given the time to study the creature, I could see that it would never be much more than it was now. This was no sinister servant of Oberon. His only crime had likely been not transferring his loyalty fast enough to the queen.

"He's your responsibility," I finally said to Fetch. At the same time, I replaced the sword in my overcoat.

"Yes . . . of course. Thank ye, Master Nicholas. Ye are too kind, Master—"

"Quiet." I waved a hand toward the trash. The other creature scurried back out of sight. Fetch looked like he wanted to follow. "I came to talk to you about Claryce."

"I'll not go near her again! Cross my heart!"

I silenced him yet again. "Actually, I want you to show me where to find her."

Fetch nodded eagerly. "I'll do that! Anything for ye, Master Nicholas! Anything!"

His exaggerated show of eagerness stirred my guilt. "Relax, Fetch. You did nothing wrong in keeping track of her, I suppose. You had the right to do that . . . and I think I'm actually glad you did."

How utterly sweet and charming. . . .

Shut up!

Fetch remained politely indifferent during my brief clash with the dragon. Only when I gave him a nod did he dare speak up.

"Don't know where she is now, but I know where she'll be later. I heard her make the appointment. Will that do?"

"Good enough. Tell me."

Fetch concentrated, then answered. "She said six-oh-two West Sixty-Third Street. I honestly tried to remember, just in case."

He wouldn't have heard the address so well unless he'd gotten a lot closer to Claryce than he'd admitted, but I let it pass. I gestured the way I'd come. "Come on. You're sticking with me until then."

"As ye like, Master Nicholas."

"Your . . . friend . . . going to stay out of trouble here when you're gone?"

"Aye, he will. I've made this place safe."

I hoped I wasn't making a mistake, but I just nodded again and started back. Within seconds, Fetch was at my side. He kept pace until we reached the end of the alley, then waited. Despite his size and appearance, Fetch could move among people without being noticed unless desired. Still, I always preferred he not take too many chances.

I went to the Packard first and casually opened the passenger door slightly as I passed it.

That was when I noticed the thug on the corner.

Not for a moment had I assumed that Moran's gang might not know who I was—or rather, who Nick Medea was. While most of those lent to Oberon by Moran had either been killed or arrested by Detective Cortez and his men, there was the chance that someone had gotten back to Moran with my description. The hood trying to look so inconspicuous as he thumbed through a copy of the *Tribune* at the newsstand was definitely a Mick like most of Moran's gang. Still, I was surprised he'd found me. Either I'd missed being tailed or he'd come across me by sheer luck.

If there was any question I was his target, that was answered the moment I climbed inside the Packard. Down went the *Trib* and off to the side went the spotter. I could already predict a car similar to my own with two other thugs inside waiting just around the corner.

"What's eating ye, Master Nicholas?" Fetch suddenly asked next to me.

"We've got friends. Maybe leftovers from Oberon?"

"Bimbos like that Doolin?"

I shook my head. "No one could be like Doolin." Oberon had found himself the nastiest of hoods to make his human enforcer. Doolin had been worthy of any of the Court. But like Oberon, Doolin was dead. "I don't want to end up leading them to Claryce."

"We behind the eight ball, then?" Fetch bared his teeth, showing me that if we were in trouble, he'd stand with me.

"We'll see. Hang on."

I started the Packard and pulled into traffic. As we reached the intersection I saw out of the corner of my eye a black Studebaker Big Six pull out to follow us. It'd be hard to lose the Big Six on speed alone; even the police were using them more and more. I had to see if the driver knew the streets of Chicago better than I did. I doubted it. I'd had more than fifty years to learn them by heart.

Even though, according to a last bit of information dragged out of Fetch, we had a few hours until Claryce would be there, I made

certain to turn away from West Sixty-Third. I moved along as if not
suspecting I was being tailed, letting them get overconfident.

"What do you see, Fetch?"

He peered behind us. "Three, Master Nicholas. Driver, two
torpedoes."

"That including the spotter?"

"Aye."

I already had a route forming in my mind, and the traffic was
building up enough to be of benefit. We had a chance to lose the
Studebaker fairly quickly after all. "How're they doing, Fetch?"

"Just with us. Should be a piece of cake for ye—"

The *second* car came out of nowhere, cutting across our path so
close all I could do was hit the brake and hope for the best.

But somehow, the other car swerved expertly out of our path. As
it did, I stared at the whitest face I'd seen outside of Max Schreck's
Count Orlok in *Nosferatu* a couple of years back. He wasn't much
better-looking than the movie vampire, either, with low-lidded pale
eyes, a lipless mouth, and barely a snub of a nose.

Behind him sat a weaselly Mick with an automatic. I dove down
behind the wheel even as I steered to the right. Not for a moment did
I assume that the gun was just a gun. If there was any chance these
were remnants of Oberon's followers, the gun probably fired something more than normal bullets. I was resilient thanks to the dragon's
power, but not invincible. I'd survived sixteen centuries through skill
and luck—especially luck.

I heard two sharp cracks. The window shattered. Fetch growled
and started to leap out.

"Get back in!" I roared. Horns honked. People screamed. I heard
at least one car hit another.

We ran up on the curb. I had no choice but to keep braking.

No more shots followed. That didn't mean we were safe. I waited
a moment before carefully peering over the cracked windshield.

There was no sign of the second car. A quick glance behind us revealed no hint of the first. I grimaced. The Studebaker'd been a distraction. They'd known the direction I'd have to first drive, then set up this ambush while I was likely still in the alley with Fetch.

A siren howled. I tried to get the Packard back into the street, but the traffic was all gnarled up now. Worse, the source of the siren was already racing into sight. The fact that it was not only a police car but also a black Ford Runabout made me more certain than ever that someone had set up the situation.

The Runabout stopped. It didn't surprise me when out of the vehicle stepped what to many Chicagoans might've been the most unlikely member of the police department. His gray suit was immaculate, his short, black hair oiled and groomed. He had in one hand a cigarette I knew probably wasn't lit. None of that mattered so much though as he was a swarthier-looking man than the two officers who got out to check the scene. Detective Alejandro Cortez was Mexican, the only one of his rank—and maybe *any* rank—on the force.

Cortez was very savvy and deserved his rank far more than a lot of those flashing badges around Chicago. Of course, he and I both knew that the only reason he'd gained that rank despite the seeping prejudice in the department was because some higher-up had hit on the idea of having someone who could not only go into the "dirty" places and get something done, but also take the fall if it didn't shine well on his so-called superiors. In the time I'd known Cortez, he'd nearly risked his life more than a dozen times for little actual gratitude.

And yet, he still went on.

"Nick Medea!" Cortez always greeted me as if we hadn't seen each other in years. In this case, it'd only been a couple of weeks, if that much. "Didn't expect you when we heard the shots! You do get into a lot of scrapes, Bo, you know?"

I took a casual glance back. The Packard was empty, of course. Even though Cortez had seen Fetch in the past, I preferred that they didn't cross paths any more than necessary. Cortez had a sharper eye than most, and he'd not been so certain of my usual explanation concerning Fetch's supposed canine background.

Of course, he'd also seen a few other things I'd had trouble explaining. This attempted hit would be one of the easier things I'd needed to clear up.

Easier . . . not easy.

The detective peered at my windshield. "Someone's tried to use a bean-shooter on you. Now why would they try to gun down a ghost-buster, Nick Medea?"

"Must be a mistake."

"Mistakes like that happen a lot around you, Bo, you know?" He straightened, his expression more serious. "You okay?"

"Not a scratch."

Cortez rummaged in his coat pocket. Somewhere along the way, he'd already lost the unlit cigarette. The detective pulled out a pack of Luckys. He took one, then, as usual, offered me the pack.

And as usual, I shook my head. Cortez put the pack away. He didn't bother to light the cigarette, just kept holding it like the last.

Cortez noticed me glancing at the cigarette. "Yeah, my Maria got on me for them again last night, but it's hard, Bo! I figure if I just hold one it might be good enough, you know?"

I shrugged. "I've told you what I know about the accident. Can I go?"

"'Accident.' Hmmph." The detective eyed the two policemen. "Yeah, I doubt much is going to happen unless you say more. We've got enough else happening, you know? Couple of small-timers rubbed out in their wagon. No hooch. Think they're tied to the Outfit, which I don't need. Happened just a couple of blocks from here. Some coincidence you were nearby."

That explained his timely appearance. It was possible it also, in part, explained my situation. Not that I was going to tell him that.

Instead, I replied, "Guess I must've accidentally gotten in their path when they were fleeing the scene. Lucky me, right?"

"Yeah. Lucky you. Better watch out for yourself next time, eh?"

He'd surprised me with his easy dismissal of my near murder, but I wasn't going to look a gift horse in the mouth, as Fetch might've said. I quickly climbed inside the Packard.

Cortez waved at me. "Hey, you get the windshield fixed quick, okay, Bo?"

I nodded. I thought that finished things, but then the detective casually stepped in front of the Packard. He stared at the windshield once more, then came around to my side.

"Listen, Nick Medea, you like strange things."

"I don't know how I'm supposed to answer that."

Cortez chuckled. He put the unlit cigarette in the side of his mouth. "Not one of your ghosts, but maybe it's close enough. Don't know exactly what to call it. Maybe you should see it."

I hid my concern. "See what?"

"You tell me . . . when you get a gander at it. Come by this station." He pulled a card from the same pocket he'd tugged the Luckys. "It's here."

The station was different from the one where Cortez actually had a desk. The detective was passed around wherever the higher-ups—especially those from the mayor's office—had a problem they didn't like. "When?"

"Tonight?"

"Not possible. Tomorrow?"

He rubbed his chin. "Good." Cortez started to turn away, then again came back. "Oh, Maria talked about you the other night."

I arched a brow. "Did she?"

"Yeah . . ." His expression darkened. "She said she wanted to say a prayer for you. You. You two have never even met. Yeah, I've mentioned you a time or two, but it really struck me funny."

It was true I hadn't met his Maria nor their two children, but I'd seen a photo of Cortez's family recently. I remembered a petite, very attractive Mexican woman a few years younger than Cortez. I also remembered that she was supposed to be very religious. Maria apparently went at least twice a week to Our Lady of Guadalupe, a church arranged for the growing population of Mexican migrants to Chicago.

"Thank her for me," I finally remarked.

"Yeah . . ." He eyed me differently now, as if mention of his Maria had sparked some other thought. "Yeah . . . see you get that windshield fixed, okay?"

Nodding, I drove off.

Fetch was at my side a moment later. I didn't question how he'd done that. He was from Feirie. It was just his way.

"All jake, Master Nicholas?"

"I don't know." My abrupt encounter with Cortez'd raised a few questions, but those had to wait for later. Right now, I was concerned with what more and more seemed like a run-in with some remnant of Oberon's gang. They'd been following me and knew what route I'd take. I could still see the pasty face, the half-finished features. Yeah, he could've been just one of many ugly mugs to be found in any of the gangs, but for some reason I didn't think so. They'd planned something, but fortunately it hadn't culminated into anything . . . not this time, anyway.

I was pretty sure they'd try again, and that made a decision for me. Sure, I was going to see Claryce, but now for an entirely different reason. I'd been planning to just take a peek at Claryce, see that she was okay, and then turn my back on her forever. I'd figured that would keep her safe enough. Now, though, if any of Oberon's followers were still active, I had to do a lot more. I had to convince her to make a very important decision.

And if I failed to make her see reason . . . she might soon be lying next to Clarissa and Claudette.

CHAPTER 4

I needed the Packard to reach Claryce, which meant driving around with the ruined windshield. Fortunately, only one cop noticed it, but he just turned his back and moved on. I didn't know if he was already on another call or thought I might be with Moran or the O'Donnells, the latter whose territory I'd just entered. Every gang had its share of beat cops on the take despite Mayor Dever's promise to clean things up after "Big Bill" Thompson's more *obliging* administration. It was possible I wrongly marked the officer, but more than five decades in Chicago had jaded me.

I turned onto Sixty-Third and headed down to the six hundred block. I wondered why Oberon'd purchased real estate in this area. It occurred to me that I should've done more to clean up after his death, but I'd wanted to separate myself from Claryce.

So much for that idea.

I was only a couple of blocks away when a shiver ran through me. I didn't have to ask myself why. The nearer I got, the more I remembered some thirty-plus years ago when the Columbian Exposition had been taking place. All the wonders of the world in one location, some had bragged outrageously. I wasn't all that far from where the White City itself had been set up.

Memories stirred. I'd gone to the World's Fair, but not so much to see the sights. Spectacles like the exposition drew the Wyld, who used them to move around among the populace without notice. In fact, it'd been shortly after the exposition that I'd crossed paths for the first time with Kravayik. He hadn't quite gotten around to converting to Christianity at that time, but the need for something to fill some hole in his existence had already been evident. I'd not met a Wyld—or in his case, a refugee from Her Lady's Court—so eager to put Feirie behind him.

The sun had already dropped so low that shadows covered much of the vicinity. A short building with empty storefronts lay across from where Fetch said Claryce would be. I parked in front of it, then headed across the street, Fetch tailing me. A sleek maroon Wills Saint Claire with a black roof sat parked in front of the address in question. I didn't recognize it, but it looked like something Oberon would've picked up in his guise as William Delke.

The building where Claryce was supposed to be was another commercial property, which meant I was able to spot her through the glass even before I reached the door. I almost turned and left then, but reminded myself about Oberon's hoods. They wouldn't leave her alone just because I did.

Despite her fair hair—bobbed like the style growing more and more popular—her full lips and the wide, expressive eyes I knew to be chocolate brown hinted at some ancient Mediterranean ancestry. She was dressed in a long, dark skirt and silk blouse, the latter mostly obscured by a jacket set to match the skirt. As usual, she had her cloche hat snugly near her brow.

Her attention was focused on a set of papers in her hands. I silently stepped inside, then cleared my throat.

Claryce looked my way. I was heartened by the widening smile she first greeted me with . . . then hesitated when the smile became a tight frown accompanied by narrowed eyes trying to burn through me.

"Nick . . ." she finally muttered. "I thought you'd forgotten all about me." With a kinder expression, she looked down at my side. "Hello, Fetch."

"Mistress Claryce," he immediately responded, his tail wagging much too merrily for my tastes.

"Claryce . . ." I began.

She tossed the papers on a plain, square table, the only furniture in the room. "You just left me *alone*. I tried to call you, tried to see you. You did *nothing*."

"I thought you were better off away from me," I quickly explained before she could cut me off again. "I didn't want you to—"

She waited, but I couldn't finish what I'd started. I didn't want to remind her about what had happened to her previous incarnations, especially now that I knew about Claudette.

"You didn't want me to *die*, is that what you were going to say? Like Clarissa and the others?"

I nodded.

Her eyes continued to burn, but not as forcefully. "*That* is my decision, not yours." Finally, she calmed. "Nick . . . Nick, you can't just leave me be after what happened . . . and I'm not talking about William."

The moment she said the name, she winced. She'd known Oberon in his human guise as boss, mentor, and friend.

"It was wrong of me," I admitted.

Claryce pursed her lips, then, "What's happened now? What's changed your mind?"

I know my cheeks flushed. She understood I hadn't come here purely because I'd missed her. She knew that there was some immediate danger that'd forced my hand. "I think some of Oberon's hoods are still around."

"That doesn't surprise me." Not too far from the papers lay her purse. Claryce reached into the purse, then pulled out a blued Smith & Wesson M1917 revolver. I didn't have to ask her if she could use it. I knew she could. "If they're human, I assume this will work on them." She frowned. "*Are* they human?"

"Not certain about one of them."

Claryce slid the gun back into the purse. "Then I'll just have to fire twice."

"This is nothing to joke about—"

"No. It isn't. Did you think about the chance there might be some of these hoods left when you decided to just vanish? Did you, Nick?"

I'd slain a dragon and the king of Feirie, among a slew of other foes. Despite that, I couldn't meet her gaze. "I thought I was doing the right thing. I've lost—you know why I did it."

"Oh, Nick . . ." Suddenly she was next to me, her hand stroking my cheek. "You're not going to lose me either way."

She kissed me, and all my troubles vanished for a moment. Then, what I considered common sense returned and I stepped back. "Claryce, I—"

"Forgive me. Have I come at an inopportune time?"

Clearing her throat, Claryce stepped around me to a very pale, mustached man in his thirties, wearing a high-collared black suit and matching Derby hat, standing just inside the door. In his left hand he held a silver pocket watch. With the other he leaned slightly on a narrow wooden cane.

As Claryce reached a hand to him, I looked down at Fetch, who cowered. I might've been distracted, but he at least could've given some warning we were no longer alone.

"Some bloodhound," I muttered just loud enough for only him to hear.

"No, you're very punctual, Dr. Bond," Claryce responded to the newcomer.

"Alexander, please. I said so on the telephone," he replied with a cultured if somewhat raspy voice. He put the watch away and switched the cane over. Only then did he finally shake her hand. "A very definite pleasure, Miss Simone."

"And you can call me Claryce." She turned to indicate me. "This is . . . this is a friend of mine, Nick Medea."

Bond smiled through his thick mustache as he extended his hand to me. I nodded and took hold. The doctor wasn't the tallest man, but he had a strong grip.

Bond smiled cheerfully. "A definite pleasure, also, Mr. Medea."

"Same here." We released hands. His grip'd been good, but had a coolness to it.

"Dr. Bond is interested in this building, Nick. He made an appointment with me last night."

"I'm looking to expand my private practice," the doctor added, his attention now drawn to Fetch. "A fine beast. Not a wolfhound. Something more exotic, I'd guess."

He had no idea. "No, just a mixed breed."

"Really? He looks like a purebred to me." Without questioning the wisdom of his action, Bond patted Fetch on the head. Fetch accepted the pat with a slow wag of his tail. He didn't seem pleased by the doctor's touch.

"Shall we look around, then, Alexander?" Claryce asked. "I know you said you'd have limited time."

"Please." He extended his arm to her. The pair walked off, talking. For some reason, I had a desire to break them apart.

I must've started to act on it, because the next thing I knew something was tugging my coat, keeping me from another step after them. It was Fetch, naturally.

He quickly released the coat. "Sorry, Master Nicholas," he muttered. "Ye had that look. . . ."

"What look?"

"*His* look. Like when he wore your body when he double-crossed ye to Oberon. . . ."

I frowned. He meant the dragon. "Don't joke."

"I'm on the up and up with ye, I swear!"

I gestured him to keep his voice down. He was dead serious. If I'd let the dragon take over for even a second, not just the good doctor but Claryce might've suffered.

Without another word, I left the building. Fetch slipped out behind me. The last glimmer of light had vanished from the street, leaving nothing but shadows. For once, I welcomed them.

Something about the empty storefronts across the street caught my attention. Still not willing to risk going back inside but not yet ready to just leave, I crossed Sixty-Third to take a better look.

"Master Nicholas—"

"Quiet." I stared inside one store, but only met darkness.

Eye can help better. . . .

He knew very well I really didn't want his help right now, but the more I stared into the storefront, the more I couldn't shake the feeling that I'd just stumbled onto something. Something too close to Claryce, too.

"All right," I whispered between clenched teeth.

"Master Nicholas—"

I shook my head. I didn't need Fetch warning me about risking even a bit of the dragon's influence on me right now. I'd had sixteen hundred years of struggle to teach me the dangers.

The world turned emerald. The shadows—most of them, anyway—gave way. I tried the door.

It wasn't locked.

The moment I opened it, I knew we'd found a lair of one of the Wyld. Its stench was strong. So strong I wondered just how long it'd been in this world. I thought about Oberon again and wondered if it'd followed him here when he'd first fled Feirie after being ousted by Her Lady. That would explain its nearness to the building Claryce was showing.

Without another thought, I drew the sword and entered. I'd not sensed something this strong since Oberon himself. This Wyld had ties to the Court. That was worrying. Not all of Oberon's high-caste supporters were accounted for.

Fetch didn't follow me inside. Instead, he was pacing around the building, looking for an alternate path inside. The store itself was walls, windows, and a wooden floor. However, there were areas in the corners that remained dark even through the dragon's gaze. I dismissed one region as too narrow even for a Wyld to hide in, but the others had potential. There was a lot of Feirie energy residue in the store.

A shadow darted by. A shadow with nothing attached to it.

I'd seen things akin to it before, spells used by Oberon to allow his human pawns to do their dirty work while their bodies remained safe farther away. This wasn't quite the same, though. This flitted along as if in a world of its own, almost like a ghost. But ghosts were rare . . . at least that was what I'd believed until the other night.

I let my gaze follow the shadow's path . . . but tilted Her Lady's gift the opposite direction.

From one of the other shadowed corners erupted a towering black form. It swelled in size as it lunged at me, growing two pairs of arching limbs that reminded me of those of a spider. As I brought the sword around, I caught a glimpse of a long, misshapen face with two cold, ivory eyes.

It nearly impaled itself on Her Lady's gift, but managed to slither to the side at the last moment. Even then, the sword severed a piece of darkness from its side, a piece that faded before it could hit the floor.

The Wyld had acted predictably, not attacking outright but trying to use distraction first. Those of Feirie generally didn't have the guts—including those who literally *had* guts—to face a foe directly if they could help it. They played tricks, used deviousness. It didn't mean that they were weak, though. The deviousness was just part of their nature.

The Wyld spun around me, its limbs stretching wider, becoming more pointed. At the same time, the ivory eyes bore into mine, trying to snare my consciousness.

I gave the dragon a moment of amusement, letting him show the Wyld just what lay behind *our* eyes.

A hiss escaped my quarry. Any eagerness it'd had faded under the dragon's baleful gaze. It had just confronted a power far older, far stronger, than anything in Feirie.

Of course, it didn't know that the dragon's full might was forever tempered inside me. All it saw was something that gave its kind nightmares. That made it hesitate.

I lunged.

Her Lady's gift came to life as it dug into the Wyld. The blade flared crimson. The moon stones glimmered.

The hiss became a shrill howl. A portion of the Wyld ripped away, the piece quickly sucked into the magical sword. Once teased, Her Lady's gift hungered for the rest of its prey.

The Wyld surprised me by managing to retreat from the blade. Once so deeply wounded by the sword, most Wyld succumbed. I found myself both impressed and concerned.

Without the ability to snare my consciousness, the Wyld couldn't use a lot of its tricks. That hardly meant it was helpless, though. Despite its wound, it spread wider, larger, growing more limbs. As that happened, I felt the floor suddenly shift.

I hadn't ignored the wooden floor when I'd come inside. Some Wyld had the ability to insinuate themselves in every nook and cranny, even those with forms like Oberon or any of the Court. Even before the floor exploded, I'd jumped to my right, Her Lady's gift always kept ready. When the tendril thrust up from beneath the ruined floorboards—a tendril I only now could see extending from the lower end of the Wyld into the floor below—I was ready to attack it in turn. The tendril pulled back, then lunged under my guard.

One of the windows near the rear of the store shattered. A long, lupine form fell upon the Wyld from behind. Fetch opened wide, his mouth stretching farther than any true hound's could. His eyes glowed moon silver. His paws twisted, looking more like hands with long claws.

Fetch tore into the Wyld, ravaging what passed for a shoulder with such abandon that one spidery limb fell free in the process. Despite the Wyld's somewhat intangible form, Fetch had no trouble keeping hold. This near me, he was better able to draw on his Feirie-spawned abilities, although even I was surprised at the gusto with which he attacked.

The other limbs twisted back to seize Fetch, bending in a manner nothing mortal could've achieved. Despite the clear threat, Fetch stayed where he was, tearing out another part of the Wyld.

I dove forward, driving the blade's point into the tendril. The black limb sizzled, then dissipated. The Wyld forgot the shapeshifter's threat as it first severed the tendril from the rest of it, then tried to retreat.

With Fetch atop it, it moved too slowly. I drove Her Lady's gift right through its center. Not through its heart—it didn't have anything remotely like that—but where its nexus of power lay. The sword fed eagerly.

The Wyld contorted as Her Lady's gift swiftly swallowed its essence. Fetch leapt free just as the Wyld vanished into the burning blade.

A moment later, Her Lady's gift stilled.

"Couldn't find a door again?" I asked Fetch as I eyed the shattered window. This wasn't the first time he'd gone for the dramatic entrance when we'd confronted a Wyld. In fact, it was beginning to become a habit of late.

He looked utterly innocent. "Might've squeaked! Would've warned the goon, ye know!"

"And the shattering glass didn't. Hmmph." The taint of Wyld had already lessened. I returned the sword to its nether-realm sheath. "I think we should get back to Claryce. This is too close by to be happenstance."

As Fetch trotted to the door, I drew out some money and dropped it near the ruined window. It was all I could do without bringing more attention to myself. What mattered now was making certain no one tied us to the damage. I didn't need the police sniffing around me. Somehow, that'd bring Cortez into the equation, I was certain.

There was no sign of either Claryce or the doctor when we stepped back out onto the street. We quickly crossed.

Just in time. The two of them stepped to the door. I didn't like Bond's hand on her arm, even if it was probably just for friendly reasons.

"I'm very interested," he said to her as we neared. "A fine location with a lot of history."

"I won't be dealing with Delke Industries in another week," Claryce returned. "If you can't decide before that, please call the number I gave you."

He tipped his hat at her. "I'll do my best to decide quickly, then." Bond turned to me. "Mr. Medea. A pleasure."

"Doctor."

With a tap of his cane, Bond strode off. Claryce pointed back inside the building. "I need to retrieve my things. Then, we go somewhere and talk, Nick."

I didn't argue. The Wyld I'd just dispatched had only emphasized to me how precarious things still were after Oberon. I wondered just how much Her Lady had not bothered to mention to me in terms of both the extent of Oberon's apparent support, even in exile, and of the turmoil in the Feirie Court in general. She was tightening her grip, but just how tight was that grip right now?

Even after sixteen hundred years, the Machiavellian intrigues of Feirie continued to surprise me.

I started inside. "Do you know anything about the building across the street? Did Oberon own that, too?"

She looked back at me. "It's not on my list. I know someone who could check." Her gaze shifted to her bag. "I haven't forgiven you yet."

"Claryce—"

"Is it because I'm *her* that I want so much to, though, Nick? Do I really not have any choice of my own?" She shouldered her bag. "I took to trusting you almost immediately when we met. Was that because of *her*, too?"

I didn't have the answer. I hadn't asked Cleolinda to be reborn over and over, and I hadn't asked her to become Claryce. I'd been close to each of the incarnations, yes, even loved most of them.

But there was something different this time. . . . "I don't want anything to happen to *you*, Claryce. You."

"You've said that." Thankfully, her expression softened. "And somehow, I also know you really mean it . . . but I can't help thinking about how much of what I do is because I want to do it or because *she* wants me to be her again." Claryce shook her head. "My God! I'd think I'm sounding crazy if I hadn't seen all I'd seen! I—"

She stared past me. I spun, fearing that now that it was actually dark outside, something I hadn't noticed in the empty store had followed me back to her.

But the only thing I saw was Fetch, nose in the air, looking as if he were trying to inhale the entire building.

"What's with you?" I asked, a little too angrily, before I could stop myself. "Smell a rat . . . or maybe Berghoff's corned beef?" While Fetch was more than happy with rats or cats for a meal, he'd developed some very human tastes as well. I'd only recently discovered his fondness for corned beef, but only if it came from Berghoff's in the Loop . . . or, at least, their garbage cans. When that happened, he wouldn't touch anything else.

Then, I saw how flattened his ears were, which I realized was why Claryce had been distracted by him in the middle of our argument. I immediately knew it couldn't be a Wyld; I'd have noticed something, too.

One other possibility came to mind. One very unsettling possibility.

"It's Dr. Bond, isn't it, Fetch? There's something about his scent you've just noticed. He have a touch of the arts on him?"

"Nay, on the contrary!" He took one more deep sniff. "I cannot smell him at all, Master Nicholas! I was partakin' of the air, as usual . . . and I realized I couldn't smell him!"

"Nick . . . what's he talking about? What's wrong with Dr. Bond?"

I kept eyeing Fetch. He could smell a rat five blocks away. Human smells at a distance might be smothered by other stronger odors like those of the rats, but this close, he should've smelled something of the man. "No scent at *all*?"

"None! I'm bein' square with ye! Honest!"

"I know you are." I slipped past him and looked outside. It came as no surprise that there wasn't a sign of the good doctor even though he'd just left. In fact, I couldn't recall even hearing another auto for the past several minutes . . . or before he'd even arrived.

I didn't know who Claryce's prospective client was, but he *wasn't* human . . . at least not anymore.

CHAPTER 5

I turned back to Claryce. "How did Bond contact you?"

"By telephone, of course." She stepped up next to me. "What does he mean, he couldn't smell the doctor? Nick . . . was he one of . . . one of what you called the 'Wyld'?"

"No." I didn't know exactly *what* Bond was. Not at all like Oberon when he'd worn a human skin in order to play the role of William Delke. There'd been something more real about the doctor.

I thought about the building across the street. Again, I didn't believe in coincidence. "Stay here, Claryce. Fetch, with me."

I'd barely taken a step when she came up next to me. "I'm not staying. Don't try to order me around again."

"It's for your own—"

She slapped me. Fetch whined and slipped outside. Smart boy, that Fetch.

A heat rose in me. I wanted to take her by the throat, then rip out that throat.

Just as quickly, I smothered the thought. I looked inward, seeking the culprit for such a horrible thought.

Eye did nothing. . . .

Not for a moment did I trust him despite the denial. Fortunately, I'd managed to keep my face from showing anything to Claryce. Instead, I silently nodded. I realized that there probably wasn't *anywhere* safe. I couldn't very well tie her up and leave her.

"Stay close, then."

She pulled out the revolver. "I'll stay close all right."

I wasn't sure what good the gun would do against whatever we might meet. Some creatures it could stop. Others . . . "What about the dagger? Do you still have that?"

"Of course." She tapped her leg. "I'm no fool. I don't want to be next in line."

I didn't respond to the last comment, although inside I felt a chill. I was glad, though, to hear that she'd continued to carry the silver-tipped dagger I'd given her during the struggle with Oberon. It'd been blessed in Constantinople over a thousand years ago and had served me well over the centuries. Claryce had shown herself handy with blades—much to my relief—so I'd left it with her. That comforted me a little bit, at least.

We crossed over to the other building.

"Why are we going here? Just what happened while I was with him?"

"Work." I pulled on the door . . . and found it locked.

"What's wrong, Nick?"

"This was open." I peered through the glass, but there was no hint that Dr. Bond was inside.

Fetch ran off around the corner. I didn't have to ask why. A few seconds later, he showed up inside by the door. He grasped the inside handle with one paw and opened it with ease.

"How did he get in there?"

"Overenthusiasm." I pulled the door open. Darkness greeted us.

Eye can help. Let Eye let you see. . . .

I ignored him. After what I'd just experienced, the thought of letting out even a hint of his power in front of Claryce bothered me.

My foot hit something metal. Whatever it was rolled across the store with a harsh echo.

Claryce leaned close. "I thought you could see in the dark—" She took my chin in her hand and turned my face to hers. "They're *yours.* Why aren't you using . . . his?"

Eye told you! Even she says so. . . .

"This is because of me, isn't it, Nick? How can you take such a risk? Change them. Now!"

I looked away. *All right. Show me.*

The dragon snickered . . . and then the world illuminated for me. Fetch, now completely visible, wagged his tail in relief.

"Anything you smell here?"

He raised his nose again. "Feirie."

I wasn't sure what he meant. "You mean the Wyld we killed in here."

"Nay, Master Nicholas . . . I smell Feirie. The realm. Didn't think of it myself at the time! Thought like ye that it was that goon we did in, but, nay, I smell Feirie itself . . . as if we stand at the Gate . . ."

Feirie. He smelled *Feirie*. I was beginning to see that there'd been more loose ends after Oberon than I'd thought.

Let me show you . . . take just a little more . . . you need it. . . .

I gritted my teeth. *Go ahead.*

The world swirled around me for a moment. I heard things differently. I could taste scents. I could smell the magic around us.

I could now sense what Fetch did. Feirie *was* here. Not in the same way as the Gate . . . but still in a potent manner.

"Do you know *anything* about this property, Claryce?"

"No. I can see what I can find out at Delke's in the morning. Maybe Will—Oberon left this place in another file. We can meet for dinner tomorrow and discuss this . . . and other things."

She knew I could see her expression, and she knew that expression was one I dared not argue against. "All right."

"I'll be near the Loop by then. We'll meet at Berghoff's."

I looked down at Fetch. He cocked his head, all innocence. I knew that he couldn't talk to her when I wasn't near, and I couldn't recall when he would've mentioned the restaurant. Certainly not in the middle of the fight with Oberon. I could only surmise she'd taken note of my brief, sarcastic comment to him and wanted to give him a better treat than garbage or rats. I would have to remind her at some point that Fetch *wasn't* a poor, stray dog.

But not now.

"Berghoff's, then," I replied as I looked at her again.

Even though I couldn't see him anymore, I knew Fetch's tail was wagging harder.

We searched, but found nothing. It was as if whatever drew the power of Feirie here didn't exist and yet did. I finally led us outside, where I took a look at the building in general.

"There used to be more," I muttered. "This used to be a taller building."

Fetch sniffed the air. "'Twas a fire here, Master Nicholas."

"How recent?"

"Oh, tens of years, I'd say. Not so long as the night *he* breathed, but some time."

There didn't seem to be a connection in that regard, but I filed away the knowledge. I noticed the place was growing darker even with the dragon's gaze. Whether that meant anything, I couldn't say and didn't want to know at the moment, especially for Claryce's sake.

"Let's go," I ordered. She looked questioningly at me, but said nothing. Fetch kept behind us, making certain nothing would catch us by surprise.

We headed for the Delke building to retrieve Claryce's things, then moved on to the Wills. Fetch kept guard while Claryce climbed inside the car.

"Nice," I commented, trying to distract her from the knowledge that once again she'd suddenly been thrust into the intrigues of my world.

"The company's given it to me in return for my work acting as executor for 'William.'" She gave me a steady stare. "It's like they all want to wash their hands of him, Nick. I can't say that they knew he was Oberon, but they seem relieved he's gone."

I found that of interest. I made another note to investigate Delke Industries deeper than I had already. After Oberon, Claryce'd given me a list of those acting as top executives. Most had quickly turned out to be innocent dupes. One had disappeared. A swarthy man named Colby Dewhurst. Two others I realized had ties to Moran's mob, but were otherwise just human. I'd seen to it that the info on their ties had gotten to Cortez without my name involved, and they'd been arrested for charges not related to the plots of the exiled lord of Feirie.

If I'd missed some others in Delke, I needed to know, but that was something that had to wait until I knew more about this building . . . and Dr. Bond. I wondered if he had a connection to Delke, too.

I wondered if what I'd thought was the end of Oberon's plots was just the beginning of them—even with him dead.

Late that same day, I phoned the Nilssons to let them know I hadn't forgotten them again . . . only to have the husband ask who I was. When I mentioned ghosts, I received a curt comment about prank telephone calls before being hung up on by him. He sounded exactly like my clients did when they began losing their memories of me once my work was done.

I decided to drive over there on my own, but then remembered that I'd promised Cortez to look at his mysterious corpse tomorrow. Despite having sworn to the detective that I'd take care of the windshield as soon as possible, I drove down to the station listed on the card as soon as I could the next morning.

I was alone, having asked Fetch to keep a secret eye on Claryce. I wasn't worried so much about Oberon's goons at the moment as I was our friend the doctor. Until I found out his place in things, I couldn't take a chance that he might not have more than passing interest in her. It was possible he'd only been interested in the building itself, but he'd called her *specifically*.

I pulled up a little away from the police station, then walked the rest of the way. Winter had come to Chicago in a rush even though it wasn't supposed to start for a few more weeks. There was about an inch of snow and winds that made not having repaired the windshield a big inconvenience. I wasn't bothered by the steep drop in temperature; both my overcoat and the dragon's presence within kept me warm enough. Traffic wasn't too bad. It was the weekend now, which meant that level-headed folks could stay at home.

The desk sergeant looked up from his copy of the *Trib* sports section in mild surprise when I entered, especially as there was no snow on me. Things looked quiet. The coroner's office had proudly announced to the *Trib* and the other papers that there'd been no unnatural deaths in the past twenty-two hours . . . a grisly record of sorts for the city. No one expected that to last, though.

"I'm looking for Detective Cortez," I told the heavyset sergeant.

He made a face that plainly noted what he thought of Cortez even though the detective outranked him. "Not in. What's your business?"

I knew I'd come earlier than expected, so I wasn't entirely surprised. I'd actually hoped to study this corpse without Cortez around. "My name is Nick Medea. He—"

"Medea," he muttered, managing to mispronounce it badly. The sergeant glanced through some papers. "From the state coroner. 'Bout time." He snapped his fingers at a fresh-faced recruit who looked like he still believed that the Chicago Police Department was a paragon of virtue and law. "Kowalski. Morgue. Now."

The rookie nodded, then gestured me to follow. No longer interested in me, the sergeant returned to reading an article about Red Grange and the Bears' latest win, this one over the Frankfort Yellow Jackets. I suspected that the sports section was going to get a lot more focus than crime today where he was concerned.

I wasn't sure why I was supposed to be from the coroner. Cortez was usually aboveboard on everything, but he'd arranged so that I'd be able to get in without a problem. There'd likely even been a bribe to the desk sergeant, who'd be willing to take money even from an upstart Mexican.

"Are you here to try to help identify the body?" Kowalski chirped as we walked. With his ruddy face and dull red hair, he looked more Irish than Polish. I judged he'd been an officer for no more than three or four months. "I've heard it looks something awful."

"I won't know what I can do until I see it. I'll need to be alone so I can concentrate better."

"Oh, sure! That's what Detective Cortez said to the sergeant. I was there."

When Kowalski spoke of Cortez, there was more respect than what the sergeant had shown. I didn't know if that was a sign of more tolerance in general or simply that the rookie was an obliging man. It probably didn't matter. The odds were good he'd either be jaded or dead in a year or two.

"There's no one in today, but since you were supposed to stop by, everything should be arranged. Michael promised."

It was all I could do to keep from stumbling. "Michael?"

"He keeps things orderly for the coroner."

"This Michael? I think I know him. Is he a Negro?"

"Yes, sir. He's a good, hard worker." Officer Kowalski gestured to the right. "Here, sir."

I nodded absently as I entered the morgue. I was about to tell him he didn't have to come inside, only to find he'd already turned around and left.

I'd thought that Cortez had gone to a lot of trouble just for me, but now I saw another's hand in the matter that might've influenced the detective without him knowing. I knew a Michael who'd made his presence felt more than once during the fight with Oberon, an elderly Negro with a habit of popping up at some opportune times.

An elderly Negro who might have been *Saint* Michael, the archangel.

To my recollection, I'd never before actually met another saint, much less an archangel. True, I spent most of my prayer in the church named for him, but I'd never expected an answer, much less a personal appearance. I wasn't even sure if I'd really met him, for that matter. I only knew that evidence suggested Saint Michael had tried to lend a hand against Oberon.

That made the corpse of even more interest to me. I didn't have to wonder which one it might be. *Someone* had marked one of the drawers with a tag on which I found my appointment written. I tore off the tag and pulled the drawer open.

The body was covered with a sheet, of course, but I judged it to be roughly my height. I assumed that meant it was male. That made sense if it was a casualty of the bootlegger war between Moran and Capone. I wondered what was so special about it that Cortez—and maybe a higher power—had wanted me to see it so badly.

I pulled back the sheet . . . and almost dropped it.

Someone had vivisected the victim from head to toe. Someone with knowledge and skill. I'd seen butchery many times in my life. This was practiced butchery. I'd no doubt that it'd been done while the victim was still living, too. I silently cursed Cortez for not warning me about what I was going to see. Clearly, he'd somehow kept the truth of the corpse's condition from the press. There wasn't a stitch of clothes nor anything that would've marked this as a gangland hit.

I looked at the face . . . or where it'd been. Something was bothering me about the body. I wondered again why . . . assuming I was right . . . powers above had also wanted me to see this.

What do you want me to see, Michael, if you want me to see anything at all? What do you—

Then, I saw the telltale details that even so much time in the water—as the one article said the body was found in the Chicago

River—couldn't hide. The narrow jaw. The slightly longer skull. The different placement of the ears—or at least the holes where the ears used to be. I took another look at the limbs, at the fingers, which stretched farther than they should've.

Inside, the dragon hissed as he, too, came to understand the truth.

This was no human corpse.

This was the mutilated shell of a high-caste elf.

CHAPTER 6

The dragon hissed again. For once, we were in concert. Yes, it saved us the job of hunting this elf down, but it also meant that there was something *worse* out there.

I knew that Her Lady had her enforcers in the mortal world. I suppose this could've been the work of one of them, but it didn't have that Feirie touch. Of course, I didn't know exactly whose touch this could be. I couldn't imagine any of Moran's or Capone's boys spending this much time and interest on a victim. Moreover, I couldn't help but think that whatever had done this had done so with some curiosity as to how this elf looked inside.

Suddenly, I was no longer concerned about Oberon or any leftovers from his supporters. Suddenly, I wondered even more just who—or maybe *what*—Alexander Bond was. If he was the physician he said he was, then this looked like something just up his alley.

Right away, I thought of Claryce. She already knew to be wary of Bond, but this added a new level of danger.

I'd seen enough. There was nothing about the corpse that would identify it as from Feirie; any normal person would either chalk it up to the mutilation of the body or maybe a problem of birth. For the sharp-sighted Cortez, I'd come up with an excuse he couldn't argue with.

After shutting the drawer, I headed out of the morgue . . . and right into Cortez himself.

"Nick Medea! With this lousy weather, I thought I'd miss you!"

I'd been hoping just that. I eyed his less formal coat and slacks. "Are you on duty?"

He toyed with an unlit cigarette. "Nah, I'm off today, you know? I was actually on my way to see my brother, but just before I left, Maria told me there was a call. Said that I was to know that you were on your way here after all, despite the lovely day."

I hadn't been aware he had a brother, not that I'd been curious. "Did she say if it was Michael who called?"

The detective frowned. "Didn't say who called. Did you want this Michael to call?"

"Never mind." There was no escaping Cortez, so I quickly went into an explanation on the corpse. "I looked it over. You may have a slasher out there. Jack the Ripper type. He did a beauty of a job on the victim."

"Yeah, some piece of work, eh? Made me cross myself when I first saw it, you know? Wanted you to see it, 'cause you work with all that spooky stuff. You ever run across anything like that?"

"I disprove ghosts, Cortez. Murder's your department."

He chewed on the Lucky. "He look a little funny to you, though? Not quite right?"

"Time in the Chicago River'll do that to you."

"Yeah. Yeah. I suppose so." Cortez turned to walk with me. I hid my frown. "Well, that's about what I thought I might get out of you, but I wanted to hear."

"Sorry you wasted your time. Hope your brother won't mind the wait."

Cortez grunted. "Pedro won't mind. He's been gone two years now."

"I'm sorry. I hope it wasn't bad."

"Killed in a construction accident while working on the new Union Station. Pedro, he came here first as a *traquero*—a railroad laborer—you know? Worked hard to save enough to bring me and the family up. No schooling like I had, but a good, honest worker."

"You have my belated sympathies."

He nodded his thanks, then grinned sadly. "I did good for him in one way, you know? I got him a nice place in Saint Boniface. Lot of Krauts there, but good, Catholic folk. He was like my Maria. Very religious. Met a Kraut priest preaching at a mission and took a liking to the father's patron saint, you know?"

I paid the rest little mind, the mention of Saint Boniface snaring my attention. I wanted to ask just where Cortez's brother was buried in the cemetery, but decided better of it.

"Listen, Nick Medea, I appreciate you coming, though." Cortez started to reach a hand to me, then, with a weak grin, pulled it back.

I took it before he could finish putting it away. I gave it a congenial shake. His expression didn't change, but there was a look in his eyes. He shook back. I doubted most of his colleagues shook hands with him. After all, he was a "wetback."

"Sorry I couldn't help more," I said as we let go.

"It's jake, Bo. Just get that windshield fixed, okay? I saw that when I got here."

"Soon as I can." A sudden thought occurred to me. I knew I shouldn't get Cortez curious on the subject, but I suspected time was of the essence. "You hear of anything that ever happened around West Sixty-Third Street? Near the six hundred block? A murder or something a long while back?"

"This got to do with your ghost work?"

It was as good an excuse as any. "Yeah. Client wants me to check out a building for him. He swears he sees shadows and hears voices." I gave the detective a look that indicated I didn't believe there was anything supernatural.

Cortez sought for another Lucky. I had no idea what'd happened to the other. "West Sixty-Third? That sounds familiar. Six hundred block, you say?"

I dared push a little more. "Six-oh-three, I think."

"A murder on West Sixty-Third . . . six-oh-three . . ." His eyes widened. He stuck the new Lucky in the corner of his mouth as he grinned. "Aaah, Nick Medea, you gotta know that one or you're no good ghostbuster! That's where the 'Murder Castle' stood, Bo! That's where the *Beast* did his dirty work! They talked all about him when I was training. It was a big thing, Bo!"

"The 'Murder Hotel.'" That rang a bell. "The World's Fair."

"Yeah, that's when. What's that, over thirty years ago?"

"Just over." The World's Fair, also known as the Columbian Exposition. I remembered now. While I'd been hunting Wyld, a monster in actual human form'd been torturing and slaughtering innocents in a hotel he'd had built with the help of an accomplice. I remembered that there'd been at least eight victims, many of them female. Rumors had had it that there'd been a lot more, though. The man the newspapers had called "the Beast of Chicago" had been very meticulous about removing all remains, from what I could recall, so it'd proved impossible to verify any count.

"The Beast," I muttered. "I'd forgotten about that. What happened to him?"

The detective shrugged. "I suppose they caught him. Don't really remember more than that. Just recall at the time thinking what a place of horrors that'd been." He exhaled. "Listen, Bo, we got enough murders going on these days, not just with the gang wars, but things like what you saw. Got two more strange murders. Not so . . . so like that . . . but more than enough to deal with, you know? Only reason I remembered the address was because my first sergeant was a beat cop when it happened and yakked about all the hubbub."

I should've left matters where they were, but again he'd mentioned something of interest. "You said 'two more' odd murders?"

"Yeah, the type that they like to drop in my lap . . . just in case."

We both knew "just in case" meant failing to solve those murders could be embarrassing, which was why they'd left them to the "wetback."

For once, the mask of congeniality fell from Cortez's face. He leaned close. "Dropped them in the lap of their own *traquero*, you know? That's the way some of them think. Well, if I'm half the *tra-*

quero my brother was, I'll do him and my family proud, Bo, and that's what matters."

Cortez tipped his hat and walked off. I had the feeling that I'd missed some earlier argument and that he'd been glad to see me just to get that off his chest. It said something that Cortez thought he could be so blunt with me. I doubted he had many friends in the department. I realized that I might be the closest thing.

The dragon chuckled at that, naturally . . . and I really couldn't blame him.

I could've had Barnaby deal with the Packard, but I knew he'd ask when we were going to see Joseph. I couldn't arrange that just yet, so despite more promises to Cortez, I toughed out driving with the bullet hole in front of me until I got out to Andersonville on the North Side just before what passed for sundown. My former clients, the Nilssons, made their home out here, and although I'd driven by once already, I wanted to take one last look around. I knew I was close when I saw several blond heads and the light jackets despite the cold. After the Night the Dragon Breathed, a good number of the Swedish immigrants to Chicago—and there'd been many who'd made the journey to the Windy City from Scandinavia—had moved up en masse to here. They were taking the storm a lot better than most of the city, which meant I couldn't just park in front of the house.

There was no good reason to come back here a second time, but I was following a hunch. I pulled up a block from the house, parked, and started walking. The houses around here weren't that old, but Wyld only cared about places to secrete themselves. The one I'd expected to find had likely figured that no one would ever think of coming to this outer neighborhood.

But what had happened to my quarry, I wanted to know. After seeing the corpse, I now wondered if something had happened to the one supposedly hiding here.

Even though it was daytime, I risked the dragon's gaze. Unfortunately, doing so revealed nothing. I shifted back to normal, then decided to take a chance and climb over the fence into their yard.

Hurrying to the house, I peered inside. There was no movement. I waited, then carefully checked the back door. Too often, people locked their front doors, then forgot about the one in back.

The knob turned. I pulled the door open slowly before stepping inside.

That was when the stench hit me.

Gritting my teeth I pulled out Her Lady's gift and moved through the kitchen. I hoped and prayed—prayed a *lot*—that I was wrong, but there was no other reason for the all-too-familiar odor permeating the house.

And there they were. She sat with her hands on her lap, her skirt neatly set . . . and her head tipping so far back due to the cut through her throat that, if she'd still lived, she'd have been staring at the front door. Her husband sat across from her, his death from some sharp point driven through the base of his skull. He still held a pipe in his hand, the remnants of the burnt tobacco trying in vain to outdo the smell of decay.

They'd died quickly if violently, but not where they'd been sitting. Someone with a sick sense of humor'd arranged them like this. Oddly, there was little blood even at the wounds. When I looked closer, I saw that the wounds had been cauterized somehow, almost as if by a weapon from Feirie.

Fetch wasn't with me, but thanks to the dragon, I could smell something else about them that bothered me even more. They'd been dead for some time. In fact, they'd already been dead when I'd called and supposedly talked to the wife.

I cursed myself for failing them. If I'd come the same day that they'd first called me, maybe they'd have still been alive.

Maybe.

The stairs beckoned me. I knew the Wyld had to have fled after its dirty work, but still I might find a clue. I no longer worried about Dr. Bond; this was a task I'd failed miserably at, and the only way to atone for my sin even the least was to see if I could track down their killer.

Give me your gaze again, I ordered the dragon.

There is nothing here. . . . The prey is gone. . . .

"We're going up," I muttered to him. "Give it to me. . . ."

I waited. Then, slowly, the world turned emerald.

The steps creaked slightly as I ascended, but I wasn't worried. If, on the off chance, the Wyld was still here, it already knew someone was in the house.

I reached the top and immediately spotted the door to the attic. The sword gripped tight, I headed toward it—

—and sensed movement in the bedroom to the right.

The weather and the angle of the house combined to provide plenty of shadows in the bedroom. Some of them were very dark even through the dragon's gaze. I focused on the areas with the blackest shadows and entered the bedroom.

There was a hint of Feirie in the shadows before me. Not much. In fact, too little to have been the source of the movement I'd noted.

I turned from the shadows to the least likely place in the room: the bed itself. Sure enough, the shadows beneath were darker than they should've been considering the dragon's eyes.

"The monster under the bed . . ." I growled as I neared. "Is that what it always was? One of you biding your time by tormenting children? Is that how powerful you are? Just a tormentor of children?"

I knew that this was more than some simple creature out of a child's nightmare, but I also knew one thing about the Wyld . . . and of Feirie folk in general. Even more than most humans, they had a vanity about them that made such a taunt often strike home. No force of Feirie liked to be reduced to a child's nightmare.

The bed rattled, then started to rise. I wasn't impressed. I'd seen Wyld do a lot worse just to show off. Still, I wondered why it was here at all anymore. I also wondered why it'd been so hard for me to sense, even with the dragon.

Then, the bed began spinning. The Wyld was strong, I knew that, but it continued to go out of its way to show off rather than attack.

I had no patience for that. Two innocents were dead, and we were both guilty in some manner or another of the crime. At least I could see that their actual murderer faced the consequences. It still wouldn't assuage my own guilt, but it would be some justice.

"Are you through?" I mocked. "I've seen better. Show me something impressive."

The bed tipped over and flew hard into the outer wall. I hoped the neighbors wouldn't hear the thud as it crashed and splintered.

And there, rising high enough to nearly touch the ceiling, stood my quarry. A living shadow. It wore a hood that gave it the look of the Grim Reaper, and even with the dragon's vision I could only make out a murky face with pits for eyes.

A pair of long, sinewy hands emerged from the shadow cloak. There were only four digits on each hand, all of them ending in nails as long as the fingers themselves. I sensed power swelling between those fingers.

Gatekeepers . . . came a familiar, haunting voice in my head.

Strike it down! Strike it down! demanded the dragon.

"Shut up. . . ." I eyed the hooded form. This was no Wyld, unless things in Feirie had gotten a hell of a lot worse than I could've imagined. Yet, this creature also shouldn't have existed. I'd seen it—*him*—tortured and executed by Oberon after he'd been sent—as the other before him—to hunt down his former liege.

"So she had a spare, did she?" I finally commented. "Twin brothers or just cut from the same cloth?"

He hissed angrily, but dismissed the energy he'd been gathering. He also shrank a bit, although still topping out over seven feet tall. As that happened, he stretched open one side of his cloak.

Instead of his body or just darkness . . . a sinister woodland scene revealed itself.

She ordered . . . when you were faced . . . she would speak with you. . . .

I didn't have to ask who he meant. He was a servant of Her Lady, queen of Feirie. A sentinel . . . a special enforcer that Kravayik had called a *Feir'hr Sein*. Kravayik, once a deadly soldier of the Court himself, had spoken of the creature with great respect, explaining that the name loosely translated into *Hunger*. I assumed that was short for "Hunger for Death" or something just as dramatic. Feirie loved its titles. Still, that meant I was facing a creature far more deadly than the usual Wyld.

It also meant that it'd hardly been the murderer of the young couple.

The Nilssons. . . . I reprimanded myself. *At least give them their due in death. The Nilssons . . . they're the latest ones you've failed.* It was a bad habit I'd developed over the centuries, too often trying to forget those I met as soon as possible so that I wouldn't think about the fact that they'd eventually join the thousands I'd known before who were now dust.

Trying to forget . . . but never actually forgetting. I had a list of sins, of lost lives, longer than the years I'd served the Gate.

"She'll have to wait her turn," I finally answered. "I've got more important things to do . . . and if you aren't what I was hunting, I'm done with you."

The sentinel didn't like that. He hissed again, then shook his cloak. The dark woodland scene rippled, but remained. *She will be obeyed!*

"She's not *my* queen." I tightened my grip on the sword. It was possible that he was immune to its abilities, but I doubted that. Her Lady had created it with her former mate in mind.

My continued disrespect for his queen proved almost too much for the sentinel. He started to lunge toward me.

I brought Her Lady's gift up, the point at his chest. "Easy, Lon!"

He pulled up short, what little I could see of his inhuman expression more puzzled than furious. I realized that in the heat of the moment, I'd used a name on him. Yes, I'd flippantly called him by that of the great actor, but he reacted as if I'd actually marked him by his true identity. Names were power in Feirie, but generally only able to be wielded by the mightiest of the Court, specifically Her Lady. That was why I and most who knew of the queen called her by the title I did, as opposed to actually using her given name—Titania. Even mentioning her true name was to risk her attention.

The sentinel wavered. *She must be obeyed. . . .*

"I'll speak with her when I need to. If you want to be any use, you can tell me right now why you're here. They were dead when you arrived, right?"

To my surprise, he readily answered, *Yesss. . . .*

I hid my relief. There'd remained a slight concern that the Nilssons had somehow gotten into the middle of Her Lady's cleansing of her domain of the unfaithful. "So how long ago did you arrive?"

In the dark of this previous night.

Not that long, then. I doubted that there was anything the enforcer could tell me. "You found no one or nothing here? No Wyld . . . especially tied to Oberon?"

The creature shifted slightly at mention of his former liege. Even in death, it seemed Oberon had some power. Her Lady wouldn't have an easy time eradicating that fear.

There is the smell of end time. . . .

"End time." That was an old Feirie term for what humans called "death."

The Nilssons weren't of Feirie, though. I hoped that they were where, from the looks of the cross on the wall across from me, they believed they'd go if they'd been decent. "Tell me something I don't know, Lon. I want to find this Wyld that did that to them."

He shimmered the moment I used the name on him again. I frowned. It seemed he was really bothered by it, which only made me more determined to use it whenever he didn't answer sufficiently.

No Wyld . . . that Wyld has seen end time here and the essence carried away. . . .

I had to digest that for a moment. Lon was telling me that his quarry and mine had not only died here along with the Nilssons, but that the remains had been dragged off. I had no sympathy for the dead Wyld . . . but who would've been hunting for him other than myself and this Feir'hr Sein?

I thought about the corpse Cortez'd wanted me to see. Another dead Wyld. One of the Court, if I was correct.

That brought me back to Alexander Bond. *Dr.* Alexander Bond.

And then I thought of what we'd come across in the building where once a human monster as horrific as anything from Feirie had tortured and slaughtered innocents. The Nilssons hadn't been cut up like either those long-dead victims or Cortez's unfortunate Wyld, but they'd been killed with sadistic precision.

One immediate question still hadn't been answered. With the tip of the sword slowly swinging toward Her Lady's enforcer, I asked him, "Who were you seeking here? One of Oberon's servants?"

Yesss. . . .

It was like slowly peeling an onion to the core, something I didn't have time for right now. "How powerful? Who—"

A siren sounded in the distance. A police siren.

I made the mistake of glancing at the nearest window. I quickly returned my attention to the Feir'hr Sein, only to find he'd taken that crucial moment to flee.

I took his unspoken advice. Hiding Her Lady's gift, I hurried out of the bedroom and down the steps. The siren was already too loud for my tastes. I'd no doubt that they were coming to the Nilsson house, maybe because of the noise raised by the shattering bed.

Just as I reached the first floor, the siren reached a crescendo out front. I spun around to the back, leaping into the yard a few seconds later. From inside the house, I heard someone knocking on the door.

I couldn't take the time to worry about what some bystander might see. The dragon understood what I wanted. My legs bent at an angle no human could've achieved and propelled me over the fence.

Fortunately, there was no one around when I landed. I pushed on immediately to where I'd left the Packard. The police would've come from a different direction. If I reached the Packard, I could be far away before anyone thought to examine the cars parked nearby.

I almost feared that I'd find something amiss with the Packard, but other than the snow, she was untouched. I started her up and drove off as casually as I could.

It wasn't more than a mile before I knew I was being followed.

CHAPTER 7

T he Studebaker that'd acted as a decoy earlier was now behind me at what the driver must've supposed was a safe distance. He probably didn't know he was dealing with someone who could not only see well in the dark, but who'd been looking over his shoulder for sixteen hundred years.

I turned south on Clark as if nothing was wrong. The Studebaker dutifully followed. The weather guaranteed that there wasn't much traffic, but I wondered exactly what they had in mind.

Then, I thought of the last time I'd been followed by them and realized I was probably being set up again.

Logic dictated I take the route I did and follow it down to Halsted toward Saint Michael's. I wasn't certain how much time I had before the other car showed up, but it couldn't be long. They couldn't have had more than a few minutes to plan this out. I doubted that they'd been waiting for me to check on the Nilssons, which meant that either I'd been followed out to Andersonville—which I thought unlikely— or they'd been watching for someone else.

The image of Her Lady's enforcer suddenly filled my thoughts. Maybe "someone" was the wrong term. Maybe they'd been on the lookout for some*thing?* Powerful as Lon was, he could be destroyed. I already knew someone was hunting down Wyld and not caring who else died in the process.

As I pondered that, Foster Avenue came up. I instinctively turned onto it . . . and nearly collided with the dark blue Chrysler Phaeton coming from the opposite direction. I had no trouble recognizing the car this time despite it being one of the company's first offerings. It wasn't just stylish, but it was practical in both size and speed, the last something whoever bossed the three figures inside must've considered, too.

I managed to veer around, cutting so close there was also no doubt as to whether or not I'd seen the figure nearest to me in the backseat. The Schreck hood already had a gun out, but it wasn't something as modern as Claryce's Smith & Wesson. Instead, he readied an old Colt Peacemaker with a shortened barrel. I doubted it fired something as simple as lead bullets.

He managed a shot just as I slammed on the gas. I heard a deadly thunk near the steering wheel as the bullet just missed my arm. Then, I was racing down Foster at far too great a speed for the slick street. I knew the Chrysler would follow, but turning around would cost them valuable time.

An arm wrapped around my throat, an arm strong enough to all but pull me from the seat. The Packard slipped to the curb, bouncing hard.

There'd been no one in the auto with me. I'd been able to see that when I'd climbed inside. I'd also been driving much too fast for anyone to jump in.

A faint odor reached my nose as I fought to pull free while still keeping the Packard from crashing into a building. It was musky, old . . . and brought to mind the inherent scent of cemeteries.

My attacker was strong, but not strong enough. I managed to peel away his arm while still using my other hand to steer. I couldn't stop; the others would catch up, and I wasn't sure what other tricks they might have.

Sharp pain roared through my neck. The dragon echoed my agony. Without thinking, my foot slipped to the brake.

The Packard shook as we stopped. The pain dwindled as what I realized was the point of some weapon or instrument slipped free of my neck. At the same time, I finally caught a glimpse of my attacker's hand.

It was as pale as the moon, not to mention long and sinewy, as if instead of fingers he had snakes at the end. Somehow, I knew that if I managed to see the face, it'd look just like Count Orlok's.

I'd never seen a Wyld or a member of Her Lady's Court who looked like my unwanted companion, but that hardly meant that he wasn't of Feirie. At the moment, though, what was more important was extricating myself from this before we drew a crowd. If that happened, I'd have to rely on luck.

Yes! encouraged the dragon. *Yes! Release me!*

If he thought I'd give him total mastery of me, he'd gone mad. I envisioned what I wanted and ignored his anger at not being fully unleashed.

My hand changed, growing longer and narrower. Scales rapidly covered it. My nails grew into claws.

With a strength now far greater than my own, I gripped his arm tight and squeezed. I felt bone break, followed by a rush of pleasure at the pain I assumed my adversary had to be suffering.

But there was no cry from behind me. Instead, he twisted free and fell into the backseat.

My foot slipped off the brake as I stretched back a hand to him. Still caught up in my bloodlust, I forgot about the street ahead and grabbed at the retreating arm. I must've let the Packard steer to the side again, for suddenly the auto bounced hard.

In the midst of the bounce, I caught sight of the ghoulish hood pressed against the backseat. His one arm dangled, but he didn't seem to care. Of more interest to my attacker was the short dagger with which he'd apparently stuck me in the neck. It was a peculiar blade, not flat but rather round, with an open point.

I hadn't seen a rondel dagger in over two hundred years. They'd been very popular in Burgundy and other parts of Europe four or five centuries ago. They'd been handy for penetrating armor at the joints, but had gone out of favor once armor had.

The open point was something I *hadn't* come across. I didn't have a chance to see more of it, though, because my attacker chose that moment to fling some sort of dust at me. I did what came normally, shielding my eyes for that brief instant while still keeping one hand in front of me in case he lunged with the dagger.

Nothing happened. The moment the dust cleared, I discovered that he was gone. The door was shut, and there was no way he could've climbed out, but he was gone.

I hadn't sensed any hint of Feirie magic, but that seemed the logical choice. I quickly peered out in time to see the Chrysler turning *from* me.

In the backseat of the departing car, I saw my attacker. He stared without blinking at me until the Chrysler was at the far end of the block.

Other vehicles began converging on the area. I didn't wait for the cops to arrive. Forcing the Packard back onto Foster, I headed off. Rubbing my neck where I'd been stuck, I knew that before I headed anywhere else, I had to make certain that Claryce was okay.

"Dear God, Nick! What happened to you?"

I didn't think I looked that bad. I went to the mirror near her apartment door and eyed myself. I was more disheveled than I'd believed. There was also a nasty red mark on my neck from the dagger.

"Is that painful?" she asked as she rushed from the room. When we'd parted, she'd given me her address and telephone number. Finding the apartment hadn't been too hard. Claryce had evidently tried to locate one as close to Saint Michael's as she could. While it made for convenience at the moment, I wished that she'd have chosen one far, far away.

Fetch watched patiently as I tried to neaten myself up. By that time, Claryce'd returned with a towel and some pharmacy medical supplies. However, she stopped short upon seeing me again. "Oh, that's right. Silly of me. I'd forgotten he could heal you."

"Hmm?" I looked back at the mirror. The wound was no longer visible. I could still feel the pinprick of pain, but my skin was good as new.

"Thanks for finally getting around to it," I muttered.

For a moment, I saw his eyes staring back at me despite not having summoned them. *Eye would not let anything happen to you. . . .*

I didn't draw much comfort from the comment. All he meant was that my body, this shell, was of importance to him. He only existed as part of me . . . unless someday I slipped and let him seize control forever. He'd come close more than once, and I had faith he would try again if he saw the opportunity.

"All copacetic, Master Nicholas?" Fetch asked with a tentative wag.

"Not at all copacetic." I pointed at Claryce's purse. "You been practicing with that thing?"

"I can hit what I aim at nine times out of ten. Will that do?"

I grunted. "So long as number ten doesn't get you afterward."

She tried to lead me to a cushioned chair, but I shook my head. I needed to stand right now.

Claryce leaned on the chair, concern still coloring her expression. "Tell me."

I went through what happened, editing out the more grotesque details. I knew that Claryce would imagine them well enough even without my help. Her face darkened when I spoke about the Nilssons, and my description of my encounter with Her Lady's enforcer brought a shiver.

"I was hoping we'd not have to deal with her for a long time once Oberon was destroyed," she commented after I'd finished.

"Unfortunately, if anything, she's encouraged. The Gate's been more porous than ever." I didn't mention the refugee Fetch'd protected, but I caught him eyeing me when I spoke of the Gate.

Claryce didn't look so much troubled now as she did frustrated. "Is the Gate always so much trouble? It seems like everything can pass through it at will despite your efforts."

I winced, but she was speaking the truth. There'd been periods throughout the centuries when the Gate'd suddenly seemed more like an open roadway rather than a treacherous portal few could breach. What I hadn't mentioned to her since we'd first met is that the Gate had never been the same after the Great Fire. Not only had it finally fixed in one place, but it'd become just as we'd discussed, an unpredictable pathway through which at times it seemed the entire population of Feirie and Chicago could come and go, if they so desired.

Even still, over the decades, I'd managed to maintain the crossovers to a minimum . . . or so I'd thought. Now I was beginning to wonder if Her Lady's suspicions that Oberon had survived the Night the Dragon Breathed had contributed. With him dead at last, I now feared that a city already in the grip of a mob war was going to become inundated with the worst of the Wyld.

She saw the change in my mood. "It's going to get worse, isn't it?"

"Maybe, but I don't think this is just a matter of the Gate being open. There's more." I told her about the corpse Cortez'd wanted me to examine.

"How much does he know about you, Nick?" she asked when I was done.

"I've not pressed that point. He knows a lot of strange things happen around me. Most of the time, people forget. Cortez doesn't."

"Is there a reason?"

I shrugged. "None that I've found. He's fairly religious. He and his Maria go to Our Lady of Guadalupe regularly." I managed a chuckle. "She's even prayed for me."

Claryce straightened. "Why would she do that? Does she know you well?"

"Never met her."

"'Never met her.'" She cocked her head. "Maybe you should sometime."

The phone rang. We both jumped. Fetch whined. When Oberon'd been alive, we'd had a few unnerving calls.

"I'd better answer that." Claryce picked up the phone and put the receiver to her ear. "Hello?" She exhaled in relief, which made me relax in turn. "Oliver? No. I have those papers. Yes, you can get them tomorrow. All right."

She hung up, then turned to a white oak table near the telephone. She thumbed through some papers there.

"What is it? What was the call?"

"Something mundane for a change. Just Oliver, a coworker from Delke. He's handling some of the other matters they're trying to clear up. Just wanted some of the papers I was given." She rubbed her forehead. "To be honest, anything that speeds up finishing this I'm happy about . . . especially after Alexander Bond."

"Have you heard from him?"

"No. Nothing so far. Don't you worry. If he calls, I'm not going to see him without you."

"You shouldn't see him again. Period."

A distinctive growl rose from Fetch's direction. Claryce chuckled. I glanced at him. He had the decency to look embarrassed. The growl had come not from his jaws but rather his stomach.

"Ye said the two of ye were going to meet at Berghoff's," the shapeshifter muttered. "Was hoping for a bite from your table. . . ."

"Poor Fetch," murmured Claryce with a slight smile. "Let me get a couple of things and we'll go." She turned the smile to me. "And I'll drive. See that you do something about the Packard. You can't go around driving with a windshield like that in this weather."

"I'll call Barnaby. I need to talk to him about something else, anyway."

The smile faded. "His son?"

"I promised I'd see Joseph."

She clutched herself. "God. Dunning. Poor man."

"I hope you're talking about Barnaby. Joseph doesn't deserve your sympathy."

"Oh, Nick!" Still, she didn't argue. "I'll be back shortly. Then we can see to keeping Fetch from starving."

"Thank ye kindly, Mistress Claryce!" His tail swept back and forth at an enthusiastic pace. For someone supposedly starving, he was looking pretty fit at the moment.

I went to the telephone and gave the operator the number I needed. As I listened to the ringing, I noticed a piece of paper behind the table where the phone stood. Still waiting for Barnaby to answer, I picked it up on the assumption it was part of the work from Delke. As Claryce'd said, anything to permanently sever her ties with Oberon's past was welcome.

"No one's answering," the nasal-toned female operator broke in. "Shall I continue to try?"

"For another minute, please," I answered as I turned over the paper. "He sometimes takes a moment to answer."

"Yes, sir." She didn't sound happy, but she let the phone ring.

She was probably even unhappier when I hung up on her. Behind me, Fetch growled. He didn't need his heightened senses to see that I'd just been startled by something.

"Master—"

"Quiet, Fetch!" I stared at the paper, well aware that it was in Claryce's clear handwriting. It was a short list of names with some information written by them. Three names, to be precise. One of them was her own, with her birthday and some basic facts about her life.

The other two names were those of Clarissa and Claudette.

Under each, she'd written their birthdays . . . and the days they had died. I'd not paid attention to one fact that she'd circled, and that was obvious when I looked. Maybe I'd been too close to the situation that I'd not seen what she had.

Of course, in many ways she was closer to what'd happened to both women than I could ever be. After all, they *had* been her.

All three women had been born on the twenty-fifth. The months were different, but the date was always the twenty-fifth.

It didn't stop there, either. She had a place of birth for both herself and Claudette. Claudette *Durand*. Both had been born in Chicago, just as I knew Clarissa'd been and Claryce had rightly assumed despite a lack of information. That wasn't the surprising part—or at least the most surprising part, considering what I'd already read. Obviously, she knew where the Gate had ended up. She'd jotted down the location, just off of Lake Michigan. However, after that, Claryce'd jotted down some numbers. It took me a moment to realize that she'd measured the exact distance not only from where she'd been born to where the Gate stood, but also the distance from where her two *previous* incarnations had been born to the portal, too.

All three were exactly the same distance.

Claryce'd made a not-so-crude drawing of the spot near the lake, then an arc running from one birthplace to the next. I shuddered, aware of what she was trying to do. She wanted to see if there were any other matches. She was looking to see how many times she'd died in Chicago.

Fetch let out a low, brief whine. I was about to tell him to quiet down when I realized he was actually trying to signal me.

"You never mentioned Claudette," she quietly commented. Although Claryce was dressed to go, she made no attempt to retrieve her purse. She just stood there, waiting.

I paused, trying hard to figure out what to say to her. I'd hardly expected to discover this. "I didn't know about her. I only found out recently. The other day, in fact."

"She and Clarissa are both buried in Saint Boniface . . . and not too far from one another. I thought from that you—" Her calm broke for a moment as she swallowed hard. "—took care of them afterward."

"Claryce." I dropped the paper by the telephone and went to her. She was a strong person, but knowing she'd been buried at least twice was a lot to take in.

Without warning, she fell into my arms. I held her while she shook. She didn't cry from what I could see, but she shook for more than a minute before recovering. By that time, Fetch'd stuck his cold nose in her left hand and tried to nuzzle her. Sometimes he forgot that he *wasn't* a dog.

"I'm sorry," Claryce finally said as she backed up slightly. "I thought I was over that after staring at it for more than a week. Last night, I wrapped myself in a blanket and drank a good portion of the last bottle of wine I got from 'William.'"

Claryce hadn't broken any laws with the wine. Prohibition forbade the manufacture, not the consumption, of alcohol. The wine Oberon'd gathered while he was William Delke had been collected before Prohibition in many cases. Claryce'd ended up with a few, thankfully.

"How long have you been looking into this?" I finally ventured.

"Since we finished with Oberon. I had a lot more time on my hands after you abandoned me."

"Claryce—"

She suddenly kissed me. For a moment, I was able to forget everything except her.

Then, of course, the dragon chuckled. *How sweet. . . . Eye always savor her kisses. . . .*

I bit back a growl. He had only a limited sense of the outside world and mainly through sight and sound. I generally had to suffer the pain. I wasn't about to share this brief pleasure with him.

Unfortunately, Claryce must've sensed something amiss. She looked up at me with a faint smile. "It's him, isn't it?"

"Yes."

"Hmm." Her smile widening—a little forcibly, I thought—she turned to Fetch. "I think we all need to get some food. I know I need to eat and poor Fetch must feel like he's got a pit in his stomach."

"I wouldn't argue with a little bit of leftover corned beef, Mistress Claryce!" His tail swept back and forth.

"Nonsense! You're going to have some fresh sausage, not some cold leftovers! You do like sausage, don't you?"

His tail beat fast enough to launch a Douglas World Cruiser biplane. "They do have a swell garlic one! I've had some fine bits from the trash bins!"

"That's all you need," I countered. "Garlic and rat. A nice combination. You can use your breath alone against the next Wyld."

He cowed, and although I'd seen this act before, this time I couldn't do anything about it because his target was Claryce.

"Nick!" She gave Fetch a gentle scratch between the ears, giving him his victory where the garlic sausage was concerned. "We'll see what we can do for you, won't we, Nick?"

"So long as afterward he sits in the backseat with his head out the side."

The telephone rang. I glanced at Claryce, who shook her head.

"Let me answer it, then." Returning to the telephone, I picked it up. "Hello?"

"Ah! Master Nicholas! It is you! I thought so, but the operator said a different number. I decided to have her ring it, regardless."

"Barnaby." With the discovery of the paper, I'd forgotten about him. "I was calling about the Packard. It's seen some damage, especially the windshield."

"I'll be happy to have it picked up, of course, but if I may, if you hadn't called me, I would've been calling you a few minutes later. Yours was a timely attempt."

"What is it?"

"I know we haven't had a chance to get to Joseph, but I did manage to finally get some information on his visitor. I thought it'd be important to get it to you as soon as possible."

I had a bad feeling. "What'd you find out?"

"Turns out, he came twice. Seems they somehow overlooked that little point when I asked the first time. I suppose it makes sense, since they thought he was one of them."

"'One of them'?"

"A physician. His name was . . . Forgive, I wrote it down."

I thought I knew already. "Let me guess. Alexander Bond."

"'Bond'? No. Here it is. H. Mudgett. There was no full first name."

H. Mudgett. "Any description?"

"No. I thought that curious, Master Nicholas. No one could describe him."

So it still could've been Bond, though why he'd chosen a different alias when visiting Dunning, I couldn't say. I wondered what he wanted with Joseph.

Barnaby cleared his throat. "I'm sorry, but there's something else and I should've told you immediately . . . but I'm still digesting it myself."

I stifled my response, wondering what could be more significant than Bond's—and I was certain it was Bond—visit to Dunning. "Spit it out, Barnaby."

"It's—it's Joseph himself. He—he *asked* to *see* you, Master Nicholas. He actually *asked* to see you."

CHAPTER 8

"Tell me more about Joseph," Claryce murmured as we finished our meal and readied to depart. Under her arm, she'd tucked the package with Fetch's sausage. The scent of garlic had already spread, and I'd warned her that her kindness was going to be something we both regretted.

I didn't say anything until we were out of Berghoff's and on to Adams Street. The weather had calmed, but it was still very cold. It didn't bother me so much, but I could see that it was affecting Claryce more than she'd thought it would.

"Joseph Sperling is the only child of Barnaby and his wife, Emma, who passed away years ago. You haven't met Barnaby—only seen him briefly at his friend's house—but you know he owns a garage and services autos."

"He calls you Master Nicholas, just like Fetch and Kravayik do. I thought that was a Feirie thing to do. Does he have some link to Feirie?"

"No. Kravayik got involved in the incident with Joseph and Barnaby, who'd just met both of us, heard him call me that. Barnaby's done the same since, despite my asking him not to."

"What happened to Joseph?"

"We were never actually certain. He and some others were supposed to use the Wingfoot Express dirigible for a spell related to the Gate, that's about all I know. They were reckless, though. Instead of what they wanted, they nearly engulfed Chicago and part of Feirie in a fire worse than . . . than what we caused."

She didn't ask who "we" were. Inside my head, the dragon chortled at the memory. *So glorious a flame . . . one of my greatest. . . . We should do it again. . . .*

I didn't reply, instead going on. "Joseph was at the nexus of the situation. I would've left him to die, but Barnaby pleaded with me to help his son if I could. I did as he asked. I still regret it."

Claryce's shiver did not have to do with just the chill air. "God! It's been six years, but I still remember hearing about the Wingfoot. Those poor people! They said thirteen died that day."

"It was more. There just weren't bodies left of the others. Don't weep for them, though. They were with Joseph. They got what they deserved."

"Why? Just what all happen—"

"Where's Fetch?" I interrupted, glad for a sudden and real excuse not to answer.

We'd reached the Wills. There was no sign of Fetch. However, from around the corner came a brief metallic clang, like something much bigger than a cat and entirely disobedient to his companions was feeding on the restaurant's trash instead of waiting like he'd been told. A moment later, Fetch came bounding into sight. He looked so eager that I almost expected him to sit up and beg for the sausage. Considering he'd disobeyed my instructions, I was tempted to make him do just that.

Claryce was more kindhearted. She opened the package. "Here you go, Fetch! Enjoy!"

"Thank ye kindly, Mistress Claryce! You're jake with me!" He thrust his muzzle into the package and snapped up the sausage.

"Take it into the alley," I ordered him. Fetch had the ability to go almost unnoticed around people at most times, but I wasn't too sure he'd remember to watch himself while he was ripping into the sausage.

"Yeth, Mathter Nicholath," he managed.

"Head to the house when you're done. Wait there. You can find your way in. Do that."

Rather than trying to speak again, the shapeshifter just nodded and rushed back into the alley. I took the empty package and threw it in a trash can, then joined Claryce in the Wills.

"Where to, Nick?"

"There's a bus stop farther down Adams. I'll take it from there."

"You will *not*. I'll drive you home or you can sleep on the couch in my apartment."

It would've been easier for both of us if I'd just accepted her second offer, but I needed to get back to the house to check my files. I had a few hunches, but it might be hours before I found anything to back them up.

"The house, then . . . and thanks."

She didn't answer, instead just working the stick and driving off.

As we drove, I decided to probe about Alexander Bond. "Do you remember anything about your initial conversation with the doctor?"

"There wasn't much special. He called up and said that he'd seen the ads concerning the properties. Delke Industries posted them in all the major papers, including the *Tribune*. He seemed especially interested in that location."

That perked my attention. "He knew the area well?"

"I suppose he did. He talked a bit about the World's Fair and the White City before we went on to arranging the appointment."

I considered very carefully before asking the next question. "Did he . . . did he mention something called the 'Murder Castle'?"

She took her eyes off the street just long enough to gape at me. "God, no! Is that something from your past? Is that what happened to Claudette?"

I started. I hadn't even been thinking of Claryce's earlier incarnations. "No. Nothing like that! The building we were in afterward. That's where Cortez told me later it was originally located."

"'Murder Castle' . . . ." She shook her head. "No, I definitely would've remembered *that*. You mean it was across the street?"

"That's what Cortez said."

"Do you remember anything about it yourself? You were here then."

"Only after it was over. I was on the hunt constantly then."

Claryce had an odd look on her face. "This was what year? I can't remember."

I blurted out the answer quickly, hoping she wasn't dwelling on the fact that I'd not aged any since then. "It was 1893."

"What, 1893? . . . Nick, that's when she died. Claudette, I mean."

It was something that'd crossed my mind, but I didn't like to think that there was a connection. "You looked her up, didn't you? Did it say how she died?"

She turned before replying. "I couldn't find that. All I found was when she died and where she was buried. When *was* the fair that year, Nick?"

I rubbed my chin as I thought. "Seems to me it ran from middle of spring to sometime in October."

The odd look grew more pronounced. "She died in that time period . . . and you say this Murder Castle existed during the fair."

I hadn't exactly said that, but I'd insinuated it well enough. I didn't say anything. She didn't say anything.

We spent the rest of the drive in silence.

The weather'd worsened by the time we got to the house. The Queen Anne looked like many another home in the neighborhood. Fetch had wondered once why I lived here instead of some secret lair in the heart of the blackest part of the Black City, a much-too-appropriate name that'd first sprung up after the advertising debacle called the White City during the exposition. I'd told him that I'd purposely chosen a place beyond the shadowed regions of the city because it *was* the least likely place the Wyld would expect me to be.

After all these years, I was still trying to convince myself I'd told him something even remotely close to the truth.

"The first bedroom upstairs is yours," I informed her when we entered. "You're not going back out there tonight. I should've let you go straight to your place."

"And I wouldn't have listened." She removed her coat. "You're sure this place is cleansed of her?"

I couldn't blame her for asking. "Let me go check, just to be cautious."

"All right. I'll go through a few papers for you."

She knew about my collection and why I kept the clippings. I just nodded, then headed upstairs.

Leonardo's painting greeted me as I entered the bedroom. There was no longer a need to hide it from Claryce. She knew it was me in all my Saint George glory facing the damned dragon in all of his . . . and with *Claryce*—or rather Princess Cleolinda—to the side of the struggle. Da Vinci'd done a masterful job, but unfortunately he'd made Claryce—well, the version of Cleolinda he'd met—and I look too much like ourselves. No one outside could ever view this work.

Eye will help you see. . . .

I let him grant me his gaze, the better to search for any overlooked traces. Yet, even when the world turned emerald, I spotted nothing immediate. As a precaution, though, I checked under the bed and inside the closet. The absurdity of the situation made me feel like I'd fallen into a Chaplin comedy, but still I searched.

Exhaling, I straightened. Only then did I see that the painting was slightly crooked—

I heard a feminine laugh.

The Saint George in the painting lunged at the dragon. The dragon roared and exhaled fire, something even the legends had forgotten. I ducked under the searing plume and charged.

Cleolinda screamed. The cry distracted me. The dragon brought one huge paw down, knocking me to the ground. The clatter of metal against rock as I tried to roll away vied with his roar in an apparent attempt to deafen me.

I was tired of this manling. Who was this presumptuous human who thought he could best me? I gave him some small credit for being nimble for one of his kind despite his metal shell. The metal shells always made me laugh; didn't they realize that the metal only helped make their blood boil and their skin burn all that much easier?

The female kept warning the manling. The fools had brought her as some sort of sacrifice to me. I liked that they had understood my supreme might, but she was hardly a morsel. She did bring me better food by living, though, so I let her stay chained by me while naive mortals like this tried to become champions—

Pain! Pain! He hurt me! How? Such pain! I slashed out at him! I snapped at him! Where is he? How did he move so quickly and—

Pain! More pain! He will pay! I will rip him into little shreds! I will scatter his innards over the landscape! I will save his skull to drink water from! I will—

Nick!

I will—

Nick!

I was in the bedroom. My hands were covered in shreds of some material. I was grateful to realize that it wasn't flesh even though there were flakes of red in it. There were also flakes of gold and other colors, I finally noticed.

Da Vinci's painting lay strewn all over the floor. The frame had been shattered and the picture ripped into small bits. Unlike last time, there'd be no repairing the painting.

Soft hands touched my cheeks. Claryce, anxious but determined, forced me to keep my eyes on her. I belatedly realized that I was looking at her through my own, not those of the dragon.

"Nick! Keep looking at me! What happened to you?"

Faint recollections of both fighting the dragon and *being* the dragon returned to me. I also remembered the feminine laugh. I was certain that it hadn't been Claryce's, and that meant only one other female.

"It was *her*!" I snapped much too angrily at her. "Titania!" For once, I didn't care if she heard my voice. "The grand queen of Feirie! She left a little prank!"

"Nick! Calm down! You're getting that look again!"

I refocused on her. I saw the open concern, the deeper feelings behind it. . . .

This time, the fury abated completely. There remained a bitterness toward the cause of it, though. Her Lady. Titania. When she'd recreated the house and the painting, she'd left some deeply hidden trace of her power in the latter. She knew what the painting meant to me. Now, with Oberon dead, evidently she thought that she could begin toying with me.

I was beginning to regret I'd finished off Oberon. I didn't know what his former mate had in mind, save seeking full control of the Gate. That boded ill.

What also boded ill was my reaction. This latest episode of rage had been the worst thus far. I feared that if they continued, there wouldn't be any difference between the dragon and me. We'd be one monstrous threat to those around us. . . .

The dragon said nothing. I could barely sense his presence, as if he was as drained as I was.

It occurred to me I still hadn't reassured Claryce. I quickly nodded. "I'm all right. I'm me again."

"Let's get out of this room," she insisted.

I didn't argue. We returned to the table where I did my research. I saw that there were a number of files on the table now.

Claryce led me to one of the chairs. "Sit. I'll get something cold from the Kelvinator. I assume you've gotten around to refilling it."

"Yes."

"What about the one in the safe house . . . just in case we have to go there?"

"No." I kept a hidden apartment over an empty establishment near the South Side, close to where Capone had some of his operations. However, things'd gotten pretty hot there during the fight with Oberon, so I hadn't been back since.

"In that case, I'm sleeping down here, too . . . until we know it is safe."

I remembered my encounter with Her Lady's enforcer. I looked forward to our next meeting. Her Lady wanted to see me? I was more than happy to oblige now.

Claryce vanished into the kitchen, returning a moment later with a dark bottle and a glass. "I hope this bottle of Bergo is good enough. I know I could do with something stronger than near beer or soda pop."

"It'll do fine. Just don't let Fetch see it. He'll think I've been going to Berghoff's without him."

She smiled, but the smile faded after she handed me the bottle. Claryce pointed at the files. "I think I've found something."

"Already?"

"You keep very organized files. I could've used you at Delke."

"Probably paid better and certainly would've had more practical hours than I have now." I set the Bergo down. "What is it?"

"I went back to your clippings from 1893. The *Chicago Times*. The *Morning Herald*. Other papers before my time I've never heard of. Most are about the World's Fair, but the last two . . . Well, look at the rest first."

Curious at what she meant, I quickly thumbed through the first batch, readily recalling things from that time. One clipping came close to reporting on the results of one of my hunts, but I chose not to mention that to Claryce.

Then, I picked up the other clippings . . . and hesitated. There was a notation on the side in my handwriting that didn't help matters, either. I'd marked the discovery of a body, vaguely noted by the police as female, but with peculiar characteristics. I dredged up the memory. What little I'd read indicated that, like Cortez's unidentified corpse, the victim had been a Wyld of high caste.

I understood Claryce's curiosity, both because of the timing and my old notation, but there was little information other than the finding. I put down the first clipping and glanced at the second.

It was about Claudette. It was about her *murder*.

After I'd had the encounter at Saint Boniface, I'd wondered how she'd died, but hadn't investigated. I could've blamed it on all that'd happened since, but the truth was I'd not wanted to know. Those incarnations I'd known had all died violently. Odd accidents or victims of either random crimes or due to becoming involved in my dark world.

Claudette'd been found with her throat cut, but that wasn't the worst of it. Whoever had done it had positioned her almost reverently, putting her hands over her heart in what seemed like prayer. In fact, she'd even been found holding her crucifix.

"I came across it by accident. I thought you didn't know about her."

"I didn't . . . or didn't make the connection. Maybe I didn't want to. I generally cut out all murders . . . just as a precaution. I store them near the top by date in each file. . . ." Suddenly, I realized how uncaring I must've sounded to her. This wasn't just *any* murder. It'd been hers.

"Don't grimace," Claryce urged. "I understand. There's no photo. You didn't know I-I'd come back. This has nothing to do with you. You see that?"

"To be honest, I don't recall even cutting this out, and I usually have some memory." I forced myself to read over the rest of the article. Claudette had been found three days before the writing. She'd had no identification, but had finally been identified by someone who knew her from where she went to church. In fact, it'd been her church that'd claimed her body for burial.

No. Not just a church. A cathedral. *The* cathedral in Chicago.

Holy Name Cathedral.

I don't believe in coincidence.

"What is it? Did you remember something?"

"No." I knew I should've been going through the files, but instead I got up and headed straight to the telephone.

"Who're you calling? Nick! Tell me what this has to do with the article?"

"Operator." After she answered, I gave her the telephone number. Claryce'd heard the number before. "Why are you calling him?"

Before I could explain, he answered. The telephone number I'd called didn't officially exist in Holy Name. Only one person used it.

"This is Kravayik. May the blessing of the Lord be upon you, Master Nicholas. How may I serve? Is it the card?"

"No." Fetch had a pretty good memory, but I knew Kravayik's to be nearly perfect. He could recite the Bible by heart, and if asked a passage, he'd know it immediately. Thirty-odd years were like yesterday to him.

"Kravayik. What drew you to Holy Name?"

"It is the seat of the diocese! How closer to God could I be here in the city?"

And I was supposed to be the saint. "Were you ever in Chicago before we met? You never made that clear."

Silence.

"Kravayik?" I considered the phrasing that might best give me answers from him. "Tell me about Claudette Durand."

The phone clicked.

He'd hung up.

Kravayik had known Claryce's previous incarnation . . . and, with his skills and background, had very possibly been her killer.

CHAPTER 9

I called back, but he didn't answer. I would've left there and then for Holy Name, but the weather had worsened. Instead, Claryce and I returned to the files, but there was nothing else we could readily match to what was going on.

Claryce again insisted on sleeping downstairs. I wasn't sure that Her Lady might not've left another cute surprise, so I didn't argue. She offered to share the couch, but I chose to stay in the chair by the table. I still remembered how the rage had taken me up there. Even if it'd been due to Her Lady, I still had my own regrets.

Claryce drifted off soon after. I pretended to sleep until I knew she wouldn't wake up easily, then headed to the kitchen and the door to the backyard.

Fetch was there, just as I'd expected. "Shake yourself off. I don't feel like mopping."

He sent a flurry of melted snow around the entrance, fortunately not getting too much in the kitchen. "Thank ye kindly, Master Nicholas. My dogs're frozen!"

"Well, wipe them on the rug, not track them on the wood."

He did the best he could, I supposed. Fetch was more nimble than any hound or wolf, but he still managed to leave a puddle. I was too distracted by everything that'd happened to care about cleaning up just yet.

A thought occurred to me. "Fetch, were you ever in the mortal world before I met you?"

"Nay! My first and only time was when she sent me to . . . you know."

"Kill me." When he started to whine, I silenced him with a dismissive wave. "We've been through this. We're . . . copacetic."

He wagged his tail with vigor. "Thank you ever for that, Master Nicholas! I still feel so bad for what I tried to do then!"

"The wound healed." Or rather, the dragon healed it. Of course, it'd taken longer for Fetch to recover from what I'd done to him. He could be grateful I'd used the blessed dagger instead of unleashing the dragon's breath on him.

Fetch finished shaking. His dark fur settled. One benefit he still had was that as a creature of Feirie, he could still manipulate his outer form a bit. He already looked nearly dry, something I couldn't say about the kitchen floor where he stood.

"Sorry, Master Nicholas. Let me try to clean it up. Please!"

"What're you going to do, lick it up?" When he gave me those pitiful eyes, I finally acquiesced. "Do what you can, but don't take long. I've got some more questions for you. About Kravayik."

"As ye say."

Claryce still slept. I sat down and began looking through the files she hadn't gotten to yet. Those involving the exposition caught my attention. Through the articles, I followed the progress of the World's Fair as it finally got underway a year later than intended. It'd supposed to have been set for the four hundredth anniversary of Columbus, but some plans had proven too ambitious. The "White City" fell into that category, a vast set of plaster and cement facades placed over the nearby buildings, painted white, then enhanced by street lamps that gave them a false glow. What was supposed to look magnificent had, to many, looked not only very gaudy, but had contrasted so sharply with the grit of the city beyond that papers had sarcastically referred to the rest of Chicago, especially the more nefarious neighborhoods, as "the Black City."

The Black City. Now a more than apt name for a place where someone would build a chamber of horrors.

Claryce shifted. I watched to see if she would wake up, then grabbed files from the years directly after the World's Fair. Once again, I looked forward to the day when the calculating machines in some of the magazine stories would become so efficient that all these files could be stored on it. Until that happened, though, I had to rely on my memory and the system I'd designed over centuries to help me locate what I wanted quickly.

I found the first clipping. Here, the chamber of horrors wasn't called something so enchanting as a castle, but a hotel. That wasn't what I was interested in, though. What I did want I found in the second paragraph.

Dr. Henry H. Holmes.

Also known as the Beast of Chicago.

There was no image of Holmes, but there was a drawing of the infamous "hotel." A three-story building with an awkward rounded appearance above the ground floor, but otherwise seemingly innocent. Inside, though, there were passages and trapdoors everywhere. There were hints in the article that Holmes had constantly switched builders to make certain no one but he knew the full details of the design.

How many victims there'd been was a controversy in itself. Nine was the least I found listed, though there were names of only a couple. Neither of them were Claudette.

I'd just started on another clipping when a slight sound in the kitchen made me wonder just what Fetch was up to. After rising quietly, I headed back and carefully peeked into the other room.

What I saw nearly made me reach for Her Lady's gift. Yes, Fetch was still at work, but not the Fetch with whom I was most familiar. This Fetch still wore a form akin to some combination of wolf and hound . . . but one just as comfortable on *two* legs as four.

I'd only seen Fetch like this once in the recent past. The night of the Frost Moon, when the influence of Feirie had been at its greatest and Oberon'd tried to slay both the dragon and me. That same influence had granted Fetch a near return to the deadly creature he'd originally been. Even now, I could see the shortness of the muzzle, the twisting of the ears as they'd looked in Feirie.

And the paws now more like hands, but hands with sharp claws for slashing.

I recalled his attack on the Wyld in the storefront on Sixty-Third. At the time, I'd not paid too much mind to how Fetch'd looked. Now, though, I thought about the changes.

With care, I stepped back. Clearing my throat, I waited a breath, then returned to the kitchen.

Fetch stood on all fours, once more the almost-hound. He took a passive lick at a tiny drop of water by the outside door, then glanced up at me in all innocence.

"Did as good as I could, Master Nicholas! All right as rain!"

"That's a little old for you. You mean it's all jake or something, don't you?"

He wagged his tail vigorously, the innocent expression remaining. "Yes, it's all jake!"

I pretended to inspect the area where he'd been working. "Pretty thorough. I couldn't have done better by hand."

"Thank ye!"

I considered confronting him, but held off. Thus far, he'd only used the transformations to help. I know that he'd briefly been seduced by Oberon with the thought of being able to again become the powerful predator he'd been, but Fetch'd turned down that opportunity in the end. He'd even turned down an offer by Her Lady to retake his place in the Court as one of her chief assassins.

At least, I'd *assumed* he'd turned her down. Thinking of what'd happened upstairs, I now wondered.

That made me think of another former servant of Her Lady. "Fetch. Did you know Kravayik when you served the Court?"

He chuckled. "Master Nicholas, whatever ye think of me, I am hardly of the same caste! The blood of the High Ones flows in Kravayik. I . . . I was only useful."

"He's better than you?"

RICHARD A KNAAK   101

"I would fight him for ye or the mistress, but I would surely perish."

I nodded my appreciation. He sounded honest, but creatures of Feirie were born with the ability to lie well. Still, I liked to think I knew Fetch.

If not . . .

"You remember the World's Fair, Fetch? Around three decades ago."

The tail wagged harder. "Oh, yes! Much hearty fare! The barrels were full of pickings! The floors a—"

"Beyond the food, if you please. Are you sure you didn't cross paths with Kravayik while we were on the hunt and forget to tell me? I won't be angry if you say you did."

The tail abruptly ceased wagging. "But I'd not be telling ye the truth if I said I did!" The ears flattened. "Master Nicholas, if I'd crossed paths with Kravayik, I'd have warned ye! He hadn't seen the light yet, as he'd say. He was still hers!"

Fetch'd verified what I'd thought. I can't say I was entirely pleased. Kravayik had a lot of questions to answer.

"All right," I finally said. "You'll be fine in here?"

"Yes."

Best to slay him while he does not suspect you know, the voice in my head suddenly warned, *lest he try to finish what he failed to do before.*

He won't do anything, I countered.

So trusting . . . it will be the death of us yet. . . .

The dragon faded back into the darkness within me. I fought to shake off the last bits of his distrust of Fetch.

"Be ye all right, Master Nicholas? Ye look like someone's just stuck a shiv in your back. Is Kravayik behind the eight ball? Do we need to treat him as a Wyld?"

"No. No. Just someone who has a few secrets he needs to spill."

"He's a tight-lipped one, that Kravayik is. He won't sing easily."

Fetch's eyes narrowed dangerously. "If we need to take him for a ride, I'll stand with ye, I swear."

"You've been hanging around the speakeasies again, haven't you? Never mind. Don't worry about Kravayik . . . until I tell you to, all right?"

"Yes, Master Nicholas."

I started to leave, then turned back. "Claryce and I are heading out to Dunning tomorrow."

"Dunning." Even though he was a creature of Feirie, the name still affected him much the way it had Claryce. "There's a sorrowful place. Got a dark magic of its own, it does."

I couldn't argue. Whatever it was that permeated Dunning, it defied any name change or cleansing. Not all magic was of Feirie . . . and not all evil, either. After all, the mortal world had produced its own monsters in the form of men like Joseph, Galerius, and H. H. Holmes.

And possibly Dr. Alexander Bond, if he was either an acolyte of Oberon or the Beast of Chicago.

Claryce hadn't moved in the time I'd been away, for which I was grateful. I returned again to the files. However, even after two more hours of steady searching, I was unable to find out much more concerning Holmes and his reign of terror. I knew that there was likely some tidbit of info somewhere else in my collection, but the trail'd gone cold for the moment.

I sat back, trying to decide what next to do . . . and promptly fell asleep.

Sleep was generally no respite for me. My slumber usually consisted of an unending series of nightmares, all revolving around the struggle that'd started everything. The dragon and I'd do battle again, with Cleolinda caught in the middle. Of late, she'd become Claryce, which only made the nightmares worse.

"Well, we just keep getting more and more intertwined no matter how we try to separate ourselves, do we not, Georgius?"

I blinked. I stood in the midst of a familiar, rocky terrain. Somewhere nearby, the dragon awaited me. Somewhere nearby, Claryce/ Cleolinda waited to be lost or killed.

But right now, it was only Diocles and me . . . only not as I often dreamed him. He was not the monster masquerading as a man or the puppet with the shadow of Galerius constantly hovering behind him. He was Diocles as I knew him *now*.

"So, you're now literally haunting my dreams? Is this some new afterlife promotion?"

The former emperor of Rome rippled. Yeah, this was no figment. This *was* Diocles in my head . . . as if my head wasn't crowded enough.

He spread his hands in that apologetic gesture he'd used even after turning down my pleas to not go through with his bloody persecution of the young Christian faith. "There is no place I would rather avoid as much as your mind, Georgius. I know the demons haunting you. They haunt me as well."

I couldn't help it. Just hearing him talk about his suffering made my heart race with growing anger. "You haunt me because you betrayed me! You haunt me because you were a friend who listened to another instead of my counsel and went on a slaughter of innocents!"

Diocles—Diocletian—faded out of existence. My hope that he'd not return was crushed immediately. Despite his regal robes and trim beard, he looked very small at the moment . . . which at least gave me some slight pleasure.

"I can only again do as I have for every day for these past sixteen hundred years," he muttered. "I have asked the Lord for forgiveness. I have asked the souls of everyone executed for their forgiveness."

Diocles himself had finally found Christianity like so many others. When he knew he was dying. To me, that made his prayers that much more hypocritical. Throughout the empire, thousands had prayed for their lives and their souls as Galerius's officers—under his dread dragon banner—had had them tortured and then executed. Young and old had been burned alive, drowned in the sea, or flayed.

I'd been told by more than one priest over the centuries that even a man who'd done what Diocles and Galerius had done could receive redemption if he was truly repentant. I don't know what version of Hell or Hades Galerius suffered in, but I suspected Diocles could never receive absolution until *I* was willing to forgive him, too. Why else was he bound to me?

Still, sixteen centuries and I wasn't ready to let him off the hook.

"Keep praying," I snarled, adjusting my grip on the spear suddenly in my hands. I could sense the dragon stirring. As astonishing and unsettling as Diocles's intrusion into my other nightmare was, he was still only a temporary distraction. My own curse was about to begin anew. Even had I wanted to talk of redemption to him, doing so was beyond both of us.

"Georgius—"

"Nick. Always Nick Medea to you," I interjected absently as under me there suddenly arose a white stallion not at all like the proud but earthy animal with whom I'd ridden into battle against the dragon. "As in Nicomedia. As in where you let Galerius have me executed."

Before he could answer, the thundering roar resounded through the land. I urged my charger on, leaving the emperor in the dust. I rode over a small hill, no longer even thinking of Diocles. There was only the dragon.

There was only death . . . again.

"Nick? Nick?"

I jerked away with such ferocity that Claryce stumbled back. My arm brushed several files to the floor. I heard the tap-tap of clawed feet on wood and knew that Fetch'd come to see what was going on.

Without thinking, I grabbed her wrist. Only then did I see that my hand was green and scaled. I looked up and saw from Claryce's abrupt change in expression that it wasn't just my hand that'd shifted form.

Take it back! I silently shouted. *Take it back! I didn't ask for anything!*

Did you not? he coldly asked in turn. *You keep declaring that, but still moments like this happen.* . . . Yet, still he vanished inside me once more, taking with him all vestiges of his monstrous glory. I shook as I returned to normal. Chicago hadn't needed someone like H. H. Holmes. I'd already set a terrible beast in its midst . . . and things were growing worse for some reason.

"Nick! Are you all right? Was it her again? What did she do?"

"It . . . wasn't . . . her."

"Not her?" Claryce glared in my direction, but not at me, I understood. "It was *him*, then. Damn him! If I could—"

I expected a mocking laugh to erupt from the depths, but he remained curiously silent. I'd noticed a few times that he might jest about Claryce, but when directly confronted by her, he seemed to shy away even though she couldn't hear him.

I noticed a slight lightening of the darkness outside. I'd slept far longer than I'd realized. "What time is it?"

"Almost eight. It's overcast, but the weather's clearer than last night."

A scent wafted past my nose, a pleasant scent that not only made my stomach growl, but made *him* stir with interest. He could only experience the world through me. In that regard, eating was one of the few sensations he enjoyed. Mostly, he stayed nicely quiet during meals—such as during dinner last night at Berghoff's—but there'd been times, especially early on in our unwilling alliance, when he'd actually tried to supervise the order of our meals. It'd been some of the few moments when we'd been at ease with one another.

Fleeting moments.

"I wanted to make some breakfast, then wake you. I asked Fetch to keep an eye out to see if you needed anything." She gave him a dramatic stare worthy of Gloria Swanson. "And of course the moment I hear a noise and come out to see what's happening, I find Fetch's been sitting in the kitchen behind me the whole time. I'm hoping that when I walk back into the kitchen, I'll find the bacon and eggs still where I put them."

Fetch's tail drooped. "The eggs are all there, Mistress Claryce."

"And *most* of the bacon?"

"A . . . good . . . share."

She sighed. "I'd better see what we've got left."

I nodded my appreciation and didn't bother to comment as Fetch followed on her heels even after having already purloined some of the bacon. Despite it being past dawn and I often staying awake for days with little repercussion, I nearly dozed a second time.

Fortunately, Claryce came back just seconds later with a cup of coffee. "Here's that black ink you like to drink. I think you need it."

"Definitely." My taste in coffee went back to an encounter in Ethiopia—or Kaffa as I'd known it. That meant my choices tended to be a lot stronger than those of most drinkers in Chicago, who leaned toward Maxwell House, Hill Brothers, or some other contemporary brand. This morning, I was doubly appreciative of its strength. I had to go to certain enclaves in the city to find it, and it was worth it.

It still took half the cup before I began to feel like myself. By that point, Claryce'd returned with a plate of food.

"He left us just enough."

"Are you sure? He didn't follow you out of the kitchen. You might have to share this with me."

"He's been warned."

The telephone rang.

We eyed one another.

"Kravayik?" she asked.

"Doubtful." I didn't waste any time. I knew it had to be only one of two things. Either my advertisement offering to help someone with their "ghost" problems had materialized before a client in need or it was Barnaby calling me about either the Packard or, more likely, when to meet him at Dunning.

I waited. When no one spoke, I finally asked, "Barnaby?"

"Shadows on the wall, shadows on the floor, shadows in my head . . . I can't take so many shadows anymore."

The line went dead.

I stood there, staring at the mouthpiece.

"Who was it?" Claryce asked. "Was it Barnaby?"

"No." I hung up the telephone. "Not exactly."

"I don't like the sound of 'not exactly.' Not when we're dealing with something like Feirie."

"This doesn't have to do with Feirie . . . at least, I don't think so. This is much closer to home." I picked up the phone again and gave the operator a number.

Claryce came up next to me. "Nick—"

The phone had barely begun ringing when someone answered.

"Hello?"

"Barnaby? It's Nick." I took a deep breath, well aware of how much what I was about to tell him might cut him deep. "I've just had a call from *Joseph*."

CHAPTER 10

We neared the eight-foot-high iron fence of Dunning just before midday. The institute lay some twelve miles northwest of the actual city, but was included in its boundaries. Beyond the fence, the Gothic-style buildings erased any last vestiges of hope that anyone who knew the asylum would ever call it other than Dunning. The trees and foliage designed to give Dunning a sense of life and hope had become in their own way twisted to reflect the darker history of the establishment. Thousands had been committed to it over its eighty and more years of existence, some of them not touched by simple madness, but the ruthless results of their sensitivity to the magics of both this world and Feirie.

But if anyone belonged in Dunning, it was Joseph.

We turned off Irving Park Road and into the entrance. Eventually we reached the main building, where I saw that Barnaby's old Whiting Runabout with its unique squared-off cowl already sat parked.

I parked the Wills, which I'd driven since I knew the way and Claryce hadn't, then looked in the back. "I told you to stay at the house, Fetch. You sure you'll be okay here?"

"Ab-so-lute-ly, Master Nicholas! I'll be good here!"

I supposed it still beat racing through the streets and alleys. "All right."

Claryce and I went inside. There was no sign of Barnaby, only a pensive-looking nurse at the front desk. I expected complications, but when I gave our names she merely handed me a paper to sign, then pointed the direction we had to go.

"No wonder he was able to get to a telephone so easily," Claryce whispered.

"Not that easily. His room should've been well-locked. In fact, I don't remember one instance when Joseph's ever escaped."

"Maybe he just never had a good reason before."

It was something I'd been considering since the call. Before we could discuss it, though, I sighted a short figure pacing the hall ahead.

Barnaby Sperling stood five feet tall at best. A crown of wild white hair circled his otherwise bald head. He was a wiry little figure dressed in a simple brown suit that spoke of much wear. Barnaby wasn't a poor man; in fact, he was pretty well-to-do, but he was also very frugal.

Our echoing footsteps made him pause and look down the hall at us. The defiant bulldog features twisted into an expression of hope.

"Master Nicholas—"

I cut him off. "It's 'Nick' to you, Barnaby. Just Nick. Let's put an end to this now. You're not Kravayik or anyone from there."

He didn't question what I meant by "there." He'd known of Feirie even before Joseph'd been born. "As you wish . . . Nick. And so this is Miss Claryce." Barnaby held out one fairly large, leathery hand. Even though he had several employees, Barnaby didn't shy from hard work himself. Not like his son. "A pleasure to finally actually meet you."

She took the proffered hand. "A pleasure for me, too. I'm sorry we didn't get the opportunity sooner."

"And I'm sorry it finally has to be under these circumstances. I hope you'll forgive me."

"What should I forgive? You've done nothing."

Barnaby grimaced. "I've brought you to Dunning."

With that, he turned to the door at his right. After pulling a key from his pocket, he started unlocking the door.

"Do they usually give relatives keys to the patients' rooms?" Claryce asked.

"No," Barnaby replied as he pushed the door open. "Not knowingly anyway."

I frowned. Barnaby had sworn off the arts years ago. Still, I understood why he might prefer easy access to his son. Joseph was a case no doctor would ever be able to solve. All Barnaby could do was pray he could keep his son secure here.

Apparently, though, even that wasn't entirely possible anymore.

He didn't look up as we entered. He didn't change his focus when Barnaby took a moment to lock the door behind us. All he did was stare at faint shadows made by the lone lightbulb high out of reach.

Barnaby stepped in front of us. "Son. Son? We've got visitors. Master Nicholas and a friend."

I bit back a sigh of frustration. Maybe Barnaby'd remember another time.

Joseph sat quietly on the edge of his simple frame bed. Some patients weren't even allowed sheets, but Joseph'd never shown any inclination for suicide or murder since he'd been committed, so eventually he'd been given a set.

While Barnaby reminded me of a bulldog, Joseph had a longer, oval face that I had to assume came from his mother, Emma. He'd been a good-looking kid once, with hints of Valentino features, but the crash'd left his nose broken and a pair of scars crosscrossing his face near his right cheek. The thick, blond hair he'd kept so well-groomed had been shaved off for the convenience of his keepers.

He wore a simple brown pants and shirt set and sandals. I wasn't sure his outfit was official Dunning wear, but I assumed anything out of the ordinary was due to some unmarked payment out of Barnaby's pocket.

We waited a moment, but Joseph didn't speak. He kept staring at the shadows.

On a hunch, I summoned the dragon's eyes. Unfortunately, even then the shadows simply remained shadows.

But it did finally serve to get a rise out of Joseph. He still stared at the shadows, but also put a hand to his scarred cheek before saying, "The shadows here, the shadows there. My soul is theirs, his to snare."

How poetic. . . . Have him do another rhyme. . . . There was that fanciful one we learned in Venice. . . .

"Quiet," I replied under my breath.

Joseph giggled. "He'd like another rhyme, but there's truly no more time. The moon is past, but its reach will last. The beast grows as the shadow flows. . . ."

Claryce and Barnaby looked puzzled, not having heard my conversation with the dragon. I stared at Joseph, wondering how he'd done that.

The dragon went a step further. Suddenly paranoid, he yelled, *Burn him! Scorch him! He is a thing of evil!*

I didn't respond to his shrieked demands save to wonder about his abrupt insistence. When Barnaby's son didn't continue, I decided to step between him and the shadows he found so fascinating.

He tried to peer around me, but I compensated. Finally, Joseph settled down again. He stared in my direction, but not at me. It was as if he could see the shadows through my body.

I leaned close. "Joseph. You know us. You called me. What did you want to tell me?"

His gaze shifted slightly. I might not've cared except for the fact that he was finally looking at something other than the shadows.

Or was he? "Claryce. What's behind me?"

"Just the wall."

"Where's my shadow?"

"Also behind you. It stretches from the floor all the way to the wall."

Of course. Still, it was at least a change of sorts. "Tell me about the beast, Joseph."

I hadn't missed his passing mention of it. Several theories passed through my mind, but I wanted to find out what I could from him before I drew conclusions.

"We had the airship headed on the path. We had the spell in progress. The river was ahead."

Suddenly, Joseph wasn't rhyming anymore. He was reliving the Wingfoot crash.

"Don't do this, Master Nicholas!" his father pleaded.

"Quiet," I warned Barnaby. I knew that the crash still affected him. He blamed himself for Joseph's actions, even though Joseph'd been of clear mind when he and his cohorts had hatched their plan to sacrifice scores of others in order to gain power. "Go on, Joseph."

"We had the matrix measured out. We had it measured out. He'd given us all we needed. There was no room for mistakes, but no mistakes to make. There was—"

I cut him off. "Who gave what to you? You've not mentioned anyone else before. Who're you talking about?"

"The dragon marches, the dragon flies, but when the beast walks, anyone dies."

Silence this fool! demanded the voice in my head. *We listen to babbling! Silence him!*

I wasn't sure which intrigued me more, Joseph's slip back into the rhyming or the dragon's abrupt insistence that I eliminate Barnaby's son for speaking. I could deal with the dragon at any time, so I finally concentrated on Joseph. "You were talking about the Wingfoot. Do you remember? He gave you what you needed. Who?"

"Is this important, Nick?" Claryce asked.

"We thought everyone was accounted for. We thought that all his remaining friends were aboard. We never knew that he had some other link with someone beyond the group." Without taking my gaze off Joseph, I asked, "Barnaby? Did you forget to mention any of his associates? Or maybe one of yours?"

"Master Nicholas, I never trafficked with the likes of Joseph's companions, and none I knew would've ever given him advice on such evil as . . . as . . ."

He trailed off, his guilt over what his son had sought to do still fresh after six years.

Joseph remained silent while we spoke, eyes still on my shadow. I decided to try something. I raised a hand and waved slightly. I knew my shadow would do the same.

A childlike smile spreading over his face, Joseph waved back at where my shadow was.

"Comes the shadow, goes the shadow," he murmured. "Comes the man, goes the man. So busy I am."

It took me a moment to understand to what he might be referring. "Yes, Joseph. You've had a lot of visitors. Your father. Me." I chose not to bring Claryce to his attention any more than I could. "And Dr. Mudgett? Or maybe Dr. Bond was his name?"

Joseph just stared.

I moved the hand back and forth. He perked up.

Continuing to move the hand, I asked, "Does Dr. Mudgett have a mustache?"

Joseph nodded.

I wished I'd had an image of Bond. I did my best to describe him. Not at all to my surprise, Drs. Bond and Mudgett appeared to be a lot alike.

"Who is this man, Master Nicholas?"

I didn't answer. I had my ideas, but I didn't want to voice them yet. Still moving the hand, I asked, "What did the doctor want from you, Joseph? Was he the one who gave you what you needed for the matrix?"

"The shadow comes, the shadow goes. With each night, the shadow grows."

I frowned. We were back to the rhyming. I thought a moment. "This shadow—"

"One shadow grows, one ebbs and flows." Joseph leaned to the side and waved at the original shadows.

That struck me. "Does one of these shadows come and visit you? Does it?"

I was rewarded with a simple nod.

"Barnaby? You know anything about this?"

"Not at all! Is it just his imagination, perhaps?"

I'd like to have thought that, but this was Joseph. It would be just like him to have sinister shadows come visiting him in Dunning. "Doubtful. Maybe something to do with the doctor."

"The moon goes, but the shadow grows . . ." Joseph pointed to his left.

I tried to think what lay in the direction beyond Dunning. The only thing I could say for certain without a map was Lake Michigan.

Joseph lowered his hand. His expression grew indifferent, and his eyes shifted to the shadows he'd been watching when we'd entered. I knew what that meant. Whatever moment of clarity—although clarity wasn't exactly the right word with Joseph—had passed. Joseph was once again Joseph as he'd been since the Wingfoot crash.

Barnaby sighed. He joined me in front of his son. As I backed up, Barnaby touched Joseph on the cheek.

Joseph's father might as well not have existed for the nonresponse the son seemed to give the touch.

"As unsettling as this was, it was still a pleasure to hear him after all this time."

Claryce put an arm on Barnaby's shoulder. "You poor man."

I said nothing. I kept thinking of the lives lost and those that *would've* been lost because of Joseph.

Turning from his son, Barnaby asked, "Did you learn enough, Master Nicholas?"

"I learned something, but what exactly it was, I'm not certain."

"But this Dr. Mudgett and your Dr. Bond are the same?"

"They sound very similar to me," Claryce responded. "Don't you think, Nick?"

"Enough for me. Just wish I knew what the doctor had in mind.

First his interest in Oberon's property across from the Murder Castle—"

"I beg your pardon?" Barnaby looked from Claryce to me. "The Murder Castle? Does this have something to do with that awful place? I remember that time . . . how curious."

I took a moment to glance at Joseph. He'd made no reaction at the mention of the place. "Why curious? Did you or Joseph have any ties to it, Barnaby? Is this something you didn't bother to get around to telling me?"

"No . . . no. It's just the timing. That you should mention it now." Barnaby's eyes widened. "Oh, dear! Joseph did mention the *moon*. He must've meant that!"

"The moon is past, but its shadow will last . . ." Joseph whispered to the wall yet again.

I waited, but he lapsed into silence. My mind raced. The moon. A particular moon. "Barnaby, was there a *Frost Moon* when all this took place?"

"Yes . . . yes, there was."

I thought of all the problems the last one had just caused. It'd not only helped Oberon with his spellwork, but it'd enabled Her Lady to get a greater foothold. "How long did that one last?"

"The moon? It was there itself like any full moon—"

I exhaled. At least that was one problem we didn't have to deal with.

"—but 'Moon's wake,' as they call it, can last anywhere from a few days to several weeks, depending on circumstances."

"*Moon's wake?*" There went my brief comfort. "What happens during Moon's wake?"

Barnaby looked guilty even though he had no reason to do so. "Where magic's concerned? Just about anything, Master Nicholas. That's why most cautious casters make use of the tremendous power of the moon itself. The wake offers incredible opportunity, but also incredible danger."

Joseph chuckled, catching our attention again. He smiled wider at the shadows before him.

"Castles in the air, once gone, now again there . . ."

And with that, Barnaby's son abruptly turned on his side, slid onto the bed, and went to sleep as if without a care in the world.

CHAPTER 11

Barnaby chose to stay with his son for a little while longer. I didn't see the point of that, but didn't say anything.

To my surprise, Fetch had remained in the Wills as promised. He rose on the backseat and wagged his tail as we climbed in.

"All jake, Master Nicholas?"

"Not really." As Claryce started the car, I leaned back. "Tell me about the Moon's wake, Fetch. Tell me the truth."

He whined, then remarked, "So ye saw me."

I'd had a suspicion after what Barnaby'd said. The only time other than on the shore of Lake Michigan during the night of Frost Moon I'd ever seen Fetch able to even partially transform was when he'd initially tried to kill me.

"Against the Wyld in the empty store and when you were trying to mop up my kitchen."

"What did he do?" Claryce asked as she drove toward the entrance.

"Remember him by the lake? Something like that."

She said nothing, but her hands tightened on the wheel.

"I swear I've never done wrong with it!" Fetch insisted as the Wills drove through the gateway. "I swear!"

I wondered how many Frost Moons there'd been since the Gate'd become fixed in Chicago. Still, even a couple of times over the past thirty years was too much.

Fetch's ears suddenly straightened. He growled at something to the right, then let his gaze go to behind the Wills.

I instinctively reached toward Her Lady's gift. "What is it?"

It was Claryce who answered. "I think we're being followed."

The news wasn't exactly surprising. Not wanting to give away the fact that we were aware of them by me actually looking behind us, I instead asked, "What do you see, Fetch?"

"Dark blue auto. Four inside."

Unlike dogs, Fetch had extremely good color vision. He'd verified with that observation that we were being followed by the Chrysler Phaeton.

"There a pasty-looking fellow among them?"

"There's two. Definitely not lookers."

"Two?" I hadn't counted on Schreck maybe having a brother.

Claryce gestured at her purse. "I've got a small mirror in there. You might be able to hold it just low enough."

I carefully pushed past the Smith & Wesson and found the mirror. Small as it was, it would definitely serve. I held it up near my shoulder.

I could see the Phaeton and the passengers, but only that the two in front were as pale as I'd thought they'd be. I couldn't make out anything else though.

Eye will help you see, the dragon offered eagerly.

The world not only shifted to emerald, but sharpened tremendously. I focused on the two hoods in the front seat, then concentrated.

The view magnified. It was almost as if the Chrysler hung on our bumper.

Schreck not only had a brother . . . he had a *twin*.

They still didn't look like anything I'd experienced with Feirie, but they also didn't look exactly like your normal hoods. I couldn't see the Peacemaker, but assumed Schreck One had it ready.

That brought another concern to mind. To Claryce, I muttered, "Don't let them get any nearer."

"Gun?"

"Unexpected passenger in our lap." I wasn't sure how close they had to be to suddenly cast themselves to our auto, but didn't want to take the risk.

Claryce accelerated. I got concerned about her speed, but she handled the Wills skillfully. Schreck Two followed suit, but then the Chrysler slid to the side as if it'd caught some slick piece of ice. The result left us far ahead.

"I saw the ice and skirted close to it," Claryce commented. "Looks like it worked. Do you want me to lose them completely?"

I had a suspicion that they knew where we could be found, anyway, but decided now was not the time to try to confront them. I'd do that when Claryce was somewhere else. "Go ahead."

With a grin, she sped up. Fetch let out a woof and stuck his head out the window so that he could catch scents in the wind. I looked in the mirror and saw the Phaeton dwindle until it disappeared from view.

We kept an eye out for our pursuers for some time, but it never reappeared. As we neared her apartment, Claryce finally slowed. "Good thing we didn't pass a police car." She cleared her throat. "That reminds me. Cortez called the other day."

"Cortez? You're just telling me this now?" I suddenly found I didn't like the way the detective kept intruding on matters, especially where she was involved. It took all my effort to keep from letting my anger show.

Unaware of my struggle, Claryce went on. "It wasn't anything important. More follow-up questions about Oberon as William. I told him what I could, and he asked how I was." She frowned. "Now that I recall, he even said his wife wanted to say a prayer for you for all your troubles."

My fury subsided. I couldn't help thinking that Maria was doing a lot of praying lately. Was Cortez talking up a storm about us, or was there something else going on?

Fetch took a big sniff of the air. His voice grew tense. "Master Nicholas . . . Wyld."

He had my attention immediately. I concentrated. There was a hint, but for some reason I couldn't exactly locate the source. It was near, yet it wasn't near.

The hoods in the car had never been too concerned about losing us. They'd known there was another pursuer that simply racing off wouldn't shake.

I'd rarely come across any Wyld who willingly came out in the daytime, but the overcast weather gave it fairly good coverage today. Still, either Fetch or I should've been able to get a fix on it by this time—

Suddenly, another presence made itself felt. The hint of Wyld faded, replaced by a stronger sense of Feirie, of Her Lady.

I looked around. "Turn into that alley."

Claryce did so without questioning. That worried me a bit. I didn't want her so used to the darkness of Feirie that she trusted me to know the right thing to do against it.

We went a few feet into the alley. Claryce stopped the Wills. I immediately jumped out.

"Stay with her, Fetch."

"Now just a minute—" she began, only to stop as a shadowed form began to coalesce a short distance ahead.

I didn't have to ask who it was. There was only one reason—other than from me—that a Wyld about to attack would flee so suddenly.

"Lose your prey again, Lon?" I asked.

Her Lady's enforcer shimmered slightly, briefly radiating that same odd uncertainty I'd noticed from him the last time I'd called him by the nickname. I still didn't understand why it put him off, but I was willing to use any tool I had to keep the advantage.

The outline of the face formed. Lon did not have a happy expression. *She still waits.*

"For me?" I hadn't obeyed the last summons. I certainly wasn't going to obey this one without a good reason. "What does she know about slaughtered Wyld? I don't like her sending a rush of fleeing shadow folk through the Gate! That goes against the pact!"

The enforcer's face faded away again. *She waits. You are summoned.*

One hand emerged from the cloak, a long, sinewy finger pointing past me. *The female, also. . . .*

Her Lady might be the most powerful force in all Feirie, but she'd crossed yet another line with me. I reached toward the inside of my overcoat. Lon would know what that meant.

"If either you or any of her other lapdogs so much as get this close to her from now on, losing your head'll be the least of your concerns."

For good measure, I summoned the dragon's eyes. Chortling, he quickly acquiesced.

A low hiss escaped the cloaked creature, but to Lon's credit, he didn't back away in the face of two overwhelming threats. Even if he had some sort of protection against the sword, he certainly had none against the dragon.

Beware the Moon's wake. . . .

"Yeah, you can thank Her Lady for not getting around to telling me about it until now. You can also tell her that I'll take any intrusion on this side other than to remove the problem as a threat I'll deal with. That includes you, too, Lon."

He shimmered. *The Gate has two sides . . . two dangers. . . .*

Right now, I was tired of Feirie's cryptic ways. "You've got something to tell me outright, you tell me—"

Beware! the dragon silently roared. *He is casting a subtle spell!*

I reacted immediately. Out came Her Lady's gift in one sweep. I heard a clicking sound behind me, but didn't register it as a threat. All that mattered was Lon.

But instead of following through with whatever attack he'd planned, Lon fled into the farther shadows. Even to the dragon's gaze, he literally scattered to pieces and vanished.

I didn't know what made me more furious, that Her Lady's servant had been trying to launch a sneak attack on me or that I'd not been able to hand him his head. My heart pounding and my breathing rapid, I turned back to Claryce and Fetch.

Her expression was enough to shake me out of my black mood. I realized I'd begun to fall into another fit of rage. I wanted to squeeze whatever passed for Lon's neck and—

—and, yet again, forced down the fury.

By that time, Claryce'd climbed out of the Wills. I saw that the click had come from the revolver, which she'd pulled out at some point. She kept the Smith & Wesson ready as she made her way toward me.

"Are you all right, Nick? What happened? What was that thing?"

"That was one of Her Lady's foot soldiers. They're not as tough as they think they are, though. Oberon dispatched the last one rather messily."

"They are very strong, very dangerous, Mistress Claryce. No simple goons. Real torpedoes."

Claryce stared at the spot where Lon'd floated. "Why did you attack him? I didn't see him do anything."

Her questioned annoyed me more than it should've. Biting back a retort, I simply answered, "He was starting a spell."

Fetch, who'd been sniffing the air, paused. "There was no spell-casting, Master Nicholas. I would've sensed that."

"Don't argue with me!"

Fetch whined. Claryce looked at me reprovingly. "Nick! Get ahold of yourself! What's happening to you?"

"Nothing. Sorry. She had the audacity to not only demand I come before her, but to bring you with me! I think maybe that's what stirred me up the most."

"Ye looked like Ed Healey about to take down a poor fool, Master Nicholas! That ye did!"

The offhand comment made me stare at him. "What? Now you're a football fan, too? You been sneaking over to Wrigley to watch the Bears?"

He looked all innocent, but I was certain he'd done just that. It was one thing to skulk around the alleys of Chicago, but I'd made him promise long ago to not go where so many people gathered. He *would* be seen if he kept growing careless like that. Someone would either take him for a loose dog or some wild animal like an oversized coyote from the west suburbs. Whichever the case, I didn't need stories of him popping up in the *Trib* and other papers.

"Is there a chance that thing'll come right back?" Claryce asked.

"No."

She finally returned the revolver to her handbag. "What's going on, Nick? Oberon's dead, isn't he? Things were supposed to calm down, weren't they?"

"Not as long as the Frost Moon's still affecting both sides of the Gate . . . something our friend here should've explained to us . . . eh, Fetch?"

"I'm sorry. . . . I didn't think it'd last long! Mostly it lasts a few days, but it has been said to go weeks on a rare occasion! What could be done, anyway?"

"A warning still would've helped." I peered over my shoulder to make certain that Lon'd actually gone. "Let's get going."

"Where to now?"

I rubbed my chin. "Now, more than ever, I want to talk with Kravayik."

The weather slowed our drive, but finally we reached Holy Name Cathedral on Wabash. I parked near a drugstore where I knew I could find a telephone. My preference would've been to surprise Kravayik after he'd hung up on me, but unfortunately, the only way I was going to get to see him at all was to give him advance warning.

The cathedral was a magnificent display of Gothic revival. True, it wasn't a humble house of God, but as the base of the diocese, I supposed it needed to be grand to attract worshippers to the faith. I'd seen a lot more ostentatious in my centuries, some of them for the sake of the Lord, others just for the sake of the ruling class's egos.

"Wait here," I told Claryce. I jumped into the drugstore and asked for the telephone. Fortunately, its location enabled me to keep an eye on Claryce and the Wills while I contacted Kravayik.

I'll give him credit. He knew it'd be me, but he still answered immediately.

"Yes, Master Nicholas."

Not a question, but a statement. "I'm outside. I'll be there in five minutes. You'll be there."

"Yes." He hung up.

Returning to the car, I told Claryce about the brief conversation.

"Should I stay here?" she asked.

"No." I still hadn't told her all my suspicions concerning Kravayik and Claudette. "No. You'll come with. Fetch—"

"Yes, Master Nicholas. I stay in the car."

"*In* the car. Not in the vicinity. Not in the neighborhood."

"I swear I will."

Hoping I could trust him, I took Claryce's arm. We headed for the arched entrance. At this time of day, there should've been little activity. The priests would be busy in other parts of the cathedral. That would leave us alone with Kravayik.

The entrance opened just enough to admit us. With no service going on, the interior was full of shadow, as the priests conserved light.

Despite some past misgivings, I instinctively made the cross as I entered. At the same time, from behind the door emerged a figure nearly as much shadow as Her Lady's enforcer . . . not a surprise considering the similar backgrounds.

Although only half as wide as me at the shoulder, Kravayik towered over both of us. He had piercing black eyes that if seen directly revealed themselves to be much too large and a nose barely more than a bump. His head stretched more than that of most humans and was flanked by ears sharply pointed. Like a monk, he had a ring of hair gracing his skull, but unlike them, his had a hint of emerald green in it.

Kravayik's employers did not see any of this. In fact, they often forgot that they'd even hired him. Kravayik remained in the shadows, tending to the cathedral and seeing to a particular task for me.

"Master Nicholas. Mistress Claryce." Finding religion'd done wonders for Kravayik, who, in my opinion, had once been an even stealthier killer than Lon. "A most pleasant surprise. Please. Follow me to my quarters. I have been experimenting—quite successfully, I think—with some gnocchi."

Kravayik had not only found religion, but he'd also found an almost religious obsession with Chicago's Italian cuisine. His first forays had bordered on the frightening, but now there were restaurants in Little Italy that would've snapped him up as a chef if he'd been so inclined . . . and looked human enough in the bright light to not scare off the customers and staff.

"Don't distract, Kravayik. We've got important business to discuss."

"Is it about—that?" He tilted his head toward the altar.

"No. No one hunts the card at the moment."

"Praise be . . ."

I suddenly realized that there was another figure in the chamber. Right on cue, he formed just beyond Kravayik barely a minute after I'd stepped into the cathedral. It didn't matter what church or similar structure I walked into; the odds were nearly overwhelming that Diocles would be there to torment me . . . and himself.

I purposely ignored him. He glared, but remained silent. I had more important things to deal with than his constant regrets or my refusals to forgive.

"You know why I called, Kravayik."

His gaze shifted ever so slightly to Claryce. "Master Nicholas—"

"Don't be afraid of disturbing me," she interjected. "I'm tired of being left in the dark. I don't know all of what Nick suspects, but I know he thinks you met my previous incarnation. A woman named Claudette."

"A very lovely name," he replied noncommittally. Kravayik indicated the hall behind him. "Please. You must try my gnocchi."

We followed him back to his spartan quarters. A cross hung on one wall. A table with chairs stood across from a narrow bed.

Behind the room was a tiny kitchen that I knew didn't appear on any of the blueprints for Holy Name. Kravayik rarely left the cathedral. He had no interest in the outside world save where it served his purpose, but his only purpose these days concerned his prayers.

Prayers and the local news, evidently. On another simple wooden table Kravayik himself might've carved sat what I recognized from its inexpensive, boxy shape as one of the Crosley 51 radios that were all the rage. Kravayik had it set on KYW, possibly meaning that in addition to religion and cooking he'd found opera as well. I pitied him if he'd done so. I'd been around when most of the operas had been written and heard them in so many variations I could hardly bear to listen to any now.

We sat at the table while he brought us two small bowls filled with gnocchi. I had to admit it—and I saw by her expression that Claryce did, too—his gnocchi was excellent. Still, I'd had about all I could take of waiting and only an occasional glance by Claryce kept me from interrupting during the small meal. I couldn't comprehend her patience, considering what this discussion concerned.

Inside me, the dragon radiated impatience of his own. He had even less love for Kravayik than he did most other creatures, something that went beyond their recent struggle when the dragon'd betrayed me and tried to steal the Clothos card from Holy Name and its guardian . . . Kravayik. The dragon'd used my body to reach the altar where we kept the artifact hidden, but the power the card emanated had enabled

Diocles of all people to warn Kravayik of the treachery. Even though Kravayik failed to stop him, the dragon had never forgiven the disruption in his plans.

Finally, I decided Kravayik'd been given enough time to stall.

"Tell me about Claudette," Claryce quietly said before I could.

"So many names. So many people I have met since I saw the light. Did you know—"

I jumped to my feet. "She's asked you much too nicely, Kravayik. If I have to ask again, it won't be me alone."

His expression remained frustratingly even, but as he took the bowl from where I'd left it, he looked at Claryce. "You can imagine my shock when Master Nicholas brought you to me recently."

"You hid it well," I pointed out.

Kravayik put the bowl aside and clasped his overly long hands together. "May the Lord forgive me; I nearly shouted out with guilt what terrible deed I'd done!"

That made both Claryce and I shift warily. I know I hadn't been alone when I'd wondered if he was responsible for Claudette's death. Claryce grew pale, and her hand kept near the purse's opening. Kravayik was fast, but if I took him on first, I was pretty certain that he'd been a part of the mortal plane long enough for bullets to work. I knew I could trust in Claryce's aim.

With one smooth motion that reminded me just how effective he'd been as one of the Court's top executioners, Kravayik lunged toward Claryce. I already had the sword out before I saw that he'd fallen into a kneeling position before her.

His tone beseeching, one of the deadliest members of the Feirie Court bent his head down in abject apology. "When I saw you with Master Nicholas, I thought that the Lord had seen fit to give me a second opportunity! I had failed to save you after you had saved me in both body and soul! I am so sorry, Mistress Claryce!"

I had only seen Feirie folk shed tears in pain, not grief, but here was Kravayik, the most staid being I knew, with streaks of water coursing down his cheeks.

Claryce sat shocked for a moment, and then, her eyes softening, she put a gentle hand on his forehead.

I wasn't as inclined to be forgiving, especially considering that he'd not gone into any detail as to how she'd passed on. "What'd you do to her, Kravayik? What happened?"

"It is my fault, of course," he muttered as he slowly rose. "My sins are legions. Pride. Hate. Sloth. Greed. I journeyed here with all the confidence of my kind and proceeded to fail at every turn."

Slowly sheathing the sword, I snarled, "Let's begin with the most basic question. Did you—" I hesitated, not wanting to say it out loud before Claryce.

"Did you kill me, Kravayik?" she asked without hesitation.

He swallowed, then, to our relief, shook his head. "Nay, Mistress Claryce, though I might as well have been the one who caused your . . . death."

"How'd it happen?" I pressed him. "How'd you two come together long enough for this to happen?" I'll admit it; there was a part of me that at that moment was grateful that apparently I'd not been responsible for the death of at least one incarnation. Yeah, it was a selfish, macabre thought, but I still welcomed it just then.

Kravayik glided to where a small, brass teapot sat. He raised it toward us.

I scowled. "Stop delaying."

He sighed. "Many are the sins I committed in the service of the Court. The—"

"Georgius. . . ."

I guess I should've expected that since Kravayik's rooms were part of the cathedral, Diocles could materialize in them. I was about to tell him to go away, when I discovered that *both* Claryce and Kravayik were looking in his direction.

"Is that—" she started.

Before Claryce could finish, Fetch howled. For his warning to reach inside with such volume spoke of just how great the danger had to be.

"Kravayik."

"Indeed." With one swift motion, he set down the teapot and scooped up Claryce. To her credit, although she looked furious, she didn't struggle. Kravayik brought her to a back wall that suddenly opened up.

I *knew* that neither the builders nor the church elders had any inkling of a secret door in this part of the cathedral.

"Something's terribly different, Georgius," Diocles announced to me as everyone else moved. "Something's *very* different. You need to follow them—"

The walls of Kravayik's quarters blackened as something *oozed* from them.

Damned moon. Damned wake. Even Holy Name wasn't safe anymore.

"Run!" Diocles warned. "It's spread through most of this part of the church!"

That stirred a fear in me, not for myself but for Claryce. I knew she was in capable hands, but until I could make sense of what was surrounding me, I couldn't be sure she'd be safe even with—

Part of the nearest wall shaped into a four-digit hand that grabbed for me. At the same time, I heard the flapping of huge wings.

Diocles formed in front of me, trying, it appeared, to act as a shield despite having no substance. "Run after—"

The grasping fingers turned into a set of small scythes that cut *through* the late emperor.

Diocles scattered into thousands of pieces, as if he'd suddenly been transformed into a miniature snowstorm.

The flapping grew ear-shattering—

Unleash me! Unleash me!

I didn't argue. I let him loose.

Or tried.

And while we were both struggling to understand just why nothing happened, something struck our head with such strength we never did stay conscious long enough to see what the hand had in mind.

CHAPTER 12

"He made you sound like much more of a threat," a voice I knew but couldn't yet identify said from what sounded like the end of a deep tunnel. "Just goes to show, you can't even believe in legends."

He seemed to amuse himself with the last statement, his chuckle echoing for several seconds in my head.

That chuckle stirred more than myself. I felt the dragon also growing conscious. Conscious and angry.

I quickly quelled him. I was still too weak to allow him to color my thoughts with his bestial rage. In fact, I was beginning to have some suspicions—

"I am a bit curious as to where it went, but we'll deal with that later."

My wits had recovered enough to recognize the voice. Of course, he'd not seemed to be interested in trying to disguise it. "Dr. Bond. Did you make up your mind about purchasing the property?"

From far away, he laughed. "You know very well it wasn't the property I wanted, but of course, with you there, I had to make an adjustment."

I bit back my anger. So, he'd wanted Claryce from the beginning. That made me worry for a moment that he now had her, but then I realized that if that'd been the case, he surely would've taunted me with the fact.

"He said you were too lucky. You so often showed up at just the right moment. 'Someone's watching over him,' he said."

Bond was being almost companionable with his conversation, giving me information I didn't even know I wanted. Still, I couldn't care less for now about his unnamed associate. Bond could tell me about that when I had Her Lady's gift at his throat.

Of course, I didn't even have the sword. Either Bond's servants had nabbed it or it'd been left behind. Whichever the case, I had to rely on myself . . . and my companion.

I kept waiting for my vision to clear, but nothing changed. Finally, I gave in to the dragon's insistence, at least in that case.

The shift came, but very gradually, almost as if something had weakened our link to each other. At last, though, I could see my surroundings, such as they were.

I was in some passage made of wood and metal, a passage that only a yard from where I sat shrank down until I would've needed to crawl to get anywhere.

The dragon laughed. *Let Eye burn away this manling's rabbit den. . . .*

I said nothing, instead reaching a hand to the nearest wall. I felt something thick and wet. Whatever it was, I was of the belief that it wouldn't be a wise idea to let the dragon's flames touch it.

"Yes, that's a wise thought," Bond commented from wherever he stood. "Fight fire with fire, you might say."

I appreciated that he'd verified my concerns about the dragon's suggestion, but I was still at the end of my patience. "What do you want, Doctor?"

"To walk beyond its shadow again, that's all." His remark was followed by a grating sound, which I suspected was the maze shifting form. There would be no use in memorizing a path. "But first, let's deal with distilling what makes you be you. Thus far, for a saint, you're not much of a dragon slayer."

The grating sound continued. I waited for Bond to speak, but there was only silence. I wasn't *just* waiting for him, though; until now, my body hadn't wanted to obey me well enough for me to trust my movements. Whatever Bond had done, he'd done it well.

If he'd wanted me dead, he'd had a better chance than many.

Instead, he clearly wanted me to follow the passage in front of me. I supposed this could be some sadistic death trap, but, if so, it was one with a certain purpose. That meant that, at least for a time, he needed me alive.

Eye can free us so quickly! Release me! Let it all burn!

"That's what the bastard wants," I muttered to him. "I'll keep in charge of things for now, you hear me?"

Eye am bound to a fool.

I didn't argue then just as I'd never much argued before. If I'd been smarter, I'd never have taken on the dragon as I had in the first place. I'd have found out why he was where he was and not just assume he was stalking prey where instead he'd actually been guarding the Gate.

All that was moot, of course. What was important was dealing with Bond. There was another reason why I'd avoided letting the dragon have his way. I still didn't know with absolute certainty if the doctor had either Claryce or Fetch—or even Kravayik, with the way things were going—and until I did, I was willing to play along a little.

Yes, Eye am definitely bound to a fool.

Ignoring him, I crawled along the passage. The same odd, moist substance covered the walls no matter where I was. It also covered the floor, which meant soon my hands and knees were covered in it. Curiously, it had no discernible scent, not even when tested with the dragon's sense of smell.

I came to a juncture. I didn't hesitate. I chose the path ahead.

My choice bent to the right . . . and ended a few yards later. With the dragon snickering, I backtracked to the juncture again. I chose the path to my left and moved on.

This time, we went a short distance until we found another intersection. Going with my success, I picked the left again. My head began to pound as I entered.

Ahead, I made out what looked like a third juncture. However, as I neared it, I saw that it opened up more. Trying to clear my head, I slowly proceeded.

It *was* another small chamber, and it *wasn't* empty. A still form stood on the other side. I blinked, but even the dragon's eyes couldn't pierce the gloom well enough. Only when I was nearly upon it did I see that it couldn't possibly have been Claryce or Kravayik.

But it *was* an elf . . . or at least the desiccated husk of one. He had that same general appearance that Kravayik did and probably had looked enough like Kravayik to have been his brother. What remained of a long, flowing cloak and an outfit that would've played well in John Gilbert's *Monte Cristo* tried in vain to still cover the corpse.

When I tried to move him, I discovered something else. He'd been sealed to the wall behind him. A quick but thorough inspection showed that the same stuff all over the walls and floor were what kept the body in place. I wasn't too thrilled about that.

Eye am stronger now. Let me take over. . . .

The idea grew more tempting by the moment, but I refused. It couldn't be that easy. I couldn't help thinking that Bond knew exactly what my relationship with the dragon was and was hoping for me to summon him into being. That might've sounded insane, but I'd confronted worse insanity during my centuries of service.

I noticed one more thing as I let go of the dead elf. Not only did he look as if something'd sucked him dry, but there was a long slit from his throat down into his midsection. In fact, when I pushed the slit a little, I found that whoever had cut him had then removed the elf's heart.

The dragon's gaze allowed me to also see the dried remnants of a dark liquid on the slit's edges. It didn't take much study to understand that there'd still been some life left when the heart had been expertly removed.

If I'd had any reservations that the good doctor'd also been responsible for the body in Cortez's morgue, they were more than dealt with now. This wasn't just the work of a mad serial killer, though; all of what I'd witnessed thus far had relevance to anyone who dealt with the darkness of Feirie and its more subtle human equivalent. Bond had something far grander in mind, and I was supposed to be part of it.

As I pushed on from the corpse, I tried more than once to seek beyond what I could see. Unfortunately, my senses remained dulled.

Apparently not so my constant companion's. *Do not turn to the left . . . there is a darkness there Eye cannot penetrate.*

It wasn't until I actually reached the next intersection that I noticed what he was talking about. No, I definitely didn't want to turn to the left. Somehow, I knew I'd be finding myself sharing the elf's fate.

"Thanks," I muttered.

You are welcome.

I didn't trust the dragon being so cooperative and congenial under the best of times, much less at this moment. If he had any reason for helping me, it was only for his own sake. That also meant that if he found a second where my control slipped enough, he would seize it as he had when Oberon'd made him a deal.

Another question began nagging at me as I turned the opposite direction. Bond had gone through a lot of trouble to take me at Holy Name. To say it'd cost any Wyld a tremendous amount to even cross the threshold of a cathedral was to make one of the greatest under-statements possible. Bond would've had to have knowledge and access to spellwork from both realms to enable the creature to succeed, and while it was clear that he had that, it had to have cost him. He'd only have risked the sudden attack for some significant reason.

There was nothing that Joseph'd said to us that would be of some value to Bond, but maybe he'd assumed otherwise. It wasn't a coinci-dence—of course—that we'd been followed from Dunning. One way or another, something that either the doctor believed Joseph'd said to us or something Barnaby's son had revealed to Bond himself had forced Bond's hand. Something involving the Moon's wake and not just its length, as important as that had to be.

I remembered the height of the Frost Moon's influence. I wondered now if the wake had a cresting point, a time when *its* effect would also be greatest.

A time for which Bond needed to be prepared.

Beware! Wyld ahead!

I hesitated. I couldn't sense anything, especially a Wyld.

"You certain?"

Eye do not lie!

I considered retreating, but then heard a low moan. Without hesitation, I pushed forward again.

Beware!

"Quiet . . ." Another chamber opened up ahead, one large enough for me to stand.

Against the other side hung another elf. He looked almost as emaciated as the corpse, and his once-fine garments were in tatters.

"All hail His Lord," I muttered.

Despite his ragged condition, the elf instinctively rasped, "May . . . may his reign be . . . eternal. . . ."

As I'd thought. One of Oberon's courtiers. He looked like he'd been here for some time, even before I'd learned about his former liege's survival. I wondered what he'd done to be left to this by Oberon.

I cautiously took a step toward him. I could feel the dragon's frustration with my choice, but I pretended to ignore him.

The elf managed to lift his head enough to look at me. Again, the similarity to Kravayik was remarkable, even in the unnatural light of the dragon's gaze. I wondered if Oberon'd had his share of dalliances on the side.

"The Gatekeepers. . . ." Despite his predicament, he tried to sneer. That was the thing about Feirie folk; they generally couldn't change their nature even when it sure as hell would've behooved them. "All . . . hail . . . His Lord. . . ."

"You do know Oberon's dead, don't you?" I asked as I moved close enough to investigate if there was some way to release him.

"His Lord is . . . eternal! Only humans . . . turn to dust."

Curiously, I could see there and then how Kravayik had so readily turned to Christianity. In Feirie, he'd lived for Oberon and then Her Lady. In the mortal realm, he'd sought for something stronger to believe in.

"He was pretty much cinders, I can promise you," I remarked.

"Stop that!"

The vehemence with which the elf managed to shout at me startled even the dragon. I stared at the prisoner. "I'm trying to free you."

"Nay! He will . . . he will punish us both severely!"

I frowned. Here was one of the highest-caste Feirie folk, a cold-hearted creature who no doubt had himself a legacy of dirty deeds done at the behest of Oberon. Despite that, I was willing to help him escape.

He spat in my face . . . or tried to. It felt more like dust than anything else. "He warned after the last time what would happen if we escaped. He warned both of us, but Jorav would not listen well enough, so he was placed near the center, where the spell's crosscurrents were strongest! We were both warned, but only I listened! I've been good! Very good! I will not let you ruin that! I will not!"

The elf became more agitated. I finally stepped back. Only when I was just out of arm's length did he calm again.

I tried one more time. "Listen to me!"

"All hail His Lord! All hail His Lord!" And with that, he began to laugh madly.

Either leave this fool or let me burn him! There is nothing worth our time here!

I had to agree with him for once. Judging by the mad look in his black eyes, the elf would do anything he could to keep me from saving him. He'd been tortured to the point where his only allegiance was to his torturer. I'd have tried much more if he'd been most humans, but I knew that, unlike Kravayik, this elf's first choice would be to try to kill me.

"I'll be leaving you, then."

This only caused him to laugh harder. He was still laughing long after I left him.

Eye say again . . . let me out . . . let me burn this place to the ground. . . . I will do a fine job. . . .

"And probably leave whatever surrounds us as ash, too. No."

You will come to beg me one day . . . and Eye will say nay.

"No, you'll chortle with glee and set fire to everything in sight until I stop you because that's your nature."

He was silent for a moment, then chuckled in a way that reminded me just a bit of the mad elf. *True. So very true.*

The path quickly forced me to my hands and knees again. That made the dragon's offer more and more tempting, but I still worried about Claryce especially. I needed to find out if Bond had her prisoner. If he did, I'd have to figure out some way to reach her. If not . . .

If not, I'd let the dragon have his way.

"This is getting monotonous, Bond!" I called. "If you've a point to all this, maybe you'd be better off explaining it."

"Call it a test," he responded cheerfully. "I've tested so many. Some were only amusing. Some gave me a hint of what I needed. A few enabled me to outwit my persecutors and linger on." Bond chuckled again. "But if he's right, you'll finally be my path all the way back."

He might've not been of Feirie, but Bond talked as cryptically as any of the shadow folk. I was about to make a remark back, but then my head began to feel as if someone had just stuck a lead weight inside my skull. I nearly collapsed face-first into the muck.

Set me free! It is our only hope! Set me free!

Bond kept talking as if he couldn't see my struggle. "Of course, there is the unexpected pleasure of renewing acquaintance with your fair lady. I have to admit that it even caught me by surprise! So many years . . ."

His mention of Claryce was enough to enable me to force my head up again . . . but that was as far as I could manage to do anything.

Set me free! Set me free!

I wanted to order him to quit badgering me, but my head felt heavier than ever. I wanted nothing better than to just lie down and let unconsciousness take me.

I must've slipped into some state where my mind was open to suggestion. I would've never allowed the dragon free rein here.

But before I knew what was happening, I felt myself *transforming*. My hands and feet splayed out and quickly grew long claws. My face stretched forward, and my teeth grew. Near my shoulder blades, protrusions pressed against my clothes and then ripped them away.

And suddenly I was in a place of darkness save for a circle of light through which I could see the passage. My view reminded me of staring through a fishbowl.

Wood cracked. Metal squealed.

The dragon laughed.

Even though we'd only gone through a portion of the transformation, he already had control. It wasn't doing him much good, though, because despite now being pressed against the walls and ceiling, he hadn't yet managed to shatter Bond's maze. More and more we were squeezed into a tighter space, something the dragon would not accept even though it meant more pain for us.

"I will be free!" he roared.

Instead, even where my mind lurked, I could feel the pressures building against us, crushing us. The maze wasn't just pinning us in, but it was adjusting, shifting.

And as it did, even through the dragon I could feel a spell taking place, a spell we were feeding.

Stop! I ordered him. *Stop!*

The dragon didn't obey. He kept trying to will the transformation further, not accepting that doing so was not only impossible, but a danger to us. The claws raked the walls. The half-formed wings sought to push through the ceiling.

The spell surrounding Bond's maze only grew stronger.

I remembered the two elves, especially the husk.

Stop! Listen to me!

The dragon roared, but this time not in triumph but agony.

His control slipped. I seized mastery again. Our body shrank. The spell around us remained strong, but not quite as strong as before.

"You want to help," I whispered to the dragon. "You'll have a chance in a moment."

Although weakened, I could sense his sudden interest. Even though the pressure in my head grew stronger and stronger again, I pushed back through the maze. I was counting on both Bond's hubris and some of the limitations this structure still had to have.

Wyld . . . the dragon cautiously warned me.

"The same?" I muttered back.

The same.

I was glad to hear that for more than one reason. What I hoped to do would be risky enough, but if there was more than one elf like the one we'd argued with, the odds against our success would be just about insurmountable.

We slipped back into the chamber. The elf failed to notice us at first, which suited me fine.

"Be ready," I warned the dragon.

He knew instantly what I wanted and eagerly awaited. I pushed forward to the elf, who finally raised his head to look at me.

"You see . . . no escape . . . we must be good! We must not stir up the Beast. . . ."

"Whatever you say." I grabbed both his arms.

The dragon chortled.

The elf screamed as we ripped him from the wall. I had no qualms about hurting him. He'd served Oberon, which meant there was a lot of blood on his hands. I knew simply killing him wouldn't work, either. The remains of the other elf indicated to me that even the corpse of one of the Feirie folk could serve Bond's spellwork for a time. Time I couldn't afford.

Much of the dark substance sealing the elf to the wall came with him, while some of the elf's skin remained on the wall. He continued to shriek, but what I'd done was still the best way to free him.

Still shrieking, he fell to his knees. I pushed the dragon's presence to the background, then tried to help the elf. Our odds would still be better if Oberon's former follower would help us.

He was having none of it, though. Face even paler than normal for one of the Court, the elf swatted my hand away, then tried to turn back to the wall.

Aware of what he had in mind, I slugged him on the jaw. One thing I'd learned—a lot of elves had glass jaws. This one proved to be of that ilk, falling in a stunned heap.

I felt the spellwork controlling the maze begin to collapse. The entire thing had worked through the body and essence of the captive.

It all falls apart! the dragon triumphantly roared in my head.

"Don't get so cocky." With some misgivings, I grabbed for the elf.

The maze exploded.

I was tossed into the air. I don't know why it happened, but suddenly the dragon had dominance again. We had wings that kept us from falling. We smelled the enticing scent of burning wood and saw a moment later flames reaching high from the building from which we'd been tossed.

But despite our wings, the tempest that rose then easily spun us around as if we were just leaves in a breeze. We both knew that the abrupt storm was magical in nature, not that it did us any good. We were cast far away, neither of us able to identify up and down anymore.

So, it wasn't all that surprising when we struck either a wall or a street with enough velocity that not only created a thundering crack, but also knocked us out.

I didn't remember the transformation back to my own shape, only that it was suddenly dark and that every bone felt as if it'd broken. I knew it couldn't have been long since we were tossed into the air, though, because suddenly I heard angry voices, some with Irish brogues.

I managed to push to my feet just as a lanky hood in a cap stepped out of a building. He pulled out an automatic when he saw me.

"Dago!" he snarled, firing.

Apparently he'd seen me well enough to think, by my somewhat Mediterranean features, that I was part of Capone's gang. The fact that even in the dark I could make out his Irish mug, not to mention hear his bloodline in his voice, meant that I was likely in North Sider territory. Bugs Moran and his chief partners, Hymie Weiss and Vincent Drucci—heirs to Deanie O'Banion's bootlegging empire—still blamed their rivals in the Outfit for their boss's murder in his flower shop. Any potential member of Capone's gang was to be shot on sight, especially if he wandered near the North Sider's distilling facilities.

Which I'd apparently done.

I couldn't say for certain whether my showing up here'd been luck or because, like Oberon, Bond had ties with Moran and his companions. For now, I had to concern myself with regaining the advantage.

The first shot went wide, no thanks to me. Fortunately, most hoods couldn't shoot straight unless at a real close distance. That gave me time to recover enough to leap at him. It wasn't a gap any normal person could've crossed in a single jump, but I had the dragon's strength to push me beyond even my abilities.

As we collided, I heard more voices. There was a clacking sound that I knew spelled far more trouble. Someone had a tommy. It didn't matter if he could shoot straight. The submachine gun could spray a hail of bullets that'd take down anything in the area.

I punched my first foe hard in the gut. As he bent, I snatched his automatic and fired in the direction of the clacking sound.

My shot was followed by a series of oaths that nearly made *my* ears burn even after centuries as a soldier and guardian. I knew my shot'd been a quick one, but had hoped it would at least keep the second hood from firing.

The rat-a-tat-tat of the tommy scratched that hope away. Evidently my shot'd convinced the second hood that his compatriot was already dead. That became a moot point as the spray ripped into the thug I was gripping.

Let me out! Let me out!

I wasn't about to go through that situation again, especially since I couldn't have witnesses seeing a mythical titan in the middle of the city. Instead, I threw the riddled body in the same direction I'd fired, then attempted a second shot.

A shadow darker than the night swept past the machine gunner. I heard a muffled cry, and suddenly the man fell forward . . . while his head fell *back*.

My first thought was of the thing I'd jokingly nicknamed Lon, but then I realized what I took for shadow was instead a robe of sorts.

The shadow turned to me. "Master Nicholas! Forgive me!"

I didn't know what Kravayik was apologizing for until the hair on the back of my head stood up. I looked over my shoulder . . . and this time *did* behold Her Lady's pet enforcer.

His cloak swept over me.

Chicago vanished . . . and Feirie in all its infernal glory surrounded me.

CHAPTER 13

There remained only one actual way to reach Feirie, and that was through the Gate. Unless something had radically changed, this could not actually be Her Lady's domain. Instead, I was in a pocket realm within the folds of the Feir'hr Sein's magical cloak. Old Lon could carry me anywhere around the city while I knew nothing but this false but still astounding version of Feirie. As much as that bothered me, what bothered me more was why he'd been able to do that.

Kravayik.

Even more than most humans, shadow folk could be slippery in their alliances. Oberon and Her Lady'd ruled through the most potent of Feirie weapons, fear. They'd earned their subjects' loyalty by emanating invincibility. Even when Oberon'd originally been exiled, his legacy was so great that there'd been many who believed that he would eventually return in triumph.

Even Fetch still showed traces of Feirie thinking at times, especially when he'd been seduced by Oberon's offers. Kravayik, though . . . I'd thought Kravayik different. He'd embraced Christianity to a depth that even few humans had. He'd seemed more like a saint to me than I'd ever actually been.

But it appeared that I'd been wrong.

I hadn't budged an inch since I'd been swallowed up. From the gnarled green oaks surrounding me, I sensed several sets of eyes watching, observing. The oaks stood in a tangle of thorny, wicked brush in which smaller but no less sinister creatures quietly moved about. As with all things in Feirie, they studied me for any weakness that they could abuse.

A raven's call broke the silence. Nothing in Feirie was ever exactly as it seemed. It was very likely the raven was one of Her Lady's spies or courtiers alerting those ahead of my presence.

A small shadow briefly poked out of the brush. I made no move. I knew a feint when I saw it.

The dragon knew what I wanted and, when it came to being in Feirie, more than willingly gave it. I reached out to the side, my hand already shaping into a paw.

"I'll gladly rip your throat out if you come even an inch nearer," I informed the tall, gaunt elf clad in forest green armor now standing at my side. In one slim, moon-white hand he held a delicate but deadly black onyx dagger.

He bared his teeth. Narrow black eyes took in what to him looked like nothing more than a puny mortal. Yet, I knew he was well aware of just who and what he faced. As Her Lady's seneschal, he was one of her very favorites. That made him very jealous of anyone who could demand her attention . . . like me.

She awaits you. . . .

Of course Feirie folk had no trouble speaking like a human being, but in the Court, and especially in front of me, he had no intention of using such a primitive method. If I couldn't cope with his projected thoughts, that just proved how much less of a creature I was.

"She better make it fast. I've no time for her little games."

He let out a hiss. The dagger inched toward me.

Another bird cawed. The seneschal flinched.

The oaks nearest us bent down, then twisted until they formed a towering throne. Lush leaves filled out the throne, creating elegant padding.

A black bird landed atop one side of the top edge. Another followed suit on the opposing end.

In the center of the throne, a black rose blossomed among the leaves. As its petals spread, it grew taller and wider. Two of the petals became arms; two more became legs. Long, very feminine legs.

I'd barely taken two breaths before Her Lady sat before me.

She could've just appeared in a puff of smoke or simply walked out from among the oaks. Shadow folk liked dramatic entrances, but I had to give it to her—this was one of the best yet.

Her darling Gatekeeper . . . the Court is honored by your presence. . . .

Standing, she would've been taller than the seneschal. Her midnight hair framed her unnaturally beautiful face. She had full pale lips and a small nose in comparison to the males of her kind. Still, however beautiful she was, I could never not think of a vampire or an animate corpse. Her beauty was death itself, both enticing and terrifying.

A musical chuckle filled my head. Her Lady's hair shifted as if snakes acting at her command. It kept her features ever somewhat obscured, but not enough so that I couldn't see her eyes.

Sometimes those eyes were simply black like the seneschal's, other times fiery as Hell's flames might be. Today, they were pools of glittering darkness in which, if I'd been anyone else, I'd likely see my soul now trapped. Whatever our pact, Her Lady never ceased trying to bend me to her will.

As before, she failed.

"I told your pet I don't have time for you just now," I muttered.

The birds cawed angrily while the seneschal inched his dagger closer. For good measure, I snatched the blade from his grip before he could even realize what was happening. There were times when I *did* enjoy our combined abilities.

From the short, deep chuckle only I heard, this was a moment that the dragon enjoyed, too.

The hiss that escaped the male elf had a hint of concern in it. To lose face before Her Lady might mean other ambitious courtiers seeking to displace him. Worse, she might see him as representing a hint of weakness in her reign. There'd been heads on pikes for less.

"That's it!" I tossed the dagger to the ground. Her Lady could stare at me all she liked; I wasn't going to be moved. "You have Lon set me back outside and take Kravayik with him instead if you want! I've had enough—"

The landscape rippled. The forest suddenly stretched, expanding to several times its size and adding hills. The nearby oaks rose higher, then created an arch over us.

The brush crawled up between the trees, forming walls. Now, instead of being outside, we stood in the midst of a throne room the envy of any king or emperor. Within the walls, silver and gold streaks pulsated, creating a constant if ever-shifting source of illumination.

Her Lady stood. She was imposing.

It still didn't impress me.

She flicked a finger toward the seneschal. He immediately bowed and retreated. As he stepped back, he literally faded into the wall.

Her darling Gatekeeper is always a guest. . . .

"Guests aren't taken by force."

The slightest hint of a smile graced her lips. It was almost always there, both mocking and tempting. *There was no force . . . by Feirie.*

She was putting the blame on Kravayik. That was fine with me, to a point. It still didn't change the current situation, though.

"I'm going to leave now, and you'd better warn Lon, if you can, that when I do, it's going to leave more than a hole in his cloak."

The smile faltered. I swear I'd only seen that happen once or twice. The last time had concerned Oberon's return. *The Feir'hr Sein will act as it must.*

I'd had enough of answers that weren't answers. I could feel the rage inside stirring beyond control. Let them see what it'd be like with the actual dragon in their midst.

Yes . . . let me out to play . . . that is it. . . .

"Nick! Nick!"

I hesitated. In the middle of the high-ceilinged chamber—in fact, only a few feet away from me—Claryce materialized.

I recovered almost immediately. This was a trick Her Lady'd played on me just recently, a trick I still resented. "Call off your changeling, Queen, or sword or not, I'll toss its bloody head at your feet!"

The eyes glittered. I tried to read them, but failed.

"Nick . . . Nick, it *is* me." The Claryce figure came around to face me. "Look at *me* and tell me you don't know that."

For good measure, she kissed me. That alone was enough to verify this wasn't any Feirie changeling.

What at first sounded like a breeze stirring arose from the walls. I knew, though, that the breeze was actually the whispering voices of the Court.

Shadows shifted along the walls. Here and there I caught glimpses of a female or male figure dressed in garments that were as much mist as they were substance.

"Nick . . . are they everywhere?"

Claryce's question surprised me. "You can see them?"

"Wherever I look, but only in bits. The only one I can actually see is *her*."

The queen of Feirie made another slight movement of her finger. The whispering subsided. Her Lady gracefully descended. As she did, the two black birds abandoned their positions and alighted on her shoulders. Behind her, her gossamer gown trailed for some distance.

Reappearing, the seneschal angrily held out his hand. His dagger flew up into his grip. Still scowling, he stepped away as his queen approached us.

Even though I'd never been certain whether or not it could work on its creator, I instinctively reached for the sword. Only when my hand was at my chest did I remember that I'd lost the weapon.

"Don't worry," Claryce murmured.

There was a muffled snarl behind me. The black birds fluttered from their mistress. She paused as if nothing was amiss, though I had to imagine she couldn't have expected such gall from him.

Fetch paused beside me. Not just Fetch, though, but Fetch with Her Lady's gift clenched by the hilt in his jaws.

"Thanks." I gingerly took the jeweled blade from him, shook off an abundance of saliva, and then brandished it.

The whispering increased noticeably. From high above, the black birds cawed angrily.

"Get behind me, Claryce."

In response, I heard the familiar click of a gun.

"I still haven't had a chance to see what this can do." Claryce drew the ready revolver out of her purse. I hadn't paid much mind to the purse when Claryce'd appeared, there having been plenty of more obvious things to worry about. It should've dawned on me that she hadn't brought it along for fashion reasons.

Her Lady showed no hint of being disturbed by either Fetch's appearance or the weapons now drawn against her Court. On the other hand, the birds and the shadows receded farther. I'd had a couple of other confrontations in the Court over the centuries, but I'd never seen the shadow folk react the way they'd just done. I'd almost have sworn that the gun was a threat to them.

Or maybe it was Claryce herself. The queen of Feirie paused before her, peering down at Claryce with unblinking eyes. Fetch growled, but Claryce met the gaze with equal strength.

Her Lady laughed. *No matter which incarnation, you are always surprising, Princess. . . .*

There was a peculiar tone in her voice, almost as if she were speaking with someone of a caste nearly as high as hers and not simply some mortal. Her use of the title only added to that effect.

But she thinks that you will be the most surprising yet. . . . Her Lady rarely referred to herself in the first person. I didn't know if that was protocol or some part of some Feirie magic.

"Nice of you to say so," Claryce replied.

The queen of Feirie reached slim fingers to Claryce's face. I was ready to intervene, but Her Lady stopped short of actually touching her. Hand still extended, she looked at me.

And so, the Beast is among us again.

I'd never heard her refer to the dragon by such a title, but merely shrugged. "He's always with me. So?"

Her other hand came up. She slowly shook a finger at me. *Not the Leviathan, though he is always welcome in her Court. . . .* Her Lady did that pout that'd begun to remind me of the actress Clara Bowe. This time, though, there was something wary in that pout. *No . . . the Beast, aptly named by mortal kind, is of your realm. A demon born of man. The Beast that feeds on Feirie.* She tilted her head toward Fetch. *The Beast that our Kravayik appears to have failed utterly to destroy.*

I wasn't sure why she looked at Fetch when she spoke about Kra-vayik, but then the full gravity of her words hit me. She was referring to Kravayik in his role as her assassin, something he hadn't been in decades . . . at least to my knowledge.

The Beast. H. H. Holmes. A demon in human form.

A *demon* born of man? Was that the irony of the two realms bound together? For Feirie, had H. H. Holmes become a true demon?

"You're talking thirty years ago," I pointed out.

Her Lady spread her hands. *A lifetime for humans. Yesterday for us.*

"Fetch . . . what do you know about this?"

He whined, which answered part of the question. He knew a lot more than he'd ever let on.

Another disappointment, along with our darling Kravayik, she went on, the slight smile back. There was no humor in that smile. *So many disappointments with Kravayik.* She looked again at Claryce. *He could have learned so much from you at that time, our sweet princess.*

"Don't call me that," Claryce responded. "And I don't know what you're talking about."

But that was the previous chapter of your oh-so-interesting life! Such a life! To renew over and over . . . to not be eternal and yet be . . . The queen of

Feirie almost looked wistful. *To experience and be so much a part of change over and over . . . and not always as the same thing . . .*

I had to interrupt. "Is the Beast why you sent Lon after me? Is that the reason?"

Again, she briefly made a face when I mentioned her ghoulish enforcer. *If Kravayik cannot perform this task, it falls to you, our Gatekeeper. Yours is to protect* both *sides of the portal, not just your favored one.*

"Yeah, fighting off Oberon didn't do a thing to help Feirie, did it?" I countered. "I know the balance has got to be maintained. It'd be a lot easier to maintain it if I'd be let in on your little troubles without all this show."

To this, Her Lady didn't reply. Instead, she drifted a few steps back, then extended one hand to her right.

Part of one wall gave way. A shadow figure with just enough semblance to a human form flittered over to her. It fell to one knee as it placed in her palm a small object.

The darkness of the Moon's wake is still spreading, our darling Gatekeeper. The Beast feeds stronger with every night . . . and will feed strongest when the wake reaches its fullest.

"What happens then?"

We do not know . . . but already he eats away at Feirie, which should not be possible. . . .

I expected some sort of game, but after a moment, I realized that she'd said what she could. Her Lady honestly didn't have much of an answer . . . and that bothered me more than if she had one. If the queen of Feirie had no notion as to what extent this human demon would affect her realm, then the risk of danger to the mortal side had to be even greater.

She eyed the object in her palm, then held it toward me. It rose from her hand and drifted to me. I easily caught it with my free hand.

It was a sphere a little bigger than a marble. There was a dark spot within and slightly to the side that even reminded me of some of the marbles I'd seen kids shooting against curbs.

But I knew right away that it wasn't some kid's marble. It wasn't as fancy as what she'd handed me to deal with Oberon, but I knew it was still something similar.

The spot was blood sealed within to keep it fresh. Feirie blood.

"From one of Oberon's followers?" I asked. One way to guarantee control over your subjects in Feirie was to keep something of importance from them. Blood was a very good choice. It could be used to punish them from afar or, as I understood Her Lady, to locate a traitor.

No.

I grunted. "One of your *own?*"

Her Lady didn't answer, which was answer enough.

I pocketed the marble. "Wouldn't he be a fool to betray you when you've got this? I can't imagine he's as powerful as Oberon was."

Her Lady didn't answer immediately . . . but someone else did.

"It's the wake, isn't it?" Claryce interjected. "There's something about its effect on things that makes the blood not so strong of a hold as it should be."

The queen of Feirie pursed her lips. *Clever in this chapter as well. But the blood may give a trail. . . .*

"This not-so-loyal servant of yours got a name?" I asked.

To my surprise, Her Lady spoke. "Lysander."

The fact that she uttered the name out loud—or at least a seductive whisper—said something about Lysander. I knew immediately what. Her Lady'd taken a lover at some point, a not uncommon thing in the Court. Lysander'd had a place of honor, but also one of a form of slavery. If he'd rejected her advances, she might've used the blood to punish or torture him.

"Lysander." I purposely pronounced the name carefully, letting each syllable hit Her Lady as hard as I hoped it would. She'd caused me a lot of trouble and hadn't bothered to tell me things that could've saved us some of this situation. She'd also continued to not only try to entice me, but also scare Claryce. "What can you tell me about . . . Lysander?"

But suddenly Her Lady faded into black mist. As she did, the throne room unraveled, the leaves dwindling and the branches returning to normal. The green oaks pulled away from one another, within seconds leaving us standing in the dark forest again.

But not immediately alone. For a moment, the seneschal stood glaring at me . . . and then he, too, faded away.

"Not a good time to be playing your games," I argued to the empty air as if it were Her Lady. "You still haven't even told me when you think this damned peak will take place—"

A strong tremor shook everything. Trying to keep a hold on the sword, I grabbed for Claryce, who seized me in turn.

We went tumbling into the air.

Feirie . . . or rather this semblance of it . . . vanished.

I braced both of us for the inevitable crash. When it came, I was lucky enough to make certain that I took the brunt of it.

My body shook. I held tight to Claryce as we settled.

Strong hands seized me. I pushed Claryce away and prepared to fight.

"Nay, Master Nicholas, it is only I, Kravayik!"

That wasn't as comforting a response as it might've once been. Making sure I kept between Claryce and him, I brought Her Lady's gift up point first at his chest. "Only *you*? Who *are* you, Kravayik?"

Behind him, the shadow I knew to be Lon flittered off . . . almost nervously, I thought. Still keeping an eye on Kravayik, I reached back for Claryce.

"Lower the sword, Nick. He came to help us."

"Help us or help himself?"

Kravayik bowed his head. "Help you, yes, but to my shame, to help assuage my great guilt as well, may the Lord forgive me."

"You made some pact with that thing of hers . . . the Feir'hr Sein, didn't you?"

"Only out of necessity, Master Nicholas. He cared for the pact as little as you or I, but your hold over it made certain that it had to agree."

"My what?"

Kravayik gave me a quizzical look. "You have a hold over it. I am not certain how, but it was clear. It is now caught between its loyalties to both you and Her Lady."

"You're making no sense." My head cleared enough that I finally paid more attention to our surroundings as well. We were in front of a church, but nothing so grand as Holy Name. Still, it had a cleanliness that showed that those who served here had a strong faith.

It was also very familiar. We were no longer in the heart of the city. Instead, we were back in North Town, near where I made my "home."

And right in front of Saint Michael's.

Its pointed tower loomed over the rest of the structure. For a brief time that tower'd made Saint Michael's the tallest building in Chicago. The Redemptorist order that oversaw the church had administered it since its building just a couple of years before the Great Fire.

I immediately looked around for Father Jonathan, the priest in charge and a light sleeper. He surely couldn't have missed the noise we'd made. Why he hadn't come out to investigate bothered me.

Kravayik crossed his heart, or at least the general location where it would've been if he'd been human. "May the Lord forgive me again . . . if that is possible. You seek the good father. I went inside just before I convinced the Feir'hr Sein of the choice it had to make between masters. The priest will sleep until we are done here."

I arched my brow. "What'd you do?"

"A simple suggestion of deeper sleep. I swear only that! My guilt is great as it is!"

"It should be a lot greater. You meet Claryce and fail to mention to either of us what happened thirty years ago?"

"Nick." Claryce pushed my sword arm down. "Nick, he's

explained. He did what he could, but I . . . Claudette . . . was very determined. I can appreciate that trait."

"Did he explain how you got involved in the first place?"

"As a matter of fact, he did." She kept pressing my arm down until the blade pointed at the ground. I wondered why I let her, but I did. "Nick, I was searching for a friend . . . I mean *Claudette* was searching . . . during the exposition. She . . . her friend disappeared. The trail led to . . . you know where."

The cold weather was also finally registering with me. I wasn't so concerned about my health, but I knew Claryce couldn't be doing that well in the thin coat she was wearing. "All right. I've got a ton of questions, but let's finish this up inside. Fetch?"

We looked around, but he was gone.

"He was with us when we came back . . . from there," Claryce murmured, answering my unspoken concern. "Was that really Feirie?"

"No . . . maybe . . . I don't know anymore. I'd have said no for certain . . . but what about it, Kravayik? That shouldn't have been the true Feirie, but things change a lot during the Frost Moon's wake, don't they?"

He exhaled. "More than I would ever wish."

The wind picked up. I led us off the middle of Cleveland Avenue to the doors of Saint Michael's. I had a key, given to me by Father Jonathan's predecessor, but suspected the door would be unlocked.

It was.

"You do this, too, Kravayik?" Only after he nodded did I open the way. I still remembered Diocles mentioning someone visiting the church in my absence. I was beginning to suspect it'd been one of the goons who apparently were working for Bond.

Thinking of Diocles, I looked past the pews, past the intricate stained glass windows and meticulous carvings of the saint and others. Yeah, Saint Michael's wasn't Holy Name—in fact, Diocles often called it rustic, though as a dead emperor he'd naturally been used to a lot more sumptuousness—but I thought its patron saint couldn't complain.

I, on the other hand, *did* have some complaints of my own for that particular saint, but he'd made certain not to cross my actual path since Oberon. Instead, I turned my thoughts to Diocles again.

"Might as well make your appearance," I muttered under my breath to the thus-far absent ghost. He was generally prompt, popping up seconds after I entered.

Not this time, though. Even after we'd moved halfway into the church the emperor'd still not made his grand entrance.

But someone else did. Someone we weren't expecting.

Father Jonathan. Father Jonathan, who should've been sleeping.

"Nick! Of course! Who else would it be?" The young priest adjusted his oversized, round glasses. "And Miss Simone!" He rubbed his thinning blond hair in concern. "Oh, dear! Are they still after you?"

Father Jonathan'd been introduced to Claryce after I'd brought her to the sanctuary of Saint Michael's during our struggle with Oberon. Oberon's Wyld servants hadn't been able to cross the threshold of the holy place. His human goons hadn't known of her presence here, either.

"Yes," I answered quickly. "Turns out there're a couple on the loose, but don't concern yourself. We just needed a moment to catch our breath. Then, we'll move on."

"Oh, that will never do! At least join me while I brew some tea for the pair of you!"

The pair of you? I looked around. Only then did I see that, like Fetch, Kravayik'd slipped away.

"Damn him," I murmured.

Claryce gave me a rebuking look, but fortunately Father Jonathan couldn't hear my blasphemy. In part to cover up any chance he might belatedly realize what I'd mouthed, I answered, "That'd be appreciated, thank you."

"Not at all." The priest paused. "Miss Simone, could I beg your assistance? I'm really sorry!"

"Not at all. I'd be glad to." She went from me to Father Jonathan.

He started to depart the room with her, then paused. "Ah! Forgot! Do you remember where the kitchen is, Miss Simone? I need to retrieve something from the altar."

"I remember." Claryce had hidden in the church while keeping out of sight of Oberon's servants, using quarters kept for a female housekeeper who came on a regular basis to deal with those matters Father Jonathan could not.

As she vanished through the doorway, Father Jonathan quickly signaled for me to join him. Frowning, I did just as he requested.

"May the Lord forgive me for the lie," he commented under his breath, sounding a lot like Kravayik. "I wasn't sure if I should mention this with Miss Simone around. This really concerns you . . . I think."

He had my attention. "What's wrong, Father?"

"I've had . . . There's been a visitor. It shames me to even speak of it . . . but I know you might listen."

"'A visitor'?" Again I recalled Diocles's vague mention of someone stopping by Saint Michael's. "Do you know who it was?"

The priest had always been a pale man, but now he was nearly as pale as the Schreck twins. "No . . . I can only describe him."

"So tell me." I knew it couldn't be the twins, but maybe Bond had tracked me to here.

Father Jonathan had a good eye for detail. He told me far more than I needed to identify his visitor. In fact, I knew who it was long before the father uttered the impossible words.

"I think . . . Nick, it could only be a *ghost*. . . ."

Yeah. He'd seen Diocles . . . and that was impossible.

CHAPTER 14

I had a lot of questions of my own that I couldn't ask with Father Jonathan around, not the least of which had to do with why Diocles was now visible to someone other than me. I had the suspicion that Diocles's situation could be blamed on the forces stirred up by the Frost Moon's wake, but couldn't be certain.

Unfortunately, it wasn't something the priest allowed me to pursue immediately. We sat in the small living room that was part of the priest's personal quarters. The three chairs and round table had been left behind by his predecessor, Father Peter, who'd served at Saint Michael's since before the Great Fire. In fact, everything in the room was exactly as the older priest had kept it. The framed pictures of the son of God and the warrior saint for whom the church was named hung just where they had so many years ago when Peter and I'd had the conversation where he'd realized just who I was.

Father Peter'd even known of Diocles, although he hadn't been able to see or hear him. When he'd left, I'd decided that his successor would be better off ignorant. Now, that was looking harder and harder to do.

Of course, as important as Father Jonathan's situation was, to me it paled beside everything involving Bond's sinister maze and what'd happened after that. It wasn't until the priest had to excuse himself for a moment that I even had a chance to broach some of the subjects with Claryce.

"What happened in Holy Name?" I quietly asked as soon as he stepped out of earshot.

She leaned forward. "After that thing took you, Kravayik leapt after it. I couldn't believe that he could move that fast. He was out of the cathedral and after it before I knew what happened!"

"He didn't take you with?"

"No. I went to the car, where Fetch still was. He'd seen the Wyld swooping in on the entrance and tried to warn us."

She'd used Fetch's senses to keep on the trail. Like the hound he somewhat resembled, Fetch had a fine nose, and he'd made the best of it. When on occasion they'd lost the shadow's trail, he'd used his familiarity with Kravayik to follow the latter's scent.

Unfortunately, they'd eventually still lost both. Hours had passed. On a hunch, though, Claryce'd turned the Wills around and headed for West Sixty-Third. She'd almost gotten there when Fetch caught scent of Kravayik again.

And there, just three blocks from where we'd first met Bond, she'd found *not* Kravayik, but me. Me in the midst of my fight with the two goons.

I was grateful she hadn't arrived before I'd regained most of the control over my body. Although she'd seen me transform into the dragon over Lake Michigan, I didn't like reminding her any more than I had to about what my tie to the dragon actually meant.

Claryce'd been just about to drive the tommy gunner down when Kravayik'd shown up. She'd also seen the Feir'hr Sein arrive a moment later and noticed how it and Kravayik had appeared to have some sort of acknowledgement of one another.

"And then Kravayik let that thing of hers envelop you," Claryce added warily.

"Did he now?" I didn't like the way Kravayik's loyalties seemed to be shifting like the tide.

"Yes. I confronted him about it, and when he said what had happened to you—how you'd been cast into some pocket variation of Feirie like what happened in your house during our fight with Oberon—I insisted on following you. Fetch, too. He grabbed the sword after you lost it."

It was nice to know I could at least rely on Fetch . . . this time. I still pictured him on the shore of Lake Michigan, debating between saving me and accepting Oberon's offer. Okay, he'd saved me, but I still couldn't forget the hesitation. I'd been betrayed too many times by those I'd thought were friends.

For a saint, I'd never been much for forgiving betrayal.

I knew what'd happened after, but another, more urgent matter needed to be addressed. "Did you see anything around me? Anything odd about the buildings?"

"No. You were in front of a warehouse. I guess that's where they keep their distillery," Claryce replied, referring to the bootleggers who'd tried to gun me down.

"No idea which direction I could've come from?"

"None. Why?"

I gave her a very brief rundown of what'd happened. As she gaped in horror, I added, "I was hoping you or Kravayik might've seen where Bond kept his little chamber of horrors. I suspect somewhere close to the original Murder Castle since he seemed very interested in that area, but exactly where, I need to know."

"From what you described, someone should have noticed all that damage. You'd think there would've been sirens immediately."

"Yeah. You'd think. We'll have to check the news—"

At that point Father Jonathan returned. We spent the next several minutes talking about the dangers Chicago faced being engulfed in the war between the two biggest gangs in the city and how things only looked to be getting worse. I hoped that might lead him to mentioning any news story fitting what I'd been going through, but instead it turned his thoughts to politics.

"I say my prayers for Mayor Dever, of course," the priest went on earnestly, "but I fear that he will be facing a major challenge next election."

He didn't have to explain the first part. Dever's predecessor, William "Big Bill" Thompson, was looking for a fight come next election. Thompson had a lot of money backing him, not to mention rumored support from most of the underworld. When he'd been mayor, corruption and gangland killings had reached new highs . . . or lows, depending on how one measured things. Dever was a fairly good man as Chicago politics went, but he'd been lucky. For reasons not entirely clear, Thompson'd stepped aside and not run, letting the local postmaster, a man named Arthur Lueder, run in his stead. Lueder'd been walloped by Dever.

Now, though, everything hinted that Thompson was through playing games. I'd seen him when he'd shown up for a special event held by Oberon in his guise as Delke. I couldn't believe that Thompson knew just who and *what* one of his biggest backers had been . . . but then again, this *was* Chicago politics. Oberon would fit right in.

"Hopefully, Mayor Dever will be reelected," Claryce said after a sip. "I've met Mr. Thompson."

Father Jonathan waited for her to continue, but when instead she took another sip, he chuckled at the unspoken intimation. "I know I am supposed to be neutral before others where politics is concerned . . . but I very much appreciate your opinion, Miss Simone."

"It's Claryce, please."

"I would prefer 'Miss Simone.' Not meaning to slight you. It's just my manner."

"It took me three years of pounding to get him to call me something other than 'Mr. Medea,'" I interjected. My cup had been empty for a couple of minutes, but I hadn't wanted to put it down too quickly even though I'd intended to move on some time ago. Now, though, I'd waited long enough. "I appreciate the tea, Father, but I'm going to have to beg a big favor of you."

He carefully set down his own cup. "What is it?"

"Keep company with Claryce for an hour or two. I need to check something out nearby."

There was a slight flickering of his eyes. He *thought* he knew what

I had in mind, and it *was* part of my reason for temporarily leaving, but he didn't know the full truth.

"Are you certain you don't need me?" Claryce asked with a hint of ice in her own gaze. It wasn't that she didn't like Father Jonathan, but I was willing to bet she didn't want me wandering off after what we'd already been through.

"I won't be far."

"In this weather, I pray not," the priest murmured. He smiled at Claryce. "I will try not to bore you, Miss Simone. Is there some subject of which you have some great interest? Perhaps we can find something we have in common."

She couldn't help smiling in return, which relieved me. I slipped out of the priest's quarters and into the main part of the church in order to take care of Father Jonathan's problem first.

And there he finally was. Diocles, looking so solid I thought that if I reached out and touched him, I'd have cloth and flesh stop my fingers.

Of course, I tried.

The fingers still went through.

"Yes, I am a ghost, a specter," the emperor remarked with a hint of amusement. "You have noticed a change, too, have you not, Georgius?"

I'd not only noticed a change in how he looked, but also the fact that he was whispering. Since the time he'd begun haunting me, Diocles's general tone of voice'd been loud and only loud. "He can hear you?"

"Hear and see." The ghost glanced past me, almost as if he expected even his whisper to bring the priest running.

"All the time?"

"Nay. Only after dark. Even then, if I keep to the shadows, he does not appear to notice me . . . unlike that Kravayik character."

"*Kravayik* can see you, too?"

"Yes. Suddenly my world has widened . . . and I am none too

happy about it, Georgius. I do not want inquisitive tourists traipsing after me."

The image forced a rare smile on my face, which only served to infuriate Diocles more. "You know roughly when this started happening?"

"Just after that damned devil of beast tried to use your body to steal that magical card from the cathedral."

It fit with the Frost Moon's presence. "It may not last, but then again, it may. You'd best be careful."

"Sound if useless advice." He stroked his beard. "I am pleased to see you are all right."

He referred to what'd happened in Holy Name. I belatedly thought about how I should've asked him how he'd done. Last I'd seen Diocles, he'd shattered like a mirror. Guess I'd just taken it for granted that he'd be fine. After all, dead was dead . . . or undead. "What happened to you back there?"

The ghost shuddered. "Gods! It was like being in a thousand places at once! Fortunately, I was able to reform a few minutes later. Regrettably, all of you were gone after that. I kept hoping that you'd end up somewhere blessed so that I could see you were all right."

I wasn't too happy with all his concern for me. "It isn't all right between us, Diocles. If you do actually need me to forgive you before you can move on, you're in for a disappointment."

"I know better than that, Georgius. It is my lot to wait and wait."

"Better that fate than losing your head."

He grimaced. "Wait for sixteen hundred years and see if you feel that way."

I refrained from remarking about my own fate, bound to the portal forever unless I let some Wyld take me. There'd been times when I'd thought about allowing that to happen, but then I'd also thought about what might happen after I was dead. There'd also been the knowledge that Cleolinda might keep reincarnating. Now that

I'd found *Claryce*, I was especially interested in not dying. At the very least, I needed to be there for her.

As I wasn't for Claudette.

"Just . . . stay out of Father Jonathan's sight and hearing." I surveyed the pews. "Did you see where Kravayik went?"

"A quiet one, he is . . . but yes. There came a tapping, a gentle tapping, at the church door."

It'd have to have been gentle for me not to hear it. "Fetch, maybe."

"The mongrel? Does he not generally howl or something?"

He had a point there, but I preferred the thought of Fetch over some other possibilities. Still, I had no choice but to take a peek outside . . . unless . . .

"Are you able to stick your head outside without opening the door?"

"I have not tried in many a century." He faded away, then reappeared next to the entrance. "Let me see."

Diocles thrust his head into the heavy door nearest him. I winced in natural anticipation of a collision, but instead an odd plume of translucent smoke formed wherever Diocles touched the door, or at least the barrier it represented.

He continued leaning into the door until his entire head had vanished. The plume grew at the same time, becoming a small cloud attached to the ghost at the shoulders.

The emperor pulled back. The plume reversed, filling in the head.

"I could see nothing past the door, not even one glimpse of the outside," Diocles bitterly reported.

"Good. Don't try that again. Especially if I'm with you."

He gave me a quizzical look as I joined him by the entrance, but kept quiet. With the utmost caution, I opened the door a crack.

Let me out! Let me out! the dragon insisted.

"For what?" Cleveland Avenue was empty. Far away, I could hear a coronet playing some faint Creole jazz worthy of Freddie Keppard, who I'd seen a few times down on the South Side. The music was likely coming from a flapper party in another part of North Town, which meant it was probably recorded, not live. Other than the coronet and its accompaniment, the rising wind was the only sound.

I stepped outside. Shutting the door behind me, I turned so that the wind was at my back, then muttered, "Come to me, Fetch."

For good measure, I whistled briefly. Yeah, he often answered just like an actual dog.

But this time, there was no replying howl. Ignoring the weather, I went to the street corner and summoned the dragon's eyes. I'd seen enough of Cleveland to know there was nothing down either direction for some distance, but only now did I have a good view of Eugenie.

There was a car three blocks down. I couldn't tell for certain, but its outline resembled the Chrysler that'd been chasing us enough for me to want to take a closer look.

Then, I caught sight of something moving near the car, something on four legs.

Fetch.

Throwing away caution, I raced toward the Chrysler. I'd barely gotten half a block when Fetch's silhouette vanished into the auto.

I expected the sounds of a violent struggle, but there was nothing. As I neared, Fetch thrust his head out of the other side of the Chrysler. He was sniffing the air. His flattened ears signaled that he wasn't liking what he did or didn't smell.

He noticed me approaching. His tongue lolled in what I knew to be relief. "Master Nicholas! Come see!"

"What happened to you?" I asked as I headed to him.

"Thought there might be some hoods following after us hoping to bump off you and Mistress Claryce! I felt like a palooka the way I let you down by the cathedral. . . ."

"You didn't let us down. You tried to warn us."

He pulled back as I leaned in to see what so bothered him about the car.

There were two gunsels in the front seat. Both looked as if they'd died screaming even though we hadn't heard anything. Other than that, they appeared untouched. A quick study of each showed no sign of what'd killed them, but I already had a suspicion.

"This breezer wasn't here when we arrived," Fetch offered, referring, in his usual manner of trying to keep up with the current human slang, to the fact that this car was a convertible. "I circled the church and there it was. I stalked it slowly, surely expecting something nasty inside . . . and found this pair of button men just like this."

He was right about them looking like more than just hoods with guns. Both men had that professional look. Unlike the pair that'd attacked me, these two had probably been pretty good shots.

Thinking about that, I looked down at the hand of the one in the passenger side. It took me a moment to find his gun, which lay on the floor between his feet. I came around then picked it up. From the unique, acrid powder smell, it'd been fired at least once . . . another sound I'd not heard.

As I leaned back, another thing bothered me. All the windows were open, certainly not something I'd expect in this weather.

I heard a slight whistling. Peeking inside I counted two bullet holes in the convertible roof.

"Fetch, I need you to use your nose again. Can you still smell the scents of these two?"

"Oh, assuredly! The driver, he smells of a dame who likes too much perfume, and the other, he likes Luckys, just like Master Alejandro!"

That was the first time I'd heard him call Cortez that. I put that aside to question later, more concerned with what'd happened here. "What else do you smell? Anyone else?"

He took a deep sniff. His tail wagged. "A third hood! He was in the backseat where I am, but his smell ain't so strong! He must've hightailed it, Master Nicholas!"

I had a growing suspicion that he'd not. Or at least, only his *body'd* moved on. "Try harder, Fetch. Any subtle traces of Wyld?"

"Nay . . . I think." His lupine/canine face twisted into what might've been a comical expression at other times. "Wait. . . ."

"How does Lon smell to you?" I asked pointedly. "The Feir'hr Sein?"

In answer, Fetch sniffed again . . . and again. Finally, "Oh, he's a sneaky one, but ye have it right, Master Nicholas! He was here! He's done these torpedoes in! He's the one!"

I'd wondered where the Feir'hr Sein had gotten to. Now I knew. He'd continued to shadow us, no doubt seeking any clue to this Lysander. These hoods had made the mistake of being here at just the wrong time.

The last Feir'hr Sein I'd had to deal with had taken the body of a guard at a bootlegging operation and tried to use that to infiltrate Oberon's operation. That hadn't gone so well, with Oberon showing why he'd once been ultimate ruler of Feirie. There'd not been much left of the Feir'hr Sein after Oberon had finished torturing him.

I wasn't sure just what Lon hoped to accomplish with the body he'd grabbed, but I couldn't let him get in the way of things. From what I'd seen, the Feir'hr Sein had no sense of justice, only fulfilling their mistress's orders. If I had to, I'd use Her Lady's gift on Her Lady's servant, and damned be any repercussions.

"What about Kravayik? Was he around here, too?"

Fetch ran his nose over part of the car before answering. "Can't smell him anywhere around this jalopy. Maybe he didn't notice it?"

"Kravayik? Even blind, deaf, and dumb, Kravayik'd be able to find this car in the middle of night and deal with all three men."

Fetch cocked his head and didn't argue.

It bothered me I didn't know where Kravayik was, but that wasn't so important a matter as doing something about this car. I didn't want the police finding two dead gunsels so near to Saint Michael's. Somehow I knew that'd catch the attention of Cortez, a headache I didn't need in addition to the rest.

"Keep in the backseat and out of sight, Fetch."

Once he'd obeyed, I quickly dragged the driver from the front seat to the back, then rolled up the windows. Satisfied that the true state of two of my passengers wouldn't be noticed in the dark, I climbed in behind the wheel. I already had an idea where to drop off the car. It'd mean a bit of a walk back, but it was necessary.

I drove to the intersection of Wells Street and North Avenue, which marked the near end of North Town and any possible connection to Saint Michael's or me—then pulled over. Fetch immediately leapt out of the car. I checked the area, then quickly transferred the driver back to his original seat.

"What now, Master Nicholas?"

"Now you talk a lot quieter," I murmured.

His tail drooped in apology. I gave him a short wave indicating I wasn't mad, then considered the trek back.

I can help . . . let me give you wings to fly, wings to ease your travels . . . wings . . .

"Get thee behind me," I growled, not for the first time in our sixteen centuries of servitude together. Whenever he talked like that, offered so much so willingly, my distrust for him grew tenfold greater than it generally was . . . which was saying a hell of a lot.

I started walking. Only when I was a good two blocks from the dead hoods did I begin to relax . . . which, of course, meant that something happened.

"Master Nicholas. Some hayburner coming from the street to our right."

The "hayburner" was an old Ford Model T that'd definitely seen better days. As it neared, I saw two male figures inside.

I hoped that the driver would just keep going. He didn't. I kept my hand where I could draw the sword if necessary. I couldn't be sure that these weren't friends of the dead goons.

The driver opened his window. It took me a second to recognize

Officer Kowalski in civilian clothes. Next to him was a slender Negro roughly the same age. Both men wore heavy coats.

I didn't believe in coincidence.

"Do you need— Hello, you're Mr. Medea, aren't you?"

"That's right. It's Kowalski, isn't it? What brings you out this way?"

"Lincoln and me"—he indicated his passenger without any hint of wariness that I'd found him in mixed company—"we were headed for a party near here."

I caught a glimpse of anxiousness from Lincoln when Kowalski mentioned the party. I knew what the rookie meant and gathered that he thought since I was so reasonable about a Mexican on the police force that I'd not have a problem with two lone men on their way to a party in this area. In my service as a tribune to the empire, I'd seen relations of all sorts. I'd also come to know the depths and—complexities—of Feirie, against which nothing human could ever compare. It wasn't my way, but it wasn't something I was concerned about, either.

"That's probably the jazz I heard earlier."

"You like jazz? Lincoln plays the horn! He's gonna be another Louie Armstrong!"

"Bill, stop it," his friend responded with a slight, sheepish grin.

Kowalski added his own grin. "It's true." To me he said, "Sorry, Mr. Medea! My mother'd hate my manners these days. It's Bill, just like Lincoln said."

And just like Bill Haines, I thought, wondering if the rookie knew how much he had in common with the actor. I doubted anyone in the precinct knew about Kowalski's outside life, considering his face was devoid of any bruises. "I'm Nick."

"We saw you out in the cold and thought we'd see if you needed a ride."

"I'm good. Just a short distance to go. Thanks, anyway."

"Are you sure?"

"Bill's gonna be a regular taxi tonight if he keeps this up," Lincoln chimed with a little more confidence. "First the old man, now you."

Kowalski glanced back at him. "Hey, Michael was the bee's knees, wasn't he?"

"Yeah, he was a funny bird, but swell."

Neither saw me stiffen at the name. "Michael? From the coroner? You picked him up near here?"

"Not so near, but on the way. He said he was heading out to see his son. Said that tomorrow they were going over to the meadows on Lawrence Street." Kowalski shook his head. "Don't know why I remember that, but that's what he said."

"The meadows on Lawrence Street," I muttered.

"Yeah." Kowalski jabbed a thumb behind him. "Sure you don't want a ride? It's not a great night."

"I'm fine. Thanks, though."

"Okay. We're gonna get a wiggle on, then!" As the rookie rolled up his window, Lincoln gave me a smile and wave.

I nodded as the pair drove off, then whispered, "Fetch."

"I am here."

"You heard?"

"Sounds like quite a blow they're going to. . . ."

I held back a growl. "I meant about *Michael*."

"He's going to a meadow with his son. That sounds like a nice time, Master Nicholas. Could we go to a meadow sometime?"

"Are you sure you aren't *really* a dog?" Before he could make some response, I went on. "Michael. You remember Michael. Like as in *Saint Michael's*."

To his credit, all trace of innocence vanished from Fetch's expression. "Oh. Not good, is that? He's a real bean-picker, that one! He only comes if there's a real problem."

We really didn't have actual proof that old Michael was actually the saint or if even that the saint had actually lent a hand—or foot or talon or whatever they were called since part of the time he'd also maybe been a black bird—but it seemed a likely bet.

And now, after popping up at the edge of things a couple of times, Michael Maybe-the-Saint'd sent what I could only imagine was a message to me through Kowalski. I didn't know why he couldn't speak directly to me, but he'd tried as much as he could, I suppose . . . if I wasn't making everything up to suit my own tastes.

Still . . . a meadow on Lawrence Street.

There was no meadow on Lawrence Street, not in the city. There was, however, a place somewhat *like* a meadow, a place Fetch and I had visited only recently.

Saint Boniface cemetery . . . where maybe this whole thing'd begun.

CHAPTER 15

By the time I left with Claryce from Saint Michael's, I'd committed several hopefully minor sins, most of them involved with lies building on other lies I'd told Father Jonathan before. Away from Claryce, I told him I hadn't found any evidence of a haunting, but that I'd look into it again shortly. That was after I'd warned Diocles to stick to the shadows as much as possible.

I also didn't tell Claryce what'd happened outside, save that Kravayik had evidently departed for Holy Name. I had no idea whatsoever whether he'd done that and couldn't worry about him at the moment, but I knew that he hadn't told us everything about what'd happened to Claudette . . . or how much he knew about this elf, Lysander.

None of that mattered, though, not to me. What did was that I needed to get to Saint Boniface . . . and without Claryce.

I suggested we drive to her apartment so that she could get a change of clothes. We didn't mention getting any rest in front of the priest, who might've taken it wrong. As it was, I knew by the time we got to Claryce's place, the question of moving on afterward would be moot.

There was no chance of getting Fetch inside, but he was happy to curl up inside the Wills, which was parked out front of the building.

She stifled a yawn as we entered. "There's some leftover ham and some fruit in the kitchen, if you want them. Some root beer, too. Sorry, none of that tar you call coffee."

"I'm fine." Ever the gracious host, Father Jonathan'd finally insisted on feeding us from his meager stores despite our protests. I'd made certain to leave a donation behind to more than cover it when he wasn't looking.

I sat down and waited. The moment I heard her returning, I leaned back and shut my eyes as if I'd been asleep for several minutes. Only when she got close did I pretend to wake.

She took the bait. "Nick, maybe we'd better get some rest before we do anything else."

"Yeah, that sounds like a good idea. We'll get some sleep, then decide what to do next." I stretched out on the couch. "We should be okay until dawn."

Claryce nodded. "All right. If you need anything, you know where I am, Nick."

I pretended not to notice her nervous but inviting tone. We'd only been thrown together a short time, yet I could see that Claryce could not only feel some of the emotions that'd traveled from one incarnation to the next, but also others unique to her. As for me, hell, I was caught between what I'd experienced for Cleolinda and some of her past lives and a new, unsettling-in-many-ways realization of how there was something different about Claryce.

How, if I didn't do every damned thing I could to keep her alive, it'd be more than just the loss of another incarnation. This time, I'd be losing a good piece of whatever was left of my soul.

That was why the minute I was certain she was asleep I got up and cautiously made a call.

"Master—er—Nick?" Barnaby answered. It wasn't all that surprising that he'd guessed it was me. No one else'd be calling at this time.

"The Packard. Is it finished?"

"Yes. Yes. I only awaited your word as to where to have it sent. Do you want it now?"

I was asking a lot from him, but I needed the Packard. "Yeah. Bring it here." I gave him Claryce's address. "Hurry, if you can."

"I will bring it myself. Ten minutes." Barnaby paused. "I went to see Joseph again. He has not changed since our last visit. He stares intently at the shadows."

"I'm sorry."

"It is what it is." He hung up.

There hadn't been much time for me to consider Joseph. I should've felt guilty, at least for Barnaby's sake, but Saint Boniface was of more immediate importance to me.

I slipped out of Claryce's apartment. Not at all to my surprise, a long, lanky, four-legged form slipped out of the shadows nearby to join me.

"Thought you were staying all cozy in the Wills," I muttered to Fetch.

He swallowed. Something the size of a rat slid down his gullet. "I got hungry."

"Of course. I'm heading to Saint Boniface."

"Without Mistress Claryce?"

A clever one, that Fetch. "Barnaby's bringing the Packard. He'll be here shortly."

Fetch wagged his tail.

The weather would've been much for any normal human, but as usual, the eternal heat of the dragon kept me warm. He said nothing, just made certain I was toasty. Still, I didn't trust his obliging nature. He was up to something. I was certain of it.

Of course, he was always up to something.

Barnaby drove up. A short distance behind him, I saw another Packard pull up with longer lines and a few more miles on it. All that could be seen of the second driver was a newsboy cap and turned-up coat collar that obscured the face.

"I trust I didn't keep you waiting?" Barnaby asked as he climbed out.

"As usual, you managed somehow to get here faster. You're a regular Peter DePaolo."

"Thank you, but I don't think I'll be entering the Indy Five Hundred too soon. Not with my stiff joints." The brief moment of levity faded away. "Master—Nick—do be careful. I don't know where you'd be heading at this time of night in this weather, but I'd guess it's not pleasant and it's something to do with my Joseph."

I wasn't sure of the connection to Joseph, but he was probably right. "Thanks for the concern, Barnaby. Don't worry. I'm resilient. You know that."

"Resilient, but not invincible. You are, if I may say so, a very mortal saint."

I decided to change the subject. "Who's your ride? That's definitely not your Runabout, and that's certainly not 'Des' O'Reilly." Something that'd been bothering me a bit, since I'd helped his friend out with a "ghost" problem during Oberon's return, finally came to the surface. "Or is it *Bobbie* like you slipped when I first met him?"

"You caught that." He looked sheepish. "I knew I'd done that, but hoped you were too occupied." A sigh. "The driver is just one of my mechanics. He just thinks we're delivering a car to a special client. Nothing to fear from him. As for Des . . . his real name's 'Bobbie' O'Hanrahan, but he hasn't used it since . . . since Harrison was shot."

"Harrison?" The name meant something to me, but I couldn't say just what.

Barnaby grimaced. "Mayor Carter Harrison Sr., Nick."

Mayor Carter Harrison Sr. Five-time leader of Chicago. His son'd gone on to do the same, but when one spoke of Mayor Harrison, he or she spoke about the father. Harrison Sr. had been assassinated just into that fifth term, supposedly by a man who believed the mayor'd let him down on a promise of a position in the administration.

I knew a little more about the assassin, a man named Prendergast, but only because, like the Leopold and Loeb kidnapping case last year, he'd been for a time represented by a much younger Clarence Darrow. Darrow hadn't known of me during the Prendergast trial, but in the process of dealing with the secret Feirie elements of the Leopold and Loeb case, I'd gone through the lawyer's older files. At the time, something about Prendergast had caught my attention, but I couldn't recall what it was other than it had to do with his supposed madness.

"All right," I finally replied. "What's Bobbie O'Hanrahan got to do with the assassination that'd make him stay in hiding for decades?"

"You won't find his name on anything official since nothing could be proved, but there was those that marked him as the assassin's cohort. They were drinking buddies, that's all. Bobbie—Des—wasn't involved in what Prendergast did, but the senior Harrison, he had a lot of influential friends, not to mention some kids with long memories. When Junior became mayor, there were suddenly cops all over the place again—cops *off duty*—looking for any trace of 'Bobbie' even though it'd been nearly twenty years. They didn't find him, but now it's only ten years since Junior left office, so there's still danger."

It didn't surprise me that even Barnaby's most innocuous-looking friend could have a troubled past. I sometimes wondered if the Gate drew such together. Either way, I didn't see it as being of any significance to what we were going through right now—

Then, I remembered just *when* Mayor Harrison'd been assassinated.

The year 1893. Only a couple of *days* before the end of the exposition.

I really wanted just *once* to believe in coincidence. I wanted to . . . but failed again.

Trying not to grit my teeth, I asked, "And Des had nothing to do with your . . . dabblings?"

He was quick and, as I read it, honest in his answer. "None."

I made a mental note to look up the assassination, Prendergast . . . and Barnaby's suddenly intriguing friend. First, though, I had to get to Saint Boniface. That meant dropping the subject of Des O'Reilly—or Bobbie O'Hanrahan—until things got calmer. "Thanks for patching up the Packard."

"Thank you for Joseph."

I thought I'd gotten the much better end of the deal, but held back out of respect for Barnaby. With a nod, I left him for the Packard.

As he turned, I watched him head to the other vehicle and its well-wrapped driver. There was nothing to hint that his companion was anything other than someone wanting to keep warm, but I couldn't help abruptly wondering if I should check and see whether Barnaby'd begun dabbling in the arts again. For the first time in six years, he'd seen some spark, however unsettling, in his son. I prayed I was wrong, but I suspected that he was hoping to capitalize on the effects of the Frost Moon's wake in order to bring his son back to his full faculties.

Fetch was already in the Packard. As I climbed inside, I asked, "You have any idea just how long we still have to worry about the wake?"

"Nay, Master Nicholas! It would take one with a fast mind for intricate calculation! Oberon himself gathered five wise ones centuries ago just to see when the next Frost Moon itself would take place in Feirie! Calculating the strength and length of the wake after would be a task very few could handle, especially alone."

I started the Packard. "A very analytical mind?"

"Couldn't be a flat tire or a dumb Dora, no sir!"

"No. I suppose not." As I drove off, I considered the type of mind he'd suggested. I'd delved enough into these matters over the centuries to appreciate just how complex such calculations could be. I knew Fetch wasn't exaggerating.

However, I also knew *one* mind that'd been more than capable of calculating something as tricky as the Frost Moon's influence during and after. One of very clever if *twisted* beliefs.

Joseph, of course.

It was still dark when we neared Saint Boniface. I took out my pocket watch and checked the time. More than three hours until sunrise . . . or at least a lessening of the darkness.

I pulled over near the same spot I'd used when visiting Clarissa's grave. Saint Boniface was closed, of course, but that didn't matter to us. I climbed over the fence, then waited for Fetch to leap after me. After a short debate with myself, I left Her Lady's gift in its safe place, then headed toward her grave. Fetch faithfully followed, proving that no one'd yet dealt with the earlier intrusion by Feirie. This part of the cemetery was still tainted.

There was no reason to think that Clarissa's last resting place had anything to do with the enigmatic message I might only have imagined I'd been given by Michael. For all I knew, I was on a wild goose chase.

The wind howled as I bent by Clarissa's stone. I thought about some of the others I'd buried before. Clara, who lay interred in New York. Clouette, who hadn't been permitted a burial because there'd been no body ever recovered from the Moselle River.

It had never been lost on me that all the names followed a pattern, with some having more similarities than others. Thinking of Clouette made me look up in the direction of the other stone, the one belonging to the incarnation I'd never known.

I left Clarissa for Claudette. With each step, I hoped her ghost might reappear and tell me what, if any, purpose she had in remaining.

"What are you doing back here, Georgius?"

Diocles. Punctual as usual. "Following a possible lead. From a maybe saint."

"The archangel?" Diocles spoke with some awe whenever Michael was brought up. As a deathbed convert, he had a bit more reverence for things than I did, even after centuries condemned to haunt yours truly.

"The maybe something," I retorted quietly. There was no point in asking him to leave, so I did my best to ignore him, however fruitless that'd been in the past.

Kneeling by Claudette's grave, I tried to imagine her as I'd seen her that brief time. It wasn't hard to picture her face; it was always a close variation of the same face. Instead, I focused on the details of her clothes to add to the strength of my image.

Still nothing happened. Exhaling, I touched the stone in silent apology to Claudette.

Fetch let out a low, almost imperceptible growl.

I looked up . . . to see a tall, strongly built figure near one of the other graves. There was just enough illumination from a nearby lamp to enable me to make out a Negro maybe a few years older than Lincoln the horn player and dressed as neatly as someone going to church. By my judgment, his coat was too thin for the weather. He also had a bowler hat in his hands and was eyeing a larger headstone shaped like a cross.

To the best of my knowledge, he'd not been there a few moments ago. I supposed I could've missed him, but even if I had, Fetch had strong hearing.

"Stay here," I whispered to Fetch. Standing, I quietly and calmly approached the figure. If he wasn't another ghost, he had a lot of explaining to do.

I'd barely gotten halfway to him when he looked over his shoulder at me.

"Greetings, sir," he commented in a deep, smooth voice. "You gave me a bit of a start."

He didn't look at all startled. "Didn't expect to see anyone here," I answered. "You know that the cemetery's not open."

That earned me a slight nod. "Makes it nice and quiet to visit loved ones, my father would say."

"Your father . . . name of Michael?"

"Yes, sir. You know him?"

"Depends. Is he a shoeshine custodian for the police?" I shouldn't have been so flippant in a cemetery, but I was growing tired of whatever game was being played on me by the maybe saint.

"Father's had a number of occupations over time, but yes."

"So, where is he? Wasn't he supposed to come here with you? A mutual friend said so."

"I'm here, sir."

Not the clear answer I wanted. I tried to remember what I'd been told by "Michael" the first time we'd met. "You the son studying at the Institute?"

"No, sir. I did my studying overseas. The three hundred sixty-ninth. Harlem Hellfighters."

I knew about the 369th, which'd consisted mainly of Negros and Puerto Ricans. They'd fought on the front lines as long as, if not longer than, many other regiments. I'd met a few of the survivors at the jazz clubs on the South Side. They'd been a pretty medaled regiment.

"So you were a soldier." I thrust a hand out. "My name's Nick. Yours?"

And, of course, he didn't disappoint me. "Michael. Named after my father."

"'Michael.'" I decided not to play any more games. "Saint Michael, is it?"

He laughed. "If I'm a saint, so are you, sir! I've seen a lot of things no saint should see! Wish I could turn back time and change that. You'd think a saint could do such a thing, wouldn't you?"

Apparently I wasn't being blunt enough. "Are you or are you not Saint Michael the archangel?"

Instead of answering, he knelt down by the cross. "You'd think a saint could also protect those around him, but that's not possible. All he can do is the best he can and pray it's enough." He brushed dead weeds from the headstone. "Shame how they don't keep things up the way they used to. Sometimes, I wonder that the dead just don't get up and walk away out of dismay."

"Listen, Michael—"

Chuckling at his own comment, he glanced past me. "Hmmph. Looks like one already did!"

I quickly followed his gaze . . . and then quietly swore.

Sure enough, by the time I looked back, Michael was nowhere to be found.

I ignored the dragon's own sarcastic laugh as I took a peek at the headstone. It wasn't some fallen fighter from the 369th, but instead that of another soldier lost during the Civil War. The German surname was in keeping with Saint Boniface's origins—the cemetery had opened in the midst of the war, which meant this was one of the first burials—but there was nothing else to hint at why this particular grave should mean anything. Of course, Michael'd always been considered the ultimate soldier, so maybe he'd kept an eye on this poor devil.

If so, he hadn't evidently done the man much good . . . which didn't ultimately bode well for me.

Only when I turned back did I realize that Fetch had never budged from where he'd been when Michael'd first appeared. His tail hung between his legs, and his ears twitched in a sign of wariness.

"You see him vanish?" I asked.

"Nay, Master Nicholas. I blinked . . . and ye were alone."

"Yeah." I was only half paying attention. What he'd said toward the end suddenly made some sense when I looked past Fetch. It wasn't that I'd forgotten the empty grave; it was just that I hadn't put it high on my list, what with everything else. I certainly hadn't forgotten the Wyld I'd battle here. Now, though, I understood that perhaps that encounter had had something to do with the events surrounding the Frost Moon's wake.

There was no sign anyone'd seen to the grave since I'd fallen into it. That bothered me. I hadn't had a chance to see if there'd been any story in the *Trib* about grave robbing, but even if there hadn't been, I would've expected them to at least cover it up. Instead, it was still open. I could only think that maybe the weather'd prevented that from being done.

Maybe.

There was nothing in the grave but the same piles of loose dirt left by the struggle. I didn't know what I'd thought I'd seen. Something.

And so, that left only the tombstone. Of course.

There wasn't much in the way of weeds in front of this one, but there was some ice and snow. I could still see enough to be puzzled by the fact that there wasn't any date. Just a name, with a symbol below it. I didn't care about the symbol. Instead, I made a fist and slammed at the hardened snow over the rest of the front. The icy mix gave with a very satisfactory cracking sound.

I brushed aside the rest . . . and although time had for some reason weathered this stone more than the others, enough remained legible for me to read. I couldn't say I was at all surprised by the name on it.

Dr. Alexander Bond.

I quickly uncovered the rest of the face. The damage to the symbol was worse. I thought it looked like some sort of creature. A serpent, maybe, or—

"The Beast's risen. The castle stands again. The stronger the wake, the stronger both become. . . ."

A shiver ran through me. I knew that voice . . . but she should've been safe and asleep in her bed in her apartment far from here. Not behind me.

Out of the corner of my eye, I caught sight of Fetch. Fetch, clearly ignorant of the voice.

"I'm so sorry . . ." the speaker softly added in the voice that sounded exactly like Claryce's.

I twisted around . . . and stared through her.

A tear coursed down Claudette's cheek. She gazed down at me in what I understood was fear . . . for me. "I'm so sorry . . . I tried. I tried, *Nick*."

She faded away.

CHAPTER 16

He answered on the first ring. I was both grateful and furious for that. Grateful I didn't have to hunt him down and furious at all he'd hidden from me.

"This is Kravayik."

I was back in the house. Seeing my mood after Saint Boniface, Fetch'd had the wisdom to jump out of the Packard as soon as we neared his home territory. As for Claryce, by now there was a good chance she'd woken up and found me gone. There'd either be a phone call or a visit, neither of which I was prepared for just yet. Right now, I could only focus on the voice on the other side of the line. "No kidding! How long've you been back at Holy Name?"

A pause. "Barely an hour, Master Nicholas."

"Anything from your hunt?" I knew he hadn't just gone for a walk after leaving us.

"No."

I tried a hunch. "Did you go back to where the Beast used to have his lair?"

"Yes. There is nothing."

"It doesn't look like it did back during the exposition?"

"No."

That crushed one theory. I'd been almost certain that whatever magic Bond yielded had enabled him to recreate H. H. Holmes's Murder Castle.

Thinking of the maze, another question came to mind. "Kravayik. I was trapped in a maze in some building. There was an elf. One of Oberon's supporters. He was being used to feed whatever spell was taking place. There was another husk there, and I've seen an eviscerated corpse. What's really going on, and does it have to do with this Lysander?"

He didn't answer at first. I could imagine his mind calculating just exactly what to tell me and how to relate it. I'd dealt with Feirie minds for sixteen centuries, so he knew I was ready for whatever convoluted tale he intended.

And that, I guess, was why when Kravayik answered, he spoke as plainly as I could imagine one of his kind able to manage. "I do not know Lysander's part in this, but I do not believe either of these you mention were him. Lysander would not so easily become prey. If anything, I suspect that the one you mentioned was a fool named Polythemus."

"What's his role?"

"He was the first to slip away from the Court when Oberon recently made his presence known to us."

Now it was my turn to pause. "So . . . you knew about that or you found out afterward? Tell me it was afterward, Kravayik. I won't believe you, but I'll try to pretend."

He cleared his throat. "Sadly, no. I was informed shortly after he slipped through the Gate. One of Her Lady's messengers."

I was really wondering whether my true purpose was not to guard the Gate, but rather to clean up after its whims. It seemed everything and everybody could pass through without me knowing anymore. That hadn't been how the Gate had worked for most of its long existence before Chicago. I wondered what'd changed to make it so.

"I'll deal with you and that later," I growled, feeling the rage stirring again. "You should know I've just come from seeing a ghost. *Claudette's* ghost." I didn't mention my other encounter. I could be as secretive as one of the Feirie folk. Besides, I wanted to hear his reaction to the ghost.

Kravayik made a sound I couldn't identify save that it wasn't a pleasant one. Then, "She . . . was a very intuitive, very adaptable human. She was strong, both in will and faith."

"'Faith'? As in Heaven?"

"As in. Master Nicholas, I have met many humans, and even you, a saint, would have come up short to the purity of faith of this incarnation . . . not to take away anything from Mistress Claryce. Claudette . . . I . . ."

I waited. And waited some more. I could hear his breathing, which was coming rapidly now.

I finally grew impatient. I could appreciate his loss, but not much else. "Kravayik, she warned me that the Beast's risen and the castle stands again. She warned that both're getting stronger."

"As . . . as I feared," he finally returned.

I threw my curveball at him. "And she apologized to *me*, Kravayik. To *me*. She knew me, Kravayik. Why would she know me? You want to tell me?"

There was another hesitation. "She is a part of Mistress Claryce."

"No. She knew me. *Claudette* knew me. Why don't I know her? I never met her."

He didn't hesitate this time, which made me listen closely. It either meant he was planning to be entirely honest with me or he'd finally put together a satisfactory lie. Or both. He was still an elf, after all.

"You have spoken to me of your curse, Saint George." He was calling me "Saint George." That couldn't be good. He never called me "Saint George." "You have told me over and over how you, the dragon, and she were forever bound, though why *she* you never understood. You only knew that she returned to you each time. No matter what city, no matter what realm, your paths always crossed."

So far, he hadn't told me anything I didn't know and *everything* I didn't like to think about. "Go on."

"You and I . . . we had crossed paths with Oberon. You saved my life. You first revealed the truth of the Word to me, then, though it did not sink in deep until later. Until she showed me its depth. Even still, when the moment came, I felt for both your sakes, I should act."

The hair on the back of my neck stiffened. In my head, I could sense that *he* was curious. She'd been instrumental in his current situation. Anything that affected her just didn't affect me; it affected him. "What did you *do*, Kravayik?"

Another pause. If he'd been in front of me, I'd have been tempted to punch him right now. "Saint George. I sought to break the curse. When she initially crossed my path in her search for her friend, it was just as you were pursuing your own efforts against the Wyld infiltrating the exposition. She saw one of the Wyld. She saw you slay it. She'd already seen more than most humans. One way or another, the curse had again worked to bring her into your world."

"*My* world." I hadn't chosen this. Not willingly. "Are you getting to the point? What did you—" Then it hit me. "Kravayik . . . you didn't . . . you didn't *tell* her how this all began, did you?"

Yet *another* pause. Another goddamned pause that said everything.

"Yes. Yes, I did. I told her all. Even about herself. I thought God had given me the chance to help both of you. I thought God had shown me the way to reward you for your servitude."

The dragon snickered. *The road to Hell is paved with good intentions . . . a truly fine human statement for this moment, would you not say?*

"Shut up!" After a moment, I realized what I'd done. "Not you, Kravayik."

There was no reply.

"Kravayik!"

He'd hung up. I couldn't blame him, but it didn't make me any less furious. I didn't know how furious until I heard a sharp crack and found the candlestick phone draped over my hand, the top half broken off by my—*our*—strength.

I threw the phone down. The dragon didn't laugh again, but I could still sense his amusement. However, I could also sense an unease akin to mine.

There was more to the story where Kravayik was concerned. He'd only peeled away a few layers for me. Claudette'd done something else that'd made her leave such a mark on him. He'd mentioned that she'd already seen more than most humans before he tried to change fate by telling her the truth about the two of us.

What're you holding back about, Kravayik? What?

Ringing arose from the second phone I'd set near the table I used for my makeshift office. At this time of night, it could only be one of three people. The first'd just hung up on me. The second—Barnaby—I doubted would be calling me now.

That left Claryce.

I moved to the second telephone but, at the last moment, held back from answering. If I wasn't fully aware of my hypocrisy after Kravayik, a brief chuckle from the dragon made certain that I was.

Trying to ignore the ringing, I started thumbing through some of the old clippings left from the search. I picked up a yellowed one, then dropped it when the phone continued. Gritting my teeth, I turned to the device . . . and someone knocked on the front door.

Even if Fetch'd come running from his usual haunts, he wouldn't have bothered to knock. Howl, maybe, but not knock.

I kept my hand ready by Her Lady's gift as I approached. Behind me, the ringing continued unabated.

The knock came again. As I approached, I heard a voice.

"Nick! Open up!"

Claryce's voice. At least, it sounded like Claryce's voice.

"Damn you, Nick! I know you're in there! Open up! You've got a lot to answer for, just leaving like that!"

It was Claryce, all right. I swung the door open and met her glare. Arms folded around her to keep her warm, she stalked toward me. I wisely backed up as quickly as I could.

And the telephone *still* kept ringing.

"Nick—"

I knew I was only going to make her angrier, but instead of trying to explain, I immediately ordered, "Shut the door, but stay by it."

I spun back to the phone. At this point, I supposed it could be Kravayik or Barnaby, but I doubted either.

Midway through the next ring, I plucked up the receiver. Raising the telephone, I said, "Hello?"

"Mr. Medea . . ."

A woman's voice. A woman's voice with which I was familiar, though I couldn't recall how.

"Yes," I finally answered. "This is Nick Medea."

"Mr. Medea . . . I don't know how to go on with this . . . but we think we have something . . . something *unnatural*. We didn't know what to do until my husband found your advertisement. I . . . I feel foolish even talking about this. . . ."

I had an uneasy feeling about the conversation, even though it was identical to any number I'd had in the past. Folks never wanted to admit that they needed my "services." Fortunately, they were always guaranteed to forget once I was finished.

"Go on . . ." I encouraged, trying to ignore Claryce's combined look of exasperation and curiosity.

"Well, it takes place upstairs and in the attic. Nothing we can actually focus on, but things move and the shadows always seem wrong. We both feel like we're being watched, and I swear I saw a tall, angular male figure."

A tall, angular figure. An elf. Not a surprise. Whenever clients spoke about figures, the figures tended to turn out to be some of the more humanoid creatures of Feirie.

"Nick . . ." Claryce muttered.

The woman on the other end didn't hear the interruption. "My husband . . . he actually saw it first. Albert said—"

"'Albert'?" I instinctively looked at Claryce, who quieted immediately. She could read my expression well enough and knew that something was very, very wrong.

She could hardly imagine. When the woman didn't continue, I repeated her husband's name. "You said 'Albert.' Your husband."

"Yes. I'm so sorry! I didn't give you our name. I'm Kaarin. Kaarin Nilsson—"

The line went dead. I immediately jiggled the earpiece cradle until the operator came on. "The call I was on. We were cut off."

The operator didn't respond right away. After what was too long a time, she finally came back and said, "I'm sorry, sir, I can't find any trace of a call to your number. In fact, I'm even having trouble identifying just what your number is. Do you have—"

I hung up. It wasn't surprising that the operator couldn't find a direct link to my number for the same reason only that those who actually needed my service saw the ad. I'd hoped she wouldn't bother checking my end of the conversation, but at least she'd done so only after trying to find out what'd happened to my "caller."

"What was that call, Nick? You look disturbed."

"A . . . ghost . . . from the past. Literally. A client recently murdered. Kaarin Nilsson." I told her all about the Nilssons.

She looked like I felt. I'd failed the Nilssons badly, and their deaths would stick with me for a long, long time.

"Then, it's a trick, then," Claryce decided. "By who?"

"Dr. Alexander Bond, I assume, who's pretty much a ghost himself." I then told her about what I'd been told and what'd happened at Saint Boniface.

"Michael again. Is he really who you think he is?"

"He sure as hell knows a lot about what's going on—"

"Nick! You shouldn't talk like that about him!"

I shrugged. "I don't see what worse can be done to me."

"I can think of too many things." She slipped off her coat. "Don't ever leave me behind again. Not in the day, not in the night. If Kravayik hadn't called me—"

"He did what?" I thought for a moment that he'd called her apartment looking for me, but the Kravayik who now served the church would never have let on that a single woman he knew might have a man in her home overnight regardless of how innocent it'd turned out.

"He called me. I don't know how he found out my number. Only the people at Delke have it . . . unless he got it through you?"

"Not me. What did he want?"

She wandered to the table and started vaguely rummaging through the old clippings. "I'm not quite certain. If I didn't know any better, I'd swear that he was trying to apologize for something he'd done to me."

"No idea what?"

"None." She picked up a clipping, glanced at it, then dropped it. "What do you think the phone call just now means? Are you sure it's Bond?"

"No. Since the Frost Moon, things've changed. There are powers stirring I never even knew existed. There are ghosts where there were none. Maybe this *was* Kaarin Nilsson, trying to keep me after who murdered her and her husband, Albert."

"Ghosts . . ." Claryce, another clipping in her hand, eyed me. "Like the one in Saint Michael's?"

I'd never gotten around to mentioning Diocles. He was part of my past I didn't want to share with her. Not because of what he'd done, but more because of what I refused to do. Forgive him and let him move on. "You know about it?"

"Father Jonathan let it slip, but I thought I saw something once or twice, including the first time you brought me there. Is there really a ghost in the church?"

"Yes, but I wouldn't bother concerning yourself with it."

Claryce frowned. "Why do I have the feeling you're hiding something . . . again?"

Instead of answering, I started organizing the clippings. As I did, I saw the paper where I'd written down the information about the Nilssons and their situation. Wondering if that meant anything, I read through the short set of notes.

Nothing. I tossed the notes aside.

"What was that?"

"The sum of my worth to the Nilssons. The information I never got around to following up on because I thought theirs was a minor matter."

"You couldn't have known it was that bad." Claryce picked up the paper. "How often do you get these calls?"

"Used to be once or twice a month. The last year, almost once a week average. More in the past three months."

"It's getting worse?"

"Much."

She pursed her lips. "So sad about them. We have to stop him, Nick."

I didn't like her use of "we." I already hated the fact that I had no choice in Claryce being in my life. Each incident meant a chance that something fatal could happen to her.

I would *not* let that happen.

She set the paper down. My guilt about the Nilssons growing by the moment, I slid it to the side and out of my immediate sight.

And there saw a file I'd not gotten to.

Claryce could clearly sense my interest in it as I pulled it from the pile. "Something?"

"I don't know." I started looking over the contents, all dated roughly three years after the exposition. The only thing that tied the file itself to our search was that it contained crimes related to Chicago no matter where they'd actually taken place.

I went through two murders and a fraud case. Two more murders after that. Then, something about the fraud case made me go back to that clipping and read more carefully.

There it was. The link.

H. Webster Mudgett.

Mudgett. The same name as Joseph's mysterious visitor. A visitor who might also be Dr. Alexander Bond.

"What do you have?"

196   BLACK CITY DEMON

"I've found our Dr. Mudgett . . . or rather, the name. A fraud case."
She saw the file. "In 1896?"

I didn't answer. I still wasn't satisfied. I'd had a strong suspicion about Bond all this time, and his use of Mudgett's name had only strengthened that suspicion. Keeping the clipping aside, I looked for any other piece concerning the fraud case.

What I found was *murder*.

I dropped the rest of the file on the table, eyeing the proof of what I'd known all along.

"Nick?"

"'H. Webster Mudgett, convicted of murder, was executed by hanging today in Moyamensing Prison in Philadelphia for the death of Benjamin Pitezel. It is believed as H. H. Holmes, Mudgett, also called the Beast of Chicago, may be responsible for more than thirty murders, many of them in his infamous Murder Castle in Chicago.'"

She shivered. "H. H. Holmes . . . so he *is* dead. Thank goodness for that at least."

She still didn't understand. For all her adaptability, Claryce was still thinking in normal mortal terms. Even me discovering this clipping hadn't been a simple matter of research. Now I saw the phone call from the late Kaarin Nilsson in a new, unsettling light. The call'd made me look at the notes, which then Claryce had done, which had led to the paper settling on top of just the right file. Justice—and vengeance—were strong factors in the supernatural world. The Nilssons were perhaps demanding justice.

Justice against a monstrosity stretching its hand again over Chicago. I handed Claryce the article. "There's a photo. Take a look."

She did. She saw. From the flashing of her eyes, she more than understood the depths of the evil rising in the Frost Moon's wake.

As I'd suspected early on, but had wanted to deny, H. Webster Mudgett, H. H. Holmes—the Beast of Chicago—and Dr. *Alexander Bond* were all one and the same.

CHAPTER 17

On May 7, 1896, H. H. Holmes had been hung until dead, his lifelessness verified. His body'd been disposed of far from Chicago. That should've been the end of it.

But the face staring at us from the old clipping was Alexander Bond. Alexander Bond, who'd somehow come to be buried in Saint Boniface shortly after. Alexander Bond, who'd not stayed buried long.

Alexander Bond. H. Webster Mudgett. H. H. Holmes.

"Did he trick them, do you think?" Claryce asked, her tone indicating she already knew my answer.

"No. I'm pretty certain that if we'd been there we'd have seen a very dead H. H. Holmes." I didn't care about either his birth name or his other identities anymore, not even that of Alexander Bond. It'd been as Holmes that he'd become known as the demon in human form, and I was more than happy to call him by that name, just so long as I was able to put him back in the grave once and for all.

"But he's human . . . or was . . . wasn't he?"

"So was I once." Before she could protest the comparison, I waved her off. "I know. Different. Think of this. You met Joseph. One of the intentions of the plot he and his comrades sought to put into motion was such power that they'd also be able to extend their lives indefinitely. It's been done before, but at horrible cost. The Clothos Deck can offer that, too . . . with a heavy price, of course. Even one card, if you make the right choice."

She was oddly silent. "You've faced people like this before? Were they all like him . . . I mean bad, evil, whatever you want to call it?"

"No. There were those who came close to being real saints. I suppose some of them might still be alive, assuming they didn't get reckless somewhere along the way. Becoming immortal tends to draw other, more unpredictable elements to you."

Claryce remained quiet for another moment, then said, "Barnaby's son keeps popping up in all this. Do you think we should try to talk with him again?"

"That was on my mind, too. The sooner better than later." I looked at the time. "Dunning won't let us in for a few hours still. I'll wait until an hour before, then call Barnaby to meet us there. This time, we'll get some honest answers out of Joseph even if I have to break every finger he has."

"God!" Her eyes widened. "You hate him that much?"

I stuffed the old clipping in a coat pocket. "If Joseph'd had his way, he'd have become something nearly as foul as our friend Dr. Bond—sorry, Dr. *Holmes*."

"It seems so impossible when I talk with Barnaby. He's such a sweet old man."

"Now." I didn't elaborate. I suddenly found myself thinking of Barnaby's covered companion. I pulled out my pocket watch. It was still early, but I decided it was already much too late. "Maybe I'll just give Barnaby a call right now."

"You're worried about something else now."

"Just taking a precaution . . . I hope." I picked up the phone. "Operator."

Fortunately, I had a different operator. This one connected me with Barnaby's number without questions about my own.

No one answered. After nearly two dozen rings, I hung up. Barnaby'd had more than enough time to return home. I also knew him as a light sleeper, which meant he hadn't snored his way through my call.

I looked at the watch again, then plucked up the telephone. This time, I didn't need a number. I knew the operator would have it herself. "Give me Dunning."

Naturally, the operator didn't correct me on the name. Claryce and I stared at one another as I waited for someone at the mental facility to answer.

Finally. "This is the Chicago State Hospital. How can I help you?"

"I know it's early, but I'd like to arrange a visit to one of your patients." I gave her Joseph's name and waited.

And waited.

"I'm sorry, sir. The gentleman is no longer a patient here. His next of kin took custody earlier this morning. I understand there was a family emergency and they needed to leave on an early train—"

I hung up. "Barnaby's taken his son out of Dunning."

"Why would he do that? Are they certain it was actually him?"

"They seemed satisfied, and it makes some sense to me. When Barnaby dropped off the Packard, he had a friend in another car, someone I couldn't make out." I had one idea, however fantastic it seemed, but I didn't mention my notion just yet. It meant aspects I'd never thought possible.

She grabbed her purse, which she'd set on the table earlier. "Where do we go? Barnaby's?"

I debated. "Let me try him one more time."

This time, I just let it ring and ring and ring. On what I counted as the thirty-third, lo and behold, someone answered.

"The shadow is waxing and waning, waning and waxing."

I gritted my teeth. "Hello, Joseph."

"Our knight in dulled armor, our flying ace in the hole . . ."

I hated madmen . . . but especially Joseph. "Were you expecting me to call? Did you want to tell me something . . . maybe in coherent sentences for a change?"

"Shadows, shadows, everywhere, beasts of all sorts, murderous and dragon, and all hail the emperor of them all! He holds the card. . . ."

The more I listened, the more I thought I heard hints of information. The only trouble was, I didn't have time to decipher which parts were significant.

At that moment, there was a muffled sound on the other end. Another voice murmured something to Joseph.

Then, "Hello, Nick."

"Just what're you up to, Barnaby? Why didn't you mention this little thing when we met during the night?"

"I was afraid you'd not be happy with it."

"You were pretty much right. What the hell are you thinking, taking Joseph out in the world again?"

After hesitating, he replied, "This is . . . this is the first time in six years that I've seen some hint of my son again. I couldn't let it just rest. They've taken care of him at Dunning, but managed little else. I thought maybe I'd have a better chance now. I could have my son back."

"This is Joseph we're talking about. We don't *want* Joseph like he was, remember, Barnaby?"

"I know, I know. I'm working toward that! I truly think that he'll be much better this time!"

I was beginning to think insanity ran in the family. Still, this at least gave me a chance to properly and privately question Joseph in depth. "Are you two alone there?"

"Yes. I thought I had Joseph . . . secure . . . but I was wrong. He's standing very quietly now."

"Where's your friend?"

"Gone." His answer came just a little too quickly, almost as if he'd known I'd ask and wanted to get the subject out of the way as soon as he could.

I decided to save that subject for when I saw Barnaby. "We're coming over. I want you to be very careful until then. I've learned a lot about our friend Bond. Mudgett wasn't his only other alias. He once went by the name of H. H. Holmes. You know that name."

"*The Beast of Chicago?*" The horror in his voice was genuine.

"Will you be okay?" I pressed.

"I have safeguards."

"We're leaving now. Keep everything secure."

I hung up without waiting for the answer. "You heard?"

Claryce nodded. "How dangerous is it that he's got Joseph with him?"

"I don't know about Joseph himself, since he seems to be eager to speak to me lately. I'm more concerned with Holmes's interest in him. I want to get to Barnaby before Holmes finds out he's no longer in Dunning. Holmes might not like that."

"Let's go, then."

We took the Packard. There was no sign of anything strange in the neighborhood as we drove off, but I kept an eye out just in case. I wasn't just concerned about my own problems, but the bootlegger war was encroaching. The heavyset doctor who lived nearby did not so secret work for the North Siders, especially Hymie Weiss, perhaps the only man Capone was actually scared of. Moran might be "Bugs," but Weiss—no Jew but a Catholic Pole named Henry Wojciechowski, according to Cortez—was a violent killer. Just a week ago, I'd seen two thugs bring a third to the doctor's home a couple of blocks down. Before this, the doctor'd always gone to *them*. If that kept up, I'd have to do something I doubted I'd like.

I turned the corner. "We're going to pass Adams near Berghoff's. I want Fetch with us."

"I thought you might want to do that."

There was little traffic, so even despite the weather, we made good time to West Adams. Berghoff's was closed, but there'd be trash from the restaurant, and where there was leftover food, there'd be vermin . . . and Fetch.

As we neared, I remembered something. "Fetch won't be alone. He's taken in a refugee from Feirie."

"A Wyld?"

"Technically. I've let it go for now, but keep watch. If anything moves toward you that isn't Fetch or me, shoot it."

She slipped her hand into the purse. "That risky?"

"That risky."

The alley was quiet. That didn't mean anything. Whether stalking a rat or a piece of corned beef, Fetch could remain as silent as the night.

I'd told Claryce to stay by the Packard, but she'd decided she preferred backing me up. I ignored the dragon's laughter at the princess protecting the knight.

There seemed no reason to be stealthy. "Fetch."

There was a slight movement from the area of the trash. He slipped into sight. "Master Nicholas. I was not expecting ye."

"We're going for a ride. I'll explain on the way."

"As ye say."

I glanced around. "Where's your friend?"

He turned his muzzle back to the trash. The Wyld revealed itself.

"He been behaving?"

"Yes, Master Nicholas! Most assuredly. All's copacetic!"

"See that it stays that way." I turned without bothering to see if Fetch followed.

Claryce kept her eyes behind me. When her expression softened, I knew Fetch was right behind me.

We hadn't used much time veering to Berghoff's, and traffic continued to be light as we neared Barnaby's neighborhood. I slowed as we came within two blocks.

"Something wrong?"

"Taking no chances. Fetch, you smell anything?"

"Nothing!"

So far, so good. "You know where Barnaby lives. Take the back-yard route."

"Yes, Master Nicholas!"

As he started to move, I added, "Don't take any foolish chances if you see anything."

"I won't take no wooden nickels, not me! I swear!" With that,

Fetch abandoned the Packard. I knew he'd reach Barnaby's before we did.

"Did he really just say that?" Claryce murmured with a smile.

"He rarely misses an opportunity, how very, very, very remote. I know. I've hoped."

The light moment passed as I turned onto Barnaby's street. All looked peaceful. The neighborhood was less cared for than where I made my base, but still a good one. Barnaby'd lived here since he and his Emma got married. Joseph'd been born and raised here, just like any normal kid.

Of course, Joseph'd also begun his plotting here, too.

I pulled over. "You want to stay here?"

"What do you think?"

"All right. Hopefully, all's just fine and we can untwist Joseph's answers into something coherent."

I made note of the fact that we weren't all that far from Des's house. I still didn't know if his past had any ties to what was happening, but maybe I'd have a chance to ask Barnaby a few questions about that while I was at it.

There was nothing about Barnaby's home that drew attention. Like the house I used, it was a Queen Anne, but of a light brown shade. The lawn was well-kept, and hedges of red roses lined the house itself. I remembered that Emma'd always loved roses. Out of love of her, Barnaby'd kept the hedges well-trimmed all these years.

"It's . . . lovely," Claryce commented, clearly surprised.

"Not the place you expect a sinister genius like Joseph to come from, eh?"

"Nick!"

Okay, it probably hadn't been her thought, but I'd contemplated the notion a time or two when I'd visited for one reason or another. Even taking Barnaby's dabbling in the arts into account, Joseph'd lived a decent life. There'd been no reason but his own darkness for the deeds to which he'd turned.

The Runabout was parked on the side of the house. I decided to just walk up to the front door and knock. Sometimes, just doing the ordinary thing worked find.

And, of course, no one answered.

Claryce looked around. "We're alone."

I didn't have to ask what she meant. Instead, after a brief try of the knob, I leaned into the door and shoved it in. It wasn't that Barnaby had a weak door; I had the dragon's strength to draw upon.

I was already reaching for Her Lady's gift as I entered. Behind me, I heard the click of Claryce's Smith & Wesson.

In front of us lay a scene of destruction.

"Dear God . . . Nick . . . did Joseph do this?"

I finished drawing the sword. "Joseph was never the overly physical type. Even in his current state, I doubt this is something he could've caused."

What I didn't add was that I was afraid we'd come across a scene identical to what'd happened to the Nilssons. A chill coursed through me that not even all the fire the dragon'd breathed on Chicago fifty-odd years ago could've burned away.

We made our way past overturned chairs, a small, shattered table, and a series of bookcases that'd been shoved around as if someone had expected to find treasure behind them. Scores of books, some of them incredibly old, lay scattered and torn. I recognized three in old Latin script, but otherwise had to ignore the damage as I searched for Barnaby and his son. If for some reason this *was* Joseph's doing, I didn't care what his father would think. I'd lay out Joseph cold if I could, and if I couldn't, Her Lady's gift was welcome to him.

Speaking of Barnaby's Emma, in one corner lay a small framed picture. The glass cover had shattered from the picture's fall from the wall behind it, but I could still make out a handsome young woman with German braids. Joseph had definitely taken after his mother, though I realized only then that his eyes—his once-penetrating eyes—favored his father's.

We went into the kitchen, where someone'd ripped open the Kelvinator and strewn all the food inside around. There wasn't much of a smell from the herring on the tile floor, so this'd happened very, very recently. That only backed up the thought that we might still find someone lurking in the house.

Claryce reached the stairs ahead of me. I moved quickly to cut her off. If we only faced a couple of cheap hoods, I'd have the utmost faith in her ability to bring them at bay. Unfortunately, I couldn't imagine that it'd just been thugs who'd overwhelmed Barnaby. As he'd hinted, he'd kept a few safeguards in place.

Too bad whatever had led this assault'd had more power.

I set one foot down on the first step. When the wood began to quietly creak, I knew our odds of reaching the upstairs this way without giving warning that we were ascending were nil. If there was someone or something waiting for us, speed was of the essence.

I measured the stairway's width, then peered back at Claryce.

Nodding, she stepped back. Smart woman; she knew I needed to get upstairs fast without making any noise. That meant some help was required.

Eye can give you wings to fly, fly high in the sky, above all else, above all lesser things. . . .

Just get me up the stairs. A good jump is all I need.

As you like.

I was surprised by his quick acquiescence, but couldn't take the time to wonder if it meant much. I felt the bones in my legs simultaneously crack and reform, the knee joint shift back. Behind me, Claryce gasped despite having prepared herself for some transformation. Seeing my legs suddenly bent backward must have been different than she'd expected.

I leapt up the stairs, landing with ease at the top. As I did, I swept

Her Lady's gift by me in case something was waiting for me. The Feirie blade met no resistance, though.

As my legs reverted to normal, Claryce, moving as quietly as she could, came running up after me. She kept her gaze on my face, though I could tell she wanted to look down at my legs to see if they might shift form again.

"Never more than necessary," I whispered. "Nothing he gives is free. He adds it all up, waiting."

The dragon said nothing, but I sensed an odd satisfaction that—I had to assume—had to do with me even needing the momentary transformation.

Claryce, meanwhile, gave me a nod, then, with a slight wave of the revolver, asked which direction. There were four bedrooms on the second floor, one behind us, two ahead on the left, and the last on the far right. The door of the farthest on the left was ajar, but otherwise there was no sign of the type of chaos we'd seen below.

The obvious choice was to go to the open door. At least, I was sure that was what someone wanted us to do. If they themselves had departed, they'd done so leaving something behind for anyone—and very likely me specifically—foolish enough to investigate.

I turned to the bedroom nearest us. I almost touched the knob, then decided to tap it with the point of the sword. If there was a spell on the knob, best to let Her Lady's gift take the brunt.

Nothing happened. I carefully opened the door.

I heard Claryce's intake of breath and couldn't really blame her. I'd never been upstairs in Barnaby's house, but had assumed that it was like any other. One bedroom for the couple—maybe *two* depending on circumstances—and the rest for whatever children they had. If there was a room left over, either the wife or the husband would likely use it for a study or guest room.

But this . . . this was a child's room. For a *girl*.

Barnaby'd clearly kept the room up, but there were telltale signs of age, especially a photograph of another house next to which a man who looked like a much younger—and better-looking—version of Barnaby stood. It *was* Barnaby and yet it wasn't.

And in his arms he held an infant. I had to assume it was a girl. *The* girl.

"You think you know someone," I muttered. "Man's got more mysteries than me, and that's saying something."

"You didn't know he had a daughter?"

"I don't know *what* he has." Whatever the story, I could see no reason to remain.

After shutting the door, I headed toward the next bedroom. My gaze shifted to the room with the open door. I *knew* it had to be a trap, but wondered whether we'd have a choice to ignore it. If the other rooms proved of no interest, we'd *have* to enter.

I repeated the same technique with the knob and got the same results. Inside, Claryce and I only found a simple room with a bed, a dresser, and an empty closet. The only clue to its use was a slight indentation in the sheets on the bed.

"This's where Joseph slept . . . at least for the few hours since Barnaby'd brought him home."

"That's odd," she remarked.

"What is?"

"The girl's room. It was well cared for. Lovingly. For years from the looks of it. Why not the same for his own son's room? Barnaby clearly loves him."

She had a point, but then, she'd also not met Joseph when he'd been of his own mind. "Look around. Barnaby's expunged everything about Joseph's past. It's not something you want Joseph remembering, trust me. Looks like Barnaby was hoping to start out fresh with his son . . . more the fool him."

"Nick . . ."

We stepped out of the room, and I shut the door behind us. We now had only two left, including the one ajar. I supposed for Barnaby's sake I should've gone straight to it. Even if it was a trap, he might be at the center of it.

"What're you doing?" Claryce whispered.

"Trying to choose between bad choices."

At that moment, the choice was taken from us. From within the room with the open door there came a crash of glass.

"Fetch!" I shouted both to Claryce and to Fetch himself. I don't know what'd caused him to enter the room, but it couldn't have been good.

Weapon ready, I barged through the door.

There was no Fetch. There *was* Barnaby, though. Barnaby on the floor in the middle of the shadowy room. Someone had shoved aside a bed and dresser to the wall next to his outstretched hand. A broken lamp lay by the dresser, the probable source of what I'd assumed had been Fetch leaping through one of the two covered windows.

I looked up, looked down, and at every wall, including the one with the closet. I could see nothing.

Eye will show you. . . .

I let his gaze take over, but even in the emerald world all seemed safe . . . thus far.

Barnaby groaned. I had no choice but to head toward him. The fact that he was still alive startled me. I'd expected to find something at least as bloody as what'd happened to the Nilssons.

"Stay in the hall," I ordered Claryce. I took a step farther inside, then another. The closet was my main concern. Children often thought there were monsters in their closets, and they were occasionally right. It was one of the places where Wyld liked to lurk as they built their power. They enjoyed toying with the open minds of children. I'd seen the results of some of their worst efforts . . . and that was enough to make me slip past Barnaby and fling open the closet door. If there was a Wyld within, it was going to discover how frightened *it* could become.

But other than a few suits that told me Barnaby had very consis-tent taste, there was nothing. No Wyld could've escaped the dragon's gaze this close.

Then, I heard a sliding sound . . . and knew I'd been thinking in all-too-human terms.

"Nick!" Claryce's warning was followed by two shots, shots that I knew wouldn't do any good.

I spun around just in time to see darkness spilling out of one of the dresser drawers, darkness swelling in size so quickly as it flew at me that a moment later I saw nothing else.

CHAPTER 18

didn't need anyone to tell me that this was the same Wyld that'd been lurking around a few other times, apparently in service to Holmes. As it spread out, I caught glimpses of dark green eyes without pupils scattered throughout the shadow.

I brought Her Lady's gift to confront the creature.

The Wyld split in two.

The action only took me by surprise for a moment, but it was a moment too many. Each half of the Wyld sprouted more than a dozen limbs, all ending in three sharp nails. The thing was versatile, I'll give it that.

I'd long ago given up trying to understand the macabre diversity of the creatures of Feirie. I could only assume that since they were in part inherently magic, it made for very fluid forms. Not one seemed the same as the last, the elves included.

I slashed at the nearest limb and watched with satisfaction as it fell cleanly away. Unfortunately, I'd not been able to make a deep cut with the point or else I'd have rid myself of at least one-half of my adversary. As it was, I continued to be assailed on both sides.

There was another shot. I didn't want Claryce wasting any more effort. "See to Barnaby! Go!"

"I can't leave you, Nick!"

"Go!" As I shouted, I lunged at the right half. Even though the blade didn't touch, the partial Wyld split into two smaller parts. Now I was confronted by *three* foes.

A set of nails rushed past my face. If I'd not jumped aside, I'd have lost a good portion of my face.

Eye can help you! Let me out! Let me breathe!

I wasn't yet desperate enough to do that. In silent reply, I used a feint to distract the largest piece and to run one of the smaller parts through. Her Lady's gift drank up the partial Wyld with gusto, the dwindling shadow's shriveling accompanied by a horrible, shrill tone.

That wasn't enough to deter the others, though. Sharp nails came at me from every direction, some scoring hits. I bit back a cry as one managed a jagged cut across my chest.

Beyond the Wyld, I heard the thumps of feet.

Its remaining parts fusing together again, the Wyld abruptly shifted aside as a new threat closed.

I stared into a familiar—and ugly—face. The deathly pale hood who'd materialized in the car and attacked me before vanishing again stood right before me . . . so close, in fact, that Her Lady's gift was all but useless.

This near, I could see the dead eyes all too well. If I hadn't known better, I'd swear he was a corpse. I still wasn't sure.

I caught his hand as it came up with the same arcane dagger with which I'd been stuck in the neck during the car chase.

"Not this time," I growled at him.

But before I could bring my other hand—and the sword—toward him, his twin materialized from nowhere and seized my wrist. The pair pinned me against the wall next to the closet.

A shot rang out. Twin One grunted and dropped the dagger, but stayed on his feet.

"Damn it!" Claryce shouted angrily. "I got him square in the back, Nick!"

I had no doubt as to her accuracy. I also had no doubt as to needing something a lot stronger to put an end to either of my new adversaries.

Eye will help you! Let me out!

I didn't have much of a choice now. I opened the way.

Nothing happened.

It came as much of a shock to him as it did to me. I could feel him pressing as hard as he could, trying to seize control and growing more and more furious that he could not. His anger spilled over on me with such intensity that I couldn't resist it. I roared at the twins, who stared back at me with their dead eyes and emotionless faces. Strong as I was even without the dragon's aid, I couldn't break their grips.

Then, another crash of glass echoed through the room. This time, I had no doubt that Fetch'd arrived.

He snarled at something. A shadow covered the area, the Wyld returning to the fray.

"Get Claryce out of here!" I managed. "Get—"

A squeal of pain that could only have come from the Wyld all but deafened me. That finally made the twins turn their heads in mirror image of one another to see what'd happened. Their reaction gave me a chance to see as well.

The shadowy Wyld writhed. In its center I could see the hilt of the blessed dagger I'd given Claryce. Teeth bared, she watched as if trying to make certain that the creature didn't shake the blade free. While not Her Lady's gift, it had strong abilities of its own just because of the blessing. Whatever the true reason, creatures of Feirie could not stand that power. The shadow literally dropped to the floor, where it continued to flail.

Fetch leapt upon it, tearing into the black mass with teeth and claw. Although shadow, the Wyld fell victim to his Feirie power.

From below, shouts and rapid footsteps warned that we had more company. I doubted they'd come to rescue us.

The dragon continued to rail against whatever unseen barrier kept him from dominating us. I became caught up between my own emotions and his to an extent I'd rarely suffered. It became impossible to focus, which didn't help when the twins returned their attention to me.

Gunshots rang out. A man cursed. Claryce'd taken the initiative and stepped out to the stairs to hold them off. Still, I hoped Fetch would listen to me and get her out of here somehow.

I screamed as, without warning, the dragon made some headway in his struggle. The world changed to emerald, and smells I could've never noticed as a human tried to overwhelm me. I could detect Claryce's nervous sweat and Fetch's odd, Feirie odor. I smelled the essence of the Wyld, including those scents indicating its near death. I could even smell the grave scent of the twins.

But what I could not smell in the least was the presence of H. H. Holmes even though he abruptly stood in the shadows just to the side of the twin on my right. Holmes tipped his bowler hat at me and smiled darkly through his mustache.

"Hold him still, lads. We're at the edge here now, but this should still work just fine!"

He drew out a small dagger akin to the one the twin'd carried, except this one had a black edge I didn't care for in the least. I struggled, but the Schrecks kept their grips. Inside me, the dragon continued his attempts.

"I can feel him now," Holmes murmured as he stepped up. His eyes grew intense with anticipation. "I can feel both of you. It's so close. So close. Yes, it was worth the risk—"

Fetch growled. I couldn't make him out, but he'd clearly lunged at Holmes.

"Damned mutt!" the Beast of Chicago snapped. He raised his free palm toward where I assumed Fetch had to be.

An unsettling thing happened. Suddenly, Holmes and I were surrounded by a throng of translucent figures. Ghosts.

Fetch whined in pain as he stumbled into view. He twisted around twice, then collapsed.

The ghosts faded away. His smile back—albeit with a touch of grimness to it—Holmes returned his attention to me.

"Keep fighting," he whispered to me. "Keep fighting. That'll make it all the better. Yes . . . fight hard . . ."

As he thrust the dagger, I realized it wasn't me he was talking to, but the dragon. I didn't know why he wanted the dragon to continue straining to take over, but I fought anew to keep control, at the same time mentally warning my constant companion to return to the recesses of my mind.

Naturally, he didn't listen.

In desperation, I threw my weight toward the twin on the opposite side. For the first time, I managed to put my captors off-balance. The twin to whom I leaned grunted as he fought to retain his footing.

My attempt still wasn't good enough. Although Holmes managed only a glancing blow with the blade, my entire body shuddered. It felt as if something slimy crawled into my veins and burrowed its way toward my heart.

Someone fired a shot. Through bleary eyes, I watched Holmes's head explode.

Then, just as quickly, I watched it reform.

Despite that miracle, Holmes looked more than a little disturbed. He shoved past Claryce—the source of the devastating shot—and leaned deeper into the shadows.

There, he melted away.

The twins released me. Groggy as I still was, I did notice that one second they were in front of me and the next they were gone.

The dragon seized control. I felt myself dwindling into that place of darkness within him.

"Nick! No! Don't lose yourself!"

I had to battle both the dragon and whatever poison Holmes's dagger had injected in me. Claryce's sudden interjection into the situation somehow gave the dragon pause. I fixed on Claryce, trying to use her to bring me back to the mortal world.

To my surprise, the dragon growled, then gave in. I stood on my two weakening legs, startled by my victory and wondering if he'd let me take over again just so the poison could do me in.

"I go, you go," I muttered. "You like to burn things, burn it away! You've done it before!"

There is nothing to burn. . . .

I didn't understand. It *felt* like poison. I'd been poisoned a hundred times and knew how poison felt.

"Nick! Hurry! They're still on the stairs!"

It took me a second to realize she was talking about Holmes's human thugs. "How . . . how many?"

"I wounded one before I came back in here. There are three others."

"Give . . . give me your hand."

I wanted it only for balance, but to my bewilderment, as we touched, I felt my focus return. I was able to look past Claryce to where the Wyld still flailed slightly. Moving over to it, I seized the dagger's hilt, then twisted the blade so it sank deeper.

A faint squeal rose from the melting darkness that was the Wyld. As I pulled the blessed weapon free, the Wyld began to melt. The other pieces followed suit.

"A nearly perfect strike," I complimented Claryce. "Did you know where to hit or just made a good guess?"

"I don't really know. It was the only spot that didn't have eyes everywhere. I thought that might mean something."

I nodded. "You thought right."

I handed her the dagger, then rushed to Barnaby's side. He'd been struck hard in the back of the head and had a knot nearly the size of my palm. He needed a doctor, but he'd live.

The fact that he'd been treated so softly compared to the Nilssons meant something. He hadn't been left alive just to draw me in. Holmes didn't strike me as the kind to plan that way. I hoped that maybe when he woke up he could fill us in.

But first we had to escape Holmes's human pawns. I didn't know who they thought he was, but clearly they had some knowledge of his arcane ways, if only because of the twins. I still had no idea what the twins were, but they had traces of Feirie on them.

I suddenly noticed that it'd grown awful quiet in the hall. With a growing suspicion, I cautiously went to the door and listened. Sure enough, it was deathly silent.

I swung the door open.

The hall and the stairs were empty. Traces of blood marked where Claryce'd hit the one man.

"They've gone?" Claryce asked as she joined me.

"Yes." That bothered me more than I let on to her. Sure, Holmes had grabbed Joseph, but he'd also set up a trap for me in particular. As far as I could tell, it hadn't quite succeeded. Whatever the dagger'd done to me had faded away. I still felt tired, but that was it.

"What do we do, Nick? Do you think they're waiting outside for us?"

"Not likely. I can't say why, but when Holmes faded into the shadows, the twins and the rest ran off." I glanced at the shadows into which the Beast vanished. For some reason, not only did they look paler, but the entire room seemed brighter to me. I asked Claryce if she noticed such a difference.

"I *think* the shadows are lighter, but I can't say about the room."

"Fetch, what about you?"

"The same as the mistress."

There was something to what we'd noticed, but I couldn't put my finger on it. Maybe the shadows had been darker only because Holmes had been using them, but I thought the reason something beyond his control. There'd been a sense of haste, of concern that if he'd remained much longer, he risked something of value to him.

I quickly returned to Barnaby. He moaned as I carefully turned him over just enough to better check his condition. There was no choice. I needed to get him to a hospital.

Eye could help him. . . .

It was true, the dragon could in limited ways heal others, but not only did I not trust him to succeed with Barnaby's injuries, but I just didn't trust him period. Not after the way he'd fought so eagerly to seize control even when I'd warned him against it.

"Fetch, check the way out." I hefted Barnaby as gingerly as I could. Fortunately, he wasn't that heavy. "Claryce, stick with me. I may need you to help shift him."

Nodding, she put away her revolver and joined me. Fetch trotted out of the room and to the stairs. He sniffed the air and the steps as we started down.

"Much blood here, Master Nicholas," Fetch remarked halfway down. "We could use a bit to follow this hood to his boss."

"If he's that bad off, he's already on his way to the river." Holmes didn't strike me as the kind to take care of the wounded. I had no sympathy for any gunsel. Throughout the centuries, I constantly had to face those like these men who'd long ago sold their souls for gold, power, and more. Galerius'd gathered himself quite a nasty bunch under his dragon banner, some of whom had taken personal parts in my beheading.

Fetch poked his head out the front door, which'd been left ajar. "All quiet."

"To the car."

He darted on. With a little assistance from Claryce, we made it to the Packard without anyone seeing us. I didn't know how well the neighbors knew Barnaby, but I doubted they'd be pleased if they saw us dragging his beaten body out of his house.

I understood enough about Barnaby's condition to risk driving him to Provident Hospital on East Fifty-First Street. It was by far neither the nearest nor largest hospital in Chicago, but I needed a place I could trust. Barnaby was no ordinary patient, and in his state he might murmur something he shouldn't.

Claryce said nothing as we pulled up at the nondescript three-plus-story building on the South Side. While I'd driven, she'd kept a constant check on Barnaby's injuries.

I drove around to the side of the hospital, parked, then ordered her and Fetch to stay inside. Now that I was here, I wasn't certain I'd made the right choice. It wasn't that I didn't trust the staff; it was I didn't know if they deserved to be involved in any way.

I knocked on the door there. A strong-looking Negro nurse opened it up and eyed me.

"You . . . Don't I know you, sir?"

"I'm a friend of Dr. Williams."

"Dr. Williams? As in Dr. Daniel Hale Williams, may God bless him?"

I tried to peer past her, but she insisted on filling the doorway. "Yes. How is Daniel?"

"Not here in a long time, sir. You know his Alice died last year?"

"I'd heard." I actually hadn't seen Williams in more than twenty years, but she wouldn't have known that. I'd actually met him shortly after he'd founded this hospital some forty years ago. It'd been a stunning thing, a Negro—well, Negro and Scots-Irish—surgeon opening a hospital willing to take those of any race. That'd caused no end of trouble for him.

He'd accidentally confronted a Wyld in the process, which was how I'd come to know him. He'd been a man of courage and conviction, always striving to save a life. Where Holmes liked to play doctor while he gutted victims, Daniel Hale Williams had sliced open a man's chest in order to save his heart.

Three times, I'd needed the services of his hospital, with Barnaby the least conspicuous of those patients. I'd known that Williams had retired—he'd be in his seventies by now—but there was another rather unorthodox doctor I'd hoped was still here—

"It is all fine, Bertha," a smooth, female voice with a hint of a German accent declared from behind the imposing nurse. "I will take care of this man and whatever troubles he brings."

"As you say, Dr. Fremd. You want me to start some paperwork?"

"No. I will attend to that, too."

Bertha gave the tall, very thin woman wearing the rounded glasses a nod, then, with a last suspicious glance at me, headed down the corridor. She no doubt believed that the doctor was dealing with a bootlegger or some other miscreant.

"Dr. Fremd."

"Mr. Medea. It has been some time."

There was a hint of gray in her bound blond hair. When I'd last met with Margaret Fremd, she'd been at least ten years younger. She was still an attractive woman, but there were now lines at the edges of her eyes. Her expression hadn't changed in a decade, though.

"Some time, yes. I have a patient."

There was an almost imperceptible flickering of the eyes. "One of those?"

"No. Just a friend who was mugged."

"'Just a friend who was mugged.' How different for you. Will he need to be overnight?"

"I think so. Maybe a few days, even."

She adjusted her jacket. Margaret Fremd had studied at both Heidelberg and Chicago, but as a female physician, she'd had few options. Of course, there were other reasons for her choice of hospitals, not the least of which had ties to something that'd happened in Germany. She'd been here the last time I'd spoken with Williams. He'd made her our liaison.

Dr. Fremd adjusted her glasses. "You will need help with him, Mr. Medea?"

"No."

"Bring him here, then."

I nodded and quickly returned to the Packard.

"Who was that?" Claryce asked.

"Someone who can watch over Barnaby." I hefted him out of the car, then carried him toward the hospital.

Dr. Fremd was waiting for me . . . along with a bull of a man who made Bertha look tiny.

"My associate will take him," she ordered. Eyeing Barnaby, the doctor asked, "How long ago did this happen?"

"A few hours ago. Will there be a problem?"

"Of course not. I suggest we put him in the fifth room, Jackson."

"Yes, Margaret."

As he carried off Barnaby, Dr. Fremd stared at me over her glasses. "Are you renewing your relationship with the hospital, Mr. Medea? I would like some warning if you are."

"No. This was unexpected."

"So was what happened with your last 'friend' you left with us. We cannot afford a repeat of that. The hospital faces trouble enough without your ways interfering."

"I'm sorry. I'll try to avoid bringing any trouble. I swear."

She gave a faint nod. "The woman with you. It is her, is it not?"

Glasses or not, the doctor had damned good eyes. "Yes."

"I see." She took off her glasses, and only then did I remember what I'd learned the first time we'd met. Margaret Fremd had grown up believing in fairy tales, only to find out the true story was darker than anything the Brothers Grimm had ever collected. "Do your best to keep her safe this time, yes?"

Before I could answer, she turned and shut the door behind her.

I headed back to the car. Claryce watched me as I seated myself. "Will he be all right there?"

"There's no place safer, I think."

"How long have you known her, Nick?" After I told her, she nodded. "I thought it was even longer. Does she know who you really are?"

"Dr. Williams—he founded the hospital—told her."

Claryce studied the building. "Does Kravayik know this place?"

"Yes. I had to bring him here once."

"How long has the hospital been here?"

I thought about it. "I believe 1891."

She leaned back. "Back in 1891."

As I started up the Packard, I wondered why she was interested. Only when I'd turned the car around and headed back for her apartment did I think about the fact that Claryce had actually still not truly fathomed my existence. I looked only a decade or so older than her; that made everything I said—even everything she'd seen—secondary.

But now . . . now maybe she was digesting the enormity.

And not liking it.

CHAPTER 19

There was a car parked near Claryce's apartment. A familiar black Ford Runabout.

Cortez.

"What's he doing here? And at this time?" I muttered.

"Is that Cortez?"

"None other." There was no chance of avoiding him seeing us unless he'd fallen asleep, which I doubted the good detective would do. Cortez was one of the sharpest, most dedicated men I'd known in centuries. Unfortunately, that meant that he often got too close to the truth where I was concerned.

Sure enough, Cortez climbed out of the Ford even as we neared. Unlit cigarette dangling from the corner of his mouth, he waited while we parked.

As we headed toward Claryce's building, Cortez stirred from his location. Plucking the cigarette out, he called, "Nick Medea! And the lovely Miss Simone, good!"

"Not exactly a good night for visiting, Cortez. That is what you're doing . . . visiting?"

"Yes and no. Mostly, I'm here to ask a few things of the lovely lady here, you know?"

I peeked past him. He'd come alone, which meant the questions might be a little more personal than we wanted. "Do you *ever* go off duty? When's your Maria and the children ever see you?"

He frowned. "She asks me that, too, sometimes. I do miss them when I'm not home, you know? I'll be getting home to them after I finish up here."

"What did you want to know, Detective Cortez?" Claryce asked, not once hinting in any manner that he should come inside with us.

Cortez chuckled. He put the cigarette back in his mouth for a moment, then commented, "Miss Simone, I'm trying to trace one Dr. Alexander Bond. Found out from a fellow employee at Delke that you'd dealt with him about a piece of property."

Claryce crossed her arms. "I'm not really an employee of Delke anymore."

"But you did see this Dr. Bond?"

"What do you want to know about him, Cortez?" I asked.

He started to reach into his coat pocket for his Luckys. I shook my head before he could get far. "Say, that's right. The property the people at Delke spoke about is right across from that place we discussed. You know, the 'Murder Castle.'"

He had a good memory. "Coincidence."

"'Coincidence.' Ha! You know what my Maria says about coincidence? She says there's no such thing. Isn't that something?"

I kept my expression neutral. "Sure is."

Cortez shrugged. "Anyway, is there something you can tell me about him? Did he mention going anywhere or say any name?"

"Nothing, Detective," she answered honestly. "I'm sorry."

"No, you should be very happy. Happy you're alive, you know? I suspect the doctor of murder."

We tried to look startled. Evidently we succeeded enough.

"You know that body I asked you to see," he said to me. "The others I talked about, too. I asked around, find this name popping up. Buys some old books from a place that gives me the heebie-jeebies. Picks up an antique knife from another. A couple of odd things here and there. Leaves his name all over, like he's daring someone to put it all together."

I had no doubt that Bond—Holmes—had been doing just that. Either he'd been mocking the city that'd once been his killing ground or he'd been daring any of his potential enemies . . . both human and Feirie.

And despite the fact that I'd never come across Holmes before all this, I couldn't help thinking that maybe he'd left the clues for me, as well. He seemed to know me, know what I was and about my link to the dragon. I was sure I could lay the blame on someone from Feirie, maybe especially this Lysander.

"So, this meeting you had with Dr. Bond, Miss Simone, that was the only contact?"

"With Dr. Bond? Other than the initial telephone call, yes."

I noticed the way she phrased it. Not exactly a lie.

"Keep an eye on her, Nick Medea. I mean it. No baloney, Bo. With things all heating up between the gangs, we don't need no madman trying to be the next Beast, you know?"

"No. Definitely."

My, we are all paragons of virtue, ever the truth dripping from our lips. . . .

Shut up!

"That's all, then." Cortez tipped his hat at Claryce, started to turn, then seemed to remember something. "Oh, Maria would tan my hide if I forgot."

From another coat pocket, he removed a small medallion. He gently placed it in Claryce's palm.

"What's this?" she asked.

"A gift from my Maria. She said she wanted you to have it."

Claryce looked from Cortez to me. "I've never actually met her. Why would she do this?"

He looked very apologetic. "My Maria, she . . . she has these feelings. She prays for people she's not met. You already know that. Sometimes she gives them things, too. Medallions. See that woman on the top? That's our Lady of Guadalupe! Maria and I, we take the children to her church at least twice a week . . . well, Maria does. I manage Sunday, mostly."

"Thank you. I mean that."

He gestured at me. "Nick here should appreciate the other side, you know? Don't know where Maria got it. Think she had it made. She does things like that."

Claryce turned it over. "I can't make it out."

"Nick will recognize it when he sees it. Saint Michael the archangel!" With that, Cortez tipped his hat at both of us and headed off.

I did a good job of acting unperturbed as the detective drove off. Claryce handed me the medallion. I summoned the dragon's vision, and sure enough, the other side had Saint Michael in all his blazing glory. The image was stylized, so it pretty much looked like every other image of an angel I'd seen.

"Coincidence?" Claryce asked.

"You know how I feel about that."

"I know. That's why I asked."

She headed toward the apartment. I followed, but not without a glance to each side.

"I am here, Master Nicholas," Fetch muttered from my right.

"Not looking for you."

He sniffed the air. "No hint of goons, Master Nicholas. All's copacetic."

I just nodded. I doubted he'd be able to smell an angel . . . especially one like Michael.

I called Dunning the next day to see if there was any clue from past visits to Joseph, but learned nothing new. I then called Provident to see if there was any change in Barnaby's condition.

Fremd wasn't there, but someone else familiar to the case answered.

"This is Jackson, Mr. Medea," he said in that deep voice. "Your friend is still unconscious, but breathing well." Jackson then went into medical detail well above my knowledge. I'd spent a lot of time patching up the wounded during my centuries, but I'd never bothered to learn any of the Latin lingo.

"Will he be fine?" I asked when he was finished.

"I still have another year of study before I can say it officially, but yes, sir, I believe he will."

I tried to imagine an imposing figure like Jackson as a healer. In the old days, his lot in life would've been determined early on, most likely as a soldier or something due simply because of his strength. Now, though, entire new avenues were open to anyone who had a good head on his shoulders and who was willing to take a risk.

After thanking him, I hung up.

Claryce entered the room, looking far too fresh considering she'd only gone off to bed about four hours earlier. "Find anything?"

"No sign of Joseph, Barnaby will be okay, and it's true, you can't judge a very large book by its cover."

"I don't even want to know what that means." She'd changed into an outfit akin to the one she'd worn yesterday, only green and clearly warmer. "What do we do next?"

"I want to go check where Holmes's old lair used to stand. He wasn't near there just for us. At the very least, there's something about the vicinity." I cleared my throat. "If you could—"

Her eyes flared with fire worthy of the dragon. "Don't say another word! I'm going with you, and that's that."

I considered knocking her out, but didn't want to leave her helpless in case Holmes sent some of his human goons looking for us. True, I could've left Fetch with her, but I needed him with me when I returned to West Sixty-Third Street. "All right. Just . . . always be careful."

"You, too. You're not exactly immortal, remember."

No, far from that, are we? my constant companion interjected snidely. *Do try to watch our back, yes? I may not always be there for you. . . .*

I gave him no response. Then, I noticed Claryce eyeing something in her hand. "Is that the medallion?"

"Yes. You know . . . it does give me some comfort, I've got to admit."

Several rather unsaintly comments came to mind, but then a notion occurred to me. "Before we head to West Sixty-Third, I want to make a stop in Saint Michael's."

"You need to discuss something with Father Jonathan?"

I scowled. "No. I'm hoping to speak to his superior."

Father Jonathan was busy with church matters, which made the situation easier. He gave me just enough time to tell me that he'd only thought he'd seen the ghost once and that was a rather questionable sighting.

Fetch waited outside in the Packard. Alone now with Claryce, I studied the altar, then eyed the image of Saint Michael. Of course, it didn't match either of my suspected Michaels, but that didn't matter.

"Okay, Michael," I muttered. "We're in your home now. I appreciate your help, such as it is, but I'd like to finally have one face-to-face with you . . . with whichever face you want to wear, just so long as you're here. What about it?"

From the front pew, Claryce gave me a look of reprimand. I just arched my brow at her. Sure, it was a long shot, but I saw no reason not to take the chance. I couldn't help wondering if my constant praying here had been one reason why Michael'd taken a hand in some situations. Still, that help had been spotty at best, certainly not reliable. I wanted to know why.

"In all the years you've prayed here, I have never seen him, Georgius."

I didn't even look to my right, where Diocles's voice had risen from. "Maybe you're just not high on Heaven's list right now."

"Perhaps, but I would think you would be."

That made me laugh, even though it wasn't at all funny. "I'm probably lower on the list than you are." Still, I felt a little foolish having tried now that Diocles was also present. "But yeah, probably not going to hear anything . . . as usual."

"Nick . . . who're you talking to? Is that . . . Diocletian?"

"She need not be so formal about me. Tell her 'Diocles' will do."

Now I finally looked at him . . . and the wall behind him, of course. "She can't see or hear you. Doesn't matter what you want her to call you."

"Nick . . ." Claryce stood. "I don't know about hearing him, but I think . . . I think . . . is he to your right . . . just beyond arm's reach?"

He was . . . and I didn't know who looked more perplexed, the emperor or me. "Yeah, that's about right. Exactly what *do* you see?"

"Just a general shape. About your height. I have to keep focusing on it, but it's definitely there."

"She does see me!" Diocles declared almost jubilantly.

"Calm yourself. She sees a blob. Nothing more." First the priest, who, being attuned to this place, had made some sense, and now Claryce.

"I thought I saw something once, when you first brought me here to hide me from Oberon's men, but this . . . this is definite, Nick."

I rubbed my chin. "How do you feel, Diocles?"

"I am dead. I do not feel."

"Comedian. Is anything different? Even from when we talked in the cemetery." I hated mentioning Saint Boniface in front of Claryce. Fortunately, she seemed too intrigued by her first run-in with a ghost.

He shimmered. "I think I can . . . manifest . . . better. It is not exactly like when the creature who shares your body sought the card in the cathedral. That was a different sensation, almost as if I lived for a moment." Diocles abruptly sighed. "If only for a moment."

The longing in his voice as he said the last disturbed me. I had my resentments where he was concerned—"resentments" a kind term considering he'd ordered my head lopped off—but for an instant, I felt for him. Even in my current condition, I didn't exactly feel alive anymore, but that hardly compared to his condition.

"And now?" I pressed when he just stood there.

"And now . . . and now I feel as if more energy coalesces in me."

If anything, his answer only worried me. I could think of just one reason why he might be growing stronger. Joseph'd talked about it in his own frustratingly mad way.

The Frost Moon's wake was affecting things more and more. It wasn't even close to starting to fade yet.

That was why Holmes had kidnapped Joseph. Joseph knew such things, even now. Holmes had something in mind that had to happen when the wake's effect was strongest. If he waited any longer, he wouldn't have access to the energies he needed.

I could only imagine just what he had in mind.

"Think hard, Diocles. Has this felt gradual, or was it in spurts?"

He smoothed his robes as he thought. It occurred to me that he was actually trying to look a little neater for Claryce even though she could only make out a shadow.

"It comes . . . as waves. Yes. Waves. That's it."

"Right now. Is it receding or rising?"

"Receding, but barely. Now that I think of it, it is strongest in the afternoon, then around midnight."

"All right. You can go now."

"Georgius—" He looked startled at my dismissal. I suppose he'd begun to think we were becoming chums again.

"*Nick*," I reminded him. "Always Nick to you. Remember?"

The emperor looked exasperated. "I remember."

He vanished.

"He's gone," Claryce remarked with a frown. "What was that, Nick? Why did you suddenly get cross with him?"

"That doesn't matter right now. What does is that from what Diocles said, whatever Holmes is up to is imminent."

"So, we should get on to West Sixty-Third, then."

I nodded. "Exactly."

I didn't know what to expect when we reached the site of Holmes's old haunts, but what we did confront was a big disappointment. Nothing'd changed. The place where the Murder Castle'd been located looked exactly as it had last time.

"Fetch, you smell anything?"

He sniffed. "Some ripe rats."

Of course. "Anything you don't count as food?"

"Nay, Master Nicholas. Don't know for nothing, sorry. I'll keep searching."

"Yeah," I responded, ignoring his tortured use of another bit of human slang.

"There's a car across the street," Claryce whispered. "I know it. It belongs to Oliver Winston. He called the apartment that one time."

"What would he be doing here?"

Claryce shrugged. "I suppose he's here on Delke business. I've been turning over more and more to him."

There was a light on in the building where we'd first met Holmes as Alexander Bond. "Maybe we should stop in and see your friend."

"Oh, God! Nick! Do you think he might—that Holmes could have—"

"I don't know." I slipped out of the Packard, my hand close to my coat.

Claryce and Fetch got out from the other side. Fetch immediately trotted off toward the side of the building. Claryce stepped up next to me, her hand in the purse.

We reached the door. I carefully tugged on it. It wasn't locked. It also didn't squeak as I pulled it open. Good.

With Claryce right behind me, I entered the empty building. From the back, someone hummed.

We were abruptly joined by a bespectacled man in his twenties. He wore a very dapper blue suit and spats on his shoes. He'd slicked his hair with oil that had a slight scent to it.

"Claryce?" he blurted in a voice a bit on the high side.

"Oliver. I didn't expect to see you here. Did—did Dr. Bond make an offer?"

He adjusted his round glasses. "Dr. Bond never called back. We might have a new prospect, so I thought I'd familiarize myself with the location. You're no longer on this, you know. I tried to call, but you weren't home."

"I understand. I only stopped by because I thought I left a book here."

"Well, I didn't see anything, but if I do, I'll be sure to send it to the address you gave us. Good-bye, Claryce." Oliver turned around and headed into the back of the store.

Not once had he paid any attention to me. "Pleasant fellow. Love to talk with him again."

She looked apologetic. "He's really not a bad person. Just . . . ambitious."

"Looking to take your old position?"

"Hmmph. More likely trying to take *William's* position as soon as possible. I said ambitious."

Oliver let out a shriek.

Despite my immediate dislike for the man, I didn't hesitate to rush back. I already had Her Lady's gift ready. There were ways of making Oliver forget anything I did, but first the man had to survive whatever was happening.

As I entered the back, I caught sight of Oliver grasping at the air next to him as if some invisible escape door stood there. His gaze was fixed on a figure standing in the back doorway, a figure who at first looked like one of Moran's gang. It was only when one stared close at the face beneath the checkered newsboy cap that the reason for Oliver's scream became even more apparent.

The goon's aquiline features were decaying.

His long nose hung slightly to the side, a ragged hole above one nostril. The right side of his lower lip had curled aside, revealing the teeth down to the blackening gums. A piece of dry flesh had begun peeling from the left cheek.

"Gah . . . gah . . . gah . . ." Oliver eloquently managed as he stumbled back.

The rotting goon took a step toward him. Behind the undead, the door shut of its own accord.

One hand was already stretched out toward Claryce's stunned coworker. The small finger dangled limply, and bits of flesh dropped from the index finger pointed at Oliver.

"Don't even think it!" I snarled, the sword flaring in response to the undead's presence. I didn't need it to tell me I faced Feirie energy here, not at all.

The eyes—or the sockets, actually—appeared to look in my direction. Then, the jaw loosely moving, the walking cadaver rasped, "Sleeeeep."

Oliver collapsed.

The ghoul and I confronted one another. He cocked his head—an act accompanied by a crackling sound—and uttered, "Gatekeeeepers . . ."

The body was the missing hood from the car I'd come across. The voice, however, belonged to Her Lady's enforcer, the thing I'd nicknamed Lon.

I'd wondered where he'd gotten to, and now I knew. His predecessor'd used a bootlegger to move around in the human world for a short time. Unfortunately, it seemed that such use burned out the corpse faster. Even though it hadn't been very long, the hood already looked several days dead, which made him no more use for the creature. I didn't know if he'd intended on using Oliver for the same thing, but that didn't matter at the moment. The more I stared at Lon, the more I realized I'd seen him in this guise elsewhere.

I'd seen him in the car waiting for Barnaby.

Yeah, I'd only made out an outline, but the cap and clothes matched what I'd seen and answered why Barnaby's companion'd taken such measures to hide himself. If I'd made the connection between the Feir'hr Sein and the missing hood, I might have realized who was in the other car.

Lon trudged forward. There wasn't much use left in his host. In fact, with the second step, the refuse that'd once been one of Holmes's puppets tumbled forward. As it did, the Feir'hr Sein peeled off the back.

Gatekeepers . . . The murky figure floated above his ruined host. To my surprise, he then tipped his hooded head forward in what I realized was almost a bow.

A bow to me.

On a hunch, I pointed at the floor right before the body. "Kneel."

And he did. Reluctantly. Resentfully. But he did.

Her Lady's enforcer was my servant as well.

I wasn't sure why, although some possibilities came to mind. I didn't think it had to do with the sword, but I wasn't about to test that at the moment. Instead, I needed to verify something and verify it quickly. There was a reason why Lon'd been in this vicinity, and I knew that it had to do with Holmes.

"You went to Barnaby, didn't you?" I asked, not bothering to explain who I meant. He knew.

Yesss. . . .

"You don't just show yourself to humans. You knew his link to the energies." I purposely put the statement in Feirie terms, rather than say Barnaby'd dabbled in magic.

Yesss . . . he repeated.

"You probably warned him that his son was in danger if he stayed at Dunning and that you'd help. Am I right?"

This time, he only nodded. I'd come to understand that the Feir'hr Sein were very good—and very relentless—at their tasks, but Lon had still surprised me. I had to believe that he'd not only taken over the hood completely, but had managed to absorb some of the man's knowledge and skills. There weren't too many cars in Feirie, so there'd been no way for Lon to learn to drive them, yet he evidently had driven fairly well when he'd followed Barnaby to me.

That brought up the point of why he'd risked discovery by me when I'd noticed the car behind the Packard. Knowing the Feirie folk as I did, I could imagine a bit of hubris. He'd known I wouldn't think of one of his kind as a mere driver.

He'd been right.

But now I treaded into territory that might bring Her Lady's gift back into play, territory that just stank of the way the powers of Feirie had no qualms about manipulating and betraying those they thought beneath them.

"Nick, we can't leave things like this here," Claryce muttered.

"I know . . . but our ghastly friend here's still hiding things. I'll bet he acted like he was working with me, but out of the goodness of his—well, whatever you have for a heart, eh, Lon?—he offered to help bring Joseph to the supposed safety that Barnaby thought he could give his son. Only, you knew not just that Barnaby couldn't provide the protection he thought he could, but you took one more step in your duty to Her Lady, didn't you?"

The shadowy creature shifted. I swore I could see anxiety in his movements.

I switched tactics for a moment. "You have to obey me, don't you?"

He didn't give any indication that he had to, but then again, he didn't deny it, which had more weight. Feirie folk did not like subservience to humans, and especially not to saints.

"But you'll do whatever you can to get around my interests without actually disobeying, isn't that so?"

I serve. . . .

It was just the not-answer answer I expected. Now I pushed the point I'd been leading to. "And you'll strive to fulfill Her Lady's desires first and foremost."

I serve . . . the Feir'hr Sein repeated.

"So you do. And in doing so, no problem with sacrificing a few humans by playing on their devotion to one another." I let the point of the sword rise until it was in line with his midsection. "And then, while your stolen body was still fresh enough, you used it to let the Beast's followers know just where they could find Joseph when they needed him."

The Feir'hr Sein hissed. I'd struck on it. Acting like he worked with me, he'd actually set things up so that Holmes could come after Joseph easier.

I didn't have to ask why. I knew. "You're waiting for it to happen, whatever it entails. You're waiting for the Beast to cast his spell because in his moment of triumph, he'll also be his most vulnerable! Am I right? Doesn't matter what might happen to a bunch of humans or even a few lesser Feirie. This is all about *her*, isn't it? She's been planning this betrayal all along! Why? So that she can better hunt down Lysander and other traitors? Is that it?"

"Yes, that is it," responded a voice from behind Claryce and me, a voice I'd been expecting. "And God help me, I aided in her treachery."

Purposely turning my back on Lon, I now aimed Her Lady's gift at someone who at the moment I loathed even more than the queen of Feirie.

"You better have a really, really good reason why I don't run you through, Kravayik."

CHAPTER 20

Kravayik didn't wear the garments we generally saw him in when visiting Holy Name. Instead, he was dressed pretty much like the dead goon, even down to a brown newsboy cap. The collar of his coat was pulled up, and his hair hung loose enough to cleverly hide the fact that he had long ears as sharp as the tip of a sword.

Anyone really looking close would have noticed those shifting features, those different eyes, but despite his conversion to the church, Kravayik still retained enough ability to keep his exact face shadowed just right.

I wondered how well he'd do if I punched him really, really hard in the jaw.

"You have every right to be furious, Master Nicholas. I continue to step far beyond my bounds, may the Lord forgive me."

"The Lord may forgive you, but I'm not so kind. I know you heard what I said to Lon here. You understand Her Lady's plotting. She doesn't care who gets killed so long as she has a chance to steal whatever power Holmes is gathering for her own. I'd think that'd be something you wouldn't like."

His gaze shifted briefly to the Feir'hr Sein. "No, not at all."

I'd known him long enough to be able to read his murky face better than most. "What do you find so amusing?"

"Why would I find anything about this amusing?"

I gave it a moment's thought, then jerked my thumb at Her Lady's enforcer, who hovered impatiently over the corpse. "It was when I mentioned Lon here."

There it was again. A slight turning up of the corners of his mouth and a shift in his eyes.

"Perhaps it is just that I also see the resemblance between the Feir'hr Sein and the great actor's latest grotesque."

It was odd to hear Kravayik call Chaney's Phantom "grotesque" as compared to the darker side of Feirie. Still, I knew there was more to it than that. "It's because I named him. That wasn't supposed to happen, was it?"

"No, Master Nicholas," Fetch responded. Somewhere along the way, he'd slipped in quietly through the front. Although he stood behind Kravayik, it was clear that, at least for now, he didn't see himself and Kravayik on the same side. "It wasn't. Ye are not supposed to have the power to give such as that a moniker that sticks. That is not just power reserved for the highest of the Feirie Court, but *impossible* for any human."

"*Any* human," Kravayik repeated quietly.

"But he'll still obey her, right?"

"Oh, yes," he answered, "and tie himself into knots worthy of Houdini doing it. You command him, but his allegiance is to her. Best to watch out for that."

"Says one who worked with him behind my back. What about that, Kravayik?"

"I have my own ties to the Feir'hr Sein. She would not have gotten what she desired, not exactly."

Spoken like a true elf. I gave up on that. Right now, I didn't like most of those I had to surround myself with as allies, but Holmes had to be stopped. "Why're you back here? I know Holmes favors this area for some reason. His old haunts used to be across the street, but I haven't found any clue. What about you?"

Kravayik lost his humor. "Sadly, the trail fades here . . . as always."

"What about Lon? He see anything?"

"Master Nicholas . . ." Fetch interrupted. "There're torpedoes about."

"'Torpedoes'? Did you and Lon know that, too?" I asked Kravayik.

"No." He reached into a pocket. I didn't think he was looking for a comb, although with the old Kravayik—who seemed to be back—even a comb was a deadly instrument. "They must have just arrived."

"Yes, Master Kravayik! Saw them parking as I came around behind you."

"You did good. I did not sense you until you reached the doorway."

Fetch growled. Clearly he hadn't actually been complimented and, already aware of my anger at Kravayik, was more than happy to side with me.

"How many, Fetch?" I asked before things could deteriorate further.

"Two hay burners. Five in each. The two pasty goons are with them."

"Know anything about the twins, Kravayik?"

He swallowed. I'd never really seen him swallow like that. I didn't find it encouraging. "No. Only that they are not of Feirie."

Things were just getting better and better. "Were they with Holmes back during the exposition?"

"Yes."

Claryce couldn't see it, but his eyes flickered to her. I remembered what'd supposedly happened to Claudette and began to wonder just what details Kravayik'd left out.

"Nick!" Suddenly, Claryce had the revolver aimed at Lon. At the same time, she moved toward him.

I spun around and found the Feir'hr Sein hovering nearer to the unconscious Oliver, the intention obvious. Unfortunately, Claryce now stood on the other side of her former coworker. She stared at the Feir'hr Sein without fear.

Fetch roared. The Feir'hr Sein reared back as without warning a thing that had to have inspired the original tales of werewolves reared up on two legs and challenged Her Lady's enforcer with gleaming claws and sharp, sharp teeth. A fiery mane of fur crowned the head, which had a muzzle shorter than that of a hound and was slightly more human in design.

"Ye'll not touch the mistress!" Fetch roared at the Feir'hr Sein. "I've ripped apart your kind before! Ye know that!"

I had to admit I expected the worst, but Lon paused. It wasn't a pause I knew had anything to do with my control, because I'd been too dull to think to order the Feir'hr Sein back.

I did that now. Lon retreated to his spot above the corpse.

"Fetch . . ." I said slowly. "This is a side of you I haven't seen since Feirie. How long?"

He'd already begun shrinking to the form with which Claryce and I were more familiar. His expression truly matched that of a beaten dog. "Three days. Stronger each day."

The Frost Moon's wake. If Fetch, who couldn't even talk to anyone other than Kravayik or me, much less revert to his true Feirie form, now had full range of his power, I wondered just what Holmes's ultimate spell would allow him to do.

I asked Kravayik what he knew about that, but he shook his head. All he—or even Her Lady—had ever known had been that here was this human who'd learned how through the dark arts to draw power from the ultimate well of magic. He had succeeded enough to even put fear into the minds of the Feirie folk.

"But what stopped him last time?" Claryce asked, still standing defensively near Oliver. We had to do something about him soon, but I was still deciding what.

I liked her question. It was one that'd been bugging me for a while. "Well, Kravayik? Why didn't Holmes succeed? It wasn't just because he was discovered by the authorities, was it? It couldn't be something that simple, could it?"

"No. The Beast was able to draw the energies thanks to the wake, but he was only human. He could not contain them well enough. They nearly destroyed him . . . and almost tore apart the royal court in the process."

That surprised me. Her Lady's Court had always struck me as

something eternal, something capable of outlasting even Feirie's ruler. "The Court, too. You were there, then, weren't you? I mean exactly when it all came down."

"Yes."

There was that glance at Claryce again. Now I knew. He'd lied to me before. Claudette'd been there at the climax, too. Been there and died.

I had no intention of saying anything in front of Claryce. We had Holmes to worry about, anyway, and very little time left, if I understood Kravayik correctly. Holmes clearly thought that he'd come up with a way to enable his mortal shell to contain the energies stirred up by the Frost Moon's wake.

"Fetch, take a peek outside and see if any of Holmes's goons are paying attention to over here."

"Yes, Master Nicholas!" He quickly trotted off, perhaps moving a little faster so as to try to help me forget what I—or more likely Claryce—had seen.

"Nick, we need to get Oliver out of here. I won't leave him in danger."

"You heard her, Kravayik. If Fetch gives us the all clear, you help her get him to his car. Then, I want both of you to drive off until you can drop him safely somewhere—"

"I'm not leaving you!" she protested.

"Only way to help him," I pointed out. "Fetch and I'll follow them. We'll stay hidden unless there's absolute reason to do something."

She frowned, but she knew I was right. It made no sense for all of us to carry Oliver off, and I wasn't about to leave the hunt for Holmes to Kravayik.

Fetch came back. "They're in the building across, in the store where we fought the Wyld."

"Yeah, I thought so. We'll slip out the back. Lon—"

Her Lady's enforcer had slipped out on us. I swore. For all I knew,

Lon had every intention of swooping in on the gang and ripping them apart until it forced Holmes's location from one of them. He'd expect that I might not like that and had made certain to leave before I could order him to not slaughter everything in sight.

"Claryce. Kravayik. Take Oliver. Fetch, to me."

I didn't bother to see if anyone obeyed. I knew that Claryce would never leave Oliver where he was and Kravayik would not abandon her in turn. That last look he'd given her had not only verified his lies concerning Claudette's death, but one shocking truth I should've seen much earlier.

Kravayik'd loved her. Not Claryce, but Claudette. The supreme assassin of the Feirie Court had fallen for a human.

It explained a bit more about his abrupt and complete conversion to the Church. I'd always wondered how the events surrounding my own encounter with Kravayik had moved him so much that he'd forsaken his eternal existence and high station.

I knew then that he'd also been the one to see to her burial in Saint Boniface.

By this time, I was around the side of the building and coming back up near the one next to it. The path wasn't the straightest, but I had to sacrifice time for stealth.

Fetch kept pace at my side. He could've easily run ahead, but I couldn't afford him being noticed. The regular thugs weren't a problem, but I had no idea what I was facing in the twins. I still wondered where Holmes had picked up that pair. For some reason, they were two pieces that didn't seem to exactly fit.

When I was certain no one was looking, I crossed to the back of the building where once the Murder Castle stood. Once there, I paused and looked up.

"Show me," I whispered.

The dragon only grunted. As the world changed to emerald, I stared with disappointment at the nothingness above the storefront.

I'd wondered if maybe the fire hadn't actually destroyed Holmes's sanctum but that rather he had hidden his sanctuary through magic. Apparently not.

I heard murmuring inside. Disgruntled voices.

Oh, allow me this grand gesture . . . the dragon mocked.

The next second, I could hear the voices clearly. The conversation concerned money . . . and the lack of it, thanks to promises Holmes had apparently made to the men.

"Five days, we been promised!" roared one man. "Five days!"

"We been promised plenty of rubes, but we seen nothin' yet," added another. "And now Frankie's gone and the others are dead!"

That furious declaration was followed by a moment of silence . . . and then a low voice that I could barely make out even with the dragon's hearing hissed, "Your needsss . . . will be addresssed."

"Yeah, so you and your bookend brother keep sayin'!" the second hood went on. "We've talked it over, and if the bucks ain't comin', we're headin' back to Hymie and the gang."

"There will be no need for that. . . ."

I heard a click behind me. I turned to face a startled hood who'd clearly chosen somewhere in the back to answer nature. Cigarette in his mouth, he gaped at me, then moved his hands from his belt—the source of the click—and grabbed for an automatic in the left-hand pocket of his coat.

Fetch moved before I did, jumping the goon. The pair went flying, the goon landing hard on his back.

Unfortunately, in the process, the gun went off.

Fetch's prey let out a howl as the bullet tore a red valley in his thigh. Fetch did him the favor of whacking him hard on the side of the head, knocking him out.

Inside, the conversation turned into a collective shout. I heard a familiar clacking noise and ducked.

Evidently not at all caring what they hit, someone fired a tommy.

The door I was standing by and its surrounding walls were quickly perforated.

The firing went on for several seconds. I gave the gunman points for spreading out his shots. Two grazed me, one in my sword arm and the other in a leg. Both were painful, but didn't slow me much.

Hoping that Claryce and Kravayik would use the confusion to flee with Oliver, I pushed myself around the corner of the building. Now, I could hear the clatter as someone shoved open the door I'd just abandoned.

It said something that they weren't afraid such noise would bring the cops. I had no doubt that someone in the nearest station had been paid well to ignore any sounds out of the ordinary.

Without warning, someone stood in front of me. There'd been no door from which he could've jumped, and the next nearest corner was too far away. That was why it didn't surprise me to see that it was one of the twins. He'd popped in the same way he or his brother had done in the car during the chase.

Like previously, he also carried a dagger with a strange hollow point. He lunged at me, not at all caring that I had Her Lady's gift drawn.

Then, a piercing pain ran through the right side of my neck. I realized I'd been tricked by distraction.

But with a growl, Fetch buried his teeth in the leg of my second attacker. Twisting his head, Fetch put the other Schreck off-balance.

The twin in front of me abruptly backed away. Fetch let out a frustrated howl the reason for which I saw as I collapsed against the wall. The twin he'd brought down had vanished.

I wasn't surprised a moment later when I discovered his companion had disappeared, too.

But that still left us with a bunch of angry mobsters.

One hood came around the corner ahead. He took a shot with his automatic, but, like so many of his kind, didn't have the best aim from such a distance. I ignored him for the moment, more concerned with who was coming through the door behind me.

Sure enough, it was the tommy gunner. He was a thin Mick who hadn't shaved in days. The tommy looked huge in his hands, but he held it like someone who'd been using it for quite a while.

He fired another burst the moment he laid eyes on me. I threw myself against the opposing building as the rain of bullets reached me. Another one caught my shoulder. I grimaced, but turned on the gunman.

The tommy gunner shifted stance. I knew I'd miscalculated. He compensated for my speed and fired.

This time, I took several bullets.

I should've been dead. I *would've* been dead, but the dragon reacted instantly. His power forced most of the bullets from my—our—body, sending them flying in several directions. At the same time, he worked to quickly heal me.

The tommy gunner gasped. I lunged the final distance, swinging at the same time.

Her Lady's gift sliced off more than half the submachine gun's barrel. The goon instinctively let go of the weapon even though it probably would've still functioned well enough at this range.

I slugged him. I tried never to use Her Lady's gift on humans, however vile they might be. I'd always had the suspicion that any human life it took meant it sucking the person's soul into its blade. I was fine with that when it came to the Wyld, who had no souls—just spirits—but not with humans.

Which didn't mean that it hadn't happened a few times over the centuries. Now and then, I was given no choice.

As the gunner fell, I stopped and groaned. The dragon had quickly done what he could, but there were still bullets lodged in me and they were wreaking hell on my body. I fell against the wall, suddenly barely able to keep my grip on the sword.

Fetch came to my side. I expected him to force his muzzle under my arm so that I could lean on him, but instead, after a brief growl, he took hold of me with *hands*.

"Forgive me, Master Nicholas," he rumbled.

"Not . . . exactly in any condition . . . to complain." I let him guide me along the wall. "Get me to—"

"Geez!" Another mobster, his automatic already pointed at us, gaped at Fetch. He was too far away for either of us to reach before he could fire, but near enough that even he could get a good bead on whoever moved.

Another hood, this one with a hooked nose and a thick, orange-red brow of hair, joined him. He didn't look as startled as the first. Like the crook at my feet, he carried a tommy.

"Don't stand there gapin'!" the second man snarled, his voice the first of those to raise a complaint inside. "They'll bleed like the others, remember? Just fire!" He aimed the tommy.

"Yeah, yeah!"

Fetch roared and threw me behind him, but before anything else could happen, a shadow spread behind the two mobsters.

Lon.

One side of the cloak, which I was beginning to believe was an actual part of the Feir'hr Sein, draped over the thug with the automatic. He vanished in the darkness without a sound.

The second hood realized something was happening behind him. He spun around, trying to fire at the same time.

One deathly pale hand thrust out, seizing him by the throat and slamming him against the wall. He dropped the tommy as he hit. His eyes bulged as Lon brought his murky face close.

As the Feir'hr Sein moved in on the second hood, the cloak unfurled from the first. A pile of dust that I realized was all that remained of the one thug scattered. A clatter on the ground proved to be the automatic and several tiny items, including buttons and other bits of metal.

"Lon!" I shouted.

The Feir'hr Sein pressed his ghoulish face against the mobster's. The crook tried to shriek . . . and Lon poured *into* his throat.

It took only a single breath. Suddenly, the thug straightened. He quietly turned to look at me.

For a brief moment, the monstrous eyes of the Feir'hr Sein shone through.

A siren screamed. Someone'd called the cops.

"Fetch!"

"Yes, Master Nicholas." He began shrinking. His hands and arms became paws and forelegs. In a moment, he was once more a four-legged beast.

I took my attention off Lon for just a second when Fetch began changing. I knew I'd made a mistake, but by the time I looked back, the Feir'hr Sein was already gone. He had a new body with which to move among mortals.

Shots rang out up front. A tommy chattered.

Something dropped on my foot. Glancing down, I saw one of the bullets I knew had come from my body. Another popped out of my chest, landing on the ground next to the first.

I felt as if a weight'd been lifted from me.

You are very welcome. . . .

"Thanks," I muttered to him. "I mean that."

Try not to get us killed so quickly again, then. . . .

I couldn't argue with him. It exerted both of us a lot when he had to do this. There was always that shared concern that one day we might not have the strength. For all we'd been through, neither of us was ready to accept death without a fight.

I doubted that Claryce'd managed to find somewhere from which to call the police. There'd been no working telephone in the building where we'd confronted Oliver, and I thought I knew Claryce well enough to think she'd see to his life first. Therefore, someone *else* had called.

The gunfire continued, mostly from the outside, I noticed. I was fine with letting the cops deal with Holmes's human goons. With Fetch trailing me, I sheathed Her Lady's gift and headed around the opposite direction. I cursed the fact that I'd parked the Packard nearby. Still, maybe the cops hadn't noticed it yet in the heat of battle.

When I thought I was far enough away, I headed back toward the street. Fetch started to move ahead of me, but I blocked him with one hand and he fell back in place behind me.

Then, Lon—or rather, the body the Feir'hr Sein wore—backed into sight. He put one hand behind him, and I saw the fingers twist until they became the clawed appendages of Her Lady's enforcer.

A figure holding a gun on the Feir'hr Sein—a gun that would do no good against the creature—stepped into view. As it did, Lon's hand briefly shut, then opened.

A small sphere of black energy formed in the palm. I didn't need sixteen hundred years dealing with Feirie to know just how wicked a thing Lon'd just created.

And only then did I see that the figure holding the gun on Lon and entirely unaware of the incredible danger he was in was none other than Detective Alejandro Cortez.

CHAPTER 21

" I've got a perfect shot on you! You don't want to do this, Bo, you know?" Cortez shouted to what he thought was just a minor hood. "Hands up!"

The Feir'hr Sein started to move the hand with the sphere.

I had no choice. "No, Lon!"

The head jerked slightly in my direction. The sphere faded away, and the hand reverted to human.

That solved one problem, but not the other. Fortunately, Cortez took care of that by jerking his eyes from the Feir'hr Sein to me. It was barely for the blink of an eye, but that was enough for Lon even in his borrowed form.

Still, Cortez reacted pretty quickly to the Feir'hr Sein, returning his gaze to Lon and firing.

Firing at nothing.

"Easy, Cortez!" I called, moving toward him. "He's not one of them."

"Nick Medea . . ." The detective didn't look very pleased with me, not that that was any surprise. "You do pop up in the oddest places, you know?"

"Not so odd for me, Cortez. I came down here for that client I mentioned earlier. Planned on giving them the story you reminded me of, the Beast of Chicago, remember?"

"Yeah, the Beast." Despite the acknowledgement of what we'd discussed, Cortez continued to eye me with more than his usual level of suspicion. "You just happen to be here when these hoods decided to gather, eh?"

I raised a hand. "I can swear by Our Lady of Guadalupe that I didn't plan on them being here."

He frowned, clearly debating on just what to believe. Farther away, the sounds of gunfire began subsiding. From the detective's calm demeanor, I wagered he was pretty certain as to the outcome. "Yeah. All right. I got enough to do without more questions that aren't going to get me anywhere, you know?" He lowered his gun. "But I got one I do want to ask you. You call and let us know this batch was here?"

"With what phone?"

"Yeah, yeah, there is that. So, not you. Funny." He holstered his gun and pulled out his Luckys. "Funny. . . ."

"What's so hilarious?" Cortez was definitely no fool. I was curious what he had in mind, just in case it might end up being a clue to my own situation.

"Well . . . maybe it was a squealer, you know? Someone doing a double-cross on the gang. Had that happen once. Might explain the suddenness of the call, eh?"

Someone shouted from the direction of the gun battle. Cortez and I looked back. A capped officer came running.

Cortez stored the Luckys away and pulled out his service weapon again. "What's going on?"

"They're all dead!"

The detective frowned. "They didn't surrender?"

"Didn't have a chance, sir." The cop was another young one. He didn't hesitate on the "sir" like maybe the sergeant at the station might've. "When they stopped firing, we moved in . . . and found the rest of them dead."

"Let's see this. Nick Medea, I want you with me."

I couldn't very well argue, but then again, I was pretty curious as to what'd happened. At first, I'd thought maybe Michael'd called, but this didn't sound like something he *might've* done. Maybe Holmes had ended up doing what I would've thought he'd do in the first place . . . cleaning house of burdensome servants . . . but I couldn't help thinking there was more to it than that.

When we got to the spot, no one questioned my being there. I found that odd, also. Once again, I considered the strange position Cortez appeared to have in the Chicago Police Department. He had no fixed beat unless you counted the entire city, and his cases seemed to be all the peculiar, even sinister, ones that'd make or break most other cops' careers.

"So, there across the street is where Miss Simone met Bond?" he asked as we walked.

"Yeah."

"Heard from him since?"

"She would've told you, Cortez."

He chuckled. "You, not her."

"Ah. No. I would've told you, too."

"Yeah, I suppose you would've. Think these poor fools had something to do with him?"

I was saved from responding by the horrific scene we encountered inside. Six bodies lay sprawled in various positions inside the building. I could see that one near the door—his hand still on the chopper he'd been firing—had probably been shot down by the cops, but the rest lay too far inside. It would've taken quite the marksman outside to hit any of them.

Two cops stepped aside from the nearest body as we entered. One nodded to Cortez.

"Got a meat wagon on the way?"

"Yeah. Two." The politeness of the first officer was noticeably lacking with this one.

Cortez gestured to the street. "Wait for them in your car."

They left without a word, the young cop following. Cortez and I walked to one of the bodies in the center. The hood stared sightlessly at the ceiling.

How lovely a scene . . . the dragon commented. *But such a waste of good flesh . . . such a shame. . . .*

I fought back any sign of my disgust with his clear longing for a snack from the corpses.

"You see anything like this in your business?" Cortez asked. "You know, sacrifices and all that spooky stuff?"

"Exactly what do you think I see in my business, detective? I help clear people's minds of any fear that there might be a ghost in their house, that's all."

"You really make a living doing that?" Instead of waiting for an answer, he bent down to the dead hood. There were two bullet holes in the chest. If one followed the line from the body to the shattered store window, it would've made sense that he'd been shot by the cops.

A well-worn revolver lay by his side. Cortez plucked out a hand-kerchief and gingerly picked up the weapon. He sniffed the barrel, then set the piece down.

"Don't suppose they really need the fingerprints," he muttered as he stood, "but some things get to be a habit, you know? Been fascinated by fingerprints since I was a kid. You around here when the Jennings case took place? Thomas Jennings? About, oh, dozen or so years ago?"

"Don't know it." I only half paid attention to his ramblings. I was noting something on the body that, with the bullet holes, made me see this scene in an entirely new light.

"It was fingerprints that did him in, you know? He tried to fight it, but they proved he did it! First big case like that. I think that's what really made me want to join the force. Fingerprints! You ever been fingerprinted, Nick Medea?"

"No." When I'd first heard about the technique, I'd made certain to avoid any situation where I'd end up fingerprinted. That didn't mean I hadn't come close. Some of Cortez's predecessors had taken too much interest in me at times.

"No," he repeated. "Never got a shot off, this one." The detective stared at the body. "Didn't bleed too much, either." He looked up, then surveyed the rest of the interior. "Not much blood anywhere besides the stiff by the door."

That was one of the things I'd been noticing. So far, though, he hadn't seen the other clue. Even if he did, I didn't think he'd be able to make anything of it.

At least, I hoped not.

"Do you really need me here, Cortez? Not much I can add to what you're saying."

"No. Thought you might." He waved toward the door. "Yeah, you're free to leave, Bo! Just let me know if you hear anything from or about our friend Bond, okay?"

"You'll be the first I call."

He chuckled, then, no longer paying attention to me, bent down to inspect another body. As I left, I caught sight of him looking at the right side of the throat.

Exactly where I'd noticed the other clue. A tiny prick on the throat. I'd been able to see two other bodies well enough to spot the same mark on them.

And even though I'd not seen my own throat at the time, I knew that these would've matched it.

Fetch was waiting for me in the Packard. He was very silent as I entered. I knew why. "Relax. You did good back there."

"Thank ye, Master Nicholas."

I started up the Packard, then tried again with him. "Did you notice anything strange after we separated?"

"I smelled . . . something."

His tone was such that I had to glance at him. "What does that mean?"

Fetch's ears flattened. "It . . . makes no sense. I'm balled up about it. . . ."

"Just tell me."

He sniffed. "I'd almost swear . . . it seemed . . . it smelled a bit like *ye*!"

"Explain."

"I cannot. It is ye and it *isn't* ye! It . . . it also smelled like Feirie! And . . . it also smelled human!"

"I *am* human."

The dragon took offense. *We are not . . . entirely . . .*

"I know, I know," Fetch continued, almost whining. "I did not even want to say something. . . ."

"Where did you smell this?"

"All over, but especially above."

I frowned. "'Above'? You mean above the stores?"

"Aye."

There was nothing above the store. I'd looked. "That's it?"

"Yes, Master Nicholas."

We drove on in silence for some time; then, I made a sudden turn.

"Are we not going back to Mistress Claryce?"

"Yeah, but first I need to go somewhere I don't want her to be."

He stifled a growl. "Ye are heading to the Gate, aren't ye?"

The dragon hissed. *Ever the fool running in . . . just what started this whole thing between us, oh noble saint. . . .*

"Quiet," I muttered. To Fetch, I replied, "Yes. To the Gate. It's time she and I had a better talk about just what she thinks she's doing . . . and why she's not going to do it or else."

"Ye are going to make an ultimatum of Her Lady?" This time, Fetch did growl. "She's a real bearcat, that one, Master Nicholas! Ye certain ye want to dare that?"

"No," I replied as we headed toward Lake Michigan. "But I've got to do it nevertheless."

When I'd fought Oberon long ago and in the process unleashed the dragon on Chicago in what humans knew as the Great Fire and what Feirie called the Night the Dragon Breathed, one of the lingering troubles had been the Gate sealing itself just off the shore of Lake Michigan. No longer would the portal gradually shift ever westward, as it had for all the sixteen centuries before.

I drove to the Municipal Pier, the closest location to where the Gate stood. I parked and then started toward the icy, yet still-choppy waters.

Fetch leapt out.

"You can stay here," I told him.

"Nay. I'll be going with ye. Ye be a real hard-boiled one, Master Nicholas, but ye need someone to watch your back there."

"Okay. Thanks."

Leave him here . . . we do not need the mutt. . . .

Instead of answering the dragon, I eyed the lake. The weather as it was, there was no one else around. That hardly mattered. Such was the Gate that no one would see what happened next. Instead, for them the weather would shift and a fog or clouds would obscure the truth.

I drew the sword. The ice on the lake cracked and crunched and swiftly began to reshape itself. A column rose into the air and arched out over the lake.

In the column, a path formed.

I stepped onto the path, then thought, *Open the way.*

As I started walking, stars formed ahead. They swirled, then coalesced into a towering, ethereal arch.

The Gate . . . or rather, its least glorious incarnation. If I'd needed to, I could've summoned its full glory, but that might've risked discovery. For my journey into Feirie, this was sufficient.

I maybe took a dozen steps . . . and then ankle-high dark green grass rose beneath my feet and huge, twisted oaks formed around me.

Fetch growled. I pointed the sword tip toward the trees on our right. The blade flared. It'd already begun glowing the moment we entered Feirie, but now it blazed bright.

"Step out. I won't ask again."

Instead of something slipping from behind the huge trunks, part of one *trunk* peeled away. A thing of rough wood with long, sharp fingers resembling small branches peered down at us. It had a crown of "hair" consisting of foliage. I couldn't see any eyes, but I could see the broad, jagged mouth in which I knew there'd be thorny, pointy teeth capable of rending flesh. Its body was broad and boxy, and the bent legs ended in lengthy toes resembling clawed roots.

Legends to the contrary, wood nymphs weren't very pretty.

They were also lethal. Often, the female aspects of Feirie were worse than the males. More so now that Her Lady was fully in charge.

Such pretty wood . . . let us see how readily she burns. . . .

His suggestion was tempting, but I passed. I'd had no bouts of fury lately, and I suspected it was because I'd tried not to rely on him any more than necessary. I'd figured out at last that these bouts weren't exactly accidental. No, the dragon had been testing me, trying to find that moment when he could take total control now and forever. Like Fetch, his power'd increased with the wake's wild growth.

I hadn't said anything, and I'd blocked off those thoughts from him, but I suspected he knew I was on to him. That was the way it was between us, an eternal war for dominance with moments of tentative alliance when others tried to do us in.

And sometimes, even those dangers weren't enough to keep him from trying to betray me.

"Tell your mistress to not play games. She knows I'm here. Let's not waste time."

To my surprise, the dryad laughed. It was a particularly feminine laugh . . . and a familiar one that made Fetch growl and even the dragon hiss.

The wood nymph melted into Her Lady.

I waited for the Court to form, but there was only the queen of

Feirie. She brushed a long lock of hair from her gloriously ivory skin and gave me that smile.

Her darling Gatekeeper . . . such a pleasant surprise. . . .

What was surprising was this peculiar encounter. Her Lady'd rarely met me outside of her Court. She liked to show off her power.

Burn her . . . my constant companion suggested.

"He doesn't trust this fine greeting," I told her, not needing to bother to tell her who I meant. "For once, I'm inclined to believe him. I suspect you've ordered your subjects far from here. Am I right?"

She no longer stood in front of me, but rather on my left. On my very *near* left.

Dear, dear Gatekeeper . . . so untrusting. . . . Why would I have anything but the greatest gratitude toward you? You have given me my kingdom. . . .

That wasn't exactly the conversation I'd just started, but that was the way with those of Feirie. They ever sought to manipulate matters in their favor, especially if they were trying to evade.

"Yes, Oberon is dead, but Lysander isn't. Still, this isn't entirely about Lysander, is it? He's a threat, but also a bit of distraction, right? You've been playing a dangerous game, haven't you?"

Feirie is all games . . . she replied without ever moving her full lips. They remained inviting, of course. *And Feirie is all serious. Very serious games, Gatekeeper . . . humans excel at such, too, you know. The Beast, he plays a strong, manipulative game worthy of the Court. . . .*

I kept my ground even though she leaned perilously close. Her Lady was inherently magic, and that magic included her power of seduction. She hadn't succeeded with me thus far, but she couldn't help herself.

"You seem to know the Beast well," I returned. Some more things were making sense. Kravayik hadn't known the entire truth. He'd been sent to stop a threat against Feirie, not realizing that the threat had also come *from* Feirie. "That must've been troubling, discovering you'd been outfoxed by a lowly human."

Suddenly, she stood against one of the oaks farther to my right.

She still wore that look of enticement, but I'd had sixteen hundred years to decipher her, and while she was still very much an enigma, I *had* figured out a couple of her tendencies. After Oberon's initial exile, Her Lady'd prided herself on being able to control all situations and foresee the treacheries of men.

But once again, she'd been outwitted.

The lives of many humans have come and gone since your servitude, Her darling Gatekeeper, so many lifetimes, so many deathtimes . . . never in that time have you seen Feirie in all her glory. . . .

"Never been interested." It was true. To me, Feirie'd always been a threat and a burden.

Now she hovered over me again, but nearer to Fetch. He snarled and, without hesitation, transformed.

The once-faithful one . . . Her Lady cooed into my ear. *Her darling Gatekeeper gathers around him Her once-most trusted servants . . . such a loyalty is so very hard to nurture either here or in the human realm. . . .*

"Have a care, Master Nicholas," Fetch growled, his voice deeper and more menacing than I'd heard it since we'd first met. "This isn't jake in the least!"

For once, she turned her attention away from me to him. *Oh, sweet Fetch, so wild, so free . . . once . . . You could be my favored again. . . .*

"Thank ye for offering again, but I'm still rather keen on staying where I am. A bit more . . . pleasant."

Her attention immediately reverted to me. Her long, smooth fingers grazed my neck before I could stop her.

We all underestimate the Beast . . . she went on. *You have not seen Feirie. You should see Feirie. . . .*

A wind swirled around us.

"Have a care, Master Nicholas!" Fetch repeated furiously.

Too late. The wind pulled both Her Lady and me into the air. Fetch snatched at me and for a moment caught my foot. A shift in the wind—intentional, no doubt—shook him off.

Eye can save us! Let me out! Let me out!

Rage filled me, a rage at Her Lady for attempting this kidnapping. The rage became uncontrollable . . . and the dragon took command.

Or rather, he *attempted* to take command.

Something went terribly wrong. I felt my face stretch and my limbs twist. Pain in my back became a pair of vestigial wings that struggled to spread.

We were caught between our two selves, our minds sharing equally yet unable to do anything because our body couldn't accept a command from either of us.

Torn free from her magical grasp by our efforts, we spiraled help-lessly. As we did, I caught glimpses of Feirie.

Or what was left of it.

I'd always understood that the magical realm itself consisted of endless forest bordered by towering mountains. Not once had I ever had any inclination to know more. There was an adage among those who knew of Feirie that to probe its secrets, even those of its very exis-tence, was to risk being seduced by its sinister beauty.

And to be seduced was to become its eternal slave.

But now . . . now I wished I'd taken a better glance at *some* point in all these centuries. I knew that what I kept glimpsing as we plum-meted couldn't be normal, not even for a fluid place such as Feirie.

Far on the horizon, the endless forest *ended*. Just like that. It was as if I'd beheld the mythical edge of the world in the mortal realm. While that wasn't possible there, here, where Feirie was magic, such an edge *could* exist . . . but shouldn't have.

And now, as we continued to drop toward the ground at an alarming rate, I understood what she'd wanted me to see. Of course, Her Lady couldn't just tell me what was happening; she'd had to use typical Feirie manipulation. Never mind that from what I saw, she clearly needed my help.

Not that I could do much. Whatever Holmes'd started, it was literally tearing Feirie apart. The magic that was Feirie was being drawn into the Gate and into whatever spell he'd begun.

Then, all concern I had for Feirie vanished as we watched the ground rush up to our face. It was not going to be a soft landing. We both knew it was going to be very, very painful.

And it was.

CHAPTER 22

"Shall we see what limitations there are?"

I screamed. . . . Only my scream came out in a different voice. A female voice.

"Now, now," murmured the speaker. "It can't be that low. You should be able to muster a little more strength . . . even summon a little power?"

All I could do was scream again in that same feminine voice.

A sigh escaped my unseen tormentor. The sigh was followed by a horrible increase in my agony.

"No. Not much better."

A face came at me out of the darkness.

Holmes. The Beast.

He had an almost clinical detachment in his expression, which made his appearance all the more monstrous. I could not only see the evil that was him, but I could feel it as well.

"Well . . . he was right after all. You are *all he promised."*

There was something different. This wasn't some memory, as I realized the previous moment'd been. This was now.

"The pound of flesh was worth it, then, I suppose," Holmes muttered almost distastefully.

His mustached face grew distorted as it filled my vision. He smiled at me.

I tried to lunge at him. I couldn't even tell if I moved at all, but suddenly his face receded.

Holmes chuckled. "Impressive. You'll last better than the others. You will *enable me to succeed at last—"*

From behind the Beast arose whispers, warning whispers. I couldn't understand the warning, but still sensed that they were trying to alert me to something about Holmes.

Instead of being disturbed by the warnings, he just laughed again. "Ah, you've woken them up. Almost forgot they were still there. Well, this should put an end to their whimpering."

His hand reached out of the darkness toward me.

Nick . . .

I knew that voice. I knew it so well.

Nick . . . please!

Claryce?

Nick . . . Georgius . . . listen to me. . . .

Holmes lost his good humor. "Now that's not a nice thing to do. . . ."

He stretched his hand closer—

Nick!

A sharp pain struck me in the heart. The dragon hissed as he shared my agony.

Nick!

The pain repeated.

Holmes's face vanished. The darkness scattered—

With a gasp, I tried to rise.

"I have him!" said Fetch from somewhere. Strong hands seized me by the shoulders.

I suddenly felt very, very cold.

Eye will . . . warm . . . us . . . the dragon said from what seemed far, far away.

But nothing happened.

"He's shivering, Fetch! Quick! Let's get him into the car!"

"I will carry him."

I shook, not only from the cold, but from Fetch evidently lifting me. I wanted to warn him to be careful that no one saw him, but couldn't form the words.

I must've passed out. The next thing I knew I was bouncing lightly in what I had to assume was Claryce's Wills. The cold had begun to recede, for which I was grateful. It hadn't been due to the dragon, though, but rather a slightly musty furred form lying against me.

"How is he?"

"Still not ducky, Mistress Claryce, but better. I think he's trying to wake up."

"Try to rest, Nick," she called. "Don't fight it."

"Gate . . ." I blurted.

"What's he saying, Fetch?"

"I think he believes he's still near the Gate. He does not know."

"We'll explain later, Nick," she answered me. "Just rest."

I didn't argue with her. I couldn't have even if I wanted to.

I vaguely remembered bouncing around a couple of times. I also recalled feeling cold briefly, but then becoming comfortably warm.

I slept . . . and so, naturally, I dreamed.

Once more, I rode my horse into battle against the dragon. In the distance, I saw Cleolinda standing behind him, her wrists manacled. This time, though, she was dressed in clothes more current to the times of the Columbian Exposition.

The dragon was sleeping when first I started riding toward him, but now he raised his head toward me. He opened his huge jaws . . . and his head became that of Kravayik.

"I am so sorry, Master Nicholas!" he roared.

My mount reared. I brought the spear up.

"Nick."

The dream faded. I used the voice to help me fight to consciousness.

Claryce's face came into view. I focused on it as best I could.

"Oh, Nick!" She leaned down and kissed me. It was as much a kiss of relief as anything, but it was just what I needed to keep awake.

"What . . . how did you find me?" I asked when she pulled back.

"*Fetch* called me."

"On the telephone?"

"Yes." She smiled at the thought. "I haven't had a chance to ask him how he managed that."

"I'm amazed he was able to drag me from Feirie and onto the pier."

"You weren't at the pier, Nick. You weren't anywhere near the lakefront."

"What's that mean?" I very distinctly recalled hitting the ground. I searched inside for the dragon and just barely felt his presence. It was surprising we were in as good a shape as we were. It was a surprise we were in any shape at all.

"First . . . if you ever go into Feirie again without me you'll wish it was Her Lady all you had to worry about. Don't *ever* do that. Understand me?" After I dutifully nodded—but didn't promise—she went on. "Fetch told me about how the encounter with her started and that damned trick she played on you."

"We were prepared for something to happen."

"You mean you and—him?" Claryce pointed at my head. "The two of you didn't do so well."

Inside, the dragon snarled halfheartedly.

"Second, from what Fetch told me, after you rose into the sky, you began to transform. Something went wrong, though. You started to fall while you were still trying to change. And then . . . and then . . . what Fetch said. It looked like the Gate opened up in reverse around you just as you hit the ground."

Despite the pain still coursing through me, that last comment pushed me to a sitting position. "Looked like what?"

"You heard me. He couldn't explain it any better save that it also seemed more like a shadow, maybe. He can explain later. He's gone after Kravayik. Fetch said that Kravayik owes you."

I didn't argue that point. "So, where did I end up?"

"West Sixty-Third Street. Near where Bond—sorry, Holmes—built that monstrosity."

"You're joking. There *again*?"

"Wish I was." She moved away from me. "Think you can eat something?"

I couldn't tell if it was my stomach that grumbled just then or the dragon stirring to life. Either way, I nodded. "Thanks."

"Just rest while I get you a sandwich and some soup. Oh, while you were asleep, I imposed on an old friend of mine in order to get the Packard back here. I didn't think you wanted to call Barnaby about it."

"No, you're right. Thanks. You've done more than enough. More than you should've."

"I did what had to be done, Nick. Now rest more. I'll be back shortly."

I laid back down on what I finally realized was her bed. The soft cotton sheets threatened to send me back to dreamland, but I tried to stay awake so that I could analyze all that'd happened. I knew that Holmes was near to completing his spell, but what worried me as much was the mere fact that he'd had some control over us at the time.

My head cleared enough that I finally figured out how. The prick I'd felt on my throat. Small wonder the daggers had that hollow point. It'd been used to draw blood or something else from me. That'd given Holmes the ability to reach out and attack the dragon and me.

But there had to be more to it than that. If he'd simply wanted to destroy us, there were easier ways than what we'd faced—

Someone whispered from my left, away from the door through which Claryce'd just gone.

When I looked, I saw no one. Still, I couldn't help feeling like I wasn't alone.

You never are. . . .

I ignored the dragon's sarcasm. Pushing myself up, I stared at the tall, glossy waterfall dresser with the rounded edges as if for some reason it would start moving. I couldn't help feeling that there was something near the dresser that I just wasn't seeing.

Seeing. I searched for the dragon. He'd receded into the back of my mind again after his remark. I finally understood that it had more to do than just with his own exhaustion. He knew I recognized that, just like Fetch, he'd been able to make use of the Frost Moon's wake. Unlike Fetch, though, he'd tried to use it to drive me to an unthinking fury strong enough for him to seize permanent control. Now, he was acting like a petulant child.

Acting like *I* was at fault.

Again, I thought I heard a whisper.

"Let me see," I murmured.

Eye . . . will let you see . . . he finally answered.

The world turned emerald . . . and revealed nothing.

No. There was movement. A shadow of a shadow. I focused on where I'd seen it.

Just as I needed to blink, I caught sight of a figure. It looked human. I had to stare again, waiting. As before, only when I finally had to blink did I see it ever so briefly.

A man. He wore an outfit outdated by several decades. He also wore a look of immense distress, as if something awful was about to befall him.

And that was it. He was there, and then he wasn't. I stared at the spot for several seconds, but there was no reappearance.

"Are you all right?"

My eyes shifted to human. Claryce came in carrying a wooden tray with a sandwich and a small bowl from which rose steam and the scent of chicken soup. My stomach rumbled, and I sensed the dragon's eagerness to have us feed.

"I need to clean up a few things. You just go ahead and eat."

"What about you?"

"I ate while you were sleeping. It kept me from going crazy waiting for you to wake up, at least for a few minutes."

I purposely stared at the neatly cut ham and Swiss cheese sandwich. "Sorry about that."

She sighed. "Eat."

Alone again, I dug into the sandwich. The first half went down quickly. The soup was boiling hot, but to someone who'd breathed fire, that was fine.

The first spoonful'd barely gone down when I heard more whispers.

The dragon didn't even wait for me to ask. The room emerald once more, I looked at the spot where I'd seen the phantasm, but saw nothing . . . until there was movement at the very edge of my vision.

This time, I didn't try to track the movement, but rather immediately looked ahead of it where I thought it might go.

A young woman pleaded to the empty air before her, her eyes as wide as the plate the sandwich had come on. She had on a faded brown dress from near the turn of the century.

In the midst of her pleading, she looked directly at me.

It wasn't just a trick of the angle. She saw me. She pleaded with *me* now.

And behind her, the man I'd seen earlier looked back at me, too. Although he simply stood there, I could sense the same despair, the same desperation, that filled her.

Then, the *rest* of them appeared.

I couldn't say how many. Two dozen. More. More unsettling than even their imploring faces were the murky shades that started to flicker in and out of existence within the gathering. They weren't exactly ghosts, as I believed these others were, but some essence of other creatures.

Can you not smell them? Can you not smell Feirie upon them?

I couldn't smell anything from any of my sudden visitors, much less the shades. Still, if they were of Feirie, I could only think that they were the essences of elves, spirits in a different sense than ghosts. Although having no souls, Feirie folk had a sentient magical essence.

A ghost is a ghost is a ghost, the dragon replied with cynicism. *We are haunted by ghosts, both human and elven. . . .*

He had a point. There was no need differentiating between specters. What was important was why they were suddenly massing around me. There were far more ghosts than I could recall ever coming across in all my centuries. Curiously, most were dressed as if from the past four or five decades—

I nearly spilled the soup as I rose from the bed. No matter how hard I tried, I still couldn't focus on any individual one for more than a breath, but there was always some figure present. Over and over they verified the two things, that they were from the same span of time and were all facing some tremendous horror. Even the murky shadows of the Feirie folk hinted at dismay.

The article we'd found concerning Holmes's execution had guessed the number of his victims. Sometimes, those kinds of articles bordered on utter conjecture, granting fiends such as the Beast of Chicago a far darker infamy than they deserved.

But this time . . . this time it was clear that only the wildest estimates had come close. What haunted me were Holmes's victims. All of them, as far as I could see.

I'd never heard of such a mass haunting, and at first I couldn't see how I'd been sought out by them. Ghosts weren't supposed to be so independent; Diocles could only materialize in holy places, and generally beyond Saint Michael's he could only form if I was present. He was bound to me . . . or I was bound to him. Either way, what little I knew of ghosts insisted that they were tied to something concerning their lives or their deaths, but especially the latter—

And that was when I clutched the side of my throat at the spot where I'd been jabbed not once but twice by hollow-tipped daggers.

That was when I realized not only just how complex Holmes's plan was, but the extent of which it'd already progressed.

Each time, those daggers had stolen some of my blood or essence. Maybe both. Either way, Holmes had not only a touch of me, but a touch of the dragon. It'd enabled him to try to draw our power when we'd begun to change. Not believing in coincidence, I suspected that our transformation had been a point where he'd actually been able to affect us . . . and he'd taken that opportunity.

But as I'd discovered in the past, those who dabbled in the use of another's magic often created a path that stretched both directions. Now that link had brought these ghosts to me, at least momentarily.

I stretched a hand toward the swirling, shifting mass. I didn't know why. A compulsion that maybe'd originated from them. All I knew was that I desperately needed to reach into their midst—

And suddenly, I was inside the damned maze Holmes'd created. I flew through it, but not so quickly that I didn't make out visions of figures trapped and tortured all along the way. Most were female. Most were human, but all had suffered at least as much as the elf I'd come across when I'd been trapped. Aware of whom they were, I didn't have that much sympathy for the Feirie folk, but I saw no reason for their lingering pain either. Holmes'd earned his moniker; he was every bit the Beast in the monstrous sense. If I could've, I'd have cast every ghost to the afterlife or oblivion that should've come to them, but that wasn't possible.

Not, at least, while Holmes existed.

Without warning, I was thrust into another chamber deep in the midst of the maze. Without understanding how I knew it—except maybe through some influence of my spectral friends—I recognized the chamber as the focal point to the entire design. All the awful energies drawn from Holmes's victims gathered here and fed his work.

And fed *him*.

Small wonder Holmes'd been able to survive hanging and time.

He'd succeeded enough in his spellwork to preserve his existence, if not his life. "Survive" hadn't quite been the right word; he was as dead as anything . . . but he was trying to change that.

"Nick?"

The vision vanished. The ghosts faded away. I stood in Claryce's bedroom, my hand still stretched toward the wall.

"So," she remarked rather dryly. "Can I assume something just happened?"

Lowering my hand, I replied, "I think . . . I think I've been begged for help . . . and warned that things're going to get a lot worse."

"Do they really need to get worse? They're pretty awful as they are."

I grunted agreement. "Think on the level of Oberon, only without his grandiose vision of a lovely world made of both our realm and Feirie. Holmes only desires one thing . . . well, maybe two. He's existing in some sort of half state and wants to become fully alive again."

"He's bad enough as he is," Claryce returned with a shudder. "And the second thing?"

"I'm still not certain about that, only that it involves tremendous power, of course."

"Oh, of course. There always has to be that. How silly of me to forget."

I knew she found the situation as humorless as I did. Whatever spellwork the Beast'd begun, it demanded literal sacrifice on an ever-expanding scale.

There was a knock on the apartment door.

"Did you tell Fetch to *knock* when he came back?"

"No, but I suppose it would make sense."

"Yeah." For some reason, I didn't feel the same. For the first time, something else occurred to me. "My overcoat—"

"Shreds. Apparently it was ripped apart when you changed. I thought you had some spell that made it vanish or something."

"Or something. It should've." I gestured at my clothes. "Just like these. Either Holmes's spells or the power of the wake must've affected things. Then, the sword . . ."

She quickly shook her head. "Not to worry. Under the bed. I wanted to keep it close for you, but I couldn't set it next to you."

"How'd you get it?"

"*She* handed it back to him after you vanished from Feirie. Apparently without a word but a look that Fetch refuses to describe but indicated unnerved him."

"I'll bet." Her Lady'd probably been stunned by Holmes's abrupt attack within Feirie. I never could've believed it, but I really did think now that it was true. Instead of being the givers of nightmare, the Feirie folk now had a human-spawned nightmare of their own. And worse, Her Lady'd given that nightmare the initial access into the power of her realm.

It served her right, but such justice didn't help the overall threat to both realms. I quickly snapped the jeweled weapon from underneath the bed, then concentrated inward. *This should be an easy one for you. You've done it before.*

Would you prefer a prettier style? the dragon mocked. *Perhaps something . . . greener?*

"Just do it, damn you," I snarled without thinking.

"Do what? What are you so mad about?"

"Not you—" Before I could explain further, a warmth surrounded me.

"Oh. I see," Claryce murmured.

A coat identical to the one I'd lost now covered me. He'd even gone overboard and recreated my hat. Of course, this "gift" also included a wave of exhaustion that reminded me of my injuries.

They will heal in a moment. . . . There was no mockery this time. It behooved him to heal our wounds as quickly and efficiently as possible, and the fact that it'd taken this long said a lot as to how much

Holmes's spell'd drained us. That made me consider just how much energy it seemed to be taking not only for him to maintain his in-between state, but how much more he'd need to fully resurrect himself.

"Stay in here," I warned her. Naturally, she didn't listen, following me out of the room and heading toward a chair where her purse sat. I decided to wait until she had the Smith & Wesson out and ready. There'd been no more knocking, but I didn't know what that might mean.

Unfortunately, the apartment had no peephole, so the first thing I did was set my ear to the door. Yeah, that offered any wily figure outside the perfect chance to blow a hole not only in the door, but through me, but I had to take the chance.

The dragon didn't like my choices. *There is only so much Eye can do. . . .*

I didn't answer. Not hearing anything outside, I prepared to open the door. If it'd been some normal visitor, I'd have heard breathing or some other sound. Besides, from Claryce's earlier reaction, I knew that she hadn't expected anyone to show up. I didn't know what she'd finally done with Oliver, but I assumed he hadn't come to see her for any reason.

There was a slight click behind me. I glanced back to see Claryce with the gun pointed at the door and slightly to my left. I readied Her Lady's gift. If it turned out to be a normal human visitor, I could use a variation of the spell that made my clients forget me afterward to erase their memory. It was also akin to what I knew the Feir'hr Sein had utilized on Oliver on my behalf.

I swung open the door.

A figure stood before me, possibly the one I'd least expected to see.

"It's cresting," Joseph commented with a childlike smile.

CHAPTER 23

Joseph continued to smile and stare at me. I pulled him inside. He was dressed in a simple brown suit and white shirt that Barnaby'd probably bought for him, a suit not at all sufficient for the cold weather. His skin felt as cold as I would've expected from someone who'd been outside for a while.

Shutting the door, I brought Joseph to the couch. He didn't get the cue when I stood him near it, so I ended up manipulating him like a doll until I had him sitting.

Claryce had set aside her revolver and had gotten a wool blanket for Barnaby's son. She covered his shoulders with it. Joseph finally showed some life by pulling the blanket tighter. The grin didn't leave his face at any moment.

"Is this a trick?" Claryce asked. "Is there someone outside right now, do you think?"

"Don't see why Holmes would pull a stunt like this. Looks to me like Joseph slipped free."

"In his condition?"

I waved a hand in front of his face. He paid it no mind. He also hadn't blinked once since showing up. "Might be the only reason he was *able* to slip free. Holmes probably assumed he'd stay docile."

"What was that he said at the door? I didn't catch it."

"It's cresting," Joseph offered helpfully, making both of us start.

"Just that," I grumbled as the dragon snickered in my head. "He must be talking about the wake. Don't know if that's the right word for what it's doing, but either way, things're coming to a head."

She leaned close. "How did he know to come here? He's never been here before. Are you sure this isn't a trap?"

"Doubtful. I can't see this benefiting Holmes in the least." I snapped my fingers in front of Joseph, which finally got his attention. "As for how he got here, I think he sensed I was here. Joseph had innate skills. He could've been someone very great. Instead, he chose to try to become infamous."

"You still really, really despise him. I can hear it."

"I don't forget treachery easily. Diocles would vouch for that if you could hear him. Not too saintly, but that's me. The Joseph I chased six years ago deserved that loathing. Barnaby's the only reason I didn't leave him to die with the rest." I glared at him. "And if he doesn't want me to regret that decision even more than I already do, he'd better start saying something."

"The Beast rises within, the Beast rises without," Joseph promptly answered.

Eye could scare the truth out of him, if you let me . . . or we could perhaps burn him a little . . . just a little, I promise. . . .

"No thanks," I muttered. I knew right after I'd spoken that Claryce'd heard me, but she didn't say anything. She'd already become accustomed to my manner in that regard. A shame.

"Any idea what we should do with him? Should we bring him back to Dunning until Barnaby recovers?"

"I doubt there's time left. Besides, Joseph's our only clue to where Holmes is doing all this. We just need to get him to show us . . . somehow."

"'Somehow.'" Grimacing, Claryce grabbed her purse and started to put the revolver back inside.

Something dropped out of it. It hit the floor with a clatter, then rolled toward me.

Joseph's hand shot out. Whatever had fallen from the purse flew from the floor into his palm. He grinned as he looked at it.

"Shiny."

Startled by his use of magic, I almost dismissed his new toy.

Joseph'd been skilled, but he hadn't shown much ability since losing his mind. I wondered how long he'd had even this much power.

Then I got a good glimpse of the object.

The coin Cortez's Maria had asked him to give to Claryce. The coin . . . with the side honoring a certain saint on top.

"Michael . . ." Barnaby's son added cheerfully.

I fought back a curse. "You know Michael, Joseph? Is Michael a friend of yours?"

In response, Joseph rose. Clutching the medallion, he stared at the door.

I joined him. "Did Michael help you escape? Can he help you help me to find out where you were?"

Joseph flipped the coin as someone might to make a decision. I tried not to get suspicious. When he'd been himself, Joseph had on occasion liked to flip a coin while he thought. I stared into his eyes, but only saw the same emptiness I'd seen since after the crash.

"Nick, try opening the door. I've got my coat. If he does anything, we can follow."

It was certainly worth a try. No sooner had I done as she'd suggested than Joseph started out.

We followed. Joseph went to the street, then turned left.

I quickly grabbed his arm. "Let's drive, Joseph. It'll be fun."

He didn't give us any trouble as we led him to the Packard. There, though, I turned to Claryce. "I think we'd better make certain that Fetch and Kravayik meet us there. Go back up and call Holy Name at this number." I gave her the one I knew only he would answer. "Tell them that we'll pick them up there. I suspect that no matter where we drive from, Joseph'll be able to lead us to where he was held."

"All right." She hurried off.

"Into the car, Joseph," I encouraged him, giving Barnaby's son the front passenger seat. I quickly slipped around to the driver's side. The moment I was inside, I started the vehicle.

She will not like you tricking her like that. . . .

"It had to be done. I'm not going to apologize for it."

Did Eye say you should? Eye would have done the same. . . .

"Great." That made me regret my subterfuge even more. The last thing I wanted was approval by the dragon.

I drove around the nearest corner, then looked at Joseph. "Which way?"

He didn't answer. He didn't even look my way, but kept staring to his right. I took that as a hint and turned again. Sure enough, Joseph looked forward.

We drove for several minutes on the same street before Joseph found interest in our left. I did as he indicated. Once more, his attention returned to the path ahead.

I'd slept most of the day and part of the night since Claryce and Fetch had brought me back. We were now deep into the night, which meant little traffic. That hardly surprised me at all. Holmes would need to perform his spellwork at night, when the moon and energies were at their optimum. Magic, especially on the human side, could involve all sorts of necessities, which was why so few here could follow the craft to any useful level. Joseph, with his aptitude for calculating when the potential for success was greatest, had far outdone his father in the arts. Had he kept to what the unknowledgeable called the "white" side, he could've accomplished miraculous things.

"But you just couldn't, could you?" I blurted. "You had to have more and more, didn't you?"

Joseph said nothing. His grin wide, he stuck his head out the window. Never mind the chill wind. None of the weather appeared to bother him. I finally refrained from trying to pull him back in.

And then . . . we turned onto West Sixty-Third. Of course. I felt like I was caught on a merry-go-round with no end to the ride. I'd been here. I'd *just* been here. There was nothing.

Nothing.

I tested Joseph by pretending to turn right. He kept his gaze on Sixty-Third. That was enough to convince me that we were still on the right route . . . and that we were heading to the site of the old Murder Castle.

A short time later, we came within two blocks of what remained of the sinister structure. I pulled over and guided Joseph out.

He immediately started down the street. I followed closely, purposely letting him go his own way.

As he walked, he occasionally flipped the coin. He also began gazing into the sky. Once, he stopped and studied the air as if fascinated by something just above a building, but I couldn't figure out exactly what.

And slowly, very slowly, we edged toward what I was certain had to be our ultimate destination.

When he reached the street corner across from where Holmes had set up his torture and murder sanctum, I thought I might be wrong. Seeing it even in the dark of night did nothing to make it any more sinister. Perhaps once it'd been a place of the darkest evil, but now it was just another street, maybe only worse because of the gangland activity it'd just suffered. Of course, there weren't many streets in Chicago that could brag they were innocent of bloodshed these days. Even before O'Banion's murder in his flower shop, Chicago had seen a regular flow of blood, dating so far back as "Big Jim" Colosimo's mysterious death five years back. That would conveniently allow his second, "Papa Johnny" Torrio, to take over just as Prohibition was turning bootlegging into a lucrative enterprise that Colosimo supposedly had rejected.

The only signs of the slaughter of Holmes's dupes were some marks on the street and some bits of glass swept over to the curb from the shattered windows, which hadn't been boarded up yet. I watched Joseph as he looked from the ruined stores to the building where Claryce and I had met Holmes, and then farther down Sixty-Third as if seeing something there more interesting.

Eye will show you. . . .

The dragon's gaze smoothly overtook mine. Unfortunately, even then I couldn't make out just what so fascinated Barnaby's wayward son.

He then looked east, toward the general direction of Lake Michigan. At some point, he'd apparently pocketed the medallion. One hand suddenly went up and began drawing invisible symbols in the air. After a moment, I realized that Joseph was doing mental calculations. It was another surprising hint at just how active his mind was. I didn't like that. Right now, he might be like an innocent child, but I didn't want any chance of the original Joseph returning. If that even looked remotely like it might happen, then I'd probably have to do something for which Barnaby'd hate me forever. I wasn't about to let Joseph find himself again; the world couldn't risk that.

For several seconds, he continued to draw in the air. Then, he looked up again in the direction of the lake. After that, another glance farther down the street.

"What the hell're you looking at?" I growled as I rejoined him. "What?"

"The crest is coming. The shadow lingers while it grows," he responded simply, as if that answered everything.

He is madder than all Feirie. . . .

"Won't argue with you there. You aren't holding back anything, are you?" I asked the dragon with some suspicion.

Nothing. . . . Eye swear on our life. . . .

That didn't really assuage me, but I chose to take it as true. Holmes's spellwork had already proven a threat to not just me, but him. I knew him well enough to be fairly certain that now he wanted the Beast destroyed as much as I did, if for more personal reasons. He hardly cared about either realm. All that mattered was his existence, even as slight as it'd become since I'd slain his physical form.

Joseph lowered his hand and took a few steps down Sixty-Third. He nodded, then turned in a complete circle.

I grew more exasperated. I could imagine Holmes laughing at us. For all I knew, he might actually be doing that.

Trying not to let my frustration get the best of me, I grabbed Joseph by the shoulder. "Listen! If you—"

I stopped, stunned. The entire scene abruptly changed. Now, instead of just seeing the world as the dragon could, I was finally getting a glimpse at what Joseph was seeing.

A different Chicago greeted my widening eyes, a Chicago that had and hadn't existed since some three decades before. Updated buildings now reverted to what they'd surely been during the exposition. There were even faint figures of people moving back and forth, people dressed as I remembered the time. These, though, didn't strike me as active ghosts, but rather mere memories. Holmes's memories.

But there were two differences that made everything else pale in comparison. The first was the sky. A huge shadow hung over it, a shadow with a distorted but still recognizable arch to it.

The Gate. I was staring at some all but invisible *shadow* of the Gate. It stretched for miles, stretched farther than the Gate itself by far. It wasn't quite black or gray. There was a crimson edge to it that pulsed consistently and seemed to be growing in intensity each time.

And slowly . . . ever so slowly . . . it was moving across Chicago, enveloping more and more of it in the process. Wherever it touched, the same unsettling crimson edge outlined what I could see. It was so massive, we'd even driven under it a good part of the time. Hell, almost all of the time during our investigation of Holmes.

I silently cursed the Gate, cursed the Frost Moon, cursed my ever having ridden against the dragon. That last, in turn, rewarded me with a snort that resounded in my mind. He'd been guardian of the Gate long before my coming. Where I'd had to put up with it for centuries, he'd done so for millennia.

And then, even the great shadow . . . created by the Frost Moon's wake, I had no doubt . . . was dwarfed by that which I'd searched for, if only because I knew it to be the locus of all the danger. It stood several stories tall, towering over all other nearby buildings and spreading an entire block . . . and the dark energies I saw radiating from it sent a chill through me.

The lair of the Beast of Chicago stood in all its hideous glory, larger than in life, more dreadful than in legend. There were windows on each floor, but all were barred to prevent escape. It had a squat, brick design that further led to its sense of a prison, a trap from which no one could escape. Even the storefronts below looked different. At the moment, I didn't know which of them, if any, had an actual store, but I suspected that Holmes had designed things so that those inside would remain innocent of what was going on above them. They, in turn, would provide him with camouflage.

Without thinking, I took my hand off Joseph's shoulder. Holmes's unsettling world vanished.

I quickly put my hand back again. Things returned to their awful magnificence.

"Almost there. Just a little longer," Joseph murmured cheerfully. "We should board the airship now. It'll be a fun ride."

I quickly looked at him, but only saw the vacant stare. It shouldn't have been surprising that little bits of his past might still exist. He thought he was getting ready to hatch his plot on the Wingfoot.

"First, we have to stop inside this fine place here," I answered, pointing at the Murder Castle. "Isn't that right?"

In response, he grinned. "I wish Father could see this."

With that, he headed on toward Holmes's sanctum.

I kept my hand on his shoulder. At some point, there had to be a way to keep everything in existence without holding onto Joseph. Otherwise, that'd make it more than a little awkward to face Holmes.

Slowly, we closed on the building. For the first time, I noticed that while there were doors, they were all sealed at the edges. I wondered how we were supposed to get inside.

Joseph didn't share this concern. He kept walking as if he intended on colliding with the sealed entrance. I trusted in his decision even though I also kept expecting him to crush his nose against the door.

But instead of colliding, he walked *through* the blocked entrance. I nearly lost my grip on his shoulder, but succeeded in keeping it enough so that when I reached the door, I, too, walked through it as if it didn't exist.

The interior was a macabre parody of a hotel lobby, with walls covered in some festering moss and a floor covered in marble segments each cracked in the center. There was a desk where one signed in and even a guest book open for use.

A couch and three chairs sat to the side, the leather an odd shade. I wanted to take a closer look, so I steered Joseph toward it.

As I neared, I noticed that it had a tanned leather covering. I hadn't seen leather like this, though. Still keeping my one hand on Joseph, I reached down with the other to feel the material.

A howl filled my head. I stumbled back as a very human cry faded away.

Catching my breath, I returned to the couch. Slowly, I reached out to touch it again.

Have a care . . . the dragon warned. From his tone, I could tell that he was very loath to repeat what'd just happened.

And again came the scream.

This time, I forced myself to keep my hand on it. The scream subsided to a consistent sob.

I recoiled. I understood what I was sensing. I also understood just what material this was which with Holmes'd covered the furniture.

I also understood that it'd taken more than one victim, too.

"All right, Joseph," I muttered as I attempted to wipe the image from my mind. I'd come across monsters in both human and Feirie form before, but Holmes guaranteed to be one of the worst and certainly living up to his infamous title. "Let's you and I get—"

Two things gave me pause. One was that I finally noticed that I wasn't holding onto him and yet still remained in Holmes's world. That solved that problem.

Unfortunately, the other thing was that Joseph was gone.

Cursing, I tried to figure out which direction he'd headed. There was a winding set of steps heading up to the next floor and beyond, but the steps were covered in moss that should've made impressions of his footprints. To the side stood a rusted elevator, its open doors not at all inviting. A regular door, not in any better shape than the elevator, hung slightly off its hinges.

I wasn't sure if all this was for effect for anyone unfortunate enough to enter Holmes's sanctum or if it was this way because it was an extension of the Beast's twisted mind. Whichever the case, I knew that I had to make a choice and make it quickly.

I was probably making the wrong decision, but I decided to take the stairway. It was wider and gave me a better view of what I was heading toward. As I started up, I drew Her Lady's gift. Anything that got in my way was going to meet its point quickly. All that mattered was reaching Holmes, preferably without him knowing I was here.

Of course, for all I knew Joseph'd already returned to him. If that was the case, Holmes was probably setting up a trap.

The second floor revealed itself to be a long series of doors supposedly leading to guest rooms. I was loath to try any of the doors, but when I saw that one was slightly ajar, I knew I had to check it out.

The knob had a dull but noticeable polish to it that indicated it'd been used often. I eyed the floor, but still saw no hint that Joseph'd headed through. Despite that, I carefully entered.

Surprisingly enough, it was a hotel room. A Victorian iron bed replete with mattress, sheets, and pillow stood on one end. There was a wooden table and chair set by a window covered with thick, dark curtains.

Opposite the bed was a closet and dresser. Recalling my recent encounter, I used the tip of the sword to check out the drawers. When I found nothing, I turned to the closet, only to come up with equally useless results.

We waste time here. . . . He will be on the highest floor. . . .

He didn't specify whether he meant Joseph or Holmes, and I didn't care. Still, this room clearly had nothing else to offer. I headed for the door—

The sound of a car on the street made me pause. I went to the curtains and shoved them aside. As I'd seen from outside, they were heavily barred. Yet, even though my view beyond Holmes's sanctum was limited, it was enough to identify just who'd arrived.

Claryce and Fetch.

Another epithet escaped me.

The dragon snickered. *Such saintly language. . . .*

Claryce climbed out of the Wills and looked directly at the castle. I was certain that she couldn't see it, but, like me, remained suspicious of the building.

I kept praying that she'd turn and leave, but then Fetch joined her and started to sniff the air. A moment later, he said something to Claryce and trotted toward my direction.

Fetch'd picked up my scent. He led Claryce toward the building. I hoped that they'd wander around the empty stores and then give up. I couldn't imagine any way they'd be able to find a path into Holmes's world.

Then, something else at the far end of the street caught my attention. Another car very slowly heading toward our location. Not at all to my surprise, it hesitated as it neared . . . as if the occupants had just taken notice of Claryce and Fetch and didn't want to be seen in turn.

I squinted. With the dragon's vision, I could just make out a very pale figure in the front passenger seat. One of the Schrecks. I couldn't see if his twin was in the back, but one was too many already.

They abandoned their car right there. I made a quick study of the rest of the gang. It didn't surprise me that there were some other goons with Holmes's lieutenant. These had a different look, though, darker and tougher. I couldn't make them out well enough, but they moved more like animals on the hunt. These clearly weren't dupes to be later sacrificed, but rather a band brought in for a specific reason. I didn't doubt for a moment that I . . . and by extension Claryce and Fetch . . . was the reason.

I couldn't help myself. Whatever Holmes had in mind, I had to let it and Joseph wait until I got Claryce to safety. At the very least, I had to warn her. I rushed back to the door and pulled it open.

It was at that point my mind brought up the fact that the door'd already been open when I'd last left it. Now, it'd been shut.

I didn't care. Claryce and Fetch were all that mattered. The sword ready, I opened the way.

The corridor was gone. Another room greeted me.

A second door beckoned from the far wall. With little choice left to me, I immediately headed toward it. Without hesitation, I tugged it open.

I faced a new corridor. Glad to find something that wasn't a room, I stepped out into it and looked for the stairway.

It wasn't there. The only exit from the floor was the elevator, which, unlike the one on the first floor, had two rusted doors tightly shut together. I didn't doubt that trying to open them would cause a lot of noise.

Eye can help us. . . .

"No thanks. Remember what happened in Feirie?"

He grumbled, but didn't argue. I still wasn't exactly certain what Holmes'd done to us or how much control he might have over our transformation, but I didn't want to test that right now. I still hoped to catch him unaware, however unlikely that was.

The elevator doors were open. I paused.

"Weren't those shut?"

Eye can tell you nothing . . . but assume that they were. . . .

He had a good point. I stood in front of the open elevator, debating.

Someone called my name. No, not just someone. Claryce.

Her call came from far away. It was enough to make me rush toward the elevator.

A hand on my shoulder held me back. The grip was a powerful one, stopping me in my tracks.

I turned on my attacker.

Joseph smiled.

"It's cresting. The shadow's everywhere."

I didn't answer him. I barely looked at him, my attention on the female figure behind him.

A ghost.

Claudette.

CHAPTER 24

Claudette's lips moved.

"The Beast is nearly complete," Joseph commented earnestly. "He and the shadow are almost one."

I looked from her to Joseph and then back again. He was repeating *her* words. He was giving her a voice in the living world.

"Follow us . . . free us . . ." Barnaby's son whispered after her lips moved again.

"Claudette . . ."

She smiled sadly.

"Oh, Kravayik . . ." Joseph dutifully repeated.

It wasn't the comment I'd expected. Before I could try to glean something from it, Claudette turned her tearful gaze down the hallway behind me. I instinctively looked where she did.

Claudette stared back at us from the *other* end. I quickly looked behind Joseph and saw that no one stood there now.

"Come on." I gently tugged Joseph by the arm and led him toward the ghost.

Claudette watched us as we neared. She was calmer than any of the other spirits I'd come across. Or—maybe not calmer, but more determined.

Actually, more real, too. I wondered if Holmes knew that. He'd been focused on how the Frost Moon's wake would enable him to magnify his abilities and his spellwork, but from what I'd seen, the wake affected nearly everything magical or supernatural, even without his actions. It'd enhanced Fetch and the dragon. I'd seen how it'd affected Diocles. Why not then the ghosts of the Beast's victims?

Claudette suddenly reached out a hand. She caressed the air at about face level.

Joseph sighed and tilted his head. Even though a short distance still separated them, he felt her caress.

She mouthed something.

"Poor Kravayik," Joseph muttered. "There is nothing to forgive. . . ."

She faded away. I shelved her words for Kravayik for a time when I saw him . . . and for when I myself had forgiven him for his lies and omissions.

Behind where Claudette'd stood there now was an open wall. I couldn't remember the wall being open before this. With a silent thanks to Claudette, I pulled Joseph along. I might've left him behind for safety reasons if not for the fact that he not only seemed to have some memory of the place, but evidently had an affinity for ghosts as well. Besides, I wasn't certain there was actually anyplace safe here at all.

We climbed through the opening . . . and entered the maze.

I might've been tempted to back out, but the choice was made by the disappearance of the opening. With no other route, I moved on. Although the outside had shown windows, none were apparent here. There was nothing I could do to warn Claryce. My only hope was to reach Holmes and force him to call off his dogs.

The maze had no intention of cooperating in that respect. The path veered abruptly to the left, away from where I thought I had to go. I wasn't helped by the fact that Joseph seemed inclined to let me lead.

All this time, Her Lady's gift had glowed a steady crimson in response to nearby Wyld. That hadn't surprised me, considering what I'd seen previously. The entire sanctum likely had traces of Wyld power. Now, though, I noticed a subtle shift in the glow, an almost imperceptible change toward gold. I had no idea what that meant, since Her Lady'd not bothered to tell me.

I tested it out in different directions. All remained the same except when I pointed the sword ahead and just a little to my right. The blade shone brighter. That made no sense, though. The wall there looked very solid.

Eye can make a path. . . .

"I don't want to bring the whole place down on us." I might've actually been tempted to do that if Claryce and Fetch hadn't shown up already.

The sword persisted in glowing strongest when facing the one wall. I let go of Joseph and swiftly ran a hand over the area in question. No secret panel opened up.

Eye could—

"Shut up." I stepped back, raised the sword, and cut into the wall.

The wood melted away as Her Lady's gift cut deep. Yes, melted. Normal physical boundaries sometimes didn't matter with the sword. It made for easy removal of the barrier, not that what I saw behind it was at all what I'd expected.

He'd been dead a long, long time. The fact that he was wearing a suit that dated back to the time of the Columbian Exposition wasn't at all surprising.

What was surprising was that, even mummified by time, I recognized a younger version of Barnaby's dear old friend . . . Des O'Reilly. The real Des O'Reilly . . . alias Bobbie O'Hanrahan.

Alias someone or something that'd been serving Holmes these past three decades.

Circumstance and discovery had forced Holmes to flee Chicago, which had in turn led to his capture. Far away from his sanctum, he'd been weak enough to be little trouble to the law. Still, I couldn't help thinking he'd planned for his body to be returned here no matter where he ended up. Death hadn't mattered to Holmes so long as a part of his bloody domain had existed beyond the mortal senses. What *had* mattered was that he be where the magical shadow of the Gate created by the wake would strike early.

Saint Boniface had been the nearest cemetery, but even then, someone would've had to bring him nearer to here for the wake to give him the strength he needed to stir again. My first thought went to Oberon, but I saw nowhere where their desires would've crossed. Yet, Holmes *had* mentioned someone else when I'd been his prisoner. Maybe he'd been talking about "Bobbie."

"This is your fault, you know," I muttered to Joseph. From what I'd learned from Barnaby back when we'd been trying to locate his son and his son's associates, Joseph'd revealed abilities very young. I didn't know when the false "Bobbie" had befriended Barnaby, but I suspect it'd happened shortly after that. It was even growing likely that one of those who'd been linked with Joseph's plot had actually also been part of Holmes's.

I exhaled in frustration. There were times when fighting a dragon to the death seemed the simple part of my existence.

The sword continued to give off its different glow. I touched the tip to the very late O'Reilly/O'Hanrahan's vest.

The glow magnified.

I brought the tip to the area just above the head.

The glow grew so blinding I had to look away at first.

"You have a lot of explaining to do," I quietly growled at the absent queen of Feirie. I'd never seen the sword do this, which made me wonder if it reacted specifically to something Holmes was doing. Just like her husband, she'd known that Holmes might somehow someday return, and she'd readied her gift for just that possibility.

And, naturally, hadn't bothered to mention it to me.

I peered above the desiccated corpse, but still didn't see anything.

I had a thought. "Joseph."

He came like an obedient puppy. I put my free hand on his shoulder, then looked again.

Sure enough, now I saw a long string of a black substance I knew well. It was metal, and it originated from Feirie.

Black silver. A deadly substance. Very rare, but not so rare as I'd once thought. Probably only rare because those who knew of its dangerous but seductive properties hoarded whatever they found.

O'Hanrahan had the string jutting out of his skull. I could imagine it having been wound through his entire system. I could also imagine it having been meticulously done while he'd still been alive. The agony would've fueled not only the black silver's latent properties, but also Holmes's monstrous work.

I studied the path of the string as it stretched up above. Although it disappeared a few feet up, I could see which direction it went. Leaning back, I eyed the walls and ceiling in that direction.

With Joseph in tow, I followed the trail. As I studied the maze's design, I noticed a system that relied on the black silver. Holmes had it running through the entire structure. Small wonder he'd been able to create and, more importantly, hide this entire place from not just the sight of men, but even from the most skilled of Feirie. Only Joseph seemed to be resistant to it. Joseph, who seemed to know it well—

Joseph, who I now believed had at some point helped Holmes complete this entire arrangement.

At that moment, he stopped dead in his tracks.

I tugged at him. "Come on! We—"

"No, that's not right." He stared at the ceiling where the first string crossed a second, then began doing silent, invisible calculations in the air.

"We don't have time for this, Joseph!"

Leave him! We do not need him!

"Not right at all," Barnaby's son went on with a strong shake of his head.

"Joseph—"

The hand I had on him began to change.

"Stop it!" I ordered the dragon.

Eye have done nothing!

Even had I not believed his words, his tone gave no doubt as to his honest answer. Then I lost all care as the transformation spread to my limbs, to my head . . . to my entire body.

My howl of pain became a dragon's furious roar. Joseph shrank before me . . . or rather I grew so large so swiftly that he was dwarfed. He appeared as if he didn't care at all, his attention still on his calculations.

"Not right," Barnaby's son continued. "That would make it do—"

I couldn't hear him anymore. Suddenly, I no longer stood in the maze. Instead, I floated above a now-familiar view. Once again, I was high above Feirie, but Feirie in turmoil. The mountains shrank and grew and shrank again like a tide, while the massive forest looked as if it were swiftly shriveling from some intense heat. Mighty oaks curled over like soft flowers under the relentless burn of fire. Their crowns browned and then blackened.

I could feel the entire realm suffering. I'd never had much sympathy for any of its inhabitants, especially those of the Court, but this was a catastrophe of astounding proportions. Feirie was not a place as huge as the mortal realm; each second meant the eradication of large portions of it.

This was certainly Holmes's doing, but I couldn't sense how it was happening. All I could sense was the raw energies arising wherever some part of Her Lady's realm collapsed. At the rate it was happening, it wouldn't take long for Feirie to completely crumble.

And if that happened, the balance between the two sides of the Gate would collapse, affecting Chicago and beyond.

I tried to move, not just for the sake of Feirie, but even more so for Claryce. However, no matter how hard I struggled, I remained where I was, hovering over the center of Feirie.

Give me control, I demanded of the dragon. *Give it to me!*

Eye have done nothing! Nothing! This is not me! This is not us, fool of a saint!

I had no idea what he meant until I tried to delve deeper. Only then did I hear the whispers, the terrified whispers.

The whispers from Holmes's tortured victims.

There was only one reason why I would hear them here in faraway Feirie. That awful conclusion was verified as the dragon body moved of its own accord . . . or rather, of H. H. Holmes's accord.

He was the dragon now . . . and we his helpless captives.

No, not exactly captives. Holmes didn't sense us, so meager a part of him we were. Even the ghosts were a stronger piece of him than we were.

And that made me look again at our own situation. If Holmes hadn't yet sensed us, that could only be because we were not actually in Feirie but still in his sanctum. We had to find our way back, so to speak. Only then could we hope to do anything more.

But doing that was turning out to be a lot harder than I could've imagined. All my willing didn't do a damned thing. It took me a moment longer to understand just why. The help I thought I'd be getting from my constant companion was proving to be just the opposite. Instead of trying to escape, he was dwelling in the power Holmes was gathering and trying to find a way to make it his own.

Give it up! I ordered him. *You won't get it that way. He's drawing from us as much as he is Feirie!*

That finally seemed to tear him from his desire. With a snarl, he joined me in trying to tear free. I focused our effort on imagining the castle and the location where we'd last been. Unfortunately, now it was my turn to become distracted, because the more I thought about Holmes's sanctum, the more I thought about the threat facing Claryce. Claudette's ghost had been yet another reminder of the constant danger to every incarnation. I couldn't bear that happening to Claryce.

Nick!

Barely had I heard her name than suddenly Feirie receded at a rapid pace. The world briefly turned black, then green, then black again.

A moment later, my head and back collided with something wooden. I knew it was wooden because the loud cracking that accompanied our collision wasn't my spine . . . something I *had* heard and felt more than once in the past. At the same time, the surface we struck partially gave way.

"Nick?"

I tried to respond to Claryce, but for the moment I didn't even have the strength to speak. It had little to do with the crash—although that hadn't helped—but mostly with our shift of perspectives. Matters weren't helped any by my fear that Holmes'd now knew we were here.

I tried to rise and failed.

"Fetch! I can't see them. Have they gone?"

"I smell them closing, Mistress Claryce! We have to move him from here."

"But where? We can't reach the car. What about the north side?"

"Let me look." I heard a soft padding of feet, Fetch trotting off.

"Claryce . . ." My own voice startled me. I sounded more like the dragon than myself.

"Nick! You should've never driven off on your own! What were you thinking . . . and where'd you just come from?"

I blinked, but still couldn't see. "Where are we?"

"In one of the empty stores. Fetch followed your trail once we arrived here, but he kept going in circles once we reached this spot!"

So Fetch hadn't been able to locate Holmes's otherworldly realm. He'd done better than I would've expected, but without the access Joseph'd provided me, he'd been stuck where he was, the trail just ending in front of him.

Then, I remembered the other situation. "I wanted to warn you about Holmes's torpedoes. How'd you notice them?"

"I can't say," Claryce muttered. "Something made the skin on my back crawl. I glanced back just in time. They were circling the block and trying to catch us by surprise, but one got too close. He started to draw, but I had the revolver out already." She paused. "That's one less, so I think no more than four."

She tried to sound detached, but I could hear the stress in her voice. It'd been one thing to shoot at monsters, another to actually kill a man. To her credit, the hand that touched mine was steady, though.

My vision returned. As she'd said, we were in one of the empty stores. I saw through my own eyes, not those of the dragon, so my view was as limited as that of Claryce or Fetch. I tried to summon the dragon's gaze, but couldn't even locate him in my mind. There'd been very few times in my life when I'd felt as if I were alone in my head.

"Great sense of timing," I muttered.

"What's wrong?"

Instead of answering, I looked around. To my relief, at least Her Lady's gift had come back with me. I grabbed it and, in a scene that would no doubt've left the queen of Feirie aghast, used the glorious magical sword as a cane to help push me to my feet.

"Claryce." I took a deep breath. "Claryce . . . I'm going to draw them off. Fetch'll help me. The moment we succeed, I need you to get to your car and drive off."

"Don't even talk nonsense like that!" She held up the Smith & Wesson. "I'm not afraid to use this again. The only one I think is a real danger is that pale one. One of the twins, I mean."

"He's bad, but Holmes is a thousand times worse. We've got to get you out of here before he notices."

"You found him? Where is he?"

"Here. And above. And in Feirie."

She helped me stabilize my footing. "I don't understand a thing you just said."

"Welcome to my world. You're still thinking in normal mortal terms. Even I still do that despite everything I've confronted over the centuries. Just know that Holmes and everything he's created is here with us, but we just can't see it. It's reaching a critical point, but I need you out of here. It's the best—"

A gun fired. The glass window to our right shattered.

Fetch came trotting back. "I smell one in the back. Nothing else." He growled at the ruined window. "I cannot say yet if the *Vyr* has any more scent than his master, though."

I caught the elven word. "The what?"

"Vyr. 'Tis a word of the Feirie folk. Means 'the hollow.'"

"Why would you call him that?"

He took a sniff of the air, then answered, "'Tis nothing special I know, Master Nicholas. 'Tis only his appearance. It struck a chord before, but I didn't think it through. Thought him just another pug-ugly torpedo. They've got some awful-looking goons in both big mobs."

"Can these Vyr pop from place to place? Magically?"

"I cannot say. If they're from Feirie, could be."

I couldn't worry about more potential Wyld until I'd gotten Claryce out of here. "Fetch, I need you to help me distract them long enough for Claryce to escape—"

"I'll do no such thing! Don't even think of it!"

"Claryce, think about it—"

She folded her arms, her hand gripping the revolver tight. "I have."

Another shot further ruined the one window. I had a suspicion that Holmes's goons were trying to manipulate where they wanted us to go. By pushing us from the one window, they limited our view of the outside world to less than half what it'd been before.

"Why do they call these Vyr 'hollow'?" Claryce asked Fetch without warning.

Fetch's brow furrowed, and one ear tilted up. "I cannot say, Mistress Claryce. None from my pack had had any experience with a Vyr. They were things in stories told to young pups!"

"Just try to stay away from him," I commented, quickly surveying every direction. There were two doors, one of which was near enough to another huge window to not be useful for whatever trick the hoods intended.

"I'll stay just far enough to get a good shot. I'm not leaving you, Nick. We've had this discussion before, and you know how it'll end."

I considered knocking her out and having Fetch carry her off, but that was too risky. Claryce wouldn't have *any* hope of defending herself if anything went awry.

She took the decision away by moving to a corner wall that gave her a view of both directions where there were windows. Fetch looked at me for guidance, but, receiving none, hurried after her. I could see where his loyalties lay.

You always have me. . . .

"Thanks a lot," I remarked, for once actually feeling a little relieved at this acknowledgement of his presence. I held up the sword, hoping that it would give me a hint as to how to get back to Holmes's sanctum. Unfortunately, it barely glowed at all now, which made me wonder about Fetch's description of the Schrecks. I didn't quite see them as these Vyr that Fetch'd spoken about, but they had some similarities. I wondered if they were some creation of Holmes's. They certainly looked like something he'd have thought of.

Then, something occurred to me. I eyed Fetch and thought about what I'd learned concerning Barnaby's supposedly good friend. Not everything was always what it seemed, especially where magic was involved.

Sword leveled toward his back, I walked silently up behind Fetch. I knew I might be wrong and actually hoped I was. If this wasn't Fetch, I had to act quickly and decisively.

"Fetch, how'd you get back to Claryce? Weren't you going after Kravayik?"

He hadn't turned yet, so he didn't see the point at his neck. Claryce *did* see it, however. Before she could react, I shook my head.

Inside, the dragon suddenly stirred. *Smell that! He must be slain! Slay him swiftly! Do not let him act!*

I almost acted, so vehement was he. Fetch looked back and stared wide-eyed at the threat I presented.

"Kravayik, he was gone already! I raced right back! I swear I am being square with you! I'm no fakeloo artist!"

If anything could've convinced me this was Fetch it was his tortured use of human slang. I lowered the sword, satisfied.

My big mistake.

He must've popped right in at the same moment. Neither Claryce nor Fetch had given any notice of the threat suddenly behind me.

The arm that wrapped around my throat ended in pale flesh that I'd seen before. The Schreck tugged me back from the others. Claryce reached for me, but I knew it was already too late. I could feel the air ripple as the pale figure magically transported us away.

But in what had to be a surprise for my adversary, what initially was our vanishing from the store became a return barely a breath later . . . albeit a few yards away from where we'd stood. More to the point, we were accompanied by none other than Joseph.

"I found it," he said to me in his childlike voice even as I struggled with Holmes' servant. "It was wrong, but I found it."

As Joseph reached to me, Fetch—fully transformed into his original Feirie form—snarled and fell upon the Schreck. Fetch managed to tear Holmes's creature from me just as Joseph took my wrist.

The world changed, becoming Holmes's twisted reflection of the exposition era. Then, it shifted again, returning us to the interior of the Murder Castle.

To a part I'd not seen yet.

To a part where the body of an elf stood strapped by black silver in the midst of the chamber. His expression was slack, and it was clear that he was dead. Still, a quick shift to the dragon's gaze revealed that energies pulsated through the corpse from one part of the string to the other.

This wasn't the same elf I'd seen earlier. This one was even more elegantly dressed and clearly had been of a much higher status. In fact, from what I knew of Feirie's caste system, especially the oak pins at each shoulder, this elf'd been among the highest of the elite.

I could see why she'd taken a shine to him. Even among the Feirie folk, he looked like he'd been a charmer. His features remind me of Valentino, but even the Great Lover couldn't compare in the end.

Of course, Valentino could at least lay claim to still being alive.

The same couldn't be said for Her Lady's Lysander, evidently.

CHAPTER 25

"I knew it was wrong," Joseph commented. "I remembered it should be different. See? He's all wrong!"

I had no idea what he was talking about and really didn't care at the moment. I was trying to figure Lysander's exact purpose. He was positioned differently from the previous pair. Lysander looked as if he were not just a key component, but *the* key component.

Of course.

Whatever else he'd done, in the end, Holmes'd still had to deal with the fact that he'd been born human. That meant that he hadn't any true link to Feirie. Without such a link, he couldn't draw upon Feirie as he seemed to be doing.

Lysander apparently provided that link in a way the other Feirie folk hadn't.

I was beginning to see the arrangement Holmes'd desired and how long he'd worked on every aspect of it. I was also beginning to see the horrible course he'd set on to make it work. Each and every horrific murder, each monstrous torture, had all been to perfect this mad design.

The clipping we'd come across concerning Holmes's capture and execution had offhandedly mentioned the destruction of his sanctum by fire months earlier. Who caused it had never been discovered, but some believed Holmes'd done it to cover his crimes. That was partially true, I realized, but hardly encompassed the truth. With what he'd drawn through his torture and slaughter of both humans and Feirie folk, the Beast had eradicated the mortal shell. The true sanctum lay hidden in a world of its own, accessible only by a select few involved in its creation . . . like Joseph, apparently.

Then, I thought of what Joseph'd just said. "How's it wrong?"

"It's wrong!" he answered unhelpfully. "All wrong!"

As I watched, he walked up to the body and started trying to work on the string rising from Lysander's left hand.

Lysander opened his eyes.

They stared sightlessly at him, then me. Sightlessly, because although they looked our ways, they did so with an odd filminess to them.

I felt a chill run down my spine. There was something else in the room.

Joseph grinned at me. "Run."

His order, spoken so softly, caught me off guard. I recalled too slowly that the last time he'd spoken like this was when Claudette'd used him to give her a voice.

Then, Joseph's grin widened more, and in a deeper voice he said, "Gatekeeper . . ."

Lysander. I couldn't swear that with all certainty, but it had to be.

Joseph's expression looked befuddled. "Mustn't touch."

His hands pulled away from his work. He let out a scowl and tried to bring them up again.

The dead eyes stared down at him again . . . and Joseph went flying across the chamber. He collided against a wall and fell into a crumpled heap. I heard a groan escape him, which surprised me.

I'll admit, I stared in disbelief. I could see the tremendous agony that the array had surely caused Lysander. I could imagine wanting to scream constantly as power pulsed along the black silver strings.

And yet . . . Lysander had evidently *willingly* accepted all that. He'd *wanted* to become part of Holmes's horrific display.

Joseph'd noticed something wrong with the arrangement. I'd have liked to know what, but I wasn't given a chance. A shadow swept over the room, a shadow that settled on the corpse.

"Gatekeeper," the body abruptly croaked. "Surely you are not surprised? Surely you understand death has different meanings in Feirie and this mud wallow!"

"Yeah, but I've forgotten to just what depths of depravity Feirie folk were willing to dive."

Despite his condition, Lysander laughed. It was a rough, painful sound. "Do not underestimate the levels to which a human can descend. He has been the master, not me. . . ."

"I stand corrected." I kept Her Lady's gift ready. Lysander hadn't done anything to attack me, which I found intriguing. He'd been quick to deal with Joseph, but not so much me.

All the while, I also continued to think of what I could do for Claryce and Fetch. Unfortunately, there was nothing at this point but to try to stop the madness.

You have me! Unleash me! Eye can tear this place apart. . . .

You don't remember last time too well, do you? I was certain that Holmes had strengthened things since we'd escaped before. There was also the consideration that Lysander appeared unconcerned about the possibility of the dragon's entrance. As one of Her Lady's most trusted, he'd have understood very well how simply I could let that happen. Yet, I was almost willing to swear that he *hoped* I would take that path.

Give me just a touch of you, I ordered my constant companion. *No more . . . for both our sakes.*

Eye will do that . . . and trust you are not more foolish than usual. . . .

I ignored his jibe as I felt his presence grow in me. Tilting the sword away, I concentrated.

My other hand transformed, the fingers becoming long, scaled digits ending in razor-sharp claws. Simultaneously, my legs bent back and I felt my face start to extend outward. Long, wicked teeth spread through my mouth. I was very grateful at that moment that Claryce *wasn't* with me.

Lysander's expression didn't change, but I sensed the array stir. Just as I'd thought, he'd hoped for me to fully release the dragon.

I thought I saw everything now. The pinprick wounds from the daggers had indeed drawn from some bit of essence from both of us. While only one of us could exist at one time, we were still forever blended together. Holmes had somehow come to realize that by using that essence, he could magnify his efforts where the Gate was concerned. With Lysander to give him a hold in Feirie and us to give him that for the portal, Holmes had all he needed to begin his final efforts.

I let the dragon recede. He did so reluctantly, naturally.

There was a flicker of frustration in the elf's eyes.

"Not what you hoped?" I asked as I moved in with Her Lady's gift. "Fully summoning the dragon would enable you pair to better draw from us, isn't that so? That's what Holmes and you wanted when we were taken last time. You wanted the dragon to keep raging long enough to take all you needed."

"We have all we need to take what we desire." Lysander managed to tilt his head toward me. Considering the black silver coursing through him, I imagined it was quite painful. He didn't seem to care, though. "And we now have enough of what we desire that we can take what else we require."

The array flared.

I started to change without *either* of us wanting to do so. The agony that accompanied it was enough to make me drop the sword and fall to our knees . . . or where the knees would've been if not for their having shifted in forming the dragon's hind legs.

Eye can save us! he started raging. *Let me flow out! Let me flow out!*

I'd come to trust the dragon only a handful of times in all the centuries since we were bound together. I supposed he might've believed what he said even now, but I was certain that Lysander still hoped we'd give in and finish the transformation ourselves. We had to be drawing valuable power from them, power they were willing to expend in order to gain so much more.

Somehow, I managed to grab hold of Her Lady's gift again. It was hard to grasp, what with a hand that continued to fight between being human and dragon. Still, regaining the weapon gave me some support.

It also gave me a moment to think. There'd been more than one reason that they'd had to wait so long to accomplish what they wanted. Something'd happened—I had to conclude Kravayik and Claudette—to force Holmes's flight in the first place. However, that'd left Lysander behind. Lysander, who'd kept the spellwork in place while they waited. He in this torturous state and Holmes in the grave. Waiting until all factors came together.

Waiting for the Frost Moon's wake to perfectly touch everywhere they needed Holmes to reach.

I forced a laugh in order to shake up Lysander. It worked. I saw his eyes flash with more life than I'd thought them capable of.

"All that . . . that suffering. All because . . . until now . . . the Frost Moons haven't touched everywhere you needed. You had to endure all . . . all this torture . . . waiting . . . wondering if the next one would . . . would reach. The previous one . . . what maybe a decade or so ago? . . . The last one enabled Holmes to reach out to Joseph, didn't . . . didn't it? Holmes brought him back to you . . . to not only calculate when the next Frost Moon would rise . . . but also where its wake would touch."

"The shadow spreads differently with each wake. We could afford to be patient, though . . . he in the ground and I . . . What is a human generation or two to one who has lived millennia?"

I didn't like that he was sounding stronger as I grew weaker. "And when . . . when did Titania realize you'd betrayed *her* plot?"

That made him wince. Few even in the mortal realm dared mention Her Lady by her given name. To do so was to risk her notice. The same had once been feared of mentioning Oberon by other than his titles, even long after he'd been ousted. They had been Feirie, and Feirie had been them.

"She is nothing . . . nothing to be feared, anymore," he responded too quickly. "No longer do I have to suffer her caresses, her kisses. . . ."

"Yeah, sounds horrible."

"Do not again judge Feirie by human standards, Gatekeeper. Love is not a common thing among our kind. Power and desire are . . . and those extend even into our relationships."

"Maybe you should've tried writing Dorothy Dix instead . . . instead of betrayal." The reference to the popular advice columnist was lost on Lysander, but I was also stalling. I'd already made a calculation as to how much time and strength I'd have left for an attack and where I'd strike. Killing Lysander might not destroy the array. Instead, I knew that I had to sever more than one string within a few seconds. If not, then I doubted I'd accomplish anything except hasten my demise.

"You should not be so kind toward her, Gatekeeper. After all, she is the one who first inferred that *you* were the key. That with you, so much could be accomplished."

I wasn't surprised that Her Lady'd entered into this, but a bit surprised at the extent. I'd thought it more recent by what she'd said, forgetting that those of Feirie talked of a hundred years ago as if it were yesterday. She'd been planning this since first we'd thought Oberon slain during the Great Fire. Or rather, *I'd* thought him slain. Obviously, she'd never assumed that. She'd been willing to bring chaos to the Gate, risk Feirie itself, just to gather the forces she thought she'd need if and when Oberon would pop up.

When he had and when he'd been destroyed for certain this time, she hadn't bothered to mention her past mistake. Instead, she kept hunters like Lon on the trail of Lysander. I wondered how many of Lon's predecessors there'd been. His kind were tough, but not as tough as some of the high caste. Oberon'd proven that.

"I'll deal with Titania later," I responded, again pointedly using her name. Sure enough, Lysander couldn't help blinking.

I felt his control slip slightly.

I lunged.

He regained his composure only a breath later, but by then I'd gained enough momentum to reach his left. Her Lady's gift cut into the string.

With most things, the blade never slowed. Flesh, bone, armor . . . there wasn't much it couldn't penetrate.

Thin as it was, though, the black silver string proved to be a stronger metal than most. The sword cut through, but only thanks to every ounce of my strength and weight thrown against it. Even then, there was a precious delay before the last bit of strand gave way.

Far too much time to allow Lysander to react.

The shadow I'd seen drape over him, the shadow that was his spirit, ripped free of the body. The head tilted to the side, and the expression went slack as only the dead could display.

The shadow moved toward me. I'd not had any experience fighting elven spirits, but I had to hope that Her Lady's gift would suffice. The flickering shape reminded me of a banshee I'd had to deal with during the battle with Oberon back in the previous century, but I doubted Lysander'd be as easy . . . not that the banshee had been simple.

He looked forward to dealing with you himself . . . he said in my mind. *But he won't mind if we take the pleasure. . . .*

"'We'?" Other than Her Lady and Oberon, I'd not heard too many elves speak of themselves so. Still, megalomania wasn't an uncommon trait for Feirie folk.

Lysander's shadow spread wider. I was reminded then that the monstrous Wyld I sometimes encountered were not all that different from the ruling caste.

From the depths of the black shape shot an inky limb ending in a clawed appendage that just barely could be called a hand. I wasn't so worried about the claws as I was the dark blue aura forming around the hand itself. I braced myself for the worst as I rushed to meet him.

But someone else leapt in front of us, gripping the spirit's out-stretched hand as if it were solid.

Someone who happened to be Kravayik.

He let out a cry as he took hold. Not a surprise since the same aura now covered him. Still, Kravayik, dressed as we'd last seen him, stood firm against Lysander's attack.

"Get . . . to . . . him!" he shouted back at me, not needing to explain just whom he meant. With Kravayik occupied, there was only me to deal with Holmes. "And forgive . . . forgive me. . . ."

Even if I hadn't noticed the change in his voice when he said the last, the flickering image I caught out of the corner of my eye was enough to let me know that it was to Claudette he begged. I wasn't certain if I'd ever get the full story out of him—assuming we all survived, that was—but I knew I'd been right about him having fallen in love with her.

I didn't flee the chamber immediately. I needed one thing, or rather, one person. Returning the sword to its hiding place, I hefted Joseph over my shoulder and dragged him off. He wasn't the lightest, but I'd had to shoulder worse. I couldn't leave him here, no matter what he'd done in the past. This Joseph was like an innocent child. An innocent and admittedly still valuable child. Holmes'd kept him alive for a reason, which meant that despite Lysander's attitude, not all was perfect with their plot. They still needed his calculations.

Holmes'd used Joseph to calculate the moment of the wake's greatest influence. What happened after that, though? How swiftly did the wake—and the shadow—recede? This was a thing of magic. It didn't necessarily follow the rules of the mortal realm. It was possible that there was some abrupt change Holmes still feared.

Which meant that by saving Joseph, I could also use him as bait.

It wasn't a very saintly notion, but I couldn't reject the consideration. If it came to sacrificing Joseph for the rest, so be it.

A crackling sound erupted behind me as I reached the door. I didn't look back. Kravayik's existence before coming to the mortal plane had been as a deadly assassin. I had to assume he could deal with Lysander . . . or at least stall him long enough for me to do whatever I could.

Whatever that was.

Someone grabbed my arm . . . and suddenly we were in the empty storefront again.

I didn't have to ask who was responsible. The pale hand on me was enough. Either the other twin had come after me or the first had been able to overwhelm both Claryce and Fetch.

I let go of Joseph. His limp body fell onto my unseen adversary. As that happened, I turned around and swung my fist.

I had the tremendous satisfaction of landing a blow as good as any Jack Dempsey or Mike McTigue could've done, sending the Schreck—who'd still been struggling with Joseph's limp body—stumbling back. Still, he quickly recovered, then pulled free the hollow-tipped dagger Joseph's body'd blocked.

A shot rang out. A hole burst open in the Schreck's throat. He dropped the dagger, then fell to his knees. He struggled to rise, but finally slumped to the floor.

Claryce grimly lowered her revolver. Her expression changed to one of relief when she looked up at me.

"Oh, thank God! Nick—"

I looked around. Fetch leaned over the body of the first twin. He was spitting out something in disgust. I'd seen him eat rats raw, so I couldn't see what would've bothered him about ripping out the throat of an adversary.

"Ah!" Fetch gasped. "Applesauce! Disgusting, that was!" He looked at us. "Like biting into soft clay and about as tasty!"

"'Clay'?" I came over to the ruined corpse. Fetch's victim lay sprawled on the floor, his head to the side. Fetch'd done a good job on the hood's throat, leaving very little intact.

Then, I saw a problem. All that carnage . . . and no blood, no moisture whatsoever. In fact, what Fetch'd said about clay made more and more sense as I inspected the wound. Instead of gobbets of flesh, small fragments of what could've passed for pottery shards lay strewn around the body.

Even more unnerving, I could see that the neck's interior was hollow.

I immediately inspected the one Claryce'd shot. Despite the damage she'd done to him, again, there was no hint of blood.

I can't say I was surprised. "Fetch. These those things you talked about? They *are* hollow."

"Nay, Master Nicholas. Not seen a thing like this, not even in Feirie. Maybe a human version?"

Shrugging, I looked at one of the open windows. "What about the others?"

"They got quiet right after you vanished," Claryce answered. "Then, suddenly, this other one showed up. He took a look at me, then at what Fetch was doing to his twin. After that, he disappeared, only to bring you back to me."

While I was as grateful to see her as she sounded about me, I couldn't help finding the second twin's antics worrisome. He'd seen his double dying and should've known that to bring me back here risked his own existence. Why then take such a suicidal tact?

Then I thought about where I was standing and knew what he'd intended. I quickly leaned over Joseph.

"What's wrong?" Claryce asked.

Instead of answering her, I ordered, "Fetch, watch the windows. Those other hoods are still going to be out there. They're setting up for something. They've been ordered to stall at all costs."

"Yes, Master Nicholas."

As Fetch rushed off, I muttered to Claryce, "We need to get Joseph conscious. You saw what happened when he showed up here?"

"Yes, both of you vanished. I was so afraid for you!"

"Holmes's entire sanctum can only be reached through those like Joseph who have a link to it. I can't return to it. They're trying to keep me out until it's too late. If Kravayik—" I stopped. "Kravayik got inside. I wonder how."

"We never saw him."

"Probably what he intended. He found a way in. But if not Joseph, then how?"

Gunfire erupted. What was left of the window Fetch'd rushed to shattered. The wind spilled inside, lowering the already cold temperature.

Claryce shivered.

Two more shots whizzed past us. Fetch leaned out, then quickly backed up as two more nearly caught him. Unless they hit him right in the head, it was doubtful that two bullets would do more than slow him a little, but there was no sense taking chances.

Although both the Schrecks had been disposed of, the gunmen one of them had brought with him were still a threat to Claryce. Despite the risk that Holmes would complete his work, I couldn't leave without making certain that she'd be safe.

Then, before we could do anything, the shooting went into a brief frenzy. I counted six, maybe seven shots in rapid succession that didn't even come close to us . . . almost as if the mobsters had a new target.

A moment later, there was silence. A single gunshot followed, and then the silence resumed.

"Fetch! What do you see?"

He peered out. "One of the torpedoes trying to run toward here. Looks scared, Master Nicholas. Looks scared."

I moved toward him. "Maybe we should grab him and see what's happening. This has to have something to do with Holmes."

"Aye. Here he comes like a bat out of hell!"

I reached the ruined window just in time to see the hood in question frantically trying to reach the last street before Holmes's building. He kept looking behind him as if, well, Hell was after him.

A second thug suddenly stepped out of the alley the first past. He rushed up behind his comrade . . . and then a black point burst out of the chest of the first man.

The skewered hood dropped his automatic. He shivered a moment, then went limp.

The point receded inside the corpse. A moment later, the body fell in a heap, just quick enough to let us see the long, sharp spike that was at the end of the second goon's arm revert to a normal-looking hand.

Lon.

He continued on toward us, moving at an incredibly rapid pace despite using a walking stance. Another time, I'd have had a word with him about his lack of consideration about just what passed for human in public, but for now I needed him desperately. I had a feeling he might be the key to reaching Holmes's sanctum.

"So, you've been lurking around here all the time," I muttered as he reached us. "You came here with Kravayik, didn't you?"

For an answer I received a slight nod. Up close, it was clear the Feir'hr Sein had pretty much worn out another body. The goon's skin was peeling off in several places, and a blackness had spread over the gums. His eyes had already begun to sink in.

"Kravayik got in. You stayed out here, but you know the way in, don't you? You can open it up or show me, can't you?"

He repeated the nod, then, in a raspy voice, murmured, "Follow. Short."

I wasn't sure what he meant by the last. I quickly turned to Fetch and Claryce. "Get out of here. Those gunshots will have to finally bring the cops around, and I can't help thinking somehow that Cortez'll be one of the first."

"Nick—"

"Get her out of here, Fetch. That's an order."

He let his ears flatten. "Yes, Master Nicholas."

To the Feir'hr Sein, I ordered, "Lead the way, Lon."

Once again, he hissed at the use of the nickname. He didn't like being bound to serve me, but I was going to use that forced obedience to my benefit. I trailed after him as he walked to the center of the room.

The moment he reached there, he sloughed off the corpse, the body nearly tumbling back into me. As that happened, I got a glimpse of a different Feir'hr Sein than that with which I was familiar. It wasn't that I hadn't seen what moved ahead of me before, just that I'd not known what it was at the time.

I hadn't had time to wonder what'd happened to the Wyld that'd attacked me near the gravesite. I *had* wondered about its tie to all these matters . . . and now I knew.

It'd been Lon.

CHAPTER 26

The stickman moved forward a few more feet, reverting in the process to the Lon I knew better. I had to assume there was a specific reason for the other shape, most likely a preferred form if and when he faced Holmes. Lon'd been on the hunt for Holmes when we'd come across each other, and as one of Her Lady's enforcers, he hadn't been concerned if he eliminated me in the process.

While matters had obviously changed, I knew that he looked for any chance to escape his servitude to me. For now, though, Holmes was the threat to all.

The Feir'hr Sein leaned down. As he did, something slipped from his bony hand. Something that made me reach for my pocket, where Her Lady's other gift—Lysander's blood—still lay nestled.

"What is that?" I asked, unable to make it out.

It is . . . he. . . .

It took me a precious moment to understand just what he meant. "That's a part of . . . him? Of Holmes?"

The price . . . for her giving him access to the power of Feirie. . . .

"Ahh." Lon didn't sound happy with the results of that pact, and I couldn't blame him. Now I understood. In Feirie, alliances were often made by giving a part of oneself to the other. When Oberon and Her Lady had wed, he'd given her a drop of his blood . . . a very precious commodity considering its potential for magic. Of course, he'd made certain to seal it so that nothing she did could penetrate.

Well, almost nothing.

And Her Lady had overstepped with Holmes, assuming all along that since he was human, she could outwit him. It was a failing with her. "What about *her* price?"

Lysander . . . she gave him Lysander, thinking her hold on that one was complete. . . . It was not. . . . Lysander and the Beast had more to bind them together. . . .

It was a long speech, for Lon. Long, but still not completely clear. Still, I didn't bother to ask what he'd left out. I swore at Her Lady again. The bit of Lysander's blood that she'd given me paled in comparison to Holmes's foul essence. That meant a link we could trust. I didn't dare attempt anything related to what Holmes had stolen from me, if only because that'd give him a much better chance to counter us.

Lon touched a finger to the spot. A flicker of crimson energy arose from the area, swirling into a whirlwind in which a vague image formed.

The Feir'hr Sein turned his half-seen, nearly fleshless face to me. *Quickly . . . this will only work with the wake so strong. . . .*

His lengthy statement surprised me for a moment. Lon straightened, then walked into the whirlwind and disappeared. I gritted my teeth and jumped in.

We ended up in chaos. I'd expected to find us wherever Holmes actually was, but instead we'd returned to Kravayik and Lysander . . . and things weren't looking good for Kravayik. The spirit of Lysander was draped over him. Kravayik was on one knee and almost to both.

From the brief hiss escaping the Feir'hr Sein, he hadn't expected to arrive here, either. It occurred to me that in the maze, everything had a touch of Holmes in it. The array probably had more, which was why we'd ended up near Lysander. Magic wasn't always perfect.

"We need to help—" I started . . . only to find Lon gone. He'd brought me here and then run off before I could demand more of him. I knew then that I'd been wrong; Lon'd diverted me to here, then continued on to Holmes.

"Dear God! What is that?"

I swore as I looked at the source of the question. Claryce, her Smith & Wesson out, stared at what was happening to Kravayik. She'd followed us through.

"Get back through before the way shuts—" I stopped as now *Fetch* jumped through. Worse, right after he did, the spell faltered and the way back dissipated.

Fetch looked rightfully ashamed. Claryce, on the other hand, glared at me. "What is that on top of Kravayik?"

"The elf."

"What, from that body? Is that what an elf's ghost is like?"

There wasn't time to explain the difference between a true ghost and an elven spirit, not that I thought Claryce would see any more sense in the definition than I really did. "Something like that. The elf—Lysander—is still alive, though."

"Would his being dead change what's happening to Kravayik?"

"Probably . . . if we could accomplish that and if Holmes weren't an even bigger, more immediate situation."

"Where's he?"

"I—" Suddenly, the world swam. Transposed over everything was a scene out of the exposition, replete with scores of people clad in the garb of the day. They strode around the area as if engrossed in the sights, especially the well over two-hundred-foot-tall marvel created by and named after steel magnate George Washington Ferris Jr. The translucent image of Ferris's gargantuan wheel with its seating for over two thousand riders added an especially surreal touch to an already madcap sensation. Holmes had dragged forward with him through the decades a spectral memory of that time, one that appeared to be strengthening as he did.

And then, the image became so real that I could barely see the chamber anymore. Now it was Claryce and the others who seemed to be ghosts.

Nick . . . Nick . . . what's happening to you?

I tried to say something, but no words escaped me. Claryce and the rest became less distinct, less visible . . . but not quickly enough to prevent me from seeing a horrific image forming behind her.

The twin whose throat'd been torn out by Fetch now grabbed for Claryce's neck.

I shouted, but still nothing came out. I realized that I was being pulled between the two visions, but was a part of neither.

Eye will give you voice!

I didn't even hesitate. I let him do it.

What felt like a volcano stirring scorched the inside of my throat. The next second, in a booming voice, I—we—shouted, "BEWARE!"

The roar shook everything, but all I cared about was that my last glimpse before Claryce faded away was her turning with her revolver to the threat behind. I didn't know if the gun would be enough, but at that moment, I thanked Heaven for her at least having a chance.

And then belatedly thanked the dragon, too.

Holmes's memory world solidified. With a ghastly creak, Ferris's wheel slowly turned, dark images I supposed were people riding in its seats. The throngs grew, but although they moved about and acted as one would've expected a crowd at such an event, their faces were blank of expression, of life. The men were also looking more and more like Holmes himself, with the women taking on faces that too much resembled Claryce . . . or maybe Claudette.

"It was a simpler time . . . but, of course, everyone says that of the past, don't they?"

Holmes sounded as if he stood right in front of me, but even with me making a swift circle revealed him nowhere in sight.

"Saint George. When I was growing up, I didn't have much use for the Church, truly. Went to it when it was necessary for the facade, but why worship a god when you can be one?"

"Is that all this is?" I asked as I continued surveying my surroundings. "Just the usual 'I will rule the world'?"

A man strolling by with a small girl looked at me as he passed. His grinning face was that of Holmes. "Well, that is a very nice benefit, if it comes to it."

He tipped his hat and continued on. The girl didn't look at me, didn't even act as if I was there.

"But ruling a world takes a lot of effort," another Holmes in a suit and long tie continued as he headed the opposite direction. Like the first, he tipped his hat as he moved on.

I reached after him, only to have my hand go through.

"All is thought," Holmes said from behind me. I spun around to find him leading a group of four other men—*all* with his countenance—across the street that'd just formed. "But I never found enough to occupy my mind . . . until I began my experiments."

"'Experiments'? Is that what you call the slaughters you committed?"

"Oh, please," the other four men chorused just before the group crossed.

"Would you be concerned over the slaughter of a cow or hog?" continued a younger male dressed in a jersey and newsboy cap. "Or weeds plucked from the ground? Hardly."

"At least I give them some worth, some overall value," Holmes added from yet another direction. This time, he wore a uniform and carried a package.

I was getting sick and tired of playing in his world. I tried to concentrate on Claryce . . . and briefly faded images of her and the rest invaded Holmes's world. I rejoiced that Claryce was not only alive but trying to get a bead on the Schreck, who at the moment had his arms pinned back by Fetch. Fetch, in his full Feirie form, was trying to take another bite out of the twin's mutilated throat. I doubted anything less than full decapitation would slow the fiend.

Meanwhile, Kravayik still struggled with Lysander's shade. Despite being nearly engulfed, Kravayik showed no sign of surrendering. From his left hand slipped a small, ebony dagger I assumed to be of black silver. He jabbed at the shadowy form, which easily shifted out of the way.

Twisting nimbly, Kravayik whirled toward Lysander's physical form and threw the dagger.

Holmes's idealized world abruptly took prominence again.

"Ah! There you are," a chorus of Holmeses announced. "It was her, wasn't it? It's always her, in one incarnation or another. It's always the princess . . . what was her original name, Cleolinda? Yes, that's what he said! And now it's Claryce, another lovely name. Were the others so vibrant? I recall Claudette, of course. A strange pairing, those two."

Holmes seemed to want to talk. I pretended rapt attention while I surreptitiously searched for where the true Holmes could be found. I didn't want to use the link he'd created for fear I'd open us up to his power. That meant that I had to be especially careful, relying mostly on my own limited human senses and my experience with others before this.

This wasn't the first time Holmes had mentioned someone else. Somehow, though, it didn't sound like he meant Lysander.

Before I could follow through, Holmes spoke again.

"I looked forward so very much to what she could offer toward my efforts. I'd researched reincarnation before, of course, but I'd never come across a reliable case. The other possible ones . . . well, they still made their contribution."

One Holmes broke off from the rest. I considered striking . . . and certainly the dragon supported that option . . . but knew that Holmes wouldn't present himself so readily.

"But when it was all said and done, when all I wanted was a simple answer as to how to extricate myself from this situation, I discovered that not all the sacrifices I made amounted to anything if I could not affect the very core of the Gate's existence."

I still hadn't located him, but couldn't help looking at his illusion. "You don't just need the Gate and the shadow, then. You're actually *bound* to them, aren't you?" I thought about all I'd seen. "Of course. You can't *exist* beyond the Gate's shadow. You're bound to it."

For the first time, I received a scowl. "Wasn't supposed to work out that way. I'd been studying life and death on the side while I

. . . shall we say 'paid' my way with various enterprises among the provincials—"

"You mean you conned and defrauded people wherever you went."

"I taught them valuable lessons. They deserved to pay a price, especially considering how long I had to put up with them and their simple ways."

I shook my head. "Some of them paid a terrible price."

"*Those* served a better purpose, you mean. My genius couldn't be allowed to dim, much less die. That *is* what this is all about! Didn't you see that?" The Holmes image removed his bowler and looked at me as if marveling that his reasoning hadn't been clear from the start. "Feirie may be a static realm . . . well, not for much longer . . . but think of all the great minds that the human race has produced! Aristotle, Caesar, and da Vinci are three names that most rubes could at least fathom. I could list a thousand artists, generals, mathematicians, athletes, and inventors who've risen among humanity to accomplish tremendous and lasting changes . . . and for what?"

I'd finally sensed something. It'd been the least of traces, but I was certain that I'd nearly pinpointed where the true Holmes was. Unfortunately, to do any better would've required utilizing our link to Holmes, something I was certain that he'd notice.

"For what?" I repeated, hoping to keep him caught up in his ego.

"For death to simply claim them in the end and leave them to be forgotten by more than a handful." Holmes put his bowler back on. "I couldn't let that happen to my genius! That's why I began gathering everything I could to at least stave off matters until a final solution could present itself!" He tapped his hat and grinned. "And I thank you for that ever so much."

A wrenching sound echoed through the memory world. Holmes turned his gaze. I couldn't help but instinctively follow suit.

Ferris's wheel had torn itself free. It rolled for some distance, crushing parts of the exposition's "White City" region in the process.

In the true world, I couldn't have seen such detail, but here in the twisted product of Holmes's thoughts, proportion meant little.

Then, with more wrenching, the wheel took on a more oval shape. Seats went flying, bodies flung from them in the process.

"You brought it to me. You gave it to me. You gave me everything, Saint George . . . and I thank you."

Even as the wheel had begun to reshape, I'd brought Her Lady's gift around at the image who'd been leading the speaking. The Feirie blade cut through his throat, neatly beheading him.

The head rolled off the left shoulder. Instead of falling, though, it spiraled in the air until it took up a position floating a foot to the side of the body. One hand reached up to where the bowler'd originally been and tipped the empty air. The bowler hat rose and then dropped onto the severed head.

"I am all I will be because of you . . ." Holmes said cheerfully. "I will always be in your debt."

He faded away, the grinning head last of all just like Alice's Cheshire cat.

I'd hated that character when Dodgson'd told me about it, not that he'd listened.

At that moment, the wheel went through one last, swift scream of metal as it concluded its transformation. I didn't need the last minute arching and gleaming stars to tell me what it'd been turning into. That'd been obvious long before it finished.

The Gate loomed over me.

Holmes's world lost cohesion as the Gate dominated all. Without warning, I stood again on the shore of Lake Michigan, watching as the Gate flared bright in a cornucopia of colors that included those I could only see because of my own ties to the portal.

And worse yet, I could also see that the key to all Holmes hoped to do—the shadow caused by the Gate itself—now draped over all Chicago.

CHAPTER 27

I am all I will be because of you. . . .

I am all I will be because of you. . . .

I knew what Holmes had meant. I couldn't be blamed for all the heinous murders he'd committed nor anything Lysander or their servants had done to achieve their goals, but still I couldn't help feeling the incredible guilt he'd probably hoped I'd feel.

If not for the Gate coming to Chicago—and then being bound there by the events of the Great Fire—Holmes's monstrous search for immortality would've ended with his neck stretched in Pennsylvania. Instead, the inroads he'd made had been just enough to enable him to keep him at the edge of death until now, until he could use me to complete matters.

I am all I will be because of you. . . .

Long ago, when I'd still been a tribune serving Diocles and naive to the cunning whispers of Galerius in his ears, I'd been troubled by the deaths that'd happened due to my role, my position. I'd taken those deaths heavily, part of the reason I'd embraced Heaven so fully. Even early on in my task as gatekeeper, I'd prayed for each individual who died as a result of the incidents influenced by the Gate and those who'd sought to misuse it.

But time *had* hardened me more than I'd realized. The Nilssons had proven an example of that. I'd had to remind myself to think of them after they'd been brutally murdered. Only when it'd come to Cleolinda and her incarnations had I retained my fullest grief . . . and that'd been for some pretty selfish reasons, I knew.

I remained aware every second that I wasn't alone in this, that

Claryce and the others were fighting alongside me. If Holmes'd thought I'd break down because of my guilt, he'd been misinformed by someone.

Despite the chill lake wind, I knew I couldn't actually be standing here. I still had to be within the matrix of Holmes's sanctum. He hadn't completed his work or else none of us would've been left alive. Holmes hadn't struck me as someone to leave his enemies behind even after triumph.

Which meant that all his talk had been, as I'd thought, an attempt to stave me off until things *did* fall into place for him. What he hadn't realized, though, was that I'd used every second on trying to understand him.

And one thing I now understood was that Lysander didn't realize that he didn't have the upper hand on his ally. Joseph'd actually tried to warn him, but the elf'd been too haughty to even listen.

The other thing I'd discovered was that Holmes couldn't possibly proceed any further *without* me. I knew he hadn't been trying to reveal that, but it made sense to me with everything else. If he hadn't needed me, he wouldn't have wasted so much time. He needed something to happen and was hoping I'd make that happen.

He wanted me to become the dragon one more time.

I turned Her Lady's gift point down and thrust hard. Dark emerald and blue energies exploded where the blade sank into what was supposedly the frosty beach.

The Gate, the violent, icy lake . . . Chicago itself . . . all vanished, replaced again by one of the chambers within the maze.

And there, of course, stood Joseph. It didn't surprise me. He was doing something with a part of the black silver array beyond Lysander's ken.

"What're you doing, Joseph?"

"The wake is nearly done, but done too soon," he answered merrily as he fiddled. "Just a tweak here. Just a tweak there. That'll fix it." He looked back at me. "Is it time to board the express?"

"Yeah, soon." I studied what he'd done. If I understood it, he'd arranged everything gathered to be drawn back to elsewhere in the maze. Away from Lysander, who'd been its true nexus for so long. That'd not only bring everything to Holmes, but burn out Lysander in the process. A simple way for Holmes to cleanly remove his ally.

I raised the sword. With one convenient slice, I could wreak havoc on all Holmes's plans. Gently pushing aside, Joseph, I focused on his work. In the midst, I noticed the place I was looking for. One cut.

One cut.

Well? asked the dragon impatiently. *Strike! Put an end to this!*

Instead of answering, I lowered Her Lady's gift. "Sorry to disappoint you, Holmes."

A sudden wave of nausea overtook me. I dropped the sword and fell to my knees.

"No matter," the Beast of Chicago remarked without a hint of disappointment. "A small matter. You and I, we're bound enough for me to go on. You see, I had Joseph do a little more work before letting you come back. The other part was just a ploy."

I didn't bother to answer. Through my nausea and pain, I sensed Holmes *physically* approach.

"The shadow's stretched as far as it can," he went on, "and I can't draw the rest of what I need from Feirie and the Gate until I make the final blending with you."

He didn't have to explain to me what he meant. The ties he'd created through my stolen blood could only go so far. Now, he needed the rest.

"I'd say if you don't struggle it won't be very painful, but, then, I'd be lying to you just as I had all the rest. It'll be very painful. So very much so. Try not to scream too much. It won't help alleviate anything. I've seen it enough."

The last few words came from very nearby. I knew where he stood.

Fighting against the strain, I shoved myself to my feet and grabbed the outstretched hand holding the hollow-tipped blade.

With pleasure, I looked into his startled face.

"After sixteen centuries, I've learned to endure more pain than you could even imagine," I replied as I twisted his wrist.

The dagger dropped to the floor with a clatter. Holmes's surprise turned to a darkness of such depth that I'd only seen on a few over the generations.

"What I can't take one way, I can take another." He grinned and, if not for our other hands coming together at that moment, would've probably even tipped his ever-present bowler.

The moment our hands touched, I understood what he meant. The fingers grasping mine weren't fingers, but the scaled digits of a monster of reptilian appearance.

A dragon.

"We are one. I will be one . . ." Holmes whispered. "You will give me what you are."

I felt an emptying. Not one of the body, but of the soul. What I'd become after my death, after inadvertently making myself successor to the dragon as guardian, was slowly but surely being drawn from me to Holmes.

Eye can stop this! Let me out and I will bite his head off!

I met Holmes's gaze and saw that if I did try to unleash the dragon on his own, I'd only magnify the rate of loss. The changes Holmes'd had Joseph make had all been to create a better conduit for stealing our mutual essence. Before, he couldn't have done it, but along with the energies he'd already drained from Feirie, he now had the strength and spellwork to take the rest.

But only if I let him. I braced myself and silently said, *If you want to save both our hides . . . or at least yours . . . then help me. . . .*

He didn't reply, but in the next instant, I felt a surge of strength. I dared not funnel it into any sort of magical reaction for fear that'd just be what Holmes wanted. Instead, I used it to create a wall against which he could strike futilely until he was weakened enough for my own attack.

Holmes grunted. A brief look of anger crossed his mustached face . . . a look that quickly faded.

"Two against one? I believe I can outdo those odds. I've been building up to this for over thirty years, after all."

And as he spoke, I sensed others forming around us, half-seen figures gathering mostly behind and beside Holmes.

"Never waste. Always save," the Beast of Chicago remarked cheerfully. "Did you think I just let them wander around for no reason?"

The ghosts gathered. Each and every victim of Holmes since he'd started his monstrous quest. Even the dread dark spirits of the Wyld who'd crossed his path.

"Two against one? How about two hundred against two?"

I didn't know if they numbered two hundred or not, only that there were many, far too many. Worse, I recognized two among them, two who'd only been recently added.

The Nilssons.

Like the rest, they stared at me with begging eyes, as if they still suffered the agonies of their deaths. The pair had an arm around each other, perhaps to draw some small comfort.

I hadn't expected them among the ghosts, but, then, I hadn't thought about the extent of the Frost Moon's wake. It'd clearly reached all the way to the Nilssons at that point.

My guilt surged . . . and almost did us in. I caught a slight glimmer in Holmes's eyes and knew he'd intended just that. I barely strengthened our wall in time to prevent him from reaching through.

"Oh, I've only begun, Saint George," he mocked. "*They've* not even joined us."

And then the dragon and I experienced the full force of Holmes's captive spirits.

It was like standing against a tidal wave or earthquake. We were battered hard, mentally thrown about as if rag dolls.

"Give in, Saint George. The shadow amplifies my power further.

Why would you want to be bound to the Gate as it is? Haven't you railed against your captivity for centuries? Doesn't Heaven owe you enough already? You've suffered enough! Let me take your burden. . . ."

My hands felt like they were on fire. A sense of displacement began growing inside me. Simultaneously, Holmes seemed to look a little more solid, a little more alive.

"Give *in*," Holmes pressed. "This is my world now. Just look at it with its gang wars and rivers of blood. You're part of a time, of a belief, so rustic, so abandoned. Heaven awaits you . . . and if you give in now I just might let it have you. The dragon'll be enough."

"You wouldn't . . . like his company . . . for very long," I managed.

"Oh, I think he and I are much alike . . . and I have another gift for him when he's mine. One you'd like, too. I can see he hates you dreadfully, and I don't doubt you hate him in turn. With the dragon mine, I won't need him anymore."

I had no idea what he meant and didn't really care. It was becoming harder and harder for us to keep the wall strong. The dragon was with me the same way that Holmes's supernatural slaves were with him. Under most circumstances, only one of us could have real substance in the world and, thus, real power. He could either augment or supersede me. There wasn't much middle ground, at least not for more than a limited time. We could never be half and half.

Actually, there *were* ways to make that happen, but to draw from the Gate in such a way was to risk a far greater danger than Holmes threatened . . . so far. Oberon'd attempted to use the Gate to meld the two realms into one; what I'd need to do was just as likely to open an abyss that would swallow much of both sides and leave a pit big enough to fit at least three or four Chicagos, including Lake Michigan.

There will be destruction no matter what. . . . Eye say do it! We are the Gatekeepers . . . it is our choice . . . our duty. . . .

No, not exactly what I'd want to be forced to do, the dragon's opinion to the contrary. The deaths of thousands wouldn't touch him,

RICHARD A KNAAK   329

but all of those losses would be added not only to the ghosts under Holmes's awful sway, but the many I'd let down long, long ago.

And yet, the strain became impossible to withstand. Once again, Holmes ate away at our defenses. Our wall crumbled in places, allowing him to feed on us.

Then, something stirred among the swirling energies. A slight shift that revealed another presence kept hidden nearby. Blinking away tears, I tried to focus on Holmes, who stood very close to where I thought the other presence materialized.

The ever so sharp black point thrust out through Holmes's chest. The Beast let out a gasp and stared down at the needlelike spear sticking more than a foot out of his body.

Lon, fully shifted into his stick figure shape, pulled the bloody point back through Holmes. Holmes shuddered and let out another gasp as the weapon withdrew.

As he pulled his sinister appendage free, Lon transformed into the shape I knew better. For the first time, I thought I saw what looked like an expression of deep satisfaction on the murky, skeletal face. This was what he had been born to do. This was his purpose, as Feirie had for millennia dictated.

Holmes shook. His eyes widened. He gasped a third time—

And then the wound sealed. Just like that. At his strongest, the dragon couldn't have healed it faster or more thoroughly. Even Holmes's shirt, vest, and coat mended.

"That might've worked . . . once," he whispered.

Another Holmes materialized behind the Feir'hr Sein. He immediately seized Lon by the approximate location of the neck.

The Feir'hr Sein let out a mournful howl as a bright glow originating from the second Holmes's hand engulfed him. Part of Lon literally burned away.

The second Holmes tossed aside the badly scorched creature. The Holmes combating me smiled wider yet. "You see? It's all becoming possible for me! I've done it, and I have you to thank for all of it, whatever he thinks of himself!"

I didn't say anything. In the moment when Lon'd used me as a distraction to aid his own attack, Holmes's control had slipped ever so slightly. Yeah, it'd been pretty impressive for him to be in two places at once as opposed to casting illusions, but it'd taken a tiny bit more out of him than I think he realized.

But equally important was that someone chose that moment to give me a hand up from behind . . . two hands, actually, as they helped me stand straight.

We give what we can when we can, a voice I couldn't identify but felt I knew said in my head. *But as strong as the sword is, the heart is stronger . . . because it is All. . . .*

I felt the dragon's presence recede as that happened, as if the voice startled him in a way few things did. I couldn't say that I blamed him.

Holmes abruptly glared at something behind me. "Who the hell are . . . Joseph?"

"Be our protection against the wickedness . . ." Barnaby's son replied much too cheerfully.

I'd heard that phrase before. It wasn't in the Bible, but it had to do with it. In fact, I knew it because it'd only been added a few years before the exposition by Pope Leo XIII as part of a prayer to one saint in particular. Not me, of course.

Michael. Now the voice in my head made sense. I'd heard it once before . . . at Saint Boniface . . . when the "son" had spoken with me.

"I fixed it," Joseph whispered as merrily as ever. "He said I was good. Said my father would be proud. Is it time to board the express?"

"Not . . . yet. . . ." I did my best to shield Joseph as Holmes threw himself into the attack again. Despite not being as cheerful as before, he'd lost none of the tremendous power at his disposal. In fact, it seemed if anything he was stronger. I wondered if Joseph'd fixed things the wrong way where I was concerned.

The ghosts didn't look as if matters had changed for the better for them, either. Their expressions had turned even more agonized, and now I could swear I heard some of their screams in my head. Bad enough that most had been tortured in life before he'd killed them; now they had to suffer by his will in order to grant him greater power.

"Your nigger friend's come and gone fast," Holmes muttered, "and done nothing for you. And don't think this addle-headed math prodigy will be of much good! I sense what he's done, but he's only made it easier for me to draw everything together!"

If I'd had any question about what he meant, it was answered a breath later as I felt a fire burning in me that had nothing to do with the dragon. It grew rapidly, and I began to wonder just what Michael'd been thinking with his little intrusion into my very desperate situation.

Then, among the ghosts, I saw Claudette. Compared to most of the rest, she was pretty composed still. There were tears streaming down her cheeks, but she'd managed to keep from screaming. I wondered what made her different, then realized that she hadn't suffered directly at Holmes's hand as the others had. She'd avoided his torture, his dark experiments.

Michael's words—or at least the words that I was fairly sure that damned elusive archangel'd muttered in my mind—came back to me. The sword was good, but the heart was better. A lot better.

It'd pushed me before. Maybe it could push a ghost to miracles.

She'd been staring at me all that time. I knew somehow that she'd become aware of what part she was in my life, that she'd been the incarnation of the woman I loved. The woman who died before me each time, rending my own heart in the process.

But she wasn't really seeing me. Of all the incarnations, this one did not see me, but another.

And so I mouthed the name Claudette would find in her soul instead of mine. I mouthed *Kravayik*.

Her expression didn't alter. I mouthed his name again, but still nothing happened.

Nothing, except that Holmes became less and less human and more like a mad mix of man and dragon such as I didn't think even I'd ever become. If I had, I prayed that, assuming we survived, Claryce would never see me like this.

He still wore the damned bowler hat and still paraded his thick mustache, but his skin had grown scaled and slightly green and his eyes had taken on a narrower, reptilian cast with which I was all too familiar. His grin hadn't changed . . . if you didn't take in account that his teeth were longer and sharper, better for tearing flesh.

"Yesss," Holmes murmured with more sibilance than even the dragon ever used. "The way isss almost clear! The way isss almost mine. . . ."

There'd been times in my existence that I would've gladly traded places with him, let him have the Gate and all its troubles. However, through the centuries, I'd gradually come to realize just what it would've meant if, say, someone like Galerius, Napoleon, or Hitler had had control. It made me wonder on occasion if it'd all been so accidental, my being the one.

Inside, there came a scream. The dragon. I'd never heard him like this before. He sounded distant, disjointed. I understood then that the fact that Holmes's transformation had continued meant that whatever there was of the dragon had, through Holmes's spellwork and the Frost Moon's wake, been ripped in part from me. The dragon was caught between both of us now and suffering as terribly as any of Holmes's victims.

I knew only one way to prevent more of it from happening. I finally urged the transformation upon me. The dragon did his best, throwing what remained of his power into the change.

"Aah, there you are!" The Beast of Chicago chuckled. "My, what a sight! Do I look like that?"

RICHARD A KNAAK   333

In response, I embraced the dragon's nature and exhaled.

Holmes did so at the same time. We bathed each other in primal flames to no avail.

"I know as you know!" he rumbled. "Nothing you do will have effect!"

A chorus of mournful cries accompanied his declaration, the ghosts' pain renewed as Holmes grew more powerful. I couldn't help but look at them for just a moment . . . and noticed then that Claudette no longer stood where she'd been. I didn't know what that meant, if anything.

Behind me, Joseph was having a mumbled conversation with himself. There was no looking for aid from Lon, who continued to burn.

He's here, I tell you! He's right here!

Fetch's voice came from within and around me, yet there was no hint of him. I knew then that he and Claryce hadn't fully melded with Holmes's foul domain, that they were in this very chamber but unable to locate us.

Holmes either couldn't sense them or paid them no mind. It didn't matter which. They couldn't do anything as they were, even Fetch.

It's all right, Fetch, I heard Claryce respond in a surprisingly calm tone. *It's all right, Kravayik.*

I shouldn't have paid any mind to the last. It wasn't surprising that Kravayik might be with her, though I'd been concerned if he'd be able to survive Lysander. Yet, the way she responded to Kravayik reminded me of something else.

It's all right, Nick.

And suddenly Claryce was in my mind. Claryce, adding an incredible strength of will that braced me like steel.

Claryce . . . and yet . . . not Claryce.

Claudette and Claryce *together.*

CHAPTER 28

"Claudette," Joseph greeted the empty air. "I missed you. I haven't seen you since I was last here. I'm glad I was able to come back to say hello. Hello."

"Nick," came Claryce's/Claudette's voice. "Nick . . . I can see you now."

Where is he, Mistress Claryce? begged Fetch from somewhere. *Where?*

Seize her hand! another voice . . . Kravayik's . . . commanded. *Seize it!*

Suddenly, the three of them stood to our side, Kravayik worn and his garments in rags, Fetch cut and bleeding, but still in his true Feirie state. Claryce stood between them, holding a hand with each.

"Claudette," Joseph repeated, slipping past. "I wish we'd met when you weren't a ghost, but that was too long ago. But we're still friends, right?"

Holmes jerked. His gaze darted to Joseph, to Claryce, then back to me. I knew then that he couldn't strike at them so long as we were locked together. We'd created a balance that for a moment meant defeat for whoever lost his concentration first.

"Yes, Joseph, we're still friends," Claryce called back with a smile. "Come." She let go of Fetch who, despite being bereft of her touch, remained solid.

Joseph vanished, materializing beside Claryce and taking up a spot next to Fetch.

"Claudette," Kravayik whispered from Claryce's other side, revealing just who now dominated the body.

Yet, as Joseph took her hand, she looked at me again. "Nick . . ."

I *knew* it was Claryce . . . but she was willingly *sharing* her consciousness with Claudette.

She, Joseph, and Kravayik vanished.

Fetch stalked toward us.

"Stay back!" I warned him.

"Nay, Master Nicholas," he returned, baring his fangs and raising his claws. "The mistress bade me do what I could at all cost if need be. I promised her scout's honor I'd do just that."

He lunged at Holmes, but suddenly froze in the air. A second later, several of Holmes's ghost slaves materialized around him, their spectral hands having no difficulty grasping the shapeshifter. Fetch let out a pained grunt as the translucent fingers enveloped him . . . and then went limp as if dead.

"A noble gesture," Holmes croaked. "A futile gesture."

But it wasn't as futile as he claimed. The slight shift in Holmes's concentration enabled me to reinforce my will. I shoved him back a step.

Hold on a moment more, Nick! Claryce pleaded. *Hold on!* Claudette begged.

In my head, a vision appeared of the other chamber as seen through her/their eyes: Joseph fiddling with the array while Kravayik climbed up to where Lysander hung limply. There was a slick black line across Lysander's throat where apparently Kravayik had finished off his fellow elf with some sharp blade. I tried not to think why Lysander's blood should be a caky black as opposed to what usually spilled out.

Kravayik tossed Lysander unceremoniously to the floor. He glanced toward me . . . Claryce/Claudette. *He must be ready! Tell him!*

Joseph! Finish! she/they implored.

This is wrong here. Let me . . . Is it time to board the express?

The vision shimmered. I felt an intrusion . . . and realized too late I'd left the vision open to Holmes.

He hissed. "They waste our time. . . . There's nothing they can do to forestall the inevitable."

The ghosts holding Fetch threw him at me. I didn't dare move.

I'd always considered Fetch light on his feet, but he certainly wasn't light when he hit. I tried to keep from moving, but it was too much. I lost my footing.

Nick! Claryce called. *Kravayik!* Claudette cried.

I had a fragmented glimpse through their eyes of Joseph stepping back and then of Kravayik . . . Kravayik . . . half-hooked into the spell array.

That should be right, Joseph commented with his usual cheer. *The moon is waning, the wake is receding, the express is flying high. . . .*

Holmes loomed over me as we grappled. He'd lost his bowler at last, and his mustache had turned into twisting, twirling tendrils as I'd seen on some images of dragons . . . but not the one true one I knew. His clothes hung in tatters, no longer able to contain his half-transformed body. At the moment, he was more bound to the Gate's power than I was.

But that was only for a moment. Then, the chamber rippled. Literally rippled.

Holmes let out an angry, startled roar. "That fool! And *her*—"

Even as he shouted, I felt something of what he did, all the energies gathered and magnified by both the array and the Frost Moon's wake swirling in an entirely different manner. I felt them regathering, coalescing, in the chamber where Kravayik had now strapped himself as best as possible.

And where Kravayik also now screamed in agony from far too much power coursing into and out of him at a rapid rate.

But where Lysander'd been drawing the stolen energies of both realms together in the mistaken belief that he and Holmes would share them, now those energies were spilling out through Kravayik and back to where they belonged. The process of doing so was ripping Kravayik apart, though.

It wasn't doing Claryce and Claudette much good either. I felt my link to them separate, come together, separate, and so on over and over. They were trying to cling together as best they could, as if their failure to do so would put everything in jeopardy.

Then, I had to focus again on Holmes, who, despite Kravayik's sacrifice, still swelled with what he'd stolen. His body radiated a dark green that reminded me of Feirie. There wasn't much of anything that looked like the dapper "doctor" we'd met. Holmes was now very much the demon, the *Beast*, he'd always been in his black soul.

He laughed. I'd heard some evil sounds before, but this was one of the worst.

"Dead or alive, they all must obey me in the end," he rasped.

I didn't know what he meant until I caught a glimpse of something detaching itself from him. A moment later, I felt it slip beyond us to where the others were.

Where it settled on Lysander's broken form.

Holmes chuckled madly. "Killing him only made him more mine to control. . . ."

Like a marionette pulled up by its strings, Lysander rose behind the suffering Kravayik. There was a hint of the haughty elf I'd seen in the eyes, yet an also monstrous glassiness.

The image rippled, then faded away. There was only Holmes and me again. The Beast and me.

The wake is receding.

It was Joseph's voice, but as ever heard only because of the connection Claryce/Claudette created. I understood then that they were battling to keep that link strong. Unfortunately, that link in part existed because of Holmes himself.

Still . . . the wake was receding.

Then I saw Claryce fire at Lysander, drawing his attention. As he turned, she fired again, striking him in the heart. It shook him, but didn't stop him.

Lysander reached for Kravayik, but Claryce took two steps forward and shot a third time.

But instead of shooting at Lysander, she fired directly at Kravayik.

Nick! she shouted in my head. Just Claryce, not Claudette. *She told me to shoot him now!*

Her voice and the image faded away. I didn't have to ask why. Claudette's ghost formed near us and did an odd thing. She bared her throat toward me.

There was no doubt in my mind what she wanted, and I thought I knew why. However, it meant putting myself at risk at a vital moment, a risk that, if I failed, would grant Holmes everything he'd murdered so many for.

I released my grip on him and immediately rolled toward her. Holmes stumbled forward. Our minds were still tied together, but the distraction caused by Claryce and Kravayik had taken his attention for a crucial breath.

Michael had whispered that the sword was good, but the heart was better. I think if he'd finished, he'd have said that better yet was using both *together*. At least, that was what I felt at that moment. Kravayik'd sacrificed for all of us, but especially Claudette's ghost. Claryce had done so for me. I couldn't do any less.

And it didn't surprise me when Her Lady's gift slid close enough for me to reach. Slid close thanks to Fetch . . . battered and drained, but still apparently conscious despite appearances . . . making use of the fact that he, too, had gained strength from the Frost Moon's wake. Strength enough to remain conscious despite what Holmes's unearthly slaves had done to him. Fetch, who'd been no doubt instructed by Kravayik on what to do and just when to do it. I hadn't seen him crawl the short distance to the sword, but neither, evidently, had Holmes, and that was the crucial point.

Taking a tremendous risk, I transformed to human, took up the sword, and, praying as quickly as I could, drove it through Claudette's throat.

She didn't scream. She just gasped, then smiled reassuringly to me. Her body shimmered, and, as the sword always did, the elven weapon flared and absorbed her. I wanted to stop it, but Claudette only shook her head before being sucked inside.

Holmes's sanctum shuddered. Walls creaked. Metal groaned.

As that happened, Holmes slashed into my back with his claws. It hurt. It hurt a lot. If I'd been a normal person, I would've bled to death right there and then. As it was, I had to struggle to keep conscious, much less maintain hold of the sword.

"For thirty years, I languished in the ground, forced to wait for my rightful immortality," Holmes rumbled. "I have waited long enough!"

"Thirty years?" I managed to retort. "Talk to me again when you've waited centuries."

Straining, I whirled and thrust Her Lady's gift in his direction.

He dodged easily.

I continued lunging, driving the sword into the midst of the ghostly throng.

If it'd been a basic weapon, I'd have been attacking empty air. But just as with Claudette, each spirit Her Lady's weapon touched was almost immediately swallowed by the sword.

Holmes groaned as his slaves . . . and thus his access to the source of his power . . . were torn away. Some of the dragon faded from him. He briefly clutched at his heart, then grabbed for my wrist. "Stop that!"

Evading him, I swept into the crowd. With each loss, Holmes grew more and more human again.

Then, suddenly the rest of the throng faded away. I swore, well aware it wasn't due to the sword's efforts.

Holmes chuckled darkly. "That will be enough of that—"

Fetch seized him from behind. "Master Nicholas—"

As weak as he was, Fetch couldn't maintain his grip. Holmes shook him off with terrible ease.

But it was all the time I needed to turn Her Lady's gift around and this time drive it into Holmes's chest.

He stood there, his gaze first on the blade, then on me. He was almost completely human by this time, but, I knew, no less dangerous.

The ghosts still under his control returned to surround Holmes defensively. There came that awful smile. "He did describe you well. Fighting nobly until the end. . . ." Holmes laughed. "And often fighting futilely."

I didn't answer. I just commanded the sword to release what it'd taken.

It wasn't a thing the weapon liked. It wasn't a thing I could do often. I'd done it only a couple of times in sixteen hundred years, and both times I'd nearly gotten myself killed in the process. It hadn't done much good for the sword, either, which meant that if I'd guessed wrong, we were all in more trouble than ever.

The blade turned an icy white. Holmes shrieked as I'd only heard one other. That one'd also been pierced by the blade when I'd attempted this.

But where that adversary had melted before my eyes . . . literally melted . . . Holmes maintained his form and even kept conscious. He did waver almost as a ghost might, the only sign that perhaps I'd done some damage.

Something was wrong. I'd been certain that Claudette'd directed me to use the sword to draw her and some of Holmes's other slaves into it in order to weaken him enough for a fatal strike to work. I could feel differences in the energies radiating from Her Lady's gift that seemed to verify that suggestion.

Yet, while Holmes'd been hurt, he'd hardly been stopped. Gritting his teeth, he grabbed the blade by the edge and started to pull free.

The blade shone brighter, the iciness nearly blinding in its dread glory.

And suddenly, the howls of ghosts resounded loudly in my head. They no longer cried out of pain, but anger. Anger . . . and freedom.

What remained of Holmes's gathered slaves faded as one. Holmes jerked as if struck. Still, he didn't fall nor did the sword do him any other damage. So long as he could draw from the Frost Moon's wake, he was still a threat—

I pulled the sword back. It slipped out of Holmes with an unsettling moist sound. The moment the point left, his wound began to seal.

But while that was still happening, I turned the point down and thrust as hard as I could.

Her Lady's gift bore through Holmes's left foot, bore through leather, flesh, bone, and more and kept going deep, deep into the floor below.

Holmes let out an inhuman roar. An invisible force hit me hard. I went flying several yards, landing with a very painful thud.

As I tried to rise, Holmes, teeth bared, tried to grip the hilt. But only a few could actually hold the weapon, much less wield it. Her Lady'd surprised me by making it possible for Claryce to use the sword, which she'd done ably against some of Oberon's Feirie servants.

His hand missed the hilt. He tried again with the same result. He could've tried a hundred times with a similar lack of success.

The wake is receding. The voice wasn't Joseph's this time, but either Claryce's or Claudette's. Just who it was didn't matter. What mattered was that Holmes apparently heard the same thing.

"No . . . no . . . no . . ." he muttered. The Beast of Chicago took another grab at the hilt. He *almost* succeeded, which was part of the weapon's cruel nature. For once, I wasn't bothered by that. I wasn't so saintly I didn't mind watching a monster discover his worst fear realized. Holmes was afraid of death, even more so than most. Maybe he knew enough about the afterlife to understand the punishment waiting for him, or maybe he was afraid there'd be nothing but oblivion.

Holmes suddenly looked up toward the ceiling. I couldn't help following his gaze, but saw nothing. However, whatever he saw made him snatch at the hilt once more, this time with great vigor but with still no luck.

Eye can let us see! Let us see! Let us!

I didn't know how much good it'd do, since without Joseph we'd not originally been able to make anything out, but I let him give me his eyes. The world turned emerald—

—except for where it was now divided between a distinct edge of darkness quickly being pushed away by a bone-white glow.

The glow of the moon . . . *through* the ceiling.

I might not've been able to see it until now . . . but Holmes certainly'd been able. He'd also had a good view of how the edge of what remained of the wake was rapidly approaching a point where he'd be beyond its shield.

I'd had a suspicion when I'd pinned him with the blade that once the wake faded, Holmes would be in trouble. I'd not expected the waning to be so abrupt, so distinct, though. I wasn't complaining, mind you.

Holmes gave up trying to grab or move the sword. Instead, he began pulling on his leg. There should've been a good deal of blood from his efforts, but, like the twins, he didn't seem to have much inside.

"Damn you!" he cursed at his foot. "Damn—"

He looked up again. With increasing speed, the shadow's receding edge had crossed most of the chamber already. It'd left me behind, left Fetch behind . . . and finally reached the sword and Holmes's foot.

"Damn you. . . ." He tugged harder.

Her Lady's gift shook slightly.

I wasn't about to let our chances slip away at the last second. Throwing myself forward, I set all my weight on the hilt and pressed down. The sword steadied.

Although now completely human in appearance, Holmes was still a wielder of power. He planted a palm against my face. An incredible dryness overtook me, as if every ounce of water was being drained from me. My legs started to buckle, but I held on, praying that I was right about how much time was left.

The glow of the moon . . . the impossible glow of the moon . . . receded from the sword, from Holmes's foot, and then his leg. Like a wild creature, he growled and fought to pull away. If he could've bitten his leg off, I suspected he would've done just that.

But all he could do was cry out as the shadow left him fully revealed to the bone-white illumination.

At that point, Holmes's body began to *flicker*. He pulled his hand back and grabbed at his throat. A tiny part of him tore free. As that happened, Holmes's voice shifted. His scream turned deeper, older . . . as if he was now someone else.

Behind him, one of the ghosts who'd earlier vanished briefly reformed. It stayed long enough for me to see the immense expression of satisfaction as it seized that piece of Holmes that'd come free and held it against where its heart had once been.

Another bit ripped free from Holmes. His voice grew higher pitched, feminine. A translucent female hand materialized around the stolen . . . or perhaps *retrieved* . . . essence and then faded with it as the first ghost'd done.

And then, faster and faster, dozens of ethereal hands gathered around Holmes. Old hands. Young hands. Male and female. Each and every one of the spirits that he'd bound to him with their horrific murders. I caught glimpses of the murky forms of elven spirits among them. Human or Feirie folk, they were united by an urge. I'd have called it justice. Someone else might've used the word "revenge." The ghosts had the right to make of it whatever they wanted.

Holmes contorted with each portion ripped away. In his eyes, I could see the growing horror as he, too, understood what was happening. No longer bound to him and with the shadow of the wake gone, they were the ones with the power. Each cry he made was a repeat of the helpless agonies inflicted upon them by the Beast of Chicago decades ago . . . with Holmes clearly reliving those tortures in rapid succession.

The hands pulled his body in a hundred directions. Holmes now looked like some macabre creation made of taffy. His suffering continued unabated even as he turned less and less substantial. Despite that, though, he still could not pull his foot free, not end his torment . . . and the ghosts' final judgment.

And as Holmes faded, so, too, did his sanctum. The glow of the moon ate away at the Murder Castle. More and more, the empty rooftop began becoming the true reality around us.

As Holmes's world lost cohesion, Claryce solidified. I couldn't see Kravayik and had no time to wonder what'd happened to him. From what I gathered he'd done . . . using Joseph's work and his own body to keep the array from feeding everything to Holmes, there was a good chance Kravayik was dead. It was a notion that bothered me more than I would've thought, and I knew that despite the secrets he'd kept from me . . . especially his Claudette . . . he was still someone I trusted more than most.

Which didn't mean that I'd forgiven him yet.

The sword shook despite my weight on it. Holmes's foot slipped free, but only because there wasn't much left of it but faded shadow. Her Lady's gift lost most of its iciness as several translucent forms flowed from it.

The last to emerge but the first to take form was Claudette.

If I'd been the focus of the expression on her face, I have to admit I'd have been more than a little shaken. I didn't want to imagine that expression coming from Claryce, but it was impossible not to.

Fortunately for me, it was Holmes who was the target of not only her fury, but that of the remaining specters. Holmes himself barely looked more cohesive than them, and if I squinted, I could just barely see through him.

He'd lost all his cockiness, all his damned coldness. The Beast of Chicago looked at least as frightened as I imagined any of his victims once had, hopefully a lot more so. He was free of the sword, but didn't have the strength to chase after the receding shadow, which had already slipped past the rooftop, anyway. There was just a vague hint of his maze remaining. It'd been designed by magic and maintained by magic, and without magic it was becoming less of a memory than the exposition.

The first of the ghosts from the sword dove into Holmes. He cried again as it emerged, its hands gripped around its prize. Holmes writhed, his voice becoming several different ones, both male and female.

The remaining specters poured into him. As loud as his shrieks were, I knew that they didn't carry into the mortal world. Only I, Fetch, and maybe Claryce could hear his suffering.

Well, the three of us and the ghosts.

I swallowed as the Nilssons formed next to Holmes. I could still see the slash marks. They took a glance back my way, their faces devoid of all emotion. I didn't know what to make of that and was more than grateful when, as one, they looked down at Holmes and took from him as the others had before.

Then, there was only Claudette. She glanced at me and for a brief moment, her supernatural rage transformed to sadness . . . and love.

Kravayik, she mouthed.

I nodded. "I'll see to him. . . ."

I was rewarded with a smile that contorted into rage again as she faced what little remained of H. Webster Mudgett, aka Dr. Alexander Bond, aka Dr. Henry Howard Holmes, aka the Beast of Chicago. He tried to crawl from her, but lacked both the physical and ethereal power to move quickly.

Claudette lunged at him. Unlike the other ghosts, she didn't just dive through Holmes, but rather seemed to take him on like a suit. I could see her within him and see that when he suddenly stood, it was because of her choice, not his.

Finally, like a hound shaking off a heavy layer of snow, Claudette, her face now one of calm, relieved herself of her hideous "coat." Holmes broke into thousands of tiny flakes, each of them screaming in a different voice that ceased as the bits themselves dissipated in the air around her.

Her hands cupped, Claudette disappeared. With her went the last hints of Holmes's sanctum.

And, of course, right then the sounds of police sirens filled the air.

CHAPTER 29

With Holmes's sanctum no more, we were back in a fully mortal world where despite the biting, snowbound weather and the dark of night, the Chicago Police were proving oddly diligent in seeing just who'd been shooting at whom.

And somehow, I had the suspicion that once again, Cortez would be with them.

Joseph sat on the edge of the roof, cheerfully watching the snow. There was only one remnant of the struggle and that was the body of the late, very unlamented Lysander. Even now, Claryce was pulling free something I saw had worked a lot better on his shambling corpse. The blessed dagger.

She wiped it off once on her arm—even though the blade was clean—then returned it to where she'd secreted it on her leg. The revolver was already gone, having no doubt been put away after it was found to be useless. "I drew him toward me with a couple of shots, then used this. I was *hoping* it'd work the way I thought."

"I didn't know it could," I answered.

"You're joking."

"No."

She bit her lip, and the two of us stepped past the body to where Kravayik lay . . . or should've.

"He was *here*," Claryce insisted. "He was still breathing last I saw him, but I don't see how he could've had the strength to even move an inch!"

My sympathy for him faded a bit with this abandonment. For someone who'd cast off the evils of Feirie for the Church years ago, he'd still been pretty damn spry.

"I know how they felt about one another," Claryce murmured as she leaned close for both warmth and support. "Claudette and Kravayik. She was me . . . but she wasn't." To my surprise and pleasure, Claryce suddenly gripped my chin, turned me toward her, and kissed me. After she stepped back again, she added, "It just happened between them. I think because she saw his dedication to you. That started it, anyway."

"Claryce, you don't have to—"

"Kravayik had gone in and disrupted the array. Holmes didn't have Joseph then, and his own calculations of the wake's waning proved inaccurate. He still might've been able to kill Kravayik, but Claudette, who'd followed, interfered. Holmes cut her throat, then had to flee Chicago without being able to complete his work."

She didn't have to explain more. Kravayik'd arranged her body out of love and respect, and then, when no one else had claimed it, he'd come forward as a servant of the Church. I doubted it'd been easy for him to see her body again and know she'd died for his sake. I knew that guilt all too well.

Fetch, once again a hound of sorts, cleared his throat. "Excuse me, Master Nicholas and Mistress Claryce, but if I may suggest, we'd better scram before the coppers get here. . . ."

"As soon as we take care of one thing." The twins'd disappeared along with the sanctum, which meant that it'd only take long enough to remove Lysander's body before we ourselves left.

Trouble was, when we turned around . . . *his* body was gone as well.

"I hate elves," I growled. Things from Feirie had a tendency to fade after a time if left out—which meant even the mutilated corpses of Holmes's elven victims would soon simply cease to be. That might leave some puzzled folks at the police department, but in a city where evidence of all sorts vanished on a regular basis, someone'd soon chalk it up to one of the gangs.

Then I recalled the other member of our little group. Lon. There was no hint of him anywhere. He'd been pretty near where Lysander's body'd been. I put two and two together and got a number I didn't like, but knew I had to leave the matter of the Feir'hr Sein and his mistress for later. With Holmes gone, I suspected that Feirie'd already begun mending. It was resilient like that, not that it deserved to be so.

I suddenly recalled the bit of Lysander's blood Her Lady'd given me. I hadn't had a chance to use it, but I wondered if it'd help me locate Lon once things settled down. With this ended, I didn't want him wandering about Chicago wearing the corpse of a dead elf noble. That was even too much for this city.

We found our way down just as the sirens became deafening. I spotted the Wills and pointed. "Claryce, you and Fetch take Joseph—damn it!" Joseph'd obediently followed us down, but now, like Lon, he was gone. Unlike Lon, I couldn't just leave it. "Claryce, the two of you go on. I'll deal with Joseph."

"Nick, we can't—"

"Don't argue. Go!"

She obeyed, albeit reluctantly. Fetch trotted after.

"You smell him?" I asked the dragon.

We inhaled through our nose. *He is around the back of the building from which we came . . . Eye think. . . .*

I could've let Fetch sniff for him, but then Claryce would've stayed. Following the dragon's suggestion, I hurried around the corner. The last time I'd been here, I'd ended up being confronted by a couple of Holmes's human pawns, one of whom Lon had taken.

This time, I ended up facing Kravayik.

You did not ask about this one. . . .

I saved my anger at the dragon for later. Kravayik didn't look good. He was as pale as ice and panting hard. There was no sign of Joseph.

"Where is he?" I asked.

"Master N-Nicholas?"

"Joseph. Barnaby's son. You know him very well. You were there six years ago, too."

"I-I have not seen him." He clutched his side near the ribs. "I have been attempting to atone." He drew in a breath, which clearly pained him. "Master Nicholas. It started out as an attempt to help save you from her dying again. I thought that if I kept her from your knowledge, she'd escape. I was wrong. Instead, I became her curse even as she became my salvation."

Somewhere on the other side of the building, the screech of tires and the roar of motors signaled the arrival of the cops. "Never mind that now. What do you mean you've been trying to atone? What'd you do?"

"They need . . . they need a murderer. A reason for all the deaths. I have arranged one of the dead . . . hoods, I believe Fetch calls them . . . to take the rap."

"'The rap'? You've been around Fetch too much, all right. Where?"

He pointed on the side of the block farthest from where the cops were. "He was closest to the Beast's general description. I do not think that the police have actually seen the Beast, so it should work."

"I can appreciate what you've done, but—"

I swore. In the two seconds I'd looked away, Kravayik'd run off.

Did I mention I hate elves?

The dragon and I tried to sniff out Joseph one more time, but there was no hint. I decided to vanish like everyone else. Cortez had his murderer, slain, I'd expect to hear, in a gangland hit. I trusted Kravayik's thoroughness, if nothing else anymore. We'd be talking soon enough. He knew that just as well as I.

The moon . . . which was *not* full now . . . lit up the area fairly well, but I made use of the dragon's gaze all the way. I slipped back around to the far side of the building. I caught a glimpse of the cops paused down the street, where the Feir'hr Sein had left a trail of bodies. He'd actually done me a favor, giving me a chance to reach the Packard while they were occupied.

There was no sign of Cortez. At least, no sign until I got to the Packard.

"Nick Medea . . . we sure do meet in the funniest places at the funniest times, you know?"

I turned to find him leaning against the wall of the nearest building. He'd chosen a spot out of the wind, but clearly he was cold despite his thick coat. As usual, an unlit Lucky dangled from the side of his mouth. A single street lamp not too far away gave him just enough light to see me . . . but not close enough to see my eyes change to normal.

"Cortez." I debated my options. He had to be suspicious.

"I got questions. I do," he commented as he walked toward me. "One of those is that I wonder if you know if our friend Dr. Bond is part of all that?"

"Could be. I'd think he'd have connections to the gangs."

"Yeah, makes sense. Someone phoned and said he'd seen someone like Bond around here, and then I get a call that some cars were headed down here because of gunfire." Cortez tugged on the cigarette. "I came here separately and drove past what I thought was your heap."

"I was here—"

Cortez shook his head. "Yeah, I know. Ghosts always show up at night. That's why you're here now, am I right?" After I nodded, he continued, "You know, my Maria, she said a special prayer for you this morning. She doesn't do that often, and she didn't explain to me why. She's like that. Finds people she thinks really need prayer. You must really need some prayer, Nick Medea."

He had no idea how much he needed prayers himself. If he pressed, I'd have to do something. I didn't know what, although the dragon was giving me a few visual suggestions I had no intention of following through on.

"You know," he went on, "if we find Dr. Bond, dead or alive, that'd make a lot of folks happy, which'd make me happy—"

At that moment, a horn honked from the direction of the police cars. Cortez tossed his cigarette in the snow.

"Told them to honk if they found something important, like maybe Dr. Bond. You think they found him, Nick Medea?"

"I hope so. He needs to face justice, one way or another."

"Yeah, that's what I think. I'll be talking with you."

He headed off in another direction where I assumed his car awaited. I quickly climbed into the Packard and got it going. I wasn't certain what'd just happened or whether I owed Cortez or he owed me, but I did know that I owed his Maria a lot for those prayers.

Those apparently powerful prayers.

Claryce and Fetch made it back to her apartment just fine. Fetch waited with her until I showed up. He looked extremely anxious to rush off, and I remembered that he still had a refugee from Feirie on his paws. He seemed very protective of this particular refugee, which made me think I'd have to keep an eye on both of them.

Nothing was ever simple.

I made a belated call to Father Jonathan as soon as I could and wasn't surprised when he hadn't seen any more signs of his ghostly visitor. Not only had Diocles done as I'd asked and stayed as far away as he could from the priest, but now that the wake had passed, I suspected that things would be back to normal . . . or as normal as they could be.

Claryce and I headed over to Provident first thing we could the next day. I didn't like having to tell Barnaby I'd lost his son somewhere, but thought maybe he'd have some notion as to where Joseph'd gone. We'd checked the house but found nothing. I'd then gone to "Des's" home and found that empty, too. I would've preferred to wrap things up nicely by dealing with Barnaby's good "friend," but from the haste which with the imposter Des had clearly fled, he was far, far away by now. It wasn't the first time that sort of thing had happened. Sometimes they were smart and never came back; sometimes they couldn't help themselves. We'd have to wait and see.

Thankfully, it was Fremd's day off. Barnaby was alone. He looked battered, but on his way to mending. We exchanged the usual pleasantries, and then he told us what he could of events. There wasn't much he could add. Mostly he remembered unexpectedly coming face-to-face with one of the twins, who was in the process of guiding Joseph out of his room. Then, someone behind Barnaby . . . someone who hadn't been there a moment before . . . beat him hard on the back of his skull. After that, there'd only been oblivion.

I was glad about that. Judging by his condition when we'd found him, he'd been worked over fairly hard. It'd been a good thing he'd not felt most of it.

Still, throughout our conversation, it was clear that there was only one thing truly on his mind . . . and mine.

"Nick. About Joseph . . ."

"I don't know where he is. I've got some ideas, but don't worry, I'll get him back for you—"

He gave me a peculiar look. "What are you talking about? I just talked to Dunning before you arrived! He's back there alive and well, brought by a friend of yours. A Negro, they said. Michael. The nurse couldn't recall his last name."

Claryce was good enough not to make a sound. I just nodded and replied, "Michael's trustworthy. So Joseph's safe and sound in Dunning. You're going to keep him in there, aren't you?"

"Yes. It's better. I thought he'd be secure with me, but then all that happened. . . ."

At that point, I explained to him about "Des." Barnaby glowered. He wasn't a man who made friends easily, but when he did, he was very loyal to them.

"A fool I am."

"This was planned over the span of thirty years," Claryce offered sympathetically.

"I suppose that's something." Barnaby grunted. "But the Beast is dead this time, isn't he?"

"He's faced his proper justice." I didn't add anything further. A long time ago, Barnaby and I had agreed that it was best he knew as little as necessary.

"Good riddance." His eyes fluttered closed for a moment.

We took that as our cue. I left a note with Bertha informing Dr. Fremd how I'd be taking care of all costs, and then we drove off.

"We need to make one more stop, if you don't mind, Nick."

I slowed the Packard. "Claryce . . ."

"I want to go there. I owe her that."

So we drove to Saint Boniface.

There was no one around . . . including Diocles. I led her toward the grave, at the same time making certain we avoided the one where Holmes as Bond had been buried. No need for reminders.

We made a brief pause at Clarissa's site. Claryce smiled sadly at me, but said nothing. She knew what'd happened to me back then and understood how much guilt I still felt for not being able to save Clarissa. After crossing herself, she moved on.

I brought her in front of Claudette's grave. Claryce knelt and gently touched the stone. "When we were together, I could feel how much she *was* me . . . but she was also herself. I suppose the others were as well, but with her, I felt it so deeply. We were one, but we were still two."

I understood what she meant. I'd always just assumed that each incarnation'd been the same soul starting over in a new body, but at least for her, things were much more complicated. Each personality had its separate essence, almost a second soul. I wasn't sure how that squared with Heaven, but to me it verified what I'd seen in Claryce. Yes, she'd been Cleolinda and all the rest, but she was also very much herself.

She had no idea, but that knowledge relieved me. More than ever, I knew what drew me to Claryce was as much *Claryce* as any link she had with those before her.

Then, I realized we were no longer alone. At the same stone where I'd last seen him was Young Michael. He peered down at the grave before him, then, seemingly aware I'd just noticed him, looked up at me.

There was no pleasure in his expression, only something I thought might be regret. He tipped his hat at me, almost as if in salute.

I must've made a sound . . . probably a growl . . . because Claryce suddenly said, "What is it, Nick?"

I looked down at her, silently berated myself for doing so, and immediately looked back at Michael.

Yep. He was gone, too.

Claryce put a hand on my arm. I realized I'd gone from growling to hissing. Hissing like my constant companion, who at the moment shared my frustration.

Eye will burn that one someday, he muttered. *Eye will . . .*

"Nick! Are you all right? Is he trying to get out?"

I shook my head. My anger began to dissipate. "No. Just a little disagreement between us. It was nothing."

"Nothing? Hmm." Her hand suddenly tightened. "That reminds me. Nick. That grave . . ."

I cursed Michael again. Thanks to him, she'd just noticed Holmes's/Bond's grave.

But I was wrong. Instead, she bent by another.

"No, not quite the same. With elves, ghosts, and such, I think I'm becoming paranoid about everything now."

"That doesn't sound paranoid. That sounds sensible."

Claryce straightened again. She grimaced. "Sensible? I see some scrollwork on a tombstone and think it's the same as that tattoo I saw on the neck of one of those ghoulish twins."

"Tattoo?"

"It was so unique, I couldn't help remembering it." She took my arm in a more comfortable way. "A stylized dragon head with a curled tail around it. At the time, I wondered if it was some magical ward or something."

"Possibly," I answered neutrally.

"Doesn't matter anymore, I guess." Claryce shivered. "We can go now. I'm starting to freeze."

"We'll get some coffee first thing."

"Just so long as it's not that tar you drink. I want to warm up, not burn a hole through my stomach."

I smiled back at her joke. I was going to do my best to at least enjoy one day with her before I let the Gate and my curse take over my existence again. Granted, it was going to be a lot harder to enjoy even this short moment, no thanks to Michael. He'd drawn my attention at that moment to get *Claryce* to notice what she had. For her, it'd just been a vague resemblance to something odd she'd seen before, but to me it was a damned warning.

I hadn't seen the tattoo, but her description had been enough. I'd seen the dragon head with the tail circling it before. Of course, that'd been sixteen centuries ago, but one doesn't forget one of the last things one sees before being beheaded. Nor could I ever forget what it'd stood for.

A dragon head circled by a tail. It'd become *his* symbol in one form or another. His take on what some called a Dacian Dragon . . . to mark the land responsible for his vile birth.

His symbol.

Galerius's.

It could've just been coincidence, a mark that happened to resemble the emblem. It was entirely possible.

The dragon hissed loudly in my head.

We do not believe in coincidence. . . .

"No," I whispered so lightly Claryce couldn't possibly hear. "No . . . we don't."

I held Claryce tighter as we walked.

ACKNOWLEDGMENTS

As usual, thanks to my editor, Rene Sears, and the rest of the Pyr gang—Sheila Stewart and Jeffrey Curry for their copyedits, Jackie Nasso Cooke for her cover design, and Jake Bonar, my publicist—for helping put this new story together into a real book. Thanks also to all the elements and history of Chicago for helping to add the city, a truly essential character, to Nick's world.

ABOUT THE AUTHOR

Richard A. Knaak is the *New York Times* and *USA Today* bestselling author of *The Legend of Huma*, *WOW: Wolfheart*, and some fifty novels and numerous shorter pieces. He is best known for his work in such shared worlds as Dragonlance, World of Warcraft, Diablo, Pathfinder, Conan, and more, plus his own stories, especially his popular Dragonrealm series. He has scripted comics, mangas, and more, and his work has been published worldwide.

Recent works include not only *Black City Saint*—first in this series—but *Reaper's Eye* for Pathfinder, a reissue of his urban fantasy, *King of the Grey*, and *The Horned Blade* for the Dragonrealm. Forthcoming releases include *Cut from the Same Shadow & Other Tales* (a Dragonrealm novella collection), *Knight of the Frost* (the first in a new Dragonrealm trilogy), and the next installment in Nick's saga. In addition to those, he is also involved in other projects to be announced. He splits his time between Chicago and northwest Arkansas.

The author invites you to join him on Facebook, Twitter, and his website http://www.richardaknaak.com.